My dear, if you meet me may I forget there are other reporters present or must I behave? I shall want to hug you to death. I can hardly wait! A world of love to you and good night and God bless you, light of my life.
—*Eleanor Roosevelt to Lorena Hickok, March 9, 1933*

I've been trying today to bring back your face—to remember just how you look. Funny how even the dearest face will fade away in time. Most clearly I remember your eyes, with a kind of teasing smile in them, and the feeling of that soft spot just north-east of the corner of your mouth against my lips.
—*Lorena Hickok to Eleanor Roosevelt, December 5, 1933*

# PROLOGUE

# Goodbye

## Hyde Park, 1962

Hick didn't go to the funeral.

Oh, she was invited, and for that she had Sisty to thank—
Eleanor's granddaughter, the one Hick had known and loved since
she was a little girl. During her grandmother's last illness, it was
Sisty who kept in touch. And who took down Eleanor's last letter
because her grandmother couldn't manage the pen: *Dearest Hick,
I'm still horribly weak, but as soon as I'm able to hold the phone I'll call you.*

But Eleanor couldn't manage the phone, either. The call came
instead from Western Union, from a bored young man who read
the telegram to Hick while she closed her eyes and tried to shut out
his voice:

THE FAMILY OF MRS. FRANKLIN D. ROOSEVELT
INVITES YOU TO THE SERVICE TO BE HELD AT
ST. JAMES EPISCOPAL CHURCH, AND TO THE
INTERMENT SERVICE IN THE ROSE GARDEN AT
SPRINGWOOD.

No, of course, she didn't go. Hick had reconciled herself to the
waning of passion many years before, had even imagined herself in
love with someone else for a while. But her love for Madam (the

5

private name she once had for Eleanor, sometimes said with a soft, sly mockery: *Mod-dom!*) was a warm river that had begun flowing out of the broken rock of her heart thirty years before, and she couldn't trust herself not to sob and gulp like a drowning fish while the rest of the mourners sat mannequin-like, hands folded, dry-eyed. She was resentful, too, not on her own but on Eleanor's account, knowing she wouldn't have the quiet service she wanted, small and simple, just a plain pine coffin covered with a blanket of pine boughs. Private, only her family and nearest friends.

"No hullabaloo, Hick," Eleanor had said once. "No pomp, no circumstance, no foolishness. Tell them to keep it private."

But Eleanor had long ago ceased to be a private person, had ceased to be Madam or Mrs. R or even Mrs. Roosevelt. She had become a *personage*, an icon, an image. She had become ER, the First Lady of the World, and her death, like her life, belonged not to herself nor to the few who loved her nor to the one who loved her longest and best. She belonged to everyone, to those who admired and respected her, even to those who ridiculed her. That's why the television networks and cameras were there. Why, in defiance of the cold November rain, the mourners stood three-and four-deep behind the ropes.

All those invited had come, Hick knew, all but herself and Cousin Alice, Eleanor's longtime antagonist, the Other Washington Monument. Two hundred and fifty political illuminati, as many as the St. James pews could hold. The president and First Lady, JFK studiously somber-faced, Jackie a porcelain doll in a black suit and black mink pillbox. Harry and Bess and Ike. (Mamie had not come, for she had once heard that Eleanor had called her an alcoholic and she had born a grudge ever since.) Ike was awkward and uneasy, a furtive Republican amid a hive of Democrats, probably remembering that he had fired ER ten years before. Adlai was there, bald as an onion, and Lyndon and Lady Bird. And David Gurewitsch, whom Eleanor had loved in her last years, and Joe Lash, whom she had loved foolishly, foolishly, twenty years before. Later, in the Rose Garden at Springwood, they stood at attention like soldiers respecting a truce, while Eleanor was laid to rest beside her husband. She wasn't the only woman to share FDR's life or his death or even his bed, but she would be the only woman to share his grave.

But person or personage, Eleanor remained the First Lady of Hick's heart, and while the mourners were displaying their public grief, she pulled a box of letters out of her closet at the Old Rectory, only a few blocks from the church. They were Eleanor's letters from their first year, their happiest, richest year, and she sat on her bed and read them, and wept. An old, sick, crippled, half-blind woman, weeping for what had once been, for what she and Madam had had together, for what was gone.

Or was it? For in the end, Hick reminded herself, wiping her eyes, there is love, love in all its many disguises, love embracing loss and death and imperfection, love changing, mutable, many-formed, but never diminishing—love, simply, and simply enduring.

And then, after the bigwigs had been bundled into their automobiles and driven away, Rev. Kidd, bless his heart, had phoned from St. James with an offer to take her to the gravesite. Hick said a grateful "thank you" and went out to the garden to gather a damp bouquet of white chrysanthemums and lamb's ear and the last goldenrod, tying them with a pink silk ribbon from the nightgown Eleanor had bought for her the summer they were in San Francisco. And then she stood stock still, seized by the memory of that time, held in its terrible, sweet grip.

Late that evening, Rev. Kidd picked her up. The guard at the Rose Garden let him park close. But it was still drizzling and as dark as the inside of a cow, and neither of them had had the good sense to bring a flashlight. They felt their way along the tall hemlock hedge for fifty yards or so, Hick with her cane, hanging onto the stalwart reverend's arm. But her arthritis wouldn't let her go the distance, damn it, so she gave it up and he went on alone, with her flowers. She waited on the outskirts of the garden as she had waited so often on the outskirts of Eleanor's life, thinking of the two of them as if they were characters in a novel, remembering them as they had been at the beginning of their story, when they had imagined they could go on loving each other forever. And so they had, each in her own way, although not as each had imagined. But wasn't that the way of love? Never going the way you would think or hope, setting its own pace, its own direction, taking you and your heart with it as far as you could go. And then farther, and then farther still, past all hope, all fear, all comprehension.

When the reverend returned, he said there was a massive eight-foot bank of flowers at the gravesite, splendid tributes from all over the world, from the governments of all the lands Eleanor had visited. But he had placed her bouquet all by itself on a corner of the white marble slab. Mrs. Roosevelt would know who left it, he said, patting her shoulder with what was meant as a comforting gesture. And that was it, her own private ceremony. No hullabaloo, no pomp. Just goodbye, dear heart.

Goodbye.


ER was gone, but Eleanor's letters remained, and as the new year opened, Hick understood, with a kind of growing desperation, that she had to decide what to do with them.

They filled more than a dozen cardboard boxes stacked in the bedroom closet at the Old Rectory and under the bed. Hick hadn't taken the time to catalog or even count them, but she reckoned offhand that there might be three thousand or more, spanning thirty years. Loving letters that told their story, its sweetness, its sadness, its promise, its pain. Two-thirds were Eleanor's, she guessed, another third hers, some creased by many readings, others still in their envelopes, read once or twice then tucked away.

Hick often thought of the collective gasp that would flutter like a panicked bird around the country if the letters from the First Lady of the World got into the papers. Especially satisfying was the thought of the discomfiture of those patronizing Oyster Bay Roosevelts, Cousin Alice especially. And the embarrassment of the Roosevelt boys—James, Elliott, Franklin Jr., John—who never for one instant thought of their mother as a flesh-and-blood woman with her own needs and desires. It would give them an awful jolt, she thought with pleasure. And damn well serve them right for the thousand ways they'd disdained and disappointed their mother over the years.

But Hick flinched at the thought of the headlines in the tabloids and the right-wing press. *Former First Lady's Secret Friendship! Eleanor's Lesbian Love Affair! ER Bares All in Love Letters to First Friend.* The press couldn't get to Eleanor; she was safely enshrined in the Rose Garden with a guard at the gate. But she, Hick, was still alive, and a rabble of reporters would be camped on her doorstep from dawn to dark, milling across the lawn like ants at a picnic, hungry for the story, the secret story, the *real* story. Photographers, too, popping their damn flashbulbs in her face as she struggled with her cane and her packages and her keys, fumbling to open her door.

And it wouldn't stop there. Hick knew reporters—of course she did, she had been one of them, hadn't she, one of th' They were like a kennel of dogs, snarling, scratching for

She understood their tricks. When they couldn't get the story from her, they'd make it up. Ethical journalism be damned, they would hint or suggest or fabricate, and what they came up with would be ugly, false, lacerating. So the letters stayed in the closet and under the bed and the Old Rectory's bedroom door stayed closed. And locked. She wasn't taking any chances.

And then there was Joe. Joseph Lash, who had fallen into Eleanor's orbit before the war. Diligent, persistent Joe, who for the last decade had been building his writing career upon ER's friendship. At her urging, he had been asked to help edit the presidential letters. And now—

And now, Joe was clamoring for the letters. He had gotten wind of them from ER's son Elliott, who had heard of them from his sister Anna, who had known from the beginning what Hick and Eleanor had been to each other. Joe had telephoned again last night, reminding Hick that he "coveted" the letters for the "little memoir" he was currently writing, which (Hick was convinced) was chiefly designed to put him into the running to write ER's official biography, which he hoped would earn him a Pulitzer. And perhaps he ought to have it—the Pulitzer, that is. Heaven knows, Joe had paid a price for the First Lady's friendship. After he was drafted, the Army Intelligence spy hunters put him on their list and began reading Eleanor's letters and following the two of them from one hotel room to another. And then he got orders for the Pacific front, courtesy of the White House (that's what he thought, anyway). But if Joe got a Pulitzer, it would be Eleanor's Pulitzer. Who in the world would remember Joseph P. Lash, if it hadn't been for the First Lady's friendship?

But jealousy quite aside (well, of course, there was jealousy), Hick wasn't going to hand the letters over to Joe, and that was all there was to it. She knew perfectly well that he would take them

straight to Elliott and Franklin Jr. They would read them with revulsion and destroy them, just as (Hick knew in her bones, though she couldn't prove it) they had bought and destroyed their mother's letters to Earl Miller, once her bodyguard, always her adoring friend. If they got their hands on the letters to Hick, all traces of Eleanor's passionate heart—revealed nowhere else on earth so fully, so intimately, over so many decades—would simply vanish. Joe and the Roosevelt boys could offer Hick all the money in the world, but it would still be *no, no, no, never.* The letters were all that was left of a lifetime of loving, to be preserved, cherished, defended. Joe Lash wasn't going to get his hot little hands on them, to trade for favors from the Roosevelts. *Oh, no. No. No. No.*

Thinking about all this, Hick almost wished she hadn't kept them, dangerous as they were. In the beginning, she had saved them because *she* was meant to write the First Lady's biography. As a reporter, a writer, an intimate friend, she had been Eleanor's best, first choice, endorsed by FDR himself, who thought it was a *delightful* idea. To that end, Hick had suggested that the First Lady include in her daily letters a diary of her activities—people she saw, places she went, projects she worked on. Once ER was out of the White House and Hick settled down to the business of writing her biography, the letters would be an invaluable source of names and dates and doings.

But Hick couldn't write Madam's biography—not because she didn't know enough about her subject but because she knew too much about Eleanor, because she loved her too much. She was defeated by the same conundrum that had evicted her from her AP career: How can you write objectively about someone you adore? And on the other, sinister side: What secrets could she reveal, what secrets must she conceal?

And there was another, even more baffling question: How

could she tell Eleanor's story without telling her own? Without laying claim to the love that had held the two of them together? The two stories were knitted together as tightly as if they had come straight off Eleanor's needles. It was impossible to tell the one without telling the other. Or, even more impossible, to tell the public story without telling the very private.

Eleanor had dealt with that problem by writing a three-volume autobiography that was, beginning to end, a masterful evasion of one important truth after another, all clothed in the most seeming frankness. She had mentioned Hick's name only casually, tacit proof to Hick that their intimate story, their *true* story, could not be published—at least, not in their lifetimes. It would rock the world. Hick herself had dealt with it a few years before by writing *The Story of Eleanor Roosevelt* for young readers and then *Eleanor Roosevelt, Reluctant First Lady*, published just last year. Both were personal enough to satisfy youngsters and to answer a few adults' questions about their friendship—although, of course, not revealing anything that would shock anybody.

But still, there were the letters. They *would* shock, and time was growing short. Hick had lived with diabetes for nearly forty years, suffering through bouts of near-blindness and poor circulation and other attendant ills, escalating from chronic to acute. She needed to do something about the letters before she was carted off to the morgue and somebody rummaged through her things and discovered the boxes and decided that the Roosevelts ought to have them. So just now, finally, in the past few weeks, she was allowing herself to think about what Ray Corry had suggested.

A stocky, soft-voiced, spectacled man in his late forties, Ray Corry was the curator of the FDR Museum, which was a part of the library, just two miles up the Albany Post Road. He was smitten by Mrs. R and had taken her his many questions about

FDR's numerous collections—books, naval drawings, ship models. For her part, Eleanor had grown fond of Ray. At her suggestion, he had knocked one afternoon at the front door of the Old Rectory and introduced himself to Hick.

"Mrs. R says you've been a very dear friend since before she went to the White House," he'd said, holding his hat in both hands. "I'm sure you must be a rich source of information about the family. I would very much like to get to know you."

It was pure flattery, but Hick didn't mind. Talking about Mrs. R was a selfish indulgence for her, and, of course, it was true that she *did* know a great deal. She had been deeply involved in Eleanor's life for so many years and knew so much about every part of it, the personal and the political, the minor and the momentous— far more than the boys and even Anna might imagine. Had Eleanor mentioned the letters to Mr. Corry? Hick thought perhaps she had, at least casually. But since he hadn't brought them up, the question went unanswered.

Ray telephoned in the evenings so they could talk, uninterrupted. He ran errands for her, buying groceries and other necessities. He stopped after work to take her shopping, something that was easier said than done, with her arthritis and her cane. He often stayed to supper, too—Hick still liked to cook, when she had a guest who appreciated good food. He was a bachelor and not very well (a "bum ticker and getting bummer," he'd said ruefully), and Hick knew that he was lonely.

Well, that made two of them, didn't it? She appreciated his many kindnesses—particularly the sly, amusing tidbits of gossip he brought about the goings-on behind the scenes at the presidential library. Hick knew its staff—especially Daisy Suckley, FDR's cousin, and the director, Elizabeth Drewry—quite well. She had spent a great many hours doing research there on *Ladies of Courage* (a book she had written and to which Eleanor had added her name), as well as her own books, biographies of FDR and ER, for young readers. While Eleanor was alive, Hick had never discussed the letters with anyone at the library. But now she was gone and Hick was beginning to feel, rather urgently, that she had to make some sort of plan, especially with Joe Lash baying like a greedy bloodhound on her heels and the Roosevelt boys behind him.

That was why, one night when she and Ray Corry were talking on the phone, she had casually mentioned that she had a few of Eleanor's letters and was wondering what she should do with them. "Joe Lash says he'd like to have them," she added, "but I don't really think..." She had let her voice trail off, and Ray—they were on a first-name basis by that time—had snapped like a trout at the lure.

"I'm sure the FDR Library would be interested," he said, not quite able to keep the excitement out of his voice. "Shall I mention them to Elizabeth?"

"If you like," Hick said, pretending indifference. But she felt she had taken the first step on a journey with an inevitable destination, and she was frightened. That night, she took a box of letters to bed with her and read until she fell asleep. Giving them up would be like giving up Eleanor herself. But the next morning, putting the box away again, she knew she had to do *something*. If she had died in the night...

Two days later, Ray came for dinner: pork chops Marsala with wild rice and fresh asparagus, which Hick could still prepare with confidence. Like a small boy with a secret, he brought up the letters the moment they sat down to eat. "Elizabeth says she'd be delighted to have them for the library." He gave a special emphasis to "delighted."

"Well," Hick said, with a feeling of resignation, "it's something to think about. Help yourself to rice. Oh, and tell me, please—how is Esther's project coming along?" Eleanor's longtime friend, Esther Lape, was possessed by the idea of getting the Nobel Committee to posthumously award the Peace Prize to ER, and everybody at the library was pitching in to help her compile the dossier.

"Esther's working hard," Ray said, "although, of course, it's a massive job. Likely to take years." He paused. "But I wonder— have you heard that Alice Longworth…"

Ray's light-hearted recital of Roosevelt gossip carried them through dinner to their coffee and dessert. They were enjoying pears flambé with crushed gingersnaps and ice cream when he propped his elbows on the table and went back to the letters.

"You know, Hick, if you're concerned that there's anything… well, a little too personal in them, you can have them sealed. Personal about yourself, I mean."

"Sealed?" Hick asked, and immediately wondered why she hadn't thought of that herself.

"Sure. That happens all the time with sensitive material. Just tell Elizabeth that you'd like them locked up for a period after your death—ten years, twenty, thirty. She'll see that the items are properly accessed and conserved but won't make them available to researchers until the date you've named."

"Ah," Hick murmured, with relish. "Of course." She would love to see Joe Lash's face when he discovered that he could have access to the letters—ten years after she was gone.

Ray smiled. "I've read your new book, *Reluctant First Lady*. It's quite charming, and, of course, it's now part of the collection as well. I believe we have two copies." He gave her a direct look. "But like your little biography of Mrs. R, it was written for young readers. I'm sure it tells only a part of the story."

Hick nodded. Yes, only a part of the story, a small part. The rest of the story, the *real* story, had to be left out—although if someone were to study the letters, the real story could be easily inferred. Neither she nor Eleanor had been very discreet.

Ray put down his coffee cup. "Both Elizabeth and I think it would be helpful if you could write a memoir to accompany the letters. Something that might fill a few gaps in the record."

*Fill a few gaps in the record.* She thought about that for a moment. "The memoir. It could be sealed, too?"

"Of course. For as long as the letters are sealed or longer, if that seems right to you. As to length, that would be entirely up to you. But your relationship with Mrs. R goes back before FDR's first term as governor. And you *are* a writer, a damned good one, too. If you feel like it, you could write about the whole course of your friendship. A kind of intimate perspective. Later researchers might find that interesting."

*I'll just bet they would,* Hick thought, and picked up the coffee pot. "Would you like another cup of coffee?"

A week later, she sat down at her typewriter.

# Part One

1928

# CHAPTER ONE

# Hello

I met Mrs. Roosevelt in 1928, the year that Herbert Hoover beat the pants off Al Smith.

I was the only woman reporter working for the Associated Press in the New York bureau that year, and I'd been handed a plum assignment: the Democratic ticket. (Not *the* plum assignment: that was Hoover, who was a sure bet to win but about as remarkable as a dead fish.) The wire services didn't fall all over themselves to hire women, but after we got the franchise in 1920 and the political parties began to lobby for the women's vote, the AP did what they had to do. They hired one woman. Me.

At first, the guys in the AP newsroom on the sixth floor at 383 Madison Avenue made me feel as welcome as a stone in a shoe. If they could've, they would've parked me on the society pages. But I had sixteen years of reporting experience to my credit—the Minneapolis *Tribune,* the Milwaukee *Sentinel,* the Battle Creek *Journal,* the *New-York Tribune,* the New York *Daily Mirror*—and I wasn't shy about slugging it out for news assignments. I had spent the previous year at the *Mirror,* stirring the usual tabloid stew of sin, sex, and sensationalism, so when Bill Chapin, the AP day city editor, assigned me to the Democrats and Tammany Hall, it was like coming home. I got out my notebook, put on my walking shoes, and went to work.

I was thirty-five that year, and in my prime. I was tall for a woman (five-foot-eight), deep-voiced, broad-shouldered, hefty. At work, I wore dark skirts and jackets, with white blouses (sometimes maybe a little rumpled or coffee-stained), bright silk scarves, low heels. An AP colleague once described me as "a big girl in a casual raincoat with a wide tailored hat, with translucent blue eyes and a mouth vivid with lipstick," adding that I managed to be "hard-boiled and soft-hearted at the same time."

That was cute. But yes, that was me: hard-boiled, soft-hearted. I could crack wise with the guys, but I liked nothing better than a human interest story with plenty of heart. And on the Democrat beat, Mrs. Roosevelt was the story with heart.

It went this way. New York's four-term governor Al Smith, the "Happy Warrior," was the Democratic candidate for president, and a political featherweight named Franklin Delano Roosevelt was aiming at the governorship. But Herbert Hoover was campaigning to the triumphant drumbeat of Republican prosperity, promising a chicken in every pot and a car in every garage—just what the American voter, always a sucker for a slogan, wanted to hear. The smart money was on Hoover.

In the state race, Roosevelt wasn't raising many hopes, either. He was a rich kid from Groton and Harvard with aristocratic good looks, a mellifluous voice, and sterling connections by blood and marriage to Teddy Roosevelt. The word around the AP office was that Roosevelt had idolized his Cousin Teddy and planned to follow his road to the White House, even going so far as to marry Eleanor, TR's favorite niece but definitely no ravishing beauty. FDR (as he was called) had served as assistant secretary of the Navy under Wilson and enjoyed a brief flurry of celebrity in 1920, on another doomed Democratic ticket: James Cox for president, FDR for vice president. FDR might've been a candidate for the presidency in 1924, but that golden dream dimmed when he was crippled by polio. Now, he wore ten-pound metal leg braces and spent months of every year paddling around at Warm Springs, a derelict health resort he'd bought in Georgia. The boys in the AP newsroom, usually pretty good judges of character, wrote him off as a well-heeled dilettante who had a boatload of charm but lacked the political muscle to steer the ship.

But Roosevelt was Al Smith's fair-haired boy and a Tammany Hall candidate, which made him very interesting copy, especially when you added in the connections to TR and the Oyster Bay Republican Roosevelts. So I spent my days loitering in the lobby at the Democratic Party headquarters in the General Motors Building at Broadway and Fifty-Seventh, picking through the flotsam and jetsam of corridor gossip. And the more I heard, the more my gut told me that the story behind *this* story was the candidate's wife, who was doing something political wives just didn't do. She was campaigning for the ticket. Openly, with enthusiasm.

Which, all by itself, was news. In Albany, Mrs. Al Smith hid behind her tea table in the governor's mansion and was off limits to the press. In Washington, Mrs. Calvin Coolidge (formerly a teacher in a school for the deaf) had been ordered by her husband not to talk to reporters. Urged to speak at a press luncheon, the story went, she had resorted to sign language—a perfect metaphor for muzzled political wives who were told to smile and keep their mouths shut.

Mrs. Roosevelt was an anomaly, and as a reporter, I loved anomalies, especially when the anomaly was a woman doing something that made her stand out as something other than a wife, a mother, and a clotheshorse. This woman went out on the campaign trail, edited the *Women's Democratic News*, wrote magazine articles on women in politics, taught at an exclusive girls' school, and, with two friends, owned a furniture factory on the Roosevelt estate. A furniture factory? Now, *there* was an anomaly for you. But she had a conventional side, as well: she was the mother of four boys and a girl, grown or away at school, and a grandmother.

It had been my experience that the fastest way to a candidate was through the candidate's secretary. In this case, the candidate's wife had a secretary—Malvina Thompson—so I knocked on her door and invited her for a late-afternoon coffee and sweet.

We met at Veniero's, on East Eleventh between First and Second Avenue, over a slice of Italian cheesecake for her and a Napoleon for me. (I knew even then that I was diabetic but didn't quite believe it. Yet.) I had stumbled onto Veniero's a decade before, during a short-lived stint on the old *New-York Tribune* during the uneasy days before the United States entered the war in 1917. I had come to the *Tribune* from the Milwaukee *Sentinel,* fired with the hope of getting credentialed as a foreign war correspondent and heading for France and the front. That's where the action was. That's where I wanted to be.

But the *Trib* editor laughed at me when I told him what I wanted to do. "Just who the hell do you think you are?" he demanded, loud enough to be heard across the newsroom. "Stick to your knittin', girlie. Females don't cover wars." Laughter stuttered from one typewriter to another as the reporters, male to a man, shared the joke.

In my anger at yet more evidence of bias against female journalists, I spouted off to the editor and got the boot for insubordination. But I had found Veniero's. When I returned to the Minneapolis *Tribune,* I missed its Napoleons. Now, a decade later, I was glad to be back.

Malvina Thompson was a dark-haired, firm-jawed woman in her mid-thirties, well-informed and politically savvy. By the time our order appeared, we were Tommy and Hick, trading Tammany Hall gossip and shaking our heads over Mayor Jimmy Walker's latest grubby, greed-stained scandal. I asked a few wary questions about what was going on at Democratic headquarters, using her answers like channel markers showing whether she'd give me access or block my way. It didn't take me long to decide that Mrs. Roosevelt's secretary knew the score, all of them. She was a source worth investing in.

Tommy asked me questions, too—where I'd been before I got to the AP, how I felt about women in politics, how I felt about the ticket, about FDR, about Mrs. R. Before I finished my Napoleon, I'd realized that she was sizing me up, vetting me in order to decide just how much access *I* should have. Each of us was using the other in the way we had learned to operate in the political universe. Neither of us could know, then, that we would be steadfast friends for as long as we lived, Tommy loving and defending her boss in one way while I loved and defended her in quite another.

Sweets finished, we both lit cigarettes and leaned back, regarding each other while the conversations from nearby tables eddied around us like smoke and the rumble of the Second Avenue El rippled the coffee in our cups.

"I think," Tommy said finally, "that you ought to meet the Boss."

*The Boss.* I had to smile at that. "You think so?" I didn't want to seem too eager.

She was slightly miffed. "Hey, she's doing good things. Those are her editorials you've been reading in the *Women's Democratic News.*" She narrowed her eyes. "You *have* been reading them, haven't you? And her *Redbook* article? You need to read that, if you want to know what she stands for."

"I read it," I said. The article was titled "Women Must Learn to Play the Game as Men Do." Not even Mrs. Roosevelt's stiff, pedantic style could mask her fuming outrage. "I agree with her basic premise. Women in politics are being exploited." Women were wooed into politics, Mrs. Roosevelt had written, because men needed their organizational talents and coveted their votes. But the minute a woman reached for real political power, her hands were slapped and she was sent back to her kitchen. Mrs. Roosevelt was not a good writer, by any measure. But she had plenty of passion and the chutzpah to go with it. That was what I admired.

"It goes beyond politics, of course," Tommy said. "Mrs. R is committed to ending exploitation for *all* women. An eight-hour day, better working conditions, the right to strike—"

"How many hours a day do you work for *her*?" I countered, amused. I'd heard the stories. "Twelve? Fourteen? Nights? Weekends?" Tommy was rumored to be married to a high school teacher named Frank Schneider. But nobody had ever seen her husband and she never seemed to leave the office before nine or ten at night. He was widely believed to be a fiction.

She had the grace to chuckle. "I do it because I want to. Because I believe in her." She became earnest. "You'll see, Hick. The Boss is just about the biggest woman in the world. Big dreams. Big heart."

I shrugged with a practiced show-me cynicism. "If you say so. When?"

"I'll set it up."

"Exclusive?"

"I'll ask."

"*Before* the election," I said firmly. Because the Happy Warrior and Franklin Roosevelt were going to lose the election. There would be no point in talking to FDR's wife after the Democratic ticket was shot down. And if he won (he wouldn't), she would be the governor-elect's wife. Muzzled, off-limits, out of the picture. If she had anything to say, she'd have to learn sign language. I had no idea then how wrong I was. How could I? She was an anomaly. There had never been anyone like her before.

"I'll give you a call," Tommy said and stubbed out her cigarette.

The AP political reporter and the Democratic political operative smiled at each other with a cautious respect. Then we gathered our things and went back out into the noise and hubbub and hurly-burly that was East Eleventh Street.

Ah, New York, New York, how I loved it!

At the end of the Twenties, the Big Apple had it all. Wheeling and dealing on Wall Street, Park Avenue for puttin' on the Ritz, Delmonico's for cocktails and dinner, followed by the theater on Broadway or the Cotton Club and the Apollo and the Savoy in Harlem. The Statue of Liberty and the Brooklyn Bridge and Central Park, the Plaza Hotel and Carnegie Hall and the Met. Yankee Stadium and Ebbets Field for baseball and Greenwich Village for intimate parties, where we played phonograph records of Bessie Smith's blues and sang Ma Rainey's "Prove It On Me": *Went out last night with a crowd of my friends. They must've been women, 'cause I don't like no men.*

But it was also the Bowery and Chinatown and the Lower East Side and Mulberry Bend and Penitentiary Row and Bandits' Roost. And sweatshop workers and street urchins and prostitutes, all dolled up, and drunken bums on the down-and-out. Prohibition had been the law since 1920, but the Volstead Act was a joke. All it took was a bottle and two chairs to make a speakeasy, and there were thirty thousand of them in the city, all under the great, greasy

Democratic thumb of Tammany Hall. The good thing was that booze was as easy to get as water. The bad thing was that you never knew what the hell you were drinking. You could order Dewar's or Gordon's at one of the dollar-a-glass clubs with brass rails and crystal chandeliers and get pretty much the same poison you got at the dime-a-shot dumps along the wharfs.

As a working reporter, I saw it all, every day, every night, and there was plenty to see, plenty to love, plenty to hate. Which suited me, because I loved and hated with equal passion and had a tough time observing the AP's cardinal rule: *Stay out of the story.* I had grown up in tiny railroad towns on the featureless prairies of South Dakota, where the wind-worn people talked only of crops and the weather and never saw a new face or heard a strange voice from one end of the month to the other.

In New York, I sometimes simply stood and *gawked.* The city's energies were hectic, electric, frenetic, chaotic. The cacophonous streets were packed curb to curb with automobiles and taxis, bicycles weaving crazily among the electric trolleys and double-decker busses. The Empire State Building was pushing up the sky at Fifth Avenue and West Thirty-Fourth, and the New York Central Building would soon straddle Park Avenue like a gray stone colossus capped with glowing gold and copper. In the Times Square district, Paramount had recently opened its thirty-six-hundred-seat movie palace, with a grand Wurlitzer theater organ that shivered my bones and turned my insides to a quivering jelly.

Those rip-roaring days were good for women, and I've always had a yen for women who aren't afraid to go for broke. The year before, Leonora Speyer had won the Pulitzer for poetry, following Amy Lowell and Edna St. Vincent Millay. Helen Wills would hold the Number One world ranking in women's tennis for eight years, not losing a set from 1927 to 1933. Fourteen-year-old ice skater

Sonja Henie won her first Olympic gold in 1928. That same year, seventeen-year-old daredevil Elinor Smith became the first pilot—the only one still, so far as I know—to fly a plane under all four East River bridges. Amelia Earhart went farther and faster, becoming the first woman to fly across the Atlantic, as a passenger in a Fokker piloted by two men. When I interviewed her, she set her jaw and said firmly, "Next time, I'm gonna do it *myself*. Alone"

I set my own records in those days, too, and I was proud of them. I was the first woman reporter in the AP's flagship office. I was the first woman political journalist in the country. I was the first woman bylined on the front page of the *New York Times*, with a story about the sinking of the steamship *Vestris*. (I beat all the guys to the dock and got a survivor's story before the others figured out what was happening.) I was the first AP reporter assigned to the Lindbergh baby kidnapping, and the only woman. What's more, my stories were carried around the country via the wire service's nearly fourteen hundred subscriber newspapers. On any given day, a quarter to a third of them would be carrying a story with my byline. "The AP's front-page girl," they called me. I resented "girl," but I damn well earned the praise and the raise—to sixty-five dollars a week—that came with it. People knew my name. Lorena Hickok was *somebody*.

And Lorena Hickok was having the time of her life. My AP colleagues and I hung out after work at Lindy's, Leo Lindemann's restaurant and deli on Broadway just below Fiftieth. Lindy's—known for its cheesecake—was the headquarters of gangster Big Arnie Rothstein, remembered by F. Scott Fitzgerald as Meyer Wolfschein, who fixed the 1919 World Series. Big Arnie collected his booty at a table in the farthest corner, where he could keep his back to the wall—but that was then. One dark night, somebody gunned him down on Seventh Avenue, where he died in a puddle of blood. For a long time, nobody would sit at his table.

Damon Runyon, then a columnist for the Hearst papers, claimed his table by Lindy's front door, where he collected characters like baseball cards—The Seldom Seen Kid, Harry the Horse, Dream Street Rose, Nicely Nicely. And big-mouthed vaudeville comedian Milton Berle, Uncle Milty even then, bounced from table to table, collecting laughs from the bit players, actors, and journalists who drank there. Lindy's didn't sell booze, but friends and friends of friends passed their flasks under the table, so we were always well served.

I shared my friends and my apartment with Prinz, my German shepherd and companion. At seventy-five dollars a month, Mitchell Place was pricey. But it was new and midtown, just off First Avenue and Forty-Ninth, and roomy enough for the two of us, with a little kitchen where I could practice cookery and a balcony where Prinz could stretch out and lust after the pigeons and seagulls winging it over the East River. Evenings and Saturdays, Prinz and I ran together along the river. On the Sundays when it was my turn to monitor the AP news ticker, he went to the office with me and curled up under my desk. On off-duty Sundays, when my AP friends came over for a brunch of bacon and eggs and croissants and my notorious Stingers, Prinz played the ham, clowning for my friends' attention.

Yes, friends, my friends—women and a few men, too, passing through my days and nights. I was young then, and I had a young person's passions, a young person's desires. But I was often lonely, and in those days, before Eleanor filled the emptiness of my heart, I was lonely for Ellie Morse.

Oh, Ellie, Ellie. We lived together for eight years back in Minneapolis, where both of us worked at the *Tribune* and shared a three-room apartment on the top floor of the swank Hotel Leamington, on Ellie's wealthy father's tab. The war was over, the times were good and getting better. At the time, Tom Dillon was the *Trib*'s managing editor. He started me on night rewrite, then moved me to the copyedit desk, and then to news and features. Mr. Dillon—the Old Man, we called him—liked my smart mouth and my moxie and assigned me to crime and politics, strong stuff for women in those days. Sports, too. I was the first woman in the country to cover a major college football team—the Minnesota Gophers. I loved the noisy crowds, the crazy excitement, the brute force of bodies against bodies. I loved being out at the field, a woman covering a man's game, a woman journalist making the news in a man's business.

And I loved coming home to Ellie. My Ellie, a wispy thing, thin, fair-haired, not at all pretty, but whose large and generous affections erased all the losses in my life. My mother had died when I was thirteen, Ellie's mother had died giving birth to her, and we two motherless daughters learned to mother one another. My alcoholic father had abused me, but Ellie's father was extravagantly loving. She shared his lavish gifts with me, so that both of us were fathered (although I'm sure that the dear, good man had no idea of the nature of our relationship). When he died and left her a potful of money, she proposed that we spend a year in San Francisco.

"You can write your novel and get a nice rest," she said. "And when that's done, we can go to Europe and have a grand romantic adventure."

"But my newspaper job," I protested. "I've invested eight years in the *Trib* and—"

Ellie might be wispy, but she knew her mind. "The doctor says stress is bad for you, Hick. If we were living a quieter life, maybe your moods wouldn't be so…" She hesitated, then put it diplomatically. "So up and down."

I had just been diagnosed as diabetic, which explained my moods. Stress pumped me up, then brought me crashing down. I hated leaving my newspaper work, but I loved Ellie, I wanted to try my hand at a novel, and the idea of San Francisco was tempting. So I took a year's leave of absence and we went.

It didn't last. Ellie had never stopped liking men and she married one of them, damn it. She didn't have the nerve to tell me what she was doing—just eloped to Yuma with Roy Dickenson, a widower she had met years before at dancing class in Minneapolis. They had their grand European adventure together, leaving me to scrabble up the pieces of my broken heart. The disaster was total, for I couldn't make myself work on the novel, which probably wouldn't have been worth much anyway. I'm a teller of true stories, and fiction feels flabby to me. I finally gave up trying.

But I couldn't face the idea of moving back to Minneapolis without Ellie, where our friends would know how utterly I had been betrayed. I needed to fill my life with new work and new people in a new place, so I took the train to the Big Apple, fast-talked myself into a job on Hearst's tabloid *Daily Mirror,* and after six or eight months, moved up to the AP. I allowed myself to be lonely now and again—who isn't? But I had Prinz and good friends and good work. If there was any lingering self-pity, I blotted it out with a romantic fling or two, and by the afternoon Tommy Thompson and I had our little talk at Veniero's, I was back on track again.

Funny thing. The day I met Eleanor Roosevelt was the first day of the rest of my life, and she would be at the very center of it. But if there was any hint of that future, I completely missed it. No beating heart, no sweaty palms, no swooning awareness. If I felt anything at that pivotal moment, it was pity.

I had heard that Mrs. Roosevelt was no beauty—"homely as a barn door," one of my AP colleagues said—and when Tommy introduced us, I saw why. She was nearly six feet tall, her shoulders sloped, and her hands flapped at the ends of her long arms as if they were hinged. Like her Uncle Teddy's, her unfortunate front teeth protruded. Her chin was severely retrograde. Her voice was high-pitched and unpredictably fluting. She wore a hairnet—a hairnet!—over her hair and a flat black pancake of a hat tilted precariously over one eyebrow. Her black skirt was six inches too long to be stylish and her moss green silk tunic made her look like a two-day-old corpse. No great beauty myself, I've always felt a comradely affiliation with unbeautiful women. This time, I felt only a subterranean compassion.

But when I followed the lady to the women's luncheon where she was scheduled to speak, I forgot about the fluty voice and the buck teeth and that fatally green tunic. I watched from the back of the room as her audience stirred, quieted, then leaned forward to listen as she talked, not about the campaign or the candidates—she mentioned neither her husband nor Governor Smith—but about issues, serious issues. About shorter hours and better pay for women, about the responsibility to vote. She talked to them as if they were her neighbors, sisters, friends. She was informed, engaged, engaging.

*Impressive,* I thought, agreeably surprised. And I was suddenly interested in Mrs. Roosevelt, not as FDR's political wife or TR's favorite niece, but as herself: editor, writer, teacher, factory owner, mother, grandmother. There was a story here. *She* was the story, and I found her on my mind several times a day. But the interview

Tommy had promised me was delayed and then delayed again, and I was beginning to think it wouldn't happen—until the day before the election, when Tommy telephoned to schedule it for the day after.

Bad timing, I thought. "Maybe we ought to put it off for a week or two," I suggested tactfully. I wanted to interview the lady, but she was going to be pretty raw on the day after her husband's defeat. Out of respect for her feelings—

"It's already on the calendar," Tommy said cheerfully and gave me the address of the Roosevelts' townhouse on East Sixty-Fifth. The interview was to take place there, rather than the office. "Fewer interruptions," she explained, when I expressed my surprise.

There was no question about the outcome of the 1928 presidential election. The Happy Warrior was a progressive Wet in a conservative nation that liked to pretend it was Dry, and rumors flew that he was an alcoholic who had promised to name a bootlegger as secretary of the treasury. Worse, he was a devout Irish Catholic who aroused the righteous ire of Protestant preachers who told their flocks that a vote for Smith was a vote for the pope and the devil disguised as the Democratic candidate. It was a dirty campaign, a smear campaign, and everybody knew that the ticket was going down.

On election night, I went to the Democratic national headquarters in the Park Avenue Armory to watch the presidential returns being posted on the big board. As predicted, the tally—Smith's trivial 87 electoral votes to Hoover's 444—was humiliating. "The time hasn't come yet when a man can say his beads in the White House," Smith growled. He clapped his brown derby on his head and stalked out. The next day at Lindy's, Uncle Milty joked that the Happy Warrior had sent the pope a one-word telegram that morning: "Unpack."

With the national GOP landslide, everybody expected that the Republican candidate would take the governor's race as well, and by the time I got to the state election headquarters at the Biltmore, Mr. and Mrs. Roosevelt had already gone home. But those of us who waited it out heard some remarkable news, along about four a.m. It was a squeaker, but when the upstate returns finally came in, Franklin Roosevelt was the state's new governor.

Bleary-eyed, I shared an early morning cigarette and a cup of black coffee with Elton Fay, AP's capital bureau chief. "Shocker, huh?" I said. "Must've been plenty of split-ticket voting."

Fay rubbed his stubbled chin. "Chalk this one up to FDR's campaign manager. Louis Howe planted Roosevelt stories in every upstate weekly. He mailed fliers to farmers and businessmen, and hounded the hell out of precinct chairmen." He squinted against the smoke of his cigarette. "But you gotta give it to FDR, you know? He stuck that battered old felt hat on his head—somebody said he wore it in the 1920 campaign, before the polio—got in an open car, and barnstormed all around the state. If anybody noticed that he's a cripple, they were too polite to say so. That wife of his helped, too, although the street says she wasn't any too eager for him to run."

"Is that so?" I said and put out my cigarette in my coffee cup. "Well, I hope she takes that hairnet off before she moves into the governor's mansion."

Fay laughed. "Makes you wonder, doesn't it?"

I filed my story, went home, took Prinz for a quick walk, and caught a couple of hours of sleep. Under the circumstances, I expected my interview with the state's new First Lady to be canceled. But when I called Tommy to check, it was still on. I wasn't getting excited, though. I figured that now that Mrs. Roosevelt was a political wife, even the AP's front-page girl would have to resign herself to a backgrounder, with no direct quotes.

There were two residences behind the single front door of the dignified four-story brick Neo-Georgian house on East Sixty-Fifth. The Franklin Roosevelts lived at Number 49; his mother, Mrs. Sara Roosevelt, lived at Number 47. Built and furnished twenty years before by the elder Mrs. Roosevelt, the townhouse had been a Christmas gift for her son and his bride—except that it wasn't a gift, for Mrs. Roosevelt had kept her son's house in her name. There were two drawing rooms, two dining rooms, two kitchens, two butler's pantries—two separate houses, but like conjoined twins, fatally fused at each floor by communicating doors that allowed the senior Mrs. Roosevelt to come and go, unannounced, at any time she wished, into the kitchen, the sitting room, the bedrooms, the nursery. As I was to learn later, the junior Mrs. Roosevelt viewed the house as a metaphor for her mother-in-law's domination of the family's life. She hated it.

But for now, all I knew was that Mrs. Franklin Roosevelt—dressed in a charming lace-trimmed hostess gown (but still wearing that appalling hairnet pulled halfway down her forehead)—was seated in a plum velvet wing chair in her elegant, flower-filled drawing room, pouring tea from a handsome silver tea service. Her black Scotty, Meggie, lay at her feet.

I'm cynical by nature and my experience as a reporter has only nurtured that natural inclination. Later that day, as I was turning my notes into newspaper copy, I would suspect that this particular presentation of the First Lady of the state of New York had been carefully staged for an audience of one—me. But at the moment, I was absorbed in the lady herself. As I watched her, I saw something. And then I saw something *else.*

I saw, and envied, the comfortable assurance that hovers like a smug ghost on the shoulders of those who have always had more than enough of everything. I recognized that easily, because for most of my young life, I never had nearly enough of anything. My father was a drunken dairyman who rarely held the same job for more than a few months at a time and moved his wife and children —two pretty daughters and me, tall and bulky for my age and strikingly *un*pretty—from one bleak prairie village to another. My mother may have loved me, but she was an ineffectual woman who wept when my father beat me but never lifted a hand to stop him. Until she died of a stroke when I was thirteen, I felt only a kind of bewildered resentment toward her. Did she fail to protect me because I wasn't pretty? Or because I wasn't as compliant as my sisters?

Yes, perhaps that was it—my defiance. I couldn't yield, somehow. I simply could not yield. My sister Ruby, younger by two years, played up sweetly to our father and later, to our stepmother. She told me that life would be easier if I did, too—if I could be submissive, if I could be meek.

"Bend a little to him," Ruby said, practical even then. "It doesn't cost anything to bend, you know."

I knew, but I couldn't. When I felt something wasn't true, I couldn't say it. When I felt it wasn't right, I couldn't do it. Perhaps I was afflicted with the moral arrogance of the young, or perhaps I knew as a child what I know as an adult: that to give in to circumstance is to fail to live fully. I refused to respect those who had not earned my respect, not even to save myself from being beaten. A year after my mother's death, my father married our housekeeper, who—sensing perhaps her new husband's incestuous interest in his daughter's maturing body, or simply tired of my rebellious obstinacy—told me to pack my things and get out.

So at an age when Miss Eleanor Roosevelt was curling her hair and going to dancing classes, I became a hired girl on the dusty Dakota plains, cooking and washing dishes, emptying chamber pots, and scrubbing floors in other people's houses. It was demeaning, spirit-destroying work, but I was protected from a fatal self-pity by the very un-girlish gift of irony. When I began to take my situation too seriously—when I hoped too much or wanted too much or even hated too much—I could hear a droll, self-mocking voice poking fun at my situation. To this day, that voice has been a strong defense against despair, for as long as I can hear it, I know there is a part of me that stands for my *self*.

I think it was that part of me that glimpsed the fearful, wistful, half-hopeful sadness and uncertainty in Eleanor Roosevelt, the deep self-doubt that gave the lie to her outward social assurance. I had come to interview a woman who seemed to be creating a place for herself, and for other women, in the male stronghold of Democratic politics. But what I saw was a diffident, lonely woman who wasn't sure who she was. This recognition touched my news-hardened heart, and as I took out my notebook and pencil, I found myself wanting to know her real story, the story of her *real* life, behind and beneath all the clamor—the opposing Roosevelt clans, the party politics, her husband's expanding ambitions. That wasn't the story the AP wanted, or would print. That was the story *I* wanted.

But I wasn't going to get it. What I got instead was the AP's story, which she rehearsed for me in that wavering, high-pitched soprano that fluttered like a lost bird somewhere above the window cornices. The story of her work, beginning with the Red Cross canteens during the Great War and continuing into her recent political activity. Her teaching—American history, literature, and public affairs—at Todhunter, a prominent private school for upper-class girls in New York. The furniture factory, a crafts workshop that she co-owned with two friends at Val-Kill Cottage, on the Roosevelt estate in Hyde Park. Her children, too: Anna, married to a Wall Street stockbroker and the mother of a baby girl; James at Harvard; the three younger boys at Groton.

She answered my questions without hesitation, speaking about the children with a mother's practiced fondness. About her political work, about the Val-Kill crafts workshop, and especially about teaching, she spoke with a different enthusiasm, her voice and face animated.

"I love teaching," she said. "It's my *life.*"

About the presidential campaign and Al Smith's defeat, she was indignant: "It was the religious issue, of course. Hoover's campaign shamelessly exploited people's fears—and their ignorance. A woman told me, quite seriously, that she couldn't vote for Smith because he intended to appoint all the pope's sons to his cabinet. Can you imagine the idiocy?"

"What did you tell her?" I asked.

"I asked her how many sons she thought the pope had," she said and relaxed into a laugh so infectious and *real* that I had to join her.

But when I asked about her husband's new job and their move to the governor's mansion, the animation disappeared from her face and voice, as if she had suddenly retreated into some kind of emotional shell concealed under that fetching hostess gown. Later, I would come to understand this ability of hers to step abruptly into a freezing reticence. But at the moment, I felt as if I were facing a blank wall, a chilly wind blowing down my neck. I had expected that excitement—about her husband's surprising victory, beating the odds, moving to Albany. Not *this*.

But thinking about what little I knew of the lady and reading between the lines (where the story usually lives), her frozen impenetrability made a certain kind of sense. Before last night, Mrs. Roosevelt had been her own independent person, a leader in national politics and women's issues, passionately committed to teaching and to the Val-Kill crafts. She had made a life for herself. Now, she was the governor's wife, expected to manage the governor's mansion, serve as the governor's hostess, dedicate herself to the governor's political career. Now, she was a character in *his* story. She didn't want to know this or feel it; she didn't want *me* to know it or feel it—and certainly not to say it in print.

I closed my notebook and laid it aside. "I'm wondering," I said mildly, "how you're going to manage."

Her glance was guarded. "Manage?"

"Yes. It will be a juggle. What will you give up?"

She tilted her head to one side, studying me, as if she were taking my measure. After a moment, she said, "I was awake all last night, thinking about that 'juggle,' as you call it." Another hesitation, then, "Can we keep this just between ourselves, Miss Hickok?"

"You mean, off the record?"

"That's what you journalists say, isn't it? Yes, off the record."

"Done." I put my pencil on my notebook.

She seemed to relax. "Perhaps you won't be surprised to hear that while I'm very glad for my husband, I'm not terribly thrilled about his election—for myself, that is." She sighed. "I know that he has to take what he thinks is the best course, and I will do my part. But for myself, I have to find a way…" She stopped.

I heard the struggle in her voice, saw it on her face, and understood. This was a woman caught between her hopes for herself and his demands, his needs. "You have to find a way to do your own work, as well as the work that's expected of you."

She was startled, as if she hadn't expected to hear her intentions in another's voice. "Yes, that's it exactly. And I mean to do it." She straightened her shoulders and began describing a complicated plan that would be my first introduction to Mrs. R's efforts to cram a great many activities into a very small space.

"Monday and Tuesday, I'll teach and do political work in New York. On Wednesday, I'll take the early train to Hyde Park, stop in at the crafts workshop, then take the afternoon train to Albany, where I'll spend the rest of the week managing cabinet dinners, afternoon teas, ladies' groups, and the like. My husband employs Miss LeHand, who is devoted to him and his work," she added. "She's coming to Albany with him, so the governor's household will be under her supervision on the days I'm not there. She is quite able."

Ah. I just managed *not* to raise my eyebrows, although I had certainly heard of Marguerite LeHand—Missy. A confident, attractive young woman, she had joined FDR's staff during the 1920 presidential campaign, stayed on during his illness, and regularly accompanied him to his spa in Georgia, where she did his secretarial work, served as his hostess, and performed other duties as required. The boys in the AP newsroom liked to grin about "the office wife" and her other duties. I had seen Missy with FDR on the campaign trail, where she seemed supremely unaware of the curious eyes that followed her attractive figure. I understood the newsroom jokes.

As if she had looked into my thoughts, Mrs. Roosevelt lifted her chin and remarked, dryly, "In Tibet, I've read, the ladies find it necessary to have three husbands each. They say that the three together add up to a nearly perfect life partner. Which seems to me a very good thing, since so many husbands have several wives."

I was startled into laughter. "Never had one husband, and certainly don't want one—let alone three." I raised my teacup in salute. "But here's to the wise ladies of Tibet."

The lines around Mrs. Roosevelt's blue eyes crinkled, and she broke into a rich, low laugh that softened her face. At that moment, she was actually rather lovely—or would be, if she would get rid of that wretched hairnet.

"To the ladies of Tibet." She raised her own cup. "May they find what they seek—although when it comes to husbands, I personally find that one is more than enough." She added hastily, "Off the record."

I chuckled. "Oh, too bad. That would have made a dandy headline." Another low laugh, and I thought again how pretty she was. I put down my teacup. "This plan of yours—can you really bring it off? The teaching, the crafts, on top of being the governor's wife?"

"I hope to—no, I *must*." She was emphatic. "My work is where I find myself. It's my salvation."

Ah, but is it where we *ought* to find ourselves? I wondered. But honesty compelled me to say, "Work keeps me going, too."

She smiled gently. "But you are so much more accomplished than I, Miss Hickok. Just look at all you've done—at all you do. I envy you, you know. You're at the top of your world. I'm at the bottom of mine."

I frowned. Surely the woman was joking. But at that moment the door opened, and a little man, scarcely five feet tall, sidled cat-like into the room. Frail and gaunt, almost skeletal, he wore a rumpled, coffee-stained white shirt and carried a cigarette in one hand, a foul-smelling Sweet Caporal. His pockmarked, gargoyle-like face had to be one of the ugliest I had ever seen, yet in that ugliness there was a compelling, almost magnetic energy.

"Good afternoon, Mrs. Roosevelt." He turned to me with a sardonic grin and a wave of his hand, ashes sifting onto his shirt, his tie, the carpet. "And Miss Hickok, the AP's celebrated girl reporter."

Mrs. Roosevelt intervened. "This is Mr. Louis Howe, Miss Hickok. He is Mr. Roosevelt's political advisor."

I knew who he was, of course. FDR's consigliere, the man who had packaged the candidate and sold him to the electorate. A political wizard, a mastermind, he was called by some; a goddamn son-of-a-bitch by others. I wasn't surprised to see him here. I knew that he had made his home with the Roosevelts, more or less, since FDR was overtaken by polio, and that during those terrible months in the summer and autumn of 1921, he and Mrs. Roosevelt had worked to exhaustion together, tending to FDR's physical needs around the clock. Howe's wife, Grace, lived in Fall River, Massachusetts, where he visited on the occasional weekend. But his personal life was completely consumed by his work for FDR, as Tommy Thompson's life was consumed by ER. I wonder now what I might have done if I had guessed, at that moment, that I would be consumed in the same way, at once filled and emptied by this woman, so tightly, so fatally fused that neither of us could let the other go. Would I have closed my notebook and left? Would I have stayed and accepted the risk? I'm glad that I didn't know, that I didn't have to choose.

"I took the liberty of telling Mr. Howe that we would be chatting this afternoon," Mrs. Roosevelt remarked in an offhand way. "He wanted to meet you."

Howe sucked on his cigarette. I could feel his dark eyes on me, at once critical, calculating, curious. He wanted to meet *me*? And then it occurred to me that perhaps the purpose of today's interview was other than I had thought. It was as if a door had opened a few inches in front of me, and I could feel a slight breeze.

I had to say something. "Congratulations on last night's win, Mr. Howe," I managed. "I'll bet there are dozens who would like to know how you pulled that split-ticket rabbit out of your hat."

"Wasn't too sure it was going to happen myself until the upstate polls reported." He sat down and accepted a cup of tea from Mrs. Roosevelt. "I've read some of your stuff, Miss Hickok. Liked the piece about the female undercover narcotics investigator." He recited the headline, using two fingers to sketch quotation marks. "'Little Woman With Brown Bobbed Hair Holds Dangerous N.Y. Police Job.' A nice, tight piece of writing. Ironic. Irreverent."

"'Little Woman' wasn't my headline," I said. "But I like writing stories about women who do things nobody expects them to do. Things that go against the grain." I grinned, feeling easier now. "Used to be a policewoman myself, down by the Navy pier."

"Really?" Mrs. Roosevelt leaned forward, her eyes on me, her gaze intent. "How *fascinating*, Miss Hickok." The corners of her mobile mouth turned upward. "You must have stories to tell about that particular work."

The conversation went on from there, but now it seemed to be more about me than the woman I had come to interview, and by the time Mr. Howe stood up and thanked Mrs. Roosevelt for the tea, I knew I was right: Louis Howe had been evaluating me, although I couldn't think why, or where that open door—if that's what it was—might lead. But I rather liked the man. He seemed to have Mrs. Roosevelt's best interests at heart, and she was relaxed and comfortable with him.

When Mr. Howe had gone, Mrs. Roosevelt walked downstairs

with me, past the dozens of framed pictures of ships and other nautical items that filled the walls. I paused to admire them.

"They're my husband's," she said. "He's always bringing home a new ship's model, or more paintings and prints. Stamps, too, and campaign buttons." Her voice was rueful. "His things are treasures, but it's hard to find room for all of them. They take up every inch of space in this house."

Exactly, I thought. And just where did FDR's wife find room for *her* treasures? What space, in the life they lived together, was left for *her* doings, her dreams?

At the door, I said goodbye. "And good luck with your juggling act," I added. "I'll be curious to see how your plan turns out."

Mrs. Roosevelt hesitated, her head on one side, considering. "You know, I think we might just go ahead and publish that bit about my plan, Miss Hickok. When my husband reads it in the newspaper, it will give him a clearer idea of what I have in mind for myself. And when it's in print, in your story, it will be settled, and he can't very well argue with it." She smiled and held out her hand. "I'll have Mrs. Thompson type up something you can quote in your article. I find that it's always nicer to be able to read someone's actual words, don't you?"

*Direct quotes?* From the governor's wife? I swallowed my surprise. "That would be swell," I said, and we shook hands warmly.

It wasn't until I was hailing a cab that I replayed her remark: once it was in print, her husband couldn't argue with it. What an odd way for a married couple to communicate, I thought. Didn't these Roosevelts *talk* to one another?

Over the coming years, as I found myself deeply, irrevocably involved with her—and inevitably with *him*, in ways I didn't like—I would wonder many times about their relationship. What *was* it? Why? How did it become what it was? Each of them kept secrets from each other, from their children, from the people who worked for them, from the public. They were not lovers (not, at least, each other's lover); sometimes they weren't even friends. That theirs became a successful political partnership was a mystery even to those who knew them best—and I think a mystery to each of them, to her, and certainly to him.

But I couldn't begin to ask myself these questions—not yet. I climbed in the taxi and went back to my AP desk, where an hour later, an envelope arrived by messenger from Mrs. Roosevelt's office. When my article appeared a couple of days later in the *New York Times* and in newspapers all over the country, it included several direct quotes from the new First Lady. The headline gave fair warning of her intentions: "Mrs. Roosevelt to Keep on Filling Many Jobs."

Many jobs. It would be the story of her life. And mine.

# Part Two

1932–1933

# Chapter Two

# Hello Again

During FDR's four years as governor, I thought of the First Lady many times—not the always-in-a-hurry woman whose name appeared daily in the newspapers, but the lonely woman whose wistful, half-hopeful vulnerability had so surprised and touched me. In the newsroom, I heard a few intriguing remarks (not all of them complimentary) about her and her friends, and I wondered whether—and how—she had been able to make time and space for herself, given the widening encroachments of her husband's political career. I kept telling myself I would follow up with her, but it was FDR who claimed my attention. I reported on the governor when he was in New York City, followed him on occasional trips around the state, and covered his successful 1930 reelection campaign. He noticed me, and since I was the only reporter who wore rouge, red lipstick, earrings, and a skirt, I got a heavy-duty dose of his banter.

"Ah, the glamorous Miss Hickok!" he would exclaim, lifting his cigarette in salute. Or with a glint in his eye: "Let's have a question from the AP's Girl Wonder."

I'm thick-skinned about my work, so while his teasing rankled, I didn't take it personally. I thought it was his way of cutting women down to size, diminishing them, especially women who amounted to something. And, like most reporters, I'd rather be noticed than overlooked.

I *was* getting noticed. On my political beat, I covered the increasingly ugly messes at Tammany Hall and the corruption in Mayor Jimmy Walker's office. I covered the Wall Street panics of 1929 and '30. I wrote about the disastrous plunge in the gross national product and the tens of thousands of banks and businesses that failed and the thirteen million workers—thirteen *million*! —who were unemployed. I wrote about the Hoovervilles in the freight yards along the East River, makeshift shelters thrown together out of used lumber, rusty sheets of corrugated metal, old tires, flattened tin cans, even cardboard. Hopeless, hungry, the occupants ate what they could get from the bread lines and soup kitchens and whatever else they could beg or scavenge. Later, I would understand just how shallow and superficial my understanding of their misery had been. But their despair made for good copy, and my stories got plenty of national play. Somebody wrote that I had "standing with the AP that no other woman can match." Somebody was right.

And then, in April of 1932, I got noticed again. My city editor, Bill Chapin, beckoned me to his desk. "I just got a call from Louis Howe. He's inviting you to take a personal, one-woman tour of the Roosevelt family estate."

"They're angling for a color piece," I said cynically. "'The Roosevelts at Springwood.' They want the public to see a scene of domestic bliss."

Chapin nodded. "The Howe publicity machine is building up a head of steam for the Democratic presidential convention. Hoover is history. If FDR gets the party's nod, he'll get the White House." He cocked his head. "You want the story or not?"

"As long as it's an exclusive," I said. "It'll be interesting to write about the rich, for a change, instead of the down-and-out."

But I had another reason. I wanted the story behind the story. I wanted to know how well Mrs. Roosevelt had managed that juggling act, commuting between New York, Hyde Park, and Albany, how well she had preserved her personal interests. And there was the most interesting question of all: How did she feel about becoming the nation's First Lady?

Before I went to Hyde Park, I did my usual background research on the estate so I'd know what I was seeing when I got there.

Springwood had been in the Roosevelt family since FDR's father bought a square mile of Hudson River farmland in 1866. Like an English country gentleman, "Mr. James" (whose money came from coal, steamships, and railroads) cantered around the Dutchess County countryside decked out in tweeds, breeches, and riding boots. Mrs. James—Sara Ann Delano Roosevelt (whose family money came from the China opium trade)—was very much the squire's lady. Franklin was her only child and the apple of her eye. When he joined the Wilson administration and his political future star seemed to glow as brightly as Cousin Teddy's, she more than doubled the size and splendor of the family home, the Big House, providing her son a suitable setting in which to entertain his political friends.

Franklin had inherited Mr. James's passionate interest in Springwood, but his father had left the family estate to his mother. Sara Roosevelt also owned the two summer houses at Campobello (one for herself, one for her son), the twin Manhattan townhouses, and the Roosevelt family bank accounts. She exercised a controlling interest in everything that went on at Springwood—except for

Val-Kill Cottage. That had been built on a small piece of land owned by FDR and now belonged to Eleanor Roosevelt and two of her friends.

Reggie Davis, an AP stringer, was glad to fill me in on the governor's wife. We sat down together one afternoon over a beer at Big Johnny's, the reporters' bar in Albany. Reggie lit a cigarette and said, "Scuttlebutt has it that Eleanor would rather stay at Val-Kill than at the Big House."

I frowned a little at the First Lady's first name, but I didn't say anything. The boys in the AP newsroom called her Eleanor and snickered at my more respectful "Mrs. Roosevelt" or even "Mrs. R."

Reggie picked up his beer mug and leaned back in his chair. "The thing is, y'see, Eleanor likes it at Val-Kill because her mother-in-law won't go on the place. Granny doesn't like Eleanor's friends." With a glint in his eye, he lowered his voice to a teasing whisper, almost drowned out by a chorus of hearty male laughter at the bar. "They're lesbians."

I didn't answer. Reggie was a good source and I liked him, but I wasn't going to rise to his bait. I had learned to keep my private life and my work life separate, and I guarded that right for others—as far as I could, given my job as a reporter. It wasn't easy now, and it would get harder as time went on, but I drew a line between what lay in the legitimate public interest and should be accessible to the press and what was nobody's damn business.

It wasn't the first time I'd heard about "Eleanor's friends," though. Nancy Cook was the executive secretary of the Women's Division of the New York State Democratic Committee, where Mrs. Roosevelt worked as a volunteer. Cook lived with Marion Dickerman, who was the principal at Todhunter, where Mrs. Roosevelt taught. And there was another pair. Elizabeth Read was

Eleanor's personal lawyer; Read's life partner Esther Lape (whom I had met and liked very much) was the founder of the League of Women Voters. Read and Lape shared a house on East Eleventh Street in Greenwich Village. "Female impersonators," somebody had called them snidely. In the AP newsroom, male eyebrows went up at the mention of their names and waggled significantly when Mrs. Roosevelt's name was added.

Somebody put a nickel in the juke box, and the sandpaper sound of Louis Armstrong singing "You Rascal You" scraped through the crowd noise.

"There's a guy, too." Reggie pursed his lips. "A real guy, I mean. A he-man."

"Oh, yeah?" I lifted my beer. This I hadn't heard. "Who?"

"Earl Miller. Sergeant Earl Miller. You go to the estate, you're likely to run into him."

Sergeant Miller. "Military?"

"State trooper. He was a guard at the mansion when the Happy Warrior was governor, and Roosevelt assigned him to Eleanor as driver and bodyguard. Big guy, Olympic boxer, circus acrobat, expert marksman. Reputation as a Casanova. Self-impressed, kind of a loudmouth." He blew out a smoke ring. "I hear Eleanor is sweet on him."

"You're kidding." It sounded like there was a story here—one the wire services wouldn't touch, of course. Which made it all the more tempting to the tabloids, as I knew from my days on the *Mirror*. I was even more intrigued. Whatever Mrs. Roosevelt was up to, I hoped for her sake that she was discreet.

"Swear to God, Hick." Reggie assumed an earnest expression. "Seen 'em together myself, his hand on her shoulder, friendly as you please. Miller lives in the governor's mansion when the family is in Albany, goes down to Hyde Park with them on weekends, eats at the family table. Drives Eleanor on weekend trips, sometimes just the two of them. He's some fifteen years younger than she is, and athletic. Goes horseback riding with her, teaches her to swim and shoot." He leaned closer, confidential. "Servants like to talk, you know. They're told to stay away from the press but that doesn't keep them from handing out a little tittle-tattle now and then. They think the Roosevelt marriage is on the rocks. The two of them don't sleep together, you know. Eleanor's got this trooper guy and the governor's got Missy LeHand." He gave me an evil grin. "Le*Hand*. Get it?"

I got it.

"And they're all one big happy family." He smirked. "Eleanor loves Missy like a sister, FDR likes having Earl around. Which makes it look innocent, if you know what I mean. Anyway, like I said, FDR's got Missy, Eleanor's got this trooper guy. Sauce for the gander, goose gets some, too."

There was a clatter of glasses at the bar and a couple of boozy male voices chimed in with Armstrong's. *I'll be glad when you're dead, you rascal you.*

"The tabloids would kill for that story," I said. "Especially now, with the nominating convention coming up."

"Oh, you bet. There's more, too." Reggie leaned forward. "One of the maids in the mansion told me that FDR set Earl up with Missy, romance-wise, figuring he could kill two birds with one stone. Shoot down the rumors about himself and Missy and Earl and Eleanor, both at the same time. But Missy wouldn't play, so he came up with another plan." He leaned back, sucking on his cigarette. "Miller's being married off. To his first wife's cousin."

I stared at him.

"Yeah, weird, you bet. The girl is seventeen, would you believe? Half Miller's age, at least. The wedding will be at Val-Kill.

And for a wedding present, FDR is giving Miller a piece of property next to Springwood." He grinned and hoisted his beer. "How d'ya like them apples, Hick? A little *quid* for the old *pro quo.*"

"Come on, now," I scoffed. "I've heard that the governor likes to play games, but surely even he wouldn't arrange a marriage just to quash a few nasty rumors."

Reggie turned serious. "Don't you bet on it, Hick. Roosevelt may look like a lightweight, but the man is devious as the devil— and he's got a sharp left hook. Comes out of nowhere when you're not looking for it. When he hits, he hurts."

I would run into that sharp left later. It would come out of nowhere, too. And it would hurt. It would hurt like bloody hell.

*You rascal you.*


When I got off the train at the Hyde Park station the following weekend, I was met by a strikingly handsome, well-built state trooper wearing a dashing uniform, polished boots, and the name *Sgt. Miller* on his breast pocket. His dark hair was parted down the middle, Hollywood style, and Brylcreemed flat to his scalp. Not my cup of tea, but as he deftly installed me in the back seat of the state car, I could see why Mrs. Roosevelt might find the man attractive —if she did.

"I understand that congratulations are in order," I said casually as we turned onto the Albany Post Road.

Startled, the sergeant glanced at me in the rear view mirror. "You heard?" He had a deep voice that resonated from somewhere in his chest.

"One of my Albany newspaper friends told me."

"Figures. You guys are all over everything." He chuckled. "Happy to say it's a big step up."

I blinked. "Pardon?"

"A big step up for me. Five prisons, two reformatories, three hundred-plus guards." He grinned at me in the mirror. "Not that I can't handle it. But it's quite a change from driving the governor and the lady here and there."

"Ah," I said, understanding. "A new job." A new job *and* a marriage. Plus a piece of property. The idea of FDR as master of ceremonies suddenly seemed a lot more credible.

He looked at me again, dark eyebrows raised. "Yeah. Director of Personnel, Department of Corrections. What'd you think?"

"I thought it was a wedding. Aren't you getting married?"

"Christ." His mouth tightened. "How'd you find out about that?"

"Supposed to be a secret?" I countered.

"From you reporters," he growled. After a moment, he added, "Keep it under your hat, okay? Off the record. Completely."

"If you say so," I said. And that's all I could get out of him for the rest of the trip.

A little later, we were turning between a pair of brownstone gateposts and down a long, maple-lined drive. At the end stood an impressive Georgian mansion with a semicircular porch, surrounded by a velvety green lawn that sloped down to a fringe of woods above the wide Hudson River. I felt an eclipsing sense of awe, tinged with a shadowy resentment. If the Depression had visited here, it had come and gone and left no signs of its passing. These Roosevelts, I thought, born to wealth and power and defined by their privilege and entitlement. Anything, everything they want is within easy reach, while the rest of us, we ordinary mortals, have to swim against the currents of fate.

But as I got out of the car, I reminded myself that I was a

reporter, not a moral philosopher. I was not part of the story. I was there to write a color feature, and that was that.

We had tea in the dark-paneled, book-lined living room, which boasted two ornate marble fireplaces, each topped by a gilt-framed Roosevelt ancestor. Several photographs of Teddy Roosevelt were prominently displayed on a shelf, an elaborate parquet floor was covered with lush Oriental rugs, and the room commanded an imposing view of the Hudson. But the rich setting wasn't what captured my attention as the hour went on. It was the relationship among the three Roosevelts that I found so fascinating. Domestic bliss? Forget about it.

The governor was seated in the leather-backed chair to the left of the fireplace, Camel cigarette jauntily canted toward the ceiling in a nicotine-stained holder. Debonair and lively, he was full of questions about the Lindbergh kidnapping case I was currently covering and brimming with political gossip about the investigation of New York's dapper playboy mayor, Jimmy Walker. The special counsel the governor had appointed had returned fifteen specific counts of corruption in the mayor's office, and it was shaping up to be a factor in the nominating process. FDR was under a great deal of pressure to remove Mayor Walker in the next month, before the Chicago Democratic convention.

But if he did, he stood to lose the support of New York's convention delegates, which he needed to win the nomination. I was covering the Walker investigation for the Associated Press, which—it now occurred to me—might be one of the reasons Louis Howe had invited me to Springwood. The governor had a hard choice to make, and it wouldn't hurt to have the AP's "front-page girl" in his pocket. But I had earned a reputation for being

carefully objective when it came to my political reporting. I didn't
intend to give it up in return for a cup of tea and a dollop of FDR's
famous patronage.

The governor's mother was seated in a chair to the right of the
fireplace, a silver-haired, imperial *grande dame* in a gray dress with a
white lace collar and a single long rope of carefully graduated
pearls. She offered me her hand with a faint smile and an air of
*noblesse oblige,* letting me know that she was not in the habit of
entertaining reporters but was making a special exception in my
case.

Mrs. Roosevelt came in a few moments after I sat down. She
was neatly dressed in a blue sweater and beige corduroy skirt, her
golden-brown hair snugged loosely back under a blue headband—
and no hairnet. She greeted me with a warm smile and a low-
voiced "Hello again, Miss Hickok." She sat down on the sofa with
her knitting—a child's sweater, it looked like—occasionally glan-
cing at me.

But that was the last time she spoke. The conversation was
entirely managed by her husband with an occasional assist from his
mother, who presided over the sumptuous silver tea tray and
chimed in now and then with choice bits of Roosevelt family lore.
Some of what the elder Mrs. Roosevelt said was clearly designed to
illustrate the political prowess of her son, on whom she obviously
doted, but some just as clearly was meant to disparage her daughter-in-law.

"If you'd take off that band and run a comb through your hair,
dear, you'd look ever so much nicer," she said, in a bladed whisper.
And then, with a small smile, she regretted aloud that I couldn't
spend more time touring the Big House instead of driving over to
see Val-Kill, the cottage that Mrs. Roosevelt shared with friends
who smoked and wore neckties and trousers, quite the done thing

in New York, she was sure, but just a little... oh, one might say, *avant garde*, here in Hyde Park, where the outlook was more... well, conservative.

The younger Mrs. Roosevelt kept her eyes on her knitting, but her shoulders were hunched against the assault and I could see the flush climbing her cheeks. In her place, I would have fired back, but whatever her feelings, she kept them to herself. Still, the tension was uncomfortable enough—*painful* enough, really—to make me squirm, and I felt deeply sorry for her. She certainly wasn't getting any help from FDR, who paid no attention to his mother's poisoned darts, airily smiling and chatting, chatting and smiling, until at last he put down his teacup, rubbed his hands together, and announced that it was time for a tour of the estate.

"We'll do this together, Hick," he said genially. "Just the two of us."

As if at a signal, Sergeant Miller and another man came into the room, made a sling of their joined arms, and carried FDR out to his specially built hand-operated Ford. I followed and climbed in beside him and we were off, followed by a second car, a blue convertible roadster driven by Mrs. Roosevelt, with Sergeant Miller beside her. Until they turned off on a different route, I could see them deep in conversation, and—by now deeply curious—I wondered.

Was there now, had there ever been, anything serious, anything romantic, between them? *Was* Miller's marriage the work of the governor, or perhaps of Louis Howe? What about that property, the wedding gift? And the supervisory job, which, as Miller himself put it, was a big step up? All designed to sweeten the pot? Good questions, the kind any experienced reporter would ask. And the tabloids had plenty of experienced reporters who knew how to craft a story out of gossip and hints and innuendo. If they began asking, there could be hell to pay.

Behind the wheel, the governor was *dee-lighted!* (an exclamation, like his pince-nez, copied from his presidential cousin Teddy) by everything he saw. In the driver's seat, his disability was invisible. He reveled in the power and mobility the car gave him, driving fast and expertly down the narrow lanes of the eleven-hundred-acre estate, proudly showing off his reforestation project, his soil conservation efforts, the farm fields that had been his father's great pleasure, even the long, steep hill he had sledded down when he was a boy. Clearly, I was meant to be impressed by these wonders and to include them in my story.

"Isn't it grand?" he exulted, over and over, a boy's gay glint in his eye. "Isn't it all just *grand*, Hick?"

Bemused, I echoed: "Grand, just grand, sir," trying to keep the sarcasm out of my voice. I was remembering the misery I saw daily on the wretched faces of the jobless, the homeless, in the railroad yards, on the dirty streets of New York City. Looking around at the rolling landscape, the woods and rich fields, I thought that this landed patrician, whom I had just seen behaving with utter insensitivity toward his wife, could never fathom the depths of their poverty. How could a man with so much ever be the president of *all* the people at a time when so many had so little?

At last we arrived at Val-Kill Cottage. It was a small, gray fieldstone house with white shutters and gables, set at the top of a gently sloping bank above a small stream and surrounded by a lawn and lovely woods. The cottage itself, Dutch Colonial, had the look of the last century, but as we drove over the log bridge and stopped next to the house, FDR told me with some pride that he had built it himself in 1926.

"Did it for my Missis," he said, "so she and her friends would have a place to get away from the city." When the cottage was finished, he had handed it and several acres over to the "girls," his wife and her two best friends, Nancy and Marion. "Now, they've built their furniture factory here." He jerked a thumb at a building behind the cottage and shot me a grin. "Keeps 'em busy, y'know." His chuckle was patronizing. "Keeps 'em off the streets and out of trouble. When my wife is here, I know where she is." The little speech was more revealing than he'd intended it to be, I thought, remembering that his mother had given the newlyweds a townhouse adjoining hers. He had given Val-Kill to his wife and her friends. The two gifts might seem different, but were they?

The governor left me and drove off. Mrs. Roosevelt came out to greet me, and I was struck by the remarkable change in her appearance. At the Big House, she had been stiff and sober-faced, clearly discomfited, even humiliated, by her mother-in-law's barbed thrusts. Here, her face was lit by a wide smile that was reflected in her large, lovely eyes, their blue heightened by the blue of her headband. All at once she seemed young and eager, almost a different person.

"Miss Hickok!" she cried, as if my arrival were a sudden surprise. "How good of you to come to the cottage! I want you to meet my very best friends, Nan and Marion. Ladies, this is Lorena Hickok. I'm sure you've seen her byline in the newspapers. She has a very long reach, you know. Her stories appear all over the country."

There was a subdued murmur of recognition and a round of handshaking. In trousers, a white shirt, and yes, a necktie, Nancy Cook was boyish, slender, and athletic-looking, with crisp brown hair and a come-and-go smile. She was a Jill of all trades, Mrs. Roosevelt said: a cabinetmaker and woodworker, a potter, a photographer, a jeweler. Marion Dickerman, tall and upright, mannish, was a study in opposites, in a dark suit and silk blouse, with severely cut dark hair, deep-set eyes, and a melancholy expression.

Nancy and Marion had been in an exclusive relationship for more than a decade, I had heard, and I caught the subtle signs of their feeling for each other, the shoulders touching, the quick sidelong glance, the secret smile. And yet Mrs. Roosevelt was clearly relaxed and comfortable, even quite happy in their company. When she was with this couple, I wondered, did she ever feel like a third wheel? Or was she the center around which the other two revolved? Did she enjoy her attachment to the two women because they were so strongly attached to each other or because they included her in their attachment? Interesting, intriguing questions that probably didn't have any answers. And weren't my business, anyway.

Mrs. Roosevelt held out her hand. "Come, Hick," she invited. "We want you to see our project." Liking the sound of my name, I took her hand and went with her into the large building.

The tables, chairs, desks, and cupboards made in the Val-Kill Industries (the name of their jointly owned business) were replicas of colonial American pieces, hand-constructed of local cherry and walnut and oak and beautifully hand-finished. I admired them with an unaffected enthusiasm and approved of the progressive scheme of employing local craftsmen who otherwise would be out of a job. A good idea, although I wondered whether the workers saw it as a bit of Roosevelt *noblesse oblige*.

But the prices put the furnishings far out of my reach—and out of the reach of all but the Roosevelts' moneyed friends, I guessed. The $125 price tag on a handsome drop-leaf dining table would buy groceries for a family of four for ten weeks. A tall secretary desk was priced at $525, when the average worker brought in

$25 a week, *if* he had a job. Luxury items, and I felt uncomfortably out of my class—my social and economic class.

And more: as Mrs. Roosevelt seemed to go out of her way to interest me in their project, the other two women almost imperceptibly pulled back, and I sensed something, faint but clear to me, of their disapproval, perhaps even their suspicion. Perhaps it was only that I was a reporter, here to collect material for a story. Maybe they feared that I might write something about their venture, or about the three of them, that they wouldn't like. Or perhaps it was something else—the first small feelings of jealousy that would become such a painful difficulty for the four of us later.

The tour over, we went back to the cottage, which was comfortable and homey, furnished with pieces from the workshop. The bookshelves were filled with books that belonged to all three, and I noticed that their three interlaced initials, E.M.N., were embroidered on a table runner—"dear Eleanor's work," Nan told me when I admired it. I caught the proprietary tone, the implicit assertion of exclusivity. I was curious about Mrs. Roosevelt's attachment to Nan and Marion, but what was their attachment to her? What claims did they make on her? I admit to being a cynical journalist, and I wondered: Was she a loved friend—or the governor's wife and an about-to-become First Lady?

The spring afternoon had turned chilly. Sergeant Miller had not only built a fire in the massive fieldstone fireplace, but also brewed tea and set out a tray of cookies and cake and then tactfully disappeared. As we settled down to our tea, I answered Mrs. Roosevelt's questions about my work at the AP. I told them about the hunt for the Lindbergh baby and about the Walker investigation.

"It's hard," I added. "Women journalists are pushed onto the society pages. We have to fight for the stories that mean something."

"We all have to fight against being pushed onto the society pages," Mrs. Roosevelt said. With an rueful little laugh, she added, "That's where they think our stories belong."

"Ah, yes," I said, struck by her remark. "And when a woman makes news, it's because she's an anomaly. She stands out in a crowd. Which makes some people uncomfortable."

"And where did you graduate college?" Marion asked, picking up her teacup.

"I didn't." I gave her a straight look. "I flunked out at Lawrence College and walked out on the University of Minnesota when the dean told me I had to live in the freshman women's dorm. You might say I got my degree from the city room, delivered with knuckles and elbows."

"Good for you, Hick!" Mrs. Roosevelt exclaimed. Marion's glance met Nancy's. I intercepted the unspoken message and understood their disapproval. Was I touchy, hypersensitive? Maybe. But I'd been in the East long enough to recognize that judgment for what it was. I was out of their league—money, class, education, profession—and always would be.

The uncomfortable silence was broken by the rattle of a teacup in the kitchen. "Oh, my goodness," Mrs. Roosevelt exclaimed and jumped to her feet. "We didn't ask Earl to join us! I'll go get him." Another glance. Marion and Nan didn't approve of Earl, either. They'd rather he stay in the kitchen.

Sergeant Miller's presence altered the chemistry in the room. He sat on the sofa beside Mrs. Roosevelt. Her fingers carelessly brushed his knee, his arm lay across the sofa back behind her shoulders, and the warmth and unaffected familiarity between them was unmistakable.

Watching, I saw a woman hungry for attention, basking in the admiration of a much younger man—a *charming* man—and I revised my understanding of her yet again. Something told me that it wasn't true that they were lovers, but that she *wanted* it to be true, that she was pretending to herself, and to Nancy and Marion, that it was true. Why? Because she desperately needed to believe that she was admired and loved? Because being loved by another was a fantasy that sustained her in the reality of her marriage? If I had been able to hold those questions in my heart over the next few years, I might have been a wiser friend to her and to myself.

But I hadn't yet learned the whole story, and the future was dark and distant. Seeing the two of them together, I knew it was no wonder that the servants were gossiping, even tattling to reporters. I no longer doubted that FDR had seen the danger in the talk and moved to put a firm stop to it before the November election. Reggie Davis could well be right about that wedding.

And Mrs. Roosevelt's feelings? Once, just once, I caught a look in her eyes when she turned to Miller that hinted of a profound sadness, and I guessed that she was resigned to his marriage but deeply unhappy about it. Did she feel that it was unwise, this virile, experienced man and a teenager? Did she know that it was her husband's doing and was disappointed that Miller had been so easily persuaded to take a wife? Or seeing the inevitable, had she tried to get the best package for him—not only the new job but the property as well?

Marion and Nancy had fallen silent. They were clearly not charmed (Miller didn't belong to their class any more than I did), and I imagined that they were relieved at the thought that his marriage was about to take him out of the picture. In any event, it wasn't long before Marion stood up and announced that she and Nan had to catch the train back to the city. That brought Miller to his feet, since he was to see me onto the same train, and ended our little tea party—although I saw Mrs. R put her hand on Miller's arm and heard her whisper that when he got back to the cottage, they would have supper together.

I had plenty on my mind as I rode back to the city, but I wasn't thinking about the color feature I would write the next morning. I was thinking instead of what I had learned: that Mrs. Roosevelt was an unhappy woman living with an ambitious and inattentive husband and a hostile and overbearing mother-in-law; that a man she cared for—how? how much?—was about to be married; and that all this was taking place dangerously close to the precinct of presidential politics. I guessed that there was a very great deal more to know. I wasn't wrong.

CHAPTER THREE

# Cheap Dresses, Budget Hats, and Dime-Store Lunches

FDR, who liked to think of himself as a Navy man, had chosen "Anchors Aweigh" as the theme song for his campaign. But when the Democratic nominating convention got underway in Chicago in late June, Louis Howe decided that the Navy hymn sounded like a dirge. His choice: "Happy Days Are Here Again." It was certainly a happy day for Franklin Roosevelt, who won the nomination on the fourth ballot.

But not for the candidate's wife. I had been at the governor's mansion in Albany, covering the convention as it was broadcast on radio. I saw Mrs. Roosevelt early on the morning of the nomination. She was remote and silent, as if she had withdrawn deep inside herself, shrinking from the impending reality of the White House. At the press conference later that day, where the nominee and his wife were boarding the plane for Chicago, a doe-eyed woman reporter burbled, "Aren't you simply *thrilled* at the possibility of living in the White House?" Mrs. Roosevelt froze her with an arctic stare and refused to answer.

It wasn't until much later that I learned what had happened in Chicago. The convention was taking its second ballot when Nancy Cook, working with Louis Howe and the nominating team, had received a letter—despairing, despondent, almost incoherent—from Mrs. Roosevelt. She simply couldn't face becoming a prisoner of the White House, being forced onto the treadmill of receptions and official dinners and dedications. She wouldn't do it. She would run away with Earl Miller, who loved her and respected her as Franklin never did. She would file suit for divorce. She...

Louis Howe tore up the letter and went to the telephone to talk sense into Mrs. R, who in the end, of course, gave up. When FDR was nominated, she flew to Chicago with him and stood on the platform while her husband accepted the nomination and promised a "new deal for the American people." And two months later, in the garden at Val-Kill, she stood beside her husband while Earl Miller exchanged vows with his pretty teenaged bride. Her daughter Anna and son Elliott served as attendants, and FDR, jovial and avuncular, posed for photographs with the bridal party. While the photographer was at work, Mrs. R went to the bathroom, closed the door, and gave way to wrenching sobs. When she came out, red-eyed but composed, she brushed off Marion's question with a careless, "Why, people always cry at weddings, don't they?"

I know this happened because I was there, assigned to cover the wedding for the AP—coverage suggested, Bill Chapin told me, by Louis Howe, who obviously wanted to get the story out there as widely as possible. There was no follow-up story a year later, however, when the bride's parents obtained an annulment. Their daughter, just seventeen at the time of the wedding, hadn't asked their permission.

But the wedding accomplished its purpose. It put Earl Miller out of Mrs. Roosevelt's reach and put an end to the gossip about her and her handsome bodyguard.

In September, FDR's presidential campaign shifted into high gear, with a thirteen-thousand-mile swing around the country by train. I was one of the three AP reporters—the only woman—assigned to cover the trip. The train made fifteen or twenty whistle-stops every day, with FDR speaking from the bunting-draped rear platform of the six-car *Roosevelt Special.* The local mayors introduced the candidate, and the small-town bands—some of them pretty ragged —played "Happy Days Are Here Again" until everybody on the train was pretty damn sick of it.

But those weren't happy days, no matter how often FDR joked with the crowds, throwing back his head and laughing that great, infectious laugh, as if he hadn't a care in the world. The Depression was biting hard into the country's flesh and muscle and the train seemed to take us further and deeper into the people's despair. In Michigan, we were met by a delegation of unemployed automobile workers. In Minneapolis, where food riots had broken out and stores had been looted, cardboard signs begged for food relief. And one blazing afternoon in Wichita, Kansas, I watched as a silent, sullen crowd gathered along the railroad track: grim-faced men with their hands in the pockets of grimy bib overalls; hollow-eyed women in thin cotton housedresses; scrawny kids, ragged and barefoot; all hopeless, despairing, desperate. Maybe it was my own failure of vision, but I couldn't see how any "new deal" could help these broken people. I wondered whether FDR even noticed what the rest of us saw all too plainly. After all, he was on a train, *his* train, passing through on its way to another whistle-stop, to another town, to the White House. Once he got to Washington, it would be too easy to forget everything he'd seen along the way.

But however haggard the people, the crowds were always large, and Louis Howe kept the press informed of the national polling. FDR was far ahead of Hoover, whom all the pundits had written off as a lost cause. The *Roosevelt Special* took us all the way to the

West Coast, turned around and came back through Arizona, where Mrs. Roosevelt boarded. Under orders from Bill Chapin, I added her to my assignment—a little grudgingly. I was there to cover the candidate.

But I was still deeply curious about his wife, and as the campaign train headed east, I found myself impressed by the easy way she dealt with people, and by her energy. FDR couldn't get off the train, so he sent his wife out to meet and talk to people. In Nebraska, she strode swiftly across a drought-stricken cornfield as I hurried after, snagged my silk stockings on a barbed wire fence, and had to sit down to catch my breath (too many Pall Malls, I suppose) while she spoke sympathetically with the farmer about the rock-bottom price of corn. One rainy morning in Missouri, she visited a barbershop, a hospital, and a school, all before lunch. In Iowa, she ate fried chicken at a church potluck and took a big slice of chocolate cake to FDR on the train, posing for photographers. My story about that cake got a nice play on the wire.

But energetic as the woman was, she also had a talent for catching a catnap. Bemused, I watched as, wedged between her husband and her son Jimmy in the stands at Wrigley Field, she slept soundly through Game Three of the World Series, the Yankees versus the Cubs. Babe Ruth made baseball history by calling the shot on Charlie Root's second pitch, a curveball, for his fifth-inning homer into the centerfield bleachers. The hit brought fifty thousand screaming fans to their feet—all but FDR, who had to lock both leg braces before he could stand up, and his wife, who was still asleep. My story about Mrs. R's unscheduled nap got a greater wire service play than any of my pieces about FDR—and got a laugh out of her, I heard later. The sports writer in me loved it, and so did Louis Howe.

"Great story, Hick," he said, with a gnomish grin. "Humanizes the Roosevelts. Worth a couple of thousand votes." As a journalist, I wasn't supposed to be in the vote-getting business, but Howe was a seasoned newspaperman himself, and I was pleased by his approval.

Once we were back in New York, however, the story about Mrs. R's nap got me pulled off the candidate and assigned, full time, to his wife. Bill Chapin stopped by my desk and gave me the news, with an air of apology.

"Sorry to do this, Hick, but I can't very well put a man on the lady, and you're the only girl I've got. What's more, your story about Mrs. R falling asleep at Wrigley Field—that was golden. I'm betting there's more where that came from."

I pulled down my mouth and Bill patted my shoulder. "Cheer up, kid. It's just from now until the election. You've seen the polls —FDR is primed to win in a walk. When he goes to the White House, the Washington bureau will cover her, and you're back at Tammany."

"I'm billing you for those goddamned stockings," I growled.

I wasn't going to let Bill Chapin see that some part of me was secretly glad to be reassigned to the candidate's wife, even if it looked like a demotion.

Mrs. Roosevelt wasn't eager to have a journalist dogging her heels, and if Louis Howe hadn't instructed her to cooperate, she might have refused. When we sat down to talk that afternoon at Democratic headquarters, I found out why.

"You're an important journalist, Hick. You should be assigned to the governor." Her voice was matter-of-fact but her shoulders were hunched, the way I had seen that afternoon at Springwood.

"He's newsworthy, I'm not. Nobody will want to read your stories about me."

"With all due respect," I said firmly, "you've got it wrong. I'll write stories about you that people will want to read. Ergo, you will be newsworthy." I gave her a grin. "See how that works?"

There was a silence as she pondered. "Ah," she said. "I see. Well, then, I suppose I shall have to do something that you'll find interesting enough to make a story out of it."

"That's the idea," I said. "You do your job, I do mine."

But the most interesting thing about the woman—to me, anyway—was something I couldn't write about, at least, not then. The day after her husband won the nomination, I had seen that she was desperately unhappy. Now that FDR was polling far ahead of Hoover and the path to the White House seemed easy, she was even unhappier, and I understood why. She was in the same situation she'd been in when I met her in 1928, except that the stakes were much higher now. She had created an identity of her own, an unconventional self she was proud of, in the gigantic shadow of her husband's political ambitions. She was afraid of losing it. She was afraid of losing *herself.* She might also have been unhappy because she had lost Earl Miller, someone who had made her feel admired, desired, loved. And there was something about Washington itself—I didn't know what, but something—that distressed her.

In what looked to me like an effort to outrun her unhappiness, Mrs. R became a dervish of frenzied activity, rushing here, hurrying there, catching a taxi, riding a bus, taking the subway, and for the next couple of weeks, I did my level best to stay with her. I hurried after her from one place to another. I waited in the hallway while she taught her Todhunter classes or sat in the back of the room while she spoke to women's groups in New York or Albany or

Syracuse or Boston. I attended afternoon teas in the governor's mansion, where she usually served a thick, rich chocolate cake, and I even joined the governor's family for Sunday night supper: scrambled eggs and sausages that she stirred together in a chafing dish at the table, with cold meats for sandwiches, salad, and dessert. (The real story there was that Mrs. R didn't know how to cook. The eggs and sausages were sent up by the kitchen, already prepared—all she did was stir them together.) There was always such a lively, intelligent discussion that somebody called those suppers "scrambled eggs with brains," and the name stuck.

For her weekday meals, Mrs. R spurned fancy restaurants in favor of a quick bowl of clam chowder or a BLT at the nearest soda fountain lunch counter. She liked no-frills clothes—ten-dollar off-the-rack dresses and inexpensive hats. I admit to being annoyed when another reporter wrote that her hats looked as if she ran in and bought them while her bus was waiting at a stoplight. But Mrs. R laughed when Tommy showed her the clipping. Her face relaxed when she laughed, and I thought she was almost pretty. I liked her sense of humor, too, and her willingness to laugh at herself. So I wrote a story about her laughing at the story about her hats.

My pieces about her frugal, plain-Jane choices—the cheap dresses, the budget hats, the dime-store lunches—played against FDR's blue-blood image and got plenty of wire service attention, not just on the women's pages, either. Meanwhile, President Hoover, always remote and inaccessible, was getting a different kind of press. In the summer, a Movietone News crew had filmed the president stiffly feeding pieces of T-bone steak to his dog. It was meant to be a down-home personality piece, but every time the newsreel was shown in a movie house, it was booed by people who hadn't been able to afford a T-bone steak in years. And then there was the ugly Bonus Army debacle, where veterans of the Great

War, camped in Washington to lobby for the early payment of their bonuses, were driven out with guns and tanks. It had been General Douglas MacArthur's decision, but it became Hoover's public relations nightmare. Even conservative *Time* magazine had to admit that Hoover—"President Reject"—was unelectable.

But FDR's election, now a virtual certainty, was not going to make his wife happy, and I finally thought of a way to write about it in the series of three stories scheduled for the week after the election. If Governor Roosevelt became President Roosevelt, Mrs. Roosevelt was going to be a singularly *reluctant* First Lady. This storyline would command plenty of interest. It would define her, give her a unique dimension. But Louis Howe, as the Roosevelt political strategist, might feel it was too negative. I thought I ought to run it by him, so that afternoon, I dropped in at his office and pitched the idea.

"Reluctant First Lady," he said, squinting at me through the haze of his cigarette smoke. "Reluctant?"

"Reluctant," I said. "It undercuts the way the right-wing papers are portraying her."

In fact, the anti-Roosevelt press had been having a field day over the past few months, reporting that Eleanor (they always called her by her first name) had set her heart on the White House the day her Uncle Teddy left it. According to them, becoming First Lady was her dream, her life's driving ambition. I had read that she wore the pants in the Roosevelt family, that FDR was subject to her "petticoat rule," and that she was secretly masterminding his presidential campaign. Of course, there was always a great deal of criticism of any woman who attempted to play a public role in politics or business. Male writers liked to argue that the world would be better off if women stayed home, kept house, and had babies, and any woman who ventured out into the world was bound to come into their line of fire. Louis was a savvy strategist, so I didn't think I needed to spell out my notion that the theme of "reluctant First Lady" might deflect some of the anti-Eleanor criticism.

I watched as, eyes closed, hands clasped across his ash-spotted vest, Louis went through all this in his head. Then he opened his eyes. "It's good, Hick. It'll get attention—although, of course, that depends on how you write it."

I gave him a straight look. "That depends on access, too, don't you think? I've noticed that Ruby Black, the new hire over at United Press, has gotten a special invitation to several of Mrs. Roosevelt's recent events." Ruby was good, and Mrs. Roosevelt seemed to feel that she should divide her attention between the two wire services. Like most journalists, I was eager for an exclusive.

Louis considered. "Tell you what," he said finally. "When you've done a piece along those lines, let me see what you've written. I'll fact-check it for you." He gave me one of his inscrutable smiles. "You can leave Ruby Black to me."

The next day, I got my exclusive. Mrs. Roosevelt invited me to go with her to visit her sons at Groton. On the train coming back, she talked about raising her children, about what a mistake it had been to hire nurses and nannies to take care of them. "If I had it to do over again, I wouldn't have any servants those first few years," she said. "My children would have had far happier childhoods if their mother had been more often with them." The sympathetic story I wrote featured a mother looking back, candidly wishing she'd done things differently. It was appealing, especially to people who thought that women ought to stay home with their kids. It made her (as Louis Howe said when he read it) more middle class, less like a Roosevelt.

Had I crossed the line? By the standards of today, yes. That kind of *quid pro quo* would be an ethical problem for a reporter now. Back then, things weren't quite so clear-cut. News and opinion were blurred together. Many newspapers—like Robert McCormick's *Chicago Tribune* for the Republicans and William Randolph Hearst's thirty-newspaper chain on the Democratic side—filtered the news through strong editorial opinions and wrapped their stories around the candidates they backed. Political candidates needed reporters to get their stories out, and reporters were encouraged to aggressively seek and cultivate access and use what they got to strengthen their reporting. Editors sometimes cautioned us against going too far, but nobody really knew what "too far" meant, so the warning didn't cut much ice.

My AP editor, Bill Chapin, was pleased when I filed stories that were rich in on-the-spot detail about Mrs. Roosevelt's activities and studded with direct quotations, which are like pure gold to a reporter. He occasionally reminded me to remember "the usual AP restraint"—corporate code words for objectivity. *Keep your distance. Don't get involved. Stay out of the story.* But Bill understood as well as I did what played on the wire. And he could count the rising number of newspapers that were running my stories about the candidate's wife.

"Good job, Hick," Bill said when he handed back the Groton copy. "And I'm glad to see that you're getting more coverage from Mrs. R than that new girl over at UP." Later that week, I got a raise.

And then… and then everything changed.

# CHAPTER FOUR

# Orbit

A week before the election, Missy LeHand's mother died, and FDR asked his wife to represent the family at the funeral in Potsdam, in upstate New York.

Odd, I thought, given what was being said about the relationship between Missy and FDR. But I was reminded of FDR smiling jovially beside Earl Miller and his bride while the photographer snapped away and thought that sending his wife might be his way of deflecting attention. Anyway, Mrs. R's sympathies were with Missy at this difficult time, and if she was affronted by her husband's request, she didn't let it show. I was invited to go along, too, since after the funeral, Mrs. R was scheduled to take a look at a new hydroelectric plant on the St. Lawrence River. The reporter covering the candidate's wife touring the power plant.

It was a gray, misty afternoon, the sky weeping softly over the late autumn trees, and after we left the plant and returned to Potsdam, Mrs. R was pensive. We went to a quiet café for supper, where she talked about personal things she'd never spoken of before, about the way she and the children, and Missy too, had ordered their lives around FDR.

"Like little moons," she said soberly, "all orbiting around a giant planet." She sighed. "Some of us might escape into outer space if we could. We might like to be somebody else, but we can't.

The pull is too great." She paused. "Even poor, sweet Missy. She's tried to leave him a time or two, you know, to escape. But she can't. She has no more choice than I do."

I held my breath. She hadn't said, "Off the record, Hick," because she wasn't thinking of me as a reporter who might use her words. She was speaking to me as a woman, as a friend, as someone who understood, and I thought, quite suddenly, that I did—more than she might guess, perhaps.

"Who would *you* be, if you could?" I asked quietly.

There was a moment's silence. "Just... myself," she said, "although I don't think I know what that means." Her little laugh was self-conscious. "I suppose I would be just Eleanor Roosevelt. That was my name before I married Franklin, you know. If I were not Mrs. Roosevelt, of the Hyde Park Roosevelts, I would still be Eleanor Roosevelt, of the Oyster Bay Roosevelts." She raised a hand, let it fall, and her face darkened. "There. You see? *I* can't escape, either."

Yes, I thought, the name hanging on her like an albatross, a millstone, a curse. I rephrased my question. "What would Eleanor Roosevelt *do*?"

She was unhesitating. "Oh, that's easy. I would live very quietly. Read, write letters, garden. Learn to cook, enjoy a few friends. Travel. But no politics at all, ever."

Was that a truthful answer? I think it was, then, or at least a wistful, wishful answer, one that might have been given by the young Eleanor, before she fell into her Uncle Teddy's orbit, or her husband's, or both.

She turned to me. "And you? Who would you be, if you could, Hick? What would *you* do?"

It was if she had opened a door and invited me inside. Her blue eyes were intent on mine, and a new thing somewhere inside me seemed to open up, to lean forward, toward her. I tried to speak, couldn't, and tried again.

"I'm not sure," I said finally, feeling breathless. In all my life no one, not even Ellie, had ever asked me those questions. Who would I be, if I could? What would I do?

"I... I love my work," I managed, still held by her gaze, as if in an embrace. "I would always want to do *that*."

She turned away. "That's the difference between us. You have important work, work that matters. You do it very well, and you're rewarded for it. I don't do... anything of consequence, except perhaps for teaching, which only matters to a few girls." Her voice flattened. "When Franklin goes to the White House, I won't even be able to do that. I will put on a gown and white gloves and stand in a receiving line and smile and say frivolous things to silly people. And the next night, I will do it all over again, and the next and the next. That's what I will do."

"I'm sorry," I said inadequately.

She gave me a regretful smile. "So am I. I can't tell you how sorry I am."

Our conversation grew lighter over dessert and coffee. But we lingered so long at the table that we had to rush to catch our train back to New York. The night had turned foggy, and when the trainmaster told us that the usual ten-hour trip was expected to take much longer, Mrs. R booked a drawing room so we could get some sleep. Then, when we reached our car, she embarrassed me by insisting that I take the lower berth. She would sleep on the narrow sofa. I protested, but I had to agree when she said, "I am longer top to toe than you are, Hick, and not quite so... well, broad."

I laughed. "Well, if you put it that way, Mrs. Roosevelt, I suppose I'll have to say yes."

"I've called you Hick." Her eyes were on mine again. "Won't you call me Eleanor? My friends do, you know."

And there, again, the door, opening. "I wish I could," I said. This was something I had already dared to think about. I might call her Eleanor in my private thoughts, and I sometimes did, but the word simply refused to form itself on my lips. Later, I would find that I could *write* about her as Eleanor, but for now: "I might call you Madam, if you don't object."

And I told her why. I had a husky contralto and, as a girl, loved to sing. Later, living with Ellie, I learned to love opera. At the Minneapolis *Tribune*, I had written an admiring story about Madam Ernestine Schumann-Heink, an operatic contralto who was giving concerts across the country on behalf of the war effort. We became friends while she was in the city, and one evening she took a gorgeous sapphire and diamond ring from her finger and pressed it on me. I tried to protest, but she wouldn't have it.

"Shut up, Hick," she said, in her thick German accent. "I love you, I give you my ring. You be a good girl and take it." That made me laugh and that was all there was to it. I had worn her ring proudly the year before, when I went to the Met to hear her sing Erda in *The Ring of the Nibelung*. Madam was past seventy by then, but her voice was still rich and strong, and I thrilled to it just as I had fifteen years before.

"Madam is perfect," Mrs. R said, smiling a little at my story. "I'm honored, Hick."

We changed into our nightclothes: my usual striped pajamas and an ankle-length pink nightgown for Madam, both flannel, because trains in those days were never very warm. But we didn't go to sleep for a very long time. Instead, she asked me to tell her about my childhood.

"It's so much easier to understand someone when you know

how they grew up," she said softly. "Understand them deeply, I mean, in all their contradictions."

And there was the door again, but this time, it opened into a darker place, into my heart. I told her what I had told only Ellie and no one else. About my childhood in a small town on the Dakota prairie; my mother's acquiescence in my father's drunken beatings; my bullying stepmother. About my stint as a hired girl in one wretched household after another—a long spiral of despair— until Mrs. O'Malley, the rouged and ancient wife of the village saloon-keeper, dispatched me to an aunt, who dispatched me to another, where I was washed and brushed and shod and sent to school while I paid for my bed and board with household help. About my failures as a student, my successes as a newspaper reporter, and then my life with Ellie. As the night slipped past the train windows, Madam heard me with an intent concern on her face, a concern for *me,* as a woman, as a friend, as a fellow human being who has lived with pain. Not even dear Ellie had heard me with such intensity, or with such an open heart.

Then it was my turn to listen. I was mesmerized by the story of her childhood, a story of cruel grief and loss and poverty of a different sort, an emotional poverty that had starved away feeling. Her extraordinarily beautiful mother, Anna, only twenty when her daughter was born, had made fun of her little girl, calling her "Granny" because she was so solemn, so old-fashioned.

"And so homely," Mrs. R added in a matter-of-fact tone. "I could see my reflection in my mother's eyes. She thought me a very unpretty child, so she rarely hugged or held me. Quite naturally, I suppose, I saw myself as homely. I knew I was doomed to failure in a society where success was based on beauty—and where social success was the whole world."

The little girl was just eight when her mother died, quite

suddenly, of diphtheria. At first, she hoped she would be sent to live with her beloved father, a charming but deeply troubled man. But Elliott Roosevelt abandoned her, too, dying of alcoholism when she was ten and ripping open a hole in her heart that was not yet healed. The deaths of both her parents sentenced her to the bleak strictures of her Grandmother Hall's Victorian household, to the cruel harassments of a nurse, and to the judgment of her pretty aunts that she was an "ugly duckling" who would never have any beaux. At fifteen, she was sent to boarding school in England, a glorious release into an exciting world of ideas. Travel, too, for she and her headmistress, Madam Souvestre, went all over Europe, just the two of them, together. At eighteen, she was back in America, where society's rituals demanded that she make her debut. And then... and then she'd been pulled into Franklin's orbit, into a Roosevelt marriage, dominated by her mother-in-law and her children and her husband's political life, until finally she had managed to pull away enough to carve out a private life for herself. And now, her husband's election and the White House threatened to obliterate it.

The night rushed like a storm past the windows as each of us listened the other into speech, until our shared confidences brought tears and the tears brought comforting embraces. We held one another in the gently swaying dark, carried along by the rhythmic pulse of the train through an uncaring world. Much was left unsaid, and I was glad, very glad, for already it seemed to me over-whelming—too much to be told, too much to be heard, too much to be *felt*. We fell silent and then fell asleep at last, and when the pale morning light flickered into our drawing room and across Madam's face and the soft gold-brown hair loose on her pillow, I watched her with a tenderness that seemed to soften my bones.

Later, I would imagine that night on the train as a metaphor for our relationship: two lonely people hurtling through the dark toward an unreachable destination, each clinging to the other as if they were the last survivors on a moon swept out of orbit by a force too powerful to be opposed. That the metaphor didn't quite fit would not be clear to me until much later, and then it would be too late. That night, I only knew that the course of my life had suddenly altered, that all the shattered and scattered pieces of my broken self had reassembled themselves around a captivating new center. I understood that this was risky and foolish, and I heard that wry, mocking hired girl's voice telling me that it made no sense to love this woman. She didn't love me. She couldn't love me. She wasn't going to know that I loved her, ever. But in that moment, nothing else mattered: not her husband nor her children nor her station in life. That I loved her—the woman, the person, Madam —was enough.

I couldn't say any of that to her, of course, any more than I could say her name. All I could do, when we were both dressed and properly combed, was to clear my throat and ask tentatively if I might use some of what she had told me about her childhood in my newspaper stories.

She gave me a direct look, long and searching. "Can I trust you, Hick?"

*With your life,* I wanted to say, loving the sound of my name on her lips. But I only nodded.

"Well, then," she said quietly, "use what you think is right." She put out her hand and touched my cheek. "I wish I could tell you what last night means to me. To know you a little, to learn what you've been through in your life, to feel that you want to share it with *me*—" She shook her head, and I saw that her eyes, those quite remarkable blue eyes, were misted with tears. "I can't explain it, my dear, but this feels very... important to me. I hope you feel that way, too."

I caught her hand and held it, feeling that I had stepped through the door, hearing it close behind me. "I do," I said.

It was a pledge, as if I were responding to *Do you take...* "Oh, yes, I do." Until death I do, although I had no idea, then, what those words might mean. I didn't know that I, like Tommy and Missy and Louis and the children, had been pulled into a Roosevelt orbit. It simply didn't occur to me that I might never be able to pull away, that I would go on circling her for as long as I lived, nearer and farther and nearer again, forever.

# CHAPTER FIVE

# Intimacies

We were back in New York, with the election only days away. FDR was in the city, staying at the Sixty-Fifth Street townhouse and, ever cheerful and confident, giving a final series of pre-election speeches. Madam was whirled into the vortex of his campaign events, and for the next two days, I was tugged along in her wake, reporter's notebook in hand. She was at the front of the room or on a stage, and I was at the back, taking notes. Or she was striding ahead, tall, erect, and I was hurrying to catch up to her—and just as I reached her, she would be engulfed by a wave of people.

But somehow we had stepped into the next improbable chapter of our story. On that first day, our glances caught often and held long enough—over heads, across crowded rooms, through the soft blue haze of cigarette smoke—to make me believe that she was remembering our time on the train. As for me, each glance seemed to stop my heart, and in that instant, I replayed the hours we had spent together, hearing our whispers in the swaying dark, sharing the private places of our hearts, clasping each other against the indifferent world rushing past the windows.

*Madam*, I wrote on the page in my notebook and then circled it, and then again and again. Orbit. Orbit.

On the second day, I managed to write the full note. *Madam, dinner tonight, my apartment? 10 Mitchell Place, 2E, off 1st & 49th.* I passed it to her and watched her unfold it and read it. She looked up, searched for me, and when she saw me, nodded and smiled. It seemed to me almost an eager smile, and my heart rang, like an answering bell.

Between covering her three events that day and rushing to the AP office to type my stories and get them on the wire, there wasn't time to cook, so I picked up egg rolls and sesame chicken and rice at a little Chinese restaurant on Forty-Ninth. At home, I scurried around cleaning up, then lit candles and put on a recording of Gieseking playing Debussy. It was just beginning to rain by the time she got there, bringing pink roses and wearing a fur wrap and an elegant maroon evening gown with pearls, a silvery glint of mist in her hair. I caught the faint, drifting scent of lilies of the valley when I took her hand. Prinz greeted her with a deferential restraint and thumped his tail on the floor as Madam turned in a circle, hands clasped, looking around the apartment, at the modest collection of modern art on the walls and the lights on the river below.

"Oh, Hick, this is a delight! A view of the river, and so quiet and *private*. It's perfect. How I envy you, having it all to yourself. And Prinz, of course." she added, bending to stroke his ears.

*It's perfect now that you're here,* I thought. "You have Val-Kill," I reminded her, putting the roses in a crystal vase on the table. "It's beautiful. And private, too."

She made a little face. "Beautiful, yes. But I share it with Nan and Marion. I've always shared my living spaces with someone— with a crowd, sometimes. This is *yours*." With a rueful laugh, she added, "And I don't see a single naval drawing. No ships' models, either."

"You're welcome here any time you can get away." I got out napkins. "Next time, I'll do the cooking. I promise it will be special."

"This is special," she said simply, still caressing Prinz's ears. "You can't know how special it is." I dared to look at her and found her smiling.

When we sat down at the table, I said, "You're dressed for a reception. How did you manage to get away?"

"It was easier than I imagined," she said. "There was a party for Franklin at the Harvard Club. I joined them for a half hour, told the host I had another engagement, got my wrap. I bought the roses from a vendor on the corner and was in the taxi two minutes later." She clapped her hands like a child delighted by her very first delicious truancy. "I simply skipped out. As simple as that, Hick!"

"Won't Franklin wonder what happened to you?"

"He won't notice. Louis might, but everyone else is focused on the election." She was suddenly sober. "That's all they talk about, of course. That, and cabinet appointments and the banking crisis."

"And if Louis notices?"

She raised her chin almost defiantly. "I'll tell him I was with you. He likes you, you know, which I must say is rather surprising. Louis is a hard man to please." Her eyes met mine. "Franklin likes you, too. At least, he likes to tease me about you." She slipped into a droll, drawling mimicry of her husband. "He says, 'You'd better stay on the right side of that Hickok woman, Babs. She's smart. And shrewd. You *listen* to her.'"

"He's right. Smart and shrewd. Take his advice." I smiled. "I advise you to play truant more often."

After we ate, we left the candles burning on the table and sat quietly together on the sofa, listening to Debussy. We talked about her projects and my work, about plays we'd seen, about ideas that interested us. We didn't say a word about the campaign or the election, or what would happen after her husband became the president of the United States. When her fingers brushed mine, my heart seemed to open, to unfold, like one of the pink rosebuds in her bouquet.

At midnight, when she sighed and said she had to go, I put on my coat and took an umbrella and Prinz and I walked with her to the corner to flag a cab. As she was getting in, I bent to kiss her.

"Good night, Madam," I whispered.

She touched my cheek. "Will you come to breakfast at the townhouse in the morning, dear?"

Somewhere deep inside me I heard the voice of the hired girl. *Don't do this, Hick. This isn't for you.* I closed my ears. "Of course I will," I said.

As Prinz and I watched, the taxi took her away through the glittering rain, its red taillights tugging my heart along behind.

"I love you," I whispered. "I love you."


There had never been any serious doubt that Roosevelt would win. In the voters' minds, the Republicans were saddled with the weighty catastrophe of the Depression. Some wag wrote that even a modestly talented dogcatcher could have been elected president on the Democratic ticket, and Hoover himself got a letter from a disgruntled farmer in Illinois who advised him to vote for Roosevelt and make it unanimous.

On election night, at the Sixty-Fifth Street townhouse, the Roosevelts hosted an early buffet supper for friends, campaign workers, and the reporters who had covered the campaign. When Mrs. Roosevelt greeted me, she held my hand a moment longer than necessary, then bent to kiss me on the cheek. As she drew me into the room, she whispered, "It's so good to have you here tonight, Hick, dear."

I stammered something unintelligible, for she had taken my

breath away, and with it my power of speech. She was wearing a long white chiffon gown with a deep V-cut neckline and a train. She was statuesque, stately, simply beautiful. I slipped to the back of the room where I exchanged meaningless words with the other reporters and watched her as she greeted guests. My feelings for her—a kind of swooning, yearning wistfulness, quite impossible to subdue or even ignore—had sharpened my already keen awareness of *her* feelings, and under her practiced smile, I saw a bleak resignation. She knew that this was the night that would change her life, that her husband was going to the White House. Her fate was irrevocably linked to his. She hated it, and I hated him for what he was doing to her.

Later that night, at Democratic headquarters at the Biltmore, each new number that was chalked up on the big board produced a jubilant cheer, a shower of confetti, and another chirpy chorus of "Happy Days Are Here Again." FDR carried 42 of the 48 states, his astonishing 472 electoral votes swamping Hoover's paltry 59. Mercifully, Hoover didn't drag it out. He conceded before midnight, and in the Biltmore ballroom, a flotilla of balloons sailed to the ceiling.

The next morning, I was awakened early by the telephone. "Please come, Hick," she said tautly. "I need you."

I went, of course. I found her in her sitting room, still in her dressing gown. The *New York Times* was on the table beside her chair, folded open to a photo of the Roosevelt family, ER crowded between her husband and her daughter, her granddaughter Sisty on her lap, the Roosevelt sons lined up like grinning mannequins behind. Under the photograph was my latest article about her, headlined *Mrs. F.D. Roosevelt a Civic Worker. Vice-Principal of School for Girls and Editor of Magazine "Babies—Just Babies."* She was red-eyed and hoarse and her hair was disheveled. I guessed that she had spent a sleepless night.

"I can't do it." She fumbled for a handkerchief. "Franklin has won the thing he always wanted, Hick, but I've lost my freedom. I will never be able to live my *own* life. Never!"

I could feel her pain like a twisting knife in my heart and I wanted to bleed with her, to fold her in my arms and comfort her. She needed that, I knew, but right now, she needed something different.

"Let's get you dressed, dear," I said briskly, "and then we'll have some breakfast. We're taking the day off."

That stopped her. "Taking the day off?" She blinked at me, her eyes focusing through tears. "But I can't, Hick. I have a full day's schedule, and I'm already late getting started. I have to see—"

"Forget the schedule," I said firmly, heading for the telephone. "You're playing hooky. You'll need a woolen suit—the one you wore to Groton is fine—and a scarf. The temperature might not get out of the fifties, and we'll be outdoors. Oh, and walking shoes."

She stared at me for a moment as if trying to decide if she should rebuke me for my audacity. Then she smiled a little. "Thank you," she said. "Self-pity is such an unrewarding emotion." With that, she went to get dressed.

I picked up the phone, dialed the office at Democratic headquarters, and reached Tommy. "Whatever's on the calendar, cancel it," I said. "The Boss is taking the day off."

"Wonderful!" Tommy exclaimed. "Just what she needs, Hick. Get her out and away so she can stop feeling sorry for herself. Where are you going?"

"This morning, the Statue of Liberty."

"Oh, grand!" Tommy said. "Do take her up to the crown. She

told me last week that she had visited the statue several times, but never gone up. What else are you planning?"

"How about this?" I asked, and told her. "Do you think you can arrange it?"

"I'm sure I can," Tommy said. "I'll phone right away."

"Good. I'll call you back before we leave here and see what you've been able to come up with." I hung up and called Bill Chapin to let him know that I would be trailing the First Lady-elect for the day and would file the story in the morning. A little later, Tommy phoned to say that it had all been arranged. A car would pick us up at Battery Place and Broadway, and our tickets would be waiting at the box office.

An hour later, Madam and I were boarding the ferry at Battery Park's Pier A. To my relief, none of the tourists on the boat with us seemed to recognize the tall woman with the fur collar of her coat pulled up around her neck and the brown felt cloche pulled down over her ears. As the ferry left the dock and moved out into the harbor, we went to stand in the bow, where we could feel the morning sun on our faces and the chilly salt breeze on our lips. Seagulls called overhead and a scattering of large ships and smaller trawlers shared the bay with us. The November wind was chilly, but there was life and energy in it and a heartening lift to the waves. I felt as if the fresh wind was blowing the past and the future away, leaving us cupped in this gray-blue circle of sea and sky, in this present moment, together.

The sight of the statue, the indomitable symbol of liberty, always awed me, and I caught a glimpse of the same feeling on Madam's face. Moved, I put my gloved hand over hers on the ferry rail. As the boat moved forward through the gray sea, she turned her palm up and clasped my fingers, and clasped my heart, as well.

Soon, too soon, we reached the dock at the island and joined the queue of people making their way up to the statue's crown. It was an easy climb for her, a breathless one for me, but when we reached the top, both of us were silenced by the panoramic view: the new George Washington Bridge over the Hudson, the jagged Manhattan skyline, the bridges over the East River, Governors Island. We lingered for an hour, then made our way down and back to the ferry and Battery Park. We had hot pastrami sandwiches and sauerkraut at a Jewish deli, and when we were finished, I looked at my watch.

"Time to go." I stood. "Come on, dear."

She took my hand like a girl, eager and caught up in the spirit of an adventure. "Where are we going?"

"It's a surprise," I said. "Trust me. It'll be fun." I delighted in the look of sheer pleasure that crossed her face. When, I wondered, was the last time anyone had made an effort to surprise her? When was the last time she'd had *fun?*

A black Buick was waiting at the corner of Broadway and Battery Place. The driver, a good-looking man in a smart gray business suit, was leaning casually against the fender. When he saw us, he straightened, took off his gray fedora, and came forward.

"Mrs. Roosevelt," he said, holding out his hand. "Congratulations on last night's landslide victory. Your friends are still celebrating." He shook hands with me. "Miss Hickok, good to see you again."

"Why, hello, Mr. Putnam," she said with a genuine smile and looked at me. "I'm to be surprised, am I, Hick?" She bent over and looked into the car. "Amelia isn't with you?" she asked the man.

"She's waiting for you at Floyd Bennett Field," he said, opening the passenger door for her.

"Does that mean—" she stopped, and her voice lifted as it did when she was excited. "Does that mean we're *flying* today?"

"Flying indeed," George Putnam said, as I got into the back seat. The man who had picked us up was Amelia Earhart's publicist, promoter, publisher, and husband. "You can thank Miss Hickok for arranging this, Mrs. Roosevelt. Amelia is looking forward to seeing you again. Today's flight is her own special congratulatory gift on your victory."

"What glorious fun!" Madam said. She turned back to me. "Such a wonderful surprise. Thank you, Hick. Thank you!"

"Thank Tommy for making the arrangements," I said. "But I'll take credit for the idea." I'd known that Putnam would say yes when Tommy called. He was always on the lookout for publicity for his wife, and he'd want to oblige the new First Lady, who had always wanted to fly. Tommy had told me that she'd applied for her student pilot's license, but that FDR wasn't happy about it.

Floyd Bennett Field, on Jamaica Bay, was New York City's municipal airport. It was usually a half-hour drive, but Putnam drove fast and we were there in twenty minutes. Amelia, looking remarkably like Charles Lindbergh in her flying outfit, was waiting for us, a Ford Tri-motor warmed up and ready to take to the air.

We all climbed aboard, Mrs. R, full of excitement, in the co-pilot's seat. From a seat behind her, I watched her with my heart, feeling her enjoyment in the takeoff as if it were my own and glad that she could be released, if only for a few hours, from the burden of her future. If I gave any thought to my own future, I don't remember it. That day was all the future I wanted.

The four of us spent a memorable hour flying over the city: up the East River, circling the new Empire State Building and skimming the length of Central Park, then north along the Hudson as far as the Palisades, where November had left a few brilliant swaths of autumn color. Then back south over the river, *under* the recently opened George Washington Bridge and across New York Harbor, over Ellis Island and around the Statue of Liberty, and back to the field.

Flying under the bridge was definitely a barnstormer's stunt, but Amelia shrugged it off. "If anybody comes looking for me," she said with her lopsided grin, "I'll just tell them that Mrs. Roosevelt was flying the plane." We all laughed with her, Madam happiest of all.

As we disembarked, George Putnam said, "We should have arranged for a photographer." Mrs. Roosevelt replied, very serious-ly, "I am so glad you didn't."

"Of course." First and last a promoter, Putnam smiled. "But soon, I hope. Amelia needs to keep her name before the public. She has big plans."

"Bigger than the transatlantic flight?" I asked in surprise.

"Oh, much bigger," Putnam said expansively. "Much, much bigger."

I would think about that when Amelia disappeared a few years later, swallowed up in the vastness of the Pacific on a flight that was to carve her place in the record books.

Looking back, I remember the glorious day like a cake glazed with happiness, *my* happiness in Madam's pleasure. And that wasn't the end of it. Putnam and Amelia drove us back to the city and dropped us at Mitchell Place, so I could look after Prinz. Then Madam and I walked a couple of blocks for dinner at a nearby Italian restaurant. Afterward, we taxied to the Alvin, on Fifty-Second, west of Broadway, just in time to pick up the tickets Tommy had arranged for us. We were in our seats when the curtain opened on *Music in the Air*, Jerome Kern and Oscar Ham-merstein's new musical. It was a wonderful end to a truly remarkable day.

I was still humming "I've Told Ev'ry Little Star"—my favorite of all the songs in the show—when the taxi pulled up at Mitchell Place. "It's just eleven," I said. "Come in with me, won't you, Madam?"

She hesitated, then shook her head. "I won't tonight, dear. But Franklin is going back to Albany tomorrow. Why don't we plan on dinner tomorrow night?"

"Nothing I'd like better, Madam." I leaned toward her to kiss her quickly on the cheek.

She stopped me with her fingers on my lips, her large eyes luminous in the dark. "Hick, I don't know how to thank you for today. You rescued me from my worst self. I dread the thought of moving back to Washington, but you've shown me that there can be moments, even hours, of freedom. Such a gift, and I love you for it." She took my hand and kissed me softly, her lips just brushing the corner of my mouth. "Sleep tight, dear one."

For the space of a half-dozen thudding heartbeats, I sat frozen, flooded by a hope I had not felt since Ellie. Was it possible? Was this to be mine?

A car honked behind us. I took a deep breath and opened the taxi door. "You, too, Madam," I said as lightly as I could. "See you tomorrow." I bounced up the stairs singing "I've told every little star" under my breath.

The next day, I filed the first of the series of three articles that were to go out on the AP wire and appear with my byline in hundreds of newspapers nationwide. It began with a direct quote meant to catch readers' attention and drop a few jaws: "'If I wanted to be selfish,' said Mrs. Franklin D. Roosevelt, "'I could wish that he hadn't been elected.'" She went on to say that she was "sincerely glad" for FDR, but "I will have to work out my own salvation."

It might be hard to understand now what a bombshell admission this was then. It was the first time a president-elect's wife had spoken so revealingly to a wire service reporter, perhaps because, for the first time, the wire service reporter was a woman. But also, I dared to hope, because *I* was that reporter and she trusted me to tell the truth—*her* truth. She trusted me to speak for her, to be her voice.

The articles didn't read like puff pieces. They followed the AP's rule of "restraint" and I got a great many compliments from colleagues who envied my near-exclusive access to the new First Lady. But I didn't tell them that while the articles might appear objective, I had done something I shouldn't have done, professionally speaking. I had shown all three stories to both Louis Howe and Mrs. Roosevelt before I filed them—ostensibly for fact-checking, but really for approval. And all three were crafted to fit the theme of the "reluctant First Lady" that Howe had approved. Even loose as things were at that time, I had crossed the line between being a reporter and being a publicist.

There's a lot of talk these days, after the Kennedy-Nixon campaign and Theodore White's *The Making of the President, 1960*, about "creating the candidate's image." The techniques and technologies of the 1930s were less sophisticated, and political strategists didn't use those words. But Louis Howe was a kingmaker, and if he had lived to write the book he planned, it might have been called *The Making of the President 1932*. It could have included a chapter on the making of the First Lady, as well. Over time, her image would become as important and enduring as her husband's—in some people's minds, even more so. It was my AP stories that crafted the new First Lady's narrative and created the first national image of her. If Bill Chapin had read all my pieces carefully and in sequence, he might have seen what I was doing, but he didn't. Was he careless—or complicit? Did Howe get to him, or was Bill simply thinking of how many wire service newspapers would pick these stories up?

But although it might have been described as "deference," complicity was the real name of the game among the reporters who covered the president-elect. In a widely distributed photo of FDR and ER taken in front of the Sixty-Fifth Street townhouse, he is standing without any visible means of support. In fact, he is clinging to Eleanor's arm and—braces locked—he's leaning against a metal railing like a life-size cardboard cutout. I know this because I was there, watching with a small cadre of reporters and photographers as two men propped him up. When Steve Early, FDR's new press secretary, gave the word, the president-elect began talking about his plans for the new cabinet and the flashbulbs began popping. The press were helping to shape the myth that Roosevelt had overcome his disability. They knew but they didn't tell the biggest story of them all, the *true* story: the man could not bathe or dress himself or walk. If one of them had told the truth, it would have spelled the end of that reporter's access, the end of his reporting career.

As far as the press were concerned, complicity was the name of the game. I wasn't the only one who played it.


Madam and I spent as much time together as we could, which was a great deal, actually. FDR was the focus of everyone's attention now. While he held center stage with the press, his wife could slip into the wings.

Oh, I did my necessary work, and she did, too. She met the last of her obligations at the governor's mansion in Albany, finished the term at Todhunter, and carried out a few First Lady duties:

buying a new wardrobe and meeting with the planners of the upcoming inaugural events. But from the November election until the March inauguration (the last of the lengthy four-month inter-regnums that once divided presidential terms), she was in New York or at Val-Kill. And I was with her.

It was usually dinner. "Italian this evening?" I would ask, or she would say, "How do you feel about Hungarian, Hick?" Or we would send out for Chinese or Cuban. But I loved it best when I could cook for her. My specialty was a hearty oven-baked steak smothered in catsup and served with a baked potato, salad, and hot dinner rolls. She enjoyed my "plain fare," as she called it, and she coveted the luxury of eating in private, without being accosted by people who recognized her. And I loved simply sitting across the table from her, watching her graceful hands, the candlelight dancing in her eyes, and feeling the mirrored light dance in my heart. After dinner, we listened to records or read aloud and then put on our coats and took Prinz for his late-night walk before she went home to Sixty-Fifth Street.

And then one night, she didn't. The evening before, she had said, "The Philharmonic is performing a Wagner program tomorrow night. Would you like to go?"

I didn't hesitate. "Oh, lovely!" I exclaimed. "I'm wild for Wagner." Since I was a very young child, music has run through me, echoing in my head, singing softly in the back of my throat. And of all composers, Wagner is to me the most powerful. I learned to love his music when Ellie and I were living together. It has a sensual, erotic quality that thrills me to my deepest center.

It had been a difficult day for Madam, with a long session on inaugural planning that once again brought her up against the implacable reality of what was to come. She was subdued when we went to dinner at our favorite mid-town French restaurant, and I tried to match her mood. It was snowing when we came out, white flakes sifting in a white silence through the incandescent halos of streetlights. At Carnegie Hall that night, Wagner seemed even more dramatically magnificent than ever, the finale of *Tristan* performed with a force that lifted me on a shining current of sound, making me weep. And weep with an even greater joy because Madam was beside me.

When the lights came up, I dashed the tears from my eyes, but not before Madam saw them. She put an arm around my shoulders and whispered, "Oh, my dear, I wish I could care as deeply as you do. Such passion must be a gift."

*Ah, passion,* I thought. Madam, you don't know the half of it.

It was still snowing after the performance, harder and with a stinging bite to the wind, and we taxied back to Mitchell Place through streets that were nearly empty of traffic. I took Prinz out while she made hot chocolate for us. ("I know how to do *that,* at least," she said with a rueful laugh.) We drank it while she talked about the day she had spent with the inaugural planners, going over details of the mammoth White House reception planned for the afternoon of the ceremony, the dinner afterward for family and friends, and the inaugural ball. The day had reawakened all her fears about Washington, and I could hear the quiet despair in her voice.

"I don't see how I can do this, Hick. It feels... it feels completely *beyond* me. Marion and Nan don't understand—they think I should be pleased by Franklin's victory. Tommy understands, but she's too busy to think about it. If it weren't for you, I would be utterly alone." She faltered. "And when I get to Washington, I won't even have you."

I reached for her hand, feeling her despair and sharing it, for I was reminded that in the time to come, she would be there and I would be here and we would have no more evenings like this. The loss suddenly felt enormous, like a gaping hole opening up in the center of my life, like a massive cloud swallowing all that I care about. And suddenly I knew what I had to do.

"You won't be alone," I said. "I'm going to Washington with you."

She stared at me, puzzled. "But you work *here*, Hick. You've made a wonderful reputation in New York, and your political reporting is so widely respected. You can't just—"

"Yes, I can. I'll ask for a transfer to the AP's Washington bureau. It's a logical request. I've been covering FDR for four years, and now you. I should be covering the White House."

"But why would you *do* that?" she asked blankly.

On the floor at our feet, Prinz sighed and turned in his sleep. "Because I love you," I said.

"I know." She smiled, patted my arm. "And I love you, Hick. I'm so grateful to you for—"

"No," I said. "I *love* you, Madam. Passionately."

There. It was said. My hired-girl self shook a scolding finger, stamped a foot, and told me that I didn't fit into her life, that there was no future in loving her, that this made no kind of sense. But it was the truth, *my* truth, and I needed to tell it. I tried to lighten it with a self-mocking chuckle.

"It's in my nature. After all, you said it yourself. 'Such passion must be a gift.' You're right. It's a gift and I'm sharing it. With you."

"Ah," she said. After a moment, she added, tentatively, sadly, "And if I can't care as deeply as you do?"

"How do you know you can't?" I challenged her and then softened my voice. "Because you don't want to? Because it isn't wise?" I paused deliberately. "Because it's against the rules?"

She weighed that for a moment. "Because if I care," she said, so softly that I had to bend toward her to hear, "you will be taken away from me."

I thought of those she had loved. Her mother and father, dead. Franklin, lost to his career and to Missy. Earl, married now. "I suppose that's true," I said, and managed a rueful smile. "But it's not going to happen tonight. I love you tonight, my dear." I raised my hand to her neck, her throat, feeling a daring tenderness. "I want you tonight. And tomorrow. Probably next week, too." I lightened it with a laugh and a little shrug. "Not sure about next year, though. We'll have to see when that time comes."

That made her smile. She took my hand and kissed my fingers. "Thank you," she said. "Oh, Hick, you don't know how much I need you."

I captured her eyes. "And want?"

There was a brief hesitation, as if she were turning the words over in her mind before she gave them voice, and I wondered if she had ever spoken them before.

"And… want," she said, even more softly.

I leaned forward and kissed her. "Then come to me, dear," I said, urgent now, direct.

And in the sweet, silent dark, she did. With only our hearts as witness, we lay together, the length of our bodies measuring our passion as we taught each other to become the lovers neither of us had ever had, the lovers both of us had only imagined.

In another space of time, I would come to understand the many differences between *wanting* and *loving* and *loving* and *needing*. But on that night and for some time to come, these words were all synonymous to me, and I think to her, as well. I wanted her and loved her and needed her. She needed me and wanted me and loved me, and I was content with that.

# Part Three

1933 – 1934

# Chapter Six

# Off the Record

*I'm going to Washington with you.*

Of course, it wasn't as simple as that, and I knew it even as I said it. While it was true that covering the White House was a logical continuation of my coverage of the Roosevelts, it was also true that in those days, the Washington AP bureau had very little to report. Harding, Coolidge, and Hoover avoided making news whenever possible, and Congress moved with glacial slowness. Asking to trade my staccato New York political beat for the adagio of the nation's capital was asking for a demotion. In terms of my journalistic career, it was worse than a bad move. It was stupid.

I did it anyway.

"Are you *nuts?*" Bill Chapin looked at me as if I'd grown an extra head. "I need you here, Hick. The Mitchell case is going to trial at the end of March, and you know that story, inside and out. Why the hell would you want to go to Washington? Roosevelt talks a good game, but when he gets there, he'll find out that the bureaucracy is so completely hidebound that he won't be able to do a damn thing. Anyway, the AP has a girl in D.C. Bess Furman, her name is. She's going to handle the White House social calendar, teas and dinners, all that society page stuff. Byron Price has already assigned her to Eleanor."

The disappointment was so sharp I could scarcely swallow it, but there was no arguing with Bill. The Mitchell case pitted an ambitious assistant U.S. attorney named Thomas E. Dewey against Charles E. Mitchell, the former director of New York's prestigious National City Bank. The case, which was the talk of the city, involved charges of tax evasion and speculation with other people's money. I understood the issues, had studied the facts, and was ready to follow the testimony when the case came to trial. Bill was right. He needed me in that courtroom.

He did, though, ask if I would be willing to stick close to Mrs. Roosevelt until she moved into the White House in March. "I hope you won't mind," he added, as if my minding mattered. "There's not much going on at Tammany, and FDR is putting his cabinet together behind closed doors. No public appearances for him—but maybe you can dig up some news on Mrs. Roosevelt."

"If that's what you want," I said in a not-quite-grudging tone and went off to my typewriter to write a note to Bess Furman, congratulating her on her assignment to the new First Lady. I couldn't help adding that I would miss Mrs. R—which was the bitter truth, so help me.

That evening, after dinner with Esther Lape and Elizabeth Read, Madam and I went back to her townhouse, where she was alone for a few days, and I told her that my request for a transfer to the Washington bureau had been turned down. I would be staying in New York.

She stared at me for a moment, incredulous. "You actually asked to leave New York? I know you said you'd do that, but I didn't believe you would."

I sighed. "I'm flattered that Bill wants me to cover the Mitchell trial. It's a plum assignment for a woman. But I'm very, very sorry that I won't be in Washington."

"I'm sorry too." She smiled softly. "But that you *want* to do it

—oh, Hick, dear, that means so much!" In an impulsive gesture, she held out her arms and drew me to her. "So very, very much."

We held one another until our tentative beginnings took on their own movement, their own motion, and pulled us forward with an energy we couldn't deny. I felt my breath come short and wished with all my heart that time would simply stop and we could hold each other forever.

In those betwixt and between months, we often went out together in the evening. The Depression had hit New York theater hard. Many venues closed and the actors had fled to Hollywood, where the movies were still making money. But Eva Le Gallienne had produced *Alice in Wonderland* at the Civic Repertory Theater, and it was quite well received. Eva (who played the White Queen) and her life partner Josephine Hutchinson (who played Alice) were friends of mine, and the four of us went out for ice cream after their performance, lingering at our table until the lights were turned out. Another night, we went with Madam's friends, Esther and Elizabeth, to see Josephine Hutchinson in *Dear Jane*, a play about the life of Jane Austen, and afterward to their brownstone on East Eleventh, a block east of Fifth Avenue, where we had dessert. I spent my days in the company of men, and Madam lived in a world dominated by them. It was a comfort to find ourselves in the companionship of women.

During those weeks, Mrs. R often included me when she entertained. At lunch on Sixty-Fifth Street one day, I was seated next to FDR's Aunt Kassie, an elderly lady who was complaining, loudly, about the number of newspaper articles in which her nephew's wife was featured—mostly my stories, I realized, with a kind of guilty pleasure. By way of veiled explanation, I suggested that it would be difficult for a woman in Mrs. Roosevelt's position to avoid the press.

"Rubbish!" The old lady's tone was acid. "The newspapers are like rats, beneath a lady's notice. I have never in my life spoken to a reporter."

Mrs. R told the story to her husband, and he couldn't resist ribbing me, the next time he saw me. "Has my dear old Aunt Kassie discovered your secret identity yet, Hick?" he asked, with a sly chortle and a sideways glance that hinted at other meanings. "Has she learned that you are a rat in female clothing?" I couldn't tell from his expression exactly what he intended, and the question about my "secret identity" made me shiver. I was afraid that for all my efforts at concealment, he might have sensed my feelings toward his wife.

Ah, my feelings. If I had imagined that they would diminish or change, I was very wrong. I understood that loving Madam was entirely hopeless. She was cultured, sophisticated, well-read, well-educated, well-traveled. She was married—to the man who would soon be president of the United States. Loving her was absurd, illogical, and unthinkable. And I was a fool.

But that didn't change a damn thing.


After the election, Mrs. R began making it clear that, while she had to include other reporters on occasion, she preferred to work with just one. I knew her calendar and was already on the scene whenever she made an unscheduled appearance. I ran interference for her with the rest of the press, sometimes handing out scraps of news so they wouldn't go away hungry. I got the exclusive on her activities and turned even the most ordinary events into stories, so that while FDR was out of the public eye, his wife was making news.

And while I was at it, I thought of a way that Mrs. R could make news on a regular basis, on her own terms, once she got to Washington. I dropped in at Louis Howe's office and pitched the idea, knowing that unless he supported it, the scheme would get nowhere fast.

"I think she should hold press conferences," I told him. "For women reporters only. *By* a woman, *for* women, *about* women. Weekly."

"Women only?" He frowned. "Never heard of such a thing."

"Women only, with a spotlight on news *for* women. Mrs. Roosevelt has ideas and she likes dealing with people. This will make her a new kind of First Lady, especially where the press is concerned. She'll be *making* news. And the Washington news-women will eat it up. They'll be delighted by the access."

I didn't have to lay out the advantages for Howe. He knew that a First Lady's press conferences would be a breath of fresh air blowing through the stuffy old White House. The male reporters and their editors would sit up and take notice. The women press corps would feel distinctly privileged. What's more, their stories wouldn't stay in Washington. They'd go out on the various news-wires and editors all over the country would grab them for their women's pages. And women voted.

"She'll have to stay out of politics," Louis said cautiously. "But I'll pass the suggestion to FDR and Early."

Everybody in the news business agreed that Steve Early had been a first-rate choice for the White House job that was, for the first time, called "press secretary." He was a talented newsman who had been at the UP, then at the AP's Washington bureau, and most recently at Paramount Pictures, where he had headed up the newsreel division. He'd convinced Roosevelt to hold twice-weekly presidential press conferences and to use radio, which Hoover had refused to do. Clearly, he was going to be one of the power people in FDR's administration. His appointment was an indication that the new administration was taking press relationships seriously.

"Let me know what you decide," I replied. "Oh, and I haven't said anything to Mrs. R about my idea. Thought I'd check it out with you first."

Louis sucked on his cigarette, then paused to cough, flicking ashes onto the papers strewn across his desk. He gave me a penetrating look and I squirmed, wondering just how deeply he could see into me.

"These women-only press conferences," he said. "Is this something the Washington AP is pushing?"

"Nope." I shook my head emphatically. "I haven't mentioned it in the bureau. I'm not going to Washington," I added, in case he was wondering if I was feathering my own nest. "Byron Price—the Washington bureau chief—has already assigned Bess Furman to the First Lady, effective on Inauguration Day." It hurt to say that.

He was silent for a moment, his large, dark eyes fixed shrewdly on my face. "You are remembering the cardinal rule of the newspaper game, aren't you, Hick?"

"Which one is that?" I managed a chuckle. "There are so many."

He sat forward, waving the smoke away with one hand, scattering ashes with the other. "A reporter shouldn't get too close to a source."

"Oh, absolutely," I said cheerfully.

But I had heard the warning, another variant on the AP's *stay out of the story*. As a political strategist, Louis had perfected the knack of reading people—understanding what they wanted, anticipating how much they would give to get it. I reminded myself that if I wasn't careful, he might guess how I felt about Madam.

Now, reflecting on that conversation across the years, I realize that he knew, even then, and knew what he might have to do.

But that came later. He didn't have to do it yet.


A few mornings later, I got the call. Louis was briskly cordial. "FDR says to tell you that the press conference idea is, and I quote, 'grand.' Early's a little doubtful—wonders whether Mrs. R can handle a mob of girl reporters without getting herself or the president into trouble. But he says for you to get him a list of correspondents and he'll certify them. You can tell Mrs. Roosevelt that she has the go-ahead from this end." He chuckled. "Too bad First Ladies don't hire press secretaries, Hick. If they did, you'd be my choice for Mrs. R's, hands down."

At lunchtime, I met Mrs. R and Tommy over a small table at the crowded Horn & Hardart Automat on Fifty-Seventh off Broadway. Mrs. R, who would be speaking at a meeting of the Women's Trade Union League, was wearing a nicely tailored gray gabardine jacket and skirt with a ruffled white blouse—one of the new "First Lady" outfits her daughter Anna had helped her pick out. But the suit was uneasily topped by an old dollar-sale hat, a maroon felt pancake with a large pink rose tipped over one eye. I had to smile. A little of the old mixed in with the new.

When Tommy went to get coffee for us, I shared the idea I had pitched to Louis.

"Press conferences?" She wrinkled her forehead doubtfully. "But I've been told to stay out of politics, Hick. There'll be nothing newsworthy about me." She raised her voice a little above the tinny rattle of coins and the clatter of the glass doors of the dispensing machines. "I've lived in Washington before. I know what the First Lady does. I'll be nothing but a hostess for social functions."

She wasn't being modest. She was genuinely unaware, I thought, of the potential of her office—which was understandable, given the limitations imposed on most previous First Ladies. But I could see it, and I knew she could, too, once she got into the habit of looking for it.

But I didn't want to overwhelm her. I shook my head firmly. "You don't have to get involved in politics." I leaned forward and punctuated my words with my fork. "*You* are the news. A weekly press conference will give you a chance to let women across the country know what *you* think is important. In case you're worrying that it'll put you in the fishbowl," I added, "remember that these press conferences will be *your* fishbowl. You'll be in charge." I had an idea for a newspaper column, too, but that could wait.

Tommy had come back to the table with three green-and-white H&H mugs filled with the Automat's legendary chicory coffee. "Whose fishbowl?" she asked.

"Hick thinks I should hold weekly press conferences at the White House," Mrs. R replied. "For women only." She pulled down her mouth. "But what would I say? And what if I say the wrong thing?"

"If you say something you didn't mean to say, just tell them it's off the record," I said. "If they don't abide by that, Early will revoke their credentials. Simple as that."

"It's a swell idea, Boss," Tommy said with a little grin. "And you'll have plenty to say. Why, if nothing else, you can hand out seating arrangements and dinner menus. It might keep them from snooping."

"Snooping?" I rolled my eyes. "Come on, now, Tommy. No reporter worth her salt would ever consider doing a thing like *that*."

We laughed. The recent administrations had been close-mouthed about everything that went on inside the White house, even social events. Reporters had been driven to bribing the servants to get the inside dope, and some of them were even rumored to keep a few servants on retainer.

"Speaking of reporters," I said, "here's something else to consider." I put down a card I hadn't played for Howe. "Newspapers are in serious trouble. Advertising revenue is dropping through the floor. Managing editors are cutting staff, and women reporters are always the first to be fired. But if the First Lady holds regular press conferences, those editors won't dare cut the women." I pointed my finger at her. "Without them, there won't be any access to *you.*"

"That's something I hadn't thought about." Still frowning and uncertain, Mrs. R put her hand over mine. "My very dear one, thank you for the vote of confidence, and for thinking of the newspaper women. But I'm sure that Louis Howe and Steve Early will think it's a terrible idea."

*My very dear one.* My heart jumped at the words and I lifted my eyes to hers, glimpsing an open, unguarded depth that startled me, and a softness around her mouth that was trembling into a smile. She had used endearments before, but not in the presence of others.

But then the look in her eyes was gone, so quickly that I wasn't sure of what I had seen, and her mouth was firm. She removed her hand. I had the feeling that we had been standing together at the edge of a very steep cliff, she and I, and that we had both stepped back at the same time. I felt Tommy's curious glance on us and heard my voice as if it were coming from a great distance.

"I took the liberty of mentioning the idea to Louis," I said. "He spoke to FDR and Steve Early, and they understand the advantages. If you decide to do it, it's okay with them."

"I see," Mrs. Roosevelt said. "Well, then, I suppose I'll have to consider it." She pushed back her chair, all business now. "I need to go to the bookshop and pick up a book I promised for Anna. Take your time, Tommy, dear. Hick, I'll see you at four, at the WTUL meeting. I'll give you a copy of my talk then. I want to mark the quotes for you." She sighed. "It's my last talk there, I'm afraid. Franklin has asked me to give it up, along with the Democratic National Committee and the League of Women Voters." She frowned at me. "You see, Hick? They really intend to keep me out of politics."

Tommy and I lingered over coffee and cigarettes, saying very little. A noisy trio took a table near us. Under their voices and the rattle of their dishes, Tommy said, "There's something I need to say to you, Hick. But it's off the record and *very* confidential." Her eyes were intent on my face. "Do I have your word?"

"Of course." I didn't stop to calculate how much I was leaving off the record these days, and what that said about my commitment to my job as a reporter.

"I've seen how much time you're spending with the Boss, and I've been glad of it. She needs a friend—someone who is more to her than a secretary. I can do a lot for her, but I can't do what you do—take her out of herself, show her that she's deeply admired, push her to do things she wouldn't undertake on her own. Earl used to do that, you know. He gave her confidence. Gave her love. You're filling his place, and that's good." She stirred her coffee, not looking at me. "Even better, you're not a man. When she was with Earl, tongues wagged." Now she glanced up. "Two women together call less attention to themselves than a woman and a man."

One of the trio at the other table dropped a fork and scraped his chair as he retrieved it. The murmur of voices around us rose like a cloud to the ceiling. I cleared my throat, not wanting to say the words but wanting to know the answer. "Do you think she's in love with Earl?"

"No," she says slowly. "Perhaps at one time, but not now. She was enormously grateful for what he offered her. He was on her side, totally. He gave her what her husband doesn't, the sense that she's a woman, a desirable woman, physically desirable, I mean." She picked up her cup, sipped, put it down again. "When the two of them were with Nancy and Marion, she liked to pretend that Earl was her lover. I'm not even sure she understood what she was doing—not fully, I mean. But *he* understood. It was a flirtatious playacting, and he played along. That's why he was so good for her." Her eyes questioned me, asking if I understand.

I nodded. Yes, I understood. Playacting. That's what I had seen that afternoon at Val-Kill. And then I wondered. I wondered about us, about her. About playacting.

She slid me another long look, then: "I'm telling you this, Hick, because much as I love and admire the woman, she *does* require a very great deal of the people who care for her. Not that she means to use anybody, not really. But she's a... a whirlwind. You and I and Earl, and even Nan and Marion—we're like scraps of paper. We get swept up into her enthusiasms and whirled along. She inspires us, and we want to do whatever we can to help her. But it's easy to get sucked in, to lose ourselves. I love my husband, but my commitment to the Boss has already caused problems. If I go to Washington with her, I might as well say goodbye to my marriage. I have to choose between Frank and—"

She was interrupted by a loud crash of china and cutlery, as a stand loaded with dirty dishes teetered and fell. She stopped, blinked, and took a deep breath. "There are demons in her, Hick, from her childhood, from her early years with FDR and his mother. Her constant busyness—it's her way of outrunning them.

But if you let yourself get in too deep, they may become your demons, too." She glanced down at her watch and pushed her chair back with the air of a woman who has just said far more than she intended. "Goodness, just look at the time. There's a stack of letters waiting on my desk. Gotta dash."

I watched Tommy as she dodged through the tables with her characteristic I-know-where-I'm-going walk and disappeared. Later, I would think again of what she had said and know that she was warning me, in the same way Louis Howe had warned me, not to get too close. Not to let myself get pulled into the whirlwind.

*Stay out of the story.* But it was already too late. Much too late.

As the days passed, Mrs. R's apprehension about going to Washington seemed to heighten, her moodiness to deepen. A reporter would ask a question, and she would harden her mouth and refuse to answer. At dinner, a friend would bring up the subject and she would turn away. I could understand that she dreaded the empty duties of the White House hostess, but it seemed to me that there was more to it than that, a dark, dangerous shadow looming just over her shoulder.

It was Bess Furman who told me. She had come up from Washington to meet Mrs. Roosevelt and Mrs. R invited both of us to lunch. I asked Bess to meet me at my office that morning so I could share background material from the AP files. The office was a hive of reporters coming and going, typewriters and teletypes clattering, telephones ringing. We found a quiet corner away from the hubbub and settled down for a working session with coffee, donuts, cigarettes, and our notebooks.

I liked Bess, I discovered. Plump and round-faced, with a frank, easy openness, she had grown up in a small town in

Nebraska. Now she was a savvy, hard-working newswoman with a Midwesterner's blunt, straight-to-the point style. I had a lot of material to cover, and Bess knew what questions to ask. By the time we were finished going through clippings and photos, I had decided I could trust her with my concern.

"May I ask you a favor, Bess?"

She closed her notebook. "Sure. I'll do what I can."

"Mrs. Roosevelt is... well, nervous about moving back to Washington. Part of it is the fishbowl life of the White House, I'm sure, and she's unhappy about giving up her personal projects. But there's something else bothering her, something deeper than that, and I don't know what it is. You might keep your eyes open. Maybe you could... well, give her a hand. If she gets into trouble, I mean."

Bess leaned back in her chair, eyeing me, half amused. "You don't know, then."

"Know what?" I lit another cigarette.

"About Franklin. And Lucy Mercer. Mrs. Winthrop Ruther-furd, she is now." She studied my expression. "Ah. I see that you don't. Well, I understand. It's never been in the newspapers, of course. And it's a Washington story. You're based in New York."

It was true. I'd been in New York for going on six years. Washington was like a foreign country. "What's there to know?" But from the tone of her voice, I could make a calculated guess. I was right.

"An affair, back in 1916, 1917. Lucy Mercer was Eleanor's social secretary. I don't know when it began, but I understand that it ended in 1918, when Eleanor found some of Lucy's letters. *Love* letters." Bess chuckled and the freckles danced across her nose. "Letters can certainly cause a lot of trouble, in the wrong hands. Better burn them before anybody gets a look, I'd say."

In later years, with several thousand of Madam's letters in my possession, I might have agreed. But at the time, I was startled, not so much by the fact of an affair, but by the awareness that it might be enough of an issue to cause trouble for Mrs. Roosevelt. Unless—

"You're not… you're not saying that the affair was public knowledge, are you?" I asked slowly. "Or that Mrs. R is concerned about people remembering *that* far back?"

Bess gave me a lopsided grin. "That's how much you know about Washington, Hick. It's nothing like New York. It's a tight-knit little town, very parochial. The people in Washington society —especially the women—know every damn thing that goes on, and they never forget. Once a story gets started, it lives eternally. This one not only lives but thrives, mostly because of Alice."

"Alice?"

"I'd better start at the beginning." Bess took a cigarette out of a monogrammed case. "Eleanor and Franklin moved to town early in the Wilson administration. They had an elegant house on R Street. Franklin was an assistant bigwig in the Navy Department, and Eleanor, as the ambitious bigwig's dutiful wife, trotted around making her duty calls, hundreds of them. She needed somebody to keep her social calendar straight, so she hired Lucy Mercer." She flicked her lighter to her cigarette. "Lucy was—and still is—an exceptionally lovely woman, graceful, elegant, light-hearted and gay." She paused, blowing out a stream of smoke. "Eleanor isn't the prettiest belle at the ball, of course. And nobody ever called her light-hearted."

"I suppose so," I said slowly, already feeling the hurt. "But she—" I caught her quizzical look and stopped. "Sorry. Go on."

"Lucy and Franklin fell in love. Franklin went to Europe—this was during the war—and there were letters. Eleanor found them when she unpacked his suitcase and the whole story came out. She was quite civilized about it. She offered Franklin his freedom, but he refused and promised never to see Lucy again." Bess pulled on her cigarette. "Or he asked for his freedom and Eleanor said yes, but Lucy said no because she was Catholic. Everybody's got a favorite explanation for what happened. Or what didn't happen. Take your pick."

"My god," I muttered, shaking my head.

"Oh, there's more. His mother is supposed to have said that she'd cut him off without a penny if he abandoned his family. And Louis Howe warned him that a divorce would make him a dead duck forever, politically speaking. Between the family money and his political ambitions, he saw his duty. He'd stick it out with his wife. In the end, Eleanor forgave him, although she never quite took him back."

*Poor, poor Madam*, I thought, heart-stricken. How deeply hurt and humiliated she must have been. It must have felt as if all her clothes were stripped off and she was forced to go naked in public.

"And then there was Alice," Bess said, dropping her lighter into her purse.

"Alice?" I asked again, and then understood. "Oh, yes. Mrs. Longworth."

"Yes. Alice Roosevelt Longworth. Teddy's daughter, Eleanor's first cousin, and an Oyster Bay Roosevelt."

Of course, I thought. Teddy Roosevelt, TR's eldest son, had been competing politically with FDR for decades. The Oyster Bay Roosevelts blamed both Franklin and Eleanor for the drubbing Teddy Junior took in the 1924 New York gubernatorial race, where Eleanor had campaigned for Al Smith and against her cousin.

"Alice is sharp-tongued and enjoys her bit of tittle-tattle," Bess went on, "and she is *not* a fan of Eleanor's. I was told that during the war, when Eleanor and the children were on holiday at Campobello, Alice invited Franklin and Lucy to dinner and seated them together. She told friends that he deserved to have a little fun, since he was married to Eleanor. Franklin was there and heard it." Bess made a little face. "He laughed."

I felt a hot, unreasoning anger boil up inside me, and in that moment, I hated him. How could Franklin Roosevelt betray his wife, and in such a careless, brutal, *public* way? I took a deep breath and steadied my voice.

"So you're telling me that Mrs. Roosevelt is going back to a place where people have nothing more important to talk about than a fifteen-year-old love affair?"

"Well, of course, FDR *is* the president," Bess said. "Which makes Mrs. Roosevelt an ideal topic of gossip. Lucy herself is out of the picture. She had to have a job, so she went to work. This time, though, she actually married her boss. Winthrop Rutherfurd —older, widowed with children, wealthy, a sterling catch. She might be forgiven, though, for thinking that if things had been otherwise, *she* would be the new First Lady."

Or not, I thought, if Louis Howe was right and a divorce put the presidency out of FDR's reach. Then she would be just plain Mrs. Roosevelt. My heart thudded. And Madam would be free. But all of this had happened long ago, and things were as they were.

I took a deep breath. "You said Mrs. R never quite took her husband back. What did you mean?"

Bess paused as one of the reporters walked past us, jauntily whistling "Oh, You Beautiful Doll." "The way Alice tells it, Elea-nor levied a penalty for her forgiveness. She agreed to go on with the marriage as if nothing had happened, but she barred Franklin from her bed. Forever."

I had to clear my throat. "You're telling me that the Roosevelts haven't been husband and wife since..."

Suddenly, Earl Miller's marriage made a different kind of sense. Perhaps FDR wasn't just silencing gossip about Eleanor, or putting Miller out of his wife's reach—although he could very well have been doing both. Perhaps he was also getting even. Taking revenge for what his wife had done to *him*.

"Well, that's the story," Bess said cheerily. "Of course, there's the thing with polio, and can he or can't he. In bed, I mean. People do wonder, especially because of that sweet little secretary who does his bidding night and day. Maybe the story about Eleanor freezing him out is just another of those poison darts that Princess Alice of Malice likes to toss."

Princess Alice of Malice. Franklin. Lucy. Good Lord. These people. I was struggling with a flooding sympathy. And with the awareness that there was more—and less—between Mrs. Roosevelt and her husband than I had imagined.

Bess picked up her notebook. "These days, the affair seems to be regarded as a funny joke that Franklin and Lucy played on poor, unwitting Eleanor, who was too naive to guess what was going on. So, to answer your initial question, I'm sure the poor woman must feel positively petrified when she thinks about living in Washington. No one deserves to be publically hurt, as she must have been. Especially because Lucy Mercer was—still is, actually—such a beauty."

She didn't say *And Mrs. Roosevelt is decidedly not,* but the unsaid words hung in the air between us.

The knowledge of Franklin's betrayal opened an even deeper and more urgent tenderness in me. I wanted to guard Madam against anything that might hurt her, to defend her against the ugliness of the world. I wanted to pull her to me as if she were a child, to embrace her and comfort her and let her know that I was on her side. That I was entirely *for her,* whatever happened. Finally, I screwed up my courage and told her all this. And for the first time, I felt able to call her by her name. Eleanor. A beautiful name.

It happened at Val-Kill, in early December. Nancy and Marion were spending the weekend with a friend on Long Island, and Madam invited me to go to the cottage with her. We were laughing and light-hearted as we drove up from the city in her blue Buick convertible, looking forward to a weekend with nothing to do. The heater in the car didn't work, and we were chilled to the bone when we arrived late on Friday afternoon. But the lamps were lit, a tidy fire was burning in the fireplace, and the lady who came in to cook had left a sandwich supper for two on a tray, with tomato soup to be heated on the stove and slices of apple pie for dessert.

After supper, we took turns reading poetry aloud to one another—the poems of Edna St. Vincent Millay, a favorite that I had brought with me. Madam's hair was softly haloed in the firelight, and as she read, her voice light and lilting, I couldn't keep my eyes from her face. She seemed to fill the space with an irresistibly radiant, magnetic energy. I found myself smiling, smiling foolishly, as if I had just learned how to smile and hadn't yet learned how to switch it off. I was smiling at the wonder that I was here, with her, alone together.

The next morning at breakfast I told her I knew about Franklin's affair with Lucy Mercer and guessed that it was one of the reasons she could not endure the thought of going to Washington.

She put down her coffee cup and regarded me for a moment, her blue eyes intent. Finally, she asked, "Who told you? Tommy?"

"I'm a journalist. I protect my sources." I took a deep breath and went on boldly, "I'm hungry to know all that there is to know about you, all the hidden things. I want to know you entirely, as I want you to know me." And then I was suddenly afraid that since I'd reminded her that I was a reporter, she might think I would somehow use her story. I added, urgently, "But this is only for the two of us, Eleanor, not to be shared with anyone else." There. I had said it. Her name

"Eleanor," she said softly. "I love the way you say it, Hick. And I trust you not to share this."

*I trust you not to share this.* Now, as I write, I look at these words on the page and wonder if, in writing them for someone else to read, I am betraying our trust, as Franklin betrayed her with Lucy. And kept on betraying her, as I know, as she discovered, up to the very day of his death. But the story about the Mercer affair came out in a book in 1947, after the Second World War, after FDR was dead. I am sure that Joe Lash intends to retell it in his memoir and in the biography of Mrs. Roosevelt that he plans to write. Others are likely to tell it, too, so that by the time this little memoir of mine is read, after *I* am dead, the story of Franklin and Lucy will no doubt have become a standard chapter in the retelling of the Roosevelts' lives.

But all that lies in a far corner of the future, dark to both of us on that Saturday morning in the winter of 1932, when Franklin's fifteen-year-old betrayal of his wife was yet a fresh hurt for her, rubbed more terribly raw by the knowledge that she would have to go to Washington and face the people who knew about it. When I let her know that I knew, her defenses against grief and loss and abandonment, the last walls between us, came down in a great crumbling tumble. There were tears and sobs and I heard the whole story, and more—more than Bess Furman knew, or Princess Alice, or even Franklin—and understood it all the better because *I* had been betrayed, too, by Ellie. I understood how utterly Eleanor had been destroyed, not just in herself and with her friends and family—the broader, Oyster Bay family—but in the unforgiving, unforgetting world that was Washington. I understood her reluctance and her fears. And understood that I would do anything, *anything*, to keep her from being hurt again.

Afterward, we put on coats and wool caps and mittens and boots and walked through the leafless woods around Val-Kill, the white birch trees like pale ghosts standing watch along the little ice-bound stream. She reached for my hand and clung to it tightly, as if I were her strength in a world that was whirling her to a place she didn't want to go. For me, it was as if the universe had been born brand new all around us, in a million dancing needles of chill December sunshine.

Later, in front of the fire, reading aloud from Ibsen's play *The Doll's House*, we sat close together, our shoulders and hands touching. And as we said goodnight, we held each other in a pledge of intimacy that was closer than close, as lovely as love.


And then things changed again—this time, for both of us.

Mrs. R continued to wrap up her obligations to her various organizations and get ready for the move to Washington. I kept on doing my job, too, following her around the city, writing a story every day for the wire and stories about other news related to the change in administrations. We spent another weekend at Val-Kill, but Nancy and Marion were there, which soured the time for me. I could feel their jealousy, like hot puffs of wind off a desert, and that defiant hired-girl self of mine, goaded by their prim disapproval, made an impolite, impetuous, indecorous fool of herself. She laughed too loudly, smoked too many cigarettes, and told coarse newsroom jokes. I could see that the two women thought of me as they did of Earl: I was rough and unmannerly, common, and socially beneath their dear Eleanor. And the sharper their disapproval, the more I acted the part.

On the train back to the city on Sunday afternoon, I told Eleanor—I was getting used to using her name—that I would not go to Val-Kill again when Nan and Marion were there. That assertion, and its many echoes, would reverberate through the rest of our years together: my wish to have her to myself, my resentment of her other friends, their dislike of me. That was understandable, wasn't it? I knew—and had to accept—the fact that her life would be filled by others, by clamoring legions, although I couldn't know then just how clamorous, and how many, those legions would become. All I knew was that, in the little time we had together, I wanted both of us to be wholly together, not parceled out among others.

"I'm sorry if I'm offending you," I said, and added quietly, "But I *care* for you, Eleanor. You come first with me, and I'm selfish. I admit it. I don't want to share you."

She smiled, wistful. "You sound a little bit like Earl, you know."

"I'm not surprised. When it comes to you, Earl and I have something in common." I took a breath and said, very seriously, "I respect the fact that Nan and Marion are your friends, and I know that you want to spend time with them. But our time is all too short as it is. The inauguration will be here before we know it and—"

"Don't say that, Hick." She put her hand over mine. "I don't want to think about what's ahead. I have the feeling—the *terrible* feeling—that these are the last weeks of freedom I'll have for the rest of my life."

Now, I know that she was right. But at the time, I was thinking only of the next four years, not knowing there would be another four, and more. "Oh, come on, now," I said soothingly. "He's only been elected for one term, dear. It's not a life sentence."

She shook her head. "You don't know, Hick. I saw how my aunt Edith—TR's wife—was changed by her years in the White House. I don't want to be changed. I don't want to become a... a public person."

She nodded toward a middle-aged lady on the other side of the aisle, a red knit cap pulled over her ears, her shoulders hunched inside her coat. She was reading *Anna Karenina*. "You see that lady? Miss Jane Doe, on her way home after an afternoon with friends in the country. If I were her, I wouldn't have to hold press conferences or state dinners or stand in reception lines." Her sigh was heavy with envy. "I could live in a little white house at the end of a pretty green village street and be just plain Jane Doe."

Could she? I wondered. Mrs. Roosevelt was used to having a maid to manage her clothes and a cook and a housekeeper to manage her household and Tommy Thompson to manage her office. Given a chance to live Miss Doe's perfectly ordinary life, Mrs. Roosevelt might find that she didn't like it very much.

But I only smiled and nodded. "And I would be your next door neighbor," I replied. "Janet Doe. We would have all the privacy we wanted, and nobody would recognize us or interfere." I chuckled. "What do you say, dear? Shall we give it a try?"

"Someday," she said. "Someday we will, Hick." I heard the promise in her voice. It was what I wanted and needed to hear and I clung to it—for longer than I should have, I know now. It was a promise she couldn't have kept, even if she'd wanted to.

That night, Eleanor came to Mitchell Place with me. We took Prinz for a walk in the early dark and fed him, then fixed an easy supper of a cheese omelet and toast and jelly and hot tea. She stayed with me all night, and then the next night. After she went back to the Sixty-Fifth Street house, we began each day with a telephone call. When we didn't spend the evening together, we ended the day with a letter, a ritual that we practiced daily, almost without interruption, for the next ten years. After that, not quite as often, but with love and affection, for the rest of our lives.

Eleanor planned to have Christmas with her family at Spring-wood, so we held our own private gift exchange the week before. After an evening of English Renaissance choral music at St. Luke's, we went back to my apartment. I had put up a small tree, and we had coffee and fruitcake and exchanged presents. She gave me a filmy blue nightgown trimmed in ivory lace—"a change from your lovely striped flannel pajamas," she said with a laugh. I gave her the sapphire and diamond ring that Madam Schumann-Heink had given to me.

"Oh," she whispered, as she opened the velvet-covered box. Her eyes widened. "Oh, my goodness!" And then, "But I can't accept this, Hick. It's much too fine. It's—"

"Shut up, Eleanor," I said, mimicking Madam Schumann-Heink's thick German accent. "I love you, I give you my ring. You be a good girl and take it." I paused. "Wear it and think of me," I added in my own voice. "For I do love you, you know."

"Oh, Hick," she said, her eyes filling with tears. "*Je t'aime et je t'adore. Je t'aime.*"

CHAPTER SEVEN

# "Empty Without You"

According to tradition, the current First Lady invited the First Lady-Elect to tour the family's White House living quarters, and as the inauguration drew closer, Mrs. Hoover asked Mrs. Roosevelt to come for a visit.

"You'll come with me, won't you, Hick?" Mrs. R asked, and I sold the AP on the story—the first time there would be press coverage of this domestic ritual. I knew it would play on every woman's page in the country.

Mrs. R made a reservation for us at the Mayflower Hotel, five blocks from the White House. One room, she told them, would do. But when we arrived, we were shown to the tenth-floor Presidential Suite. "Much too grand," she muttered. But she had to laugh when her friend Janet Doe confessed to being impressed by the size and magnificence of the suite, whose last occupants had been the Hoovers.

"After all," I said, gazing at the huge bouquet of hothouse flowers that spilled over the foyer table, "this Miss Doe grew up in South Dakota, where she scrubbed people's floors and washed their dishes. She thinks this is incredibly *swell*. She intends to enjoy every minute of it."

"Then I will, too," Mrs. R said firmly.

The next morning, we were treated to a lavish breakfast, served with fine china and crystal at the damask-covered table in the suite's dining room. Mrs. R—wanting to be as anonymous as possible—had declined Mrs. Hoover's offer of a car, so we set off on foot up Connecticut, through a park, and across Pennsylvania. We said goodbye at the iron gate at the northwest entry to the White House and she went alone to her meeting with Mrs. Hoover, who would never have tolerated a reporter tagging along As I waited there for her, I thought of the hired girl and the incredible journey that had brought her from South Dakota to the White House gate and tried *not* to think about Inauguration Day. Eleanor would be the nation's First Lady, Bess Furman would be covering her, and I would go back to New York, alone.

That afternoon, I saw Eleanor and her son Elliott onto a small plane (no Amelia this time, however) and off to Warm Springs, where FDR was celebrating his fiftieth birthday. As I waved goodbye, I wondered—a little maliciously, I confess—if the president-elect would be getting a birthday card from Mrs. Lucy Mercer Rutherfurd or if he would invite her to his inauguration.

Later, I would learn from the backstairs gang at the White House that FDR did in fact send a limousine for Mrs. Rutherfurd, so that she could be there when he was sworn in. The way the servants told it (they were silent witnesses to everything that went on every day at 1600 Pennsylvania Avenue), Franklin saw her occasionally after the inauguration, concealing her visits not just from his wife but also from Missy LeHand. Missy, the servants said, was kept in the dark about Lucy because she was wildly jealous. Which was ironic, they thought, since the First Lady didn't seem to be at all jealous of Missy.

But while Eleanor made every effort to overlook Missy's relationship with her husband, it sometimes arose in uncomfortable ways. One of the things she feared most about Washington was that she would have no work there. So she approached Franklin with an offer to take over some of the president's mail. He had given her a long, strange look, then shook his head at her offer. "Missy handles the mail, Babs. If you stepped in, she might think you were… well, interfering."

I heard the hurt in her voice when she told me this and remembered the letters that had precipitated the crisis of the Lucy Mercer affair. Was FDR thinking of that episode when he told his wife she wasn't welcome to open his presidential mail?

I remembered, too, what Reggie Davis had said about the man's left hook and wondered whether he was being intentionally cruel by preferring his secretary to his wife. Or whether he simply thought of no one's feelings but his own.

Three weeks before the inaugural, the president-elect narrowly escaped assassination.

Eleanor and I had eaten an early supper at my favorite Armenian restaurant. Later that evening, we were to catch a train to Ithaca, where she'd been invited to speak at Cornell University. On our way back uptown, the taxi dropped me off at the AP office to file the day's story, then took her home to Sixty-Fifth Street. We were to meet later at Grand Central Station.

I was sitting down to my typewriter when the night city editor yelled at me. "Some guy just tried to kill FDR, Hick. Where's Mrs. Roosevelt?"

I was reaching for my coat. "On her way back up to Sixty-Fifth Street."

"Get a taxi," the editor snapped. "Get that story. *Now.*" He didn't have to tell me. I was already heading for the elevator.

The shooting had happened in Miami, where FDR had docked

after two weeks fishing in the Caribbean on Vincent Astor's yacht. He had just finished speaking to a crowd from the back of his car, when an emigrant Italian anarchist fired five bullets, hitting Chicago Mayor Anton Cermak in the chest and slightly wounding four other people. Roosevelt was unharmed, but Cermak died two days after the inauguration. His unrepentant killer, Giuseppe Zangara was executed in Florida's electric chair two weeks later. In those days, justice was swift.

Mrs. Roosevelt was shaken, but calm, and when FDR telephoned to tell her that the Secret Service was insisting on assigning agents to her, she refused, firmly.

"I understand that you have to have security, Franklin. But I don't—and I *won't*. I am not going to have men following me around. That's all there is to it." At the time, the law mandated that the president (and president-elect) be protected. But agents were assigned to family members only at the president's request. If FDR didn't insist, the Service was out of luck.

Her voice may have sounded firm enough to her husband, but I heard the strain in it. I knew why she didn't want the Secret Service keeping tabs on her. So far, I had been just another female reporter assigned to the new First Lady, and nobody paid much attention to our comings and goings together, especially early in the morning or late at night. Both of us were relieved when FDR gave a resigned sigh and said, "Well, if that's the way you want it, Babs."

"That's the way I want it," she said. "Thank you, Franklin."

We took a later train to Ithaca. The next day, she spoke at a faculty breakfast, gave a talk to a crowd of three thousand people, and attended a luncheon, an afternoon tea, and a dinner at which the governor spoke. Sometime that day, answering a reporter's question, she said, "A man in public life has to face the possibility that he'll be a target. He can't live in fear, and neither can his family." I couldn't have been prouder.

That wasn't the end of it, of course. When she moved into the White House, the Secret Service code-named her "Rover" and the chief, Bill Moran, increased his efforts to get her to accept protection. (She said she didn't know whether to be pleased that they knew she was always on the move or annoyed that they had named her for somebody's pooch.) She managed to keep the Service at bay in the summer of that first year, when the two of us took our long driving trip into the Canadian provinces. As time went on, however, it wouldn't be just the Secret Service keeping tabs on her. It would be the FBI and J. Edgar Hoover.

I have often wondered what would have happened if one of those five anarchist bullets had killed FDR. John Nance Garner, Roosevelt's vice president, would have moved into the White House. The "new deal," if there was one, would certainly have been different, for Garner was a conservative Texan who support-ed the poll tax, opposed the executive branch's "meddling" in congressional affairs, and, as *Time* magazine later characterized him, stood for "oil derricks, sheriffs who use airplanes, prairie sky-scrapers, mechanized farms, and $100 Stetson hats."

Mrs. R was already on her way to a public life, so I think it's fair to say that she would never have become Mrs. Jane Doe. But if she hadn't moved into the White House, her life, and mine, would have been very different.

Most certainly mine.

I had a great deal on my mind as the inauguration drew closer. Much of it was personal, of course. My relationship with Eleanor lightened my days and lit my nights with a fierce joy. Love has a way of creating its own truth, of writing its own story.

But love couldn't change the truth of what was happening across the country. The nation was living through its darkest days, and as a reporter, I saw them firsthand. More than a quarter of the American workforce was out of a job, and homes and farms were being lost by the thousands each week. The newspapers were an avalanche of bad news. Well over a billion dollars in gold had flown out of the country. The banks were falling like November leaves, taking with them the failed economies of towns all across the country. Businesses and industries could not pay their creditors, and the creditors could not pay *their* creditors. Cities—New York, Chicago, and Cleveland among them—couldn't meet their payrolls. Mayors across the country were expecting riots, and some state governors predicted a violent revolution.

"If the nation can get past the inaugural without blowing itself all to hell," Louis Howe told me, quite seriously, "we may have a chance. But right now, the whole country is scared to death. Anything can happen. I don't give a good goddamn what else Franklin says in his inaugural address as long as he tells the people that the only thing they have to fear is *fear*."

Mrs. R and I had planned to drive to Washington for the inaugural, loading up her Buick with the family's two dogs—Meggie and Major—and her personal belongings. I had even written a story that made the front pages of many newspapers under the headline, "Wife of Next President to Drive Alone to Capital."

But FDR vetoed the plan. He had already arranged for a train party, with the press, cabinet members, and special guests, and he insisted that his wife go with him as his hostess, adding flatly, "No argument, Babs." Louis Howe said FDR was concerned about the

possibility of an accident, but in a moment of personal paranoia—
it wasn't the first and wouldn't be the last—I wondered whether he
was trying to separate Mrs. R and me. But that was silly, I told
myself. The man had more on his mind than his wife's friendships.
Anyway, if that was his (or Howe's) intention, it didn't work. She
asked me to go with her on the train and to stay with her at the
Mayflower.


The day before the inauguration, Washington was an armed camp.
Army machine gunners and sharpshooters were installed at
strategic locations along the parade route, and armed police
guarded federal buildings. Rumors swirled like dust devils from
office building to office building. Roosevelt was going to impose
martial law. He would seize control of the country and assume
dictatorial powers, like Mussolini (which some thought would be a
very good idea). The inaugural bunting that hung everywhere
reminded me of a brightly colored shroud, and "Happy Days Are
Here Again" sounded like an unfunny parody.

That night, the ornate Mayflower Hotel lobby was jammed
with reporters from newspapers all over the country. I was headed
for the elevator when I was waylaid by Mack Petrie, who had been
night city editor of the Minneapolis *Tribune* when I left. Mack was a
big man, burly, with a voice like an auctioneer. He and I had been
on a number of assignments together over the years. He knew Ellie
—and he knew that we had lived together for the eight years I'd
worked at the *Trib*.

"Hey, Hick!" Mack cried, and heads turned. "How the hell are
you, kiddo? The *Trib*'s been running your AP pieces almost every
day. You're doing swell—all kinds of great access to the Roose-

velts." He flashed me a broad wink. "Especially Eleanor, huh? Kinda tight with the old girl, aintcha?"

I gave him what passed for a smile. "Good to see you, Mack. In town for the big day, huh?" I glanced around the crowded room. They had the look of hungry hyenas, keen to snatch up any juicy bit that another hyena might miss. They were just doing their job, but all of a sudden, their job seemed ugly, menacing.

Stepping closer, Mack pulled out his notebook and lowered his voice. "Say, Hick, do you remember that tip I gave you on the Carter arraignment, years back? You told me then that you owed me one. Now's your chance to pay up." He took his pencil from behind his ear and poised it over his open notebook. "I need a couple of names, like who's upstairs in that suite with Roosevelt. I'm guessing his boy Jimmy. Likely Louis Howe—maybe Woodin, too, huh?" William Woodin, a Republican businessman, had been a director of the Federal Reserve Bank of New York. FDR had named him secretary of the treasury. "Maybe you've got some word on how he and FDR intend to handle the banking crisis." He was already scribbling. "I won't identify you, of course—just 'a source close to the family.'"

"Sorry." I was backing toward the elevator, hands out, demonstrating that they were empty. "Wish I could help you out, Mack, but I don't know any more than you do."

It was a lie, of course. I'd been in the suite all afternoon and I knew who was there and what they were doing. But if I handed out any inside dope, it would go to the AP, not the *Trib*. I didn't blame Mack for trying, though, and if I'd thought for a moment, I would have wondered why I felt so defensive. Who was I protecting? Why? And what did it say about me, as a reporter?

Mack wasn't buying my refusal. "Come on, kiddo, you've got access. You've got a wire service byline. You're a *star*." He raised his voice, teasing, mocking—with Mack, it was always hard to tell the difference. "Ain't she, boys? Ain't Hick a star?"

I looked up and realized that we were encircled by reporters watching and listening with avid attention, waiting for the kill, for the carcass, for some little scrap of news they could pounce on and snap up.

A star? I didn't want to be a star. I just wanted to get away.

An hour later, Mrs. R and I were poking at the dinner she'd had sent up for us to her sitting room in the Mayflower's presidential suite, where we had stayed on our earlier trip to Washington. Neither of us felt much like eating, or even admiring the new suit —a brown, beige, and blue tweed—that Anna (in charge of the First Lady's wardrobe) had brought for her mother to wear the next morning. Inauguration Day promised to be cold, and Mrs. R would be outdoors for the ceremony, the address, and the parade. For the inaugural ball, she would wear an evening gown that the press was calling "Eleanor blue," sleeveless, with simple lines and a deep décolleté back, of silk crepe embroidered with a leaf-and-flower design in gold thread. I admired its severity and felt that it matched the temper of the time. However, my hired-girl self thought that too much money had been spent on Mrs. R's new clothes—two ball gowns, several daywear ensembles, nine dresses, four hats, and three pairs of shoes—when too many people didn't have a warm winter coat. Reasonably, Eleanor retorted that her spending had boosted both the economy and the careers of a couple of designers, as well as giving work to a number of people in the clothing business.

She was right, of course. Her new job as First Lady required more than the ten-dollar off-the-rack dresses, and she had to meet the expectations of the people who wielded power in the city. But our exchange reminded me, once again, that Eleanor and I came from different places in the world of haves and have-nots.

Mrs. R settled down with her knitting, as usual. But I'm a pacer, and I prowled, listening to the rise and fall of men's voices that came from the next room. Finally, I went to stand in the open door, where I could watch FDR working on his inaugural address. There was a continuous stream of traffic in and out of the suite that night—Brain Trusters, advisers, new cabinet members, Roosevelt sons, waiters with food and mixers for the smuggled-in liquor, people with urgent messages for the president-elect about the dire financial conditions around the country. President Hoover telephoned twice, urging FDR ("begging him," according to Louis Howe) to issue a joint statement halting the disastrous flow of gold out of the banks and overseas. FDR refused. He was playing his cards even closer to the chest than usual. Nobody knew what he intended to do.

Finally, at midnight, at the moment when Hoover's term officially ended, Roosevelt announced to the hushed gathering that he would declare a four-day bank holiday and call Congress into extraordinary session to pass an emergency banking bill. There was a loud whoosh, as everybody in the room let out his breath. Watching from the door, I knew that the president's declaration would generate banner headlines in newspapers across the country. It would be a career-topping grand slam for any reporter, and I was within arm's reach of the telephone. I could pick it up and call Byron Price, chief of the AP's Washington bureau, and tip him off. I looked at it for a moment, put out my hand, and then pulled it back.

Hours later, I would realize that this was a remarkable moment. But just as remarkable was the fact that not one of FDR's team appeared to notice that an AP reporter was in the suite. Perhaps I had been seen with Mrs. R on so many occasions that I was accepted as part of the Roosevelt family, rather than as a reporter. Or perhaps—and this is the explanation I eventually settled on— the president's team paid no attention to me that night for the same reason that they paid no attention to Mrs. R. We were both women, and when it came to politics, governance, and the gold crisis, women didn't count.

But at two a.m., when we were about to go to bed, Louis Howe brought us the final draft of FDR's inaugural address. Mrs. R read it aloud to me, pausing to emphasize the ten words that everyone would remember: "The only thing we have to fear is fear itself." I recognized the sentence from an earlier conversation. It was Howe's, a memorable turn of phrase that would soon be repeated like a mantra everywhere. I took the draft back to Louis, who went off with it to the hotel business office, which he had put on standby. To make sure there were no leaks, he would wait there until it was retyped and mimeographed, then bring it back to the suite for distribution to the press the next morning.

The rooms emptied out as everybody finished their drinks and headed for bed. Eleanor went to say goodnight to her husband, and I went into the bedroom, got ready for bed, and lay down. On the small table between our beds was a telephone, and I looked at it for a moment, considering whether to call Byron. But I was weary to the bone and I chose to do… nothing. I turned over and pulled up the covers. I was asleep by the time Eleanor came back to the room.

It wasn't until I woke up the next morning that I realized what I had done—or rather, what I had failed to do. I hadn't phoned the AP with FDR's plan to declare a bank holiday and call an emergency session of Congress. I hadn't phoned in a synopsis of FDR's inaugural speech or Howe's memorable line: "The only thing we have to fear…" I was standing in the middle of the biggest breaking news on the planet. If I had filed even a couple of paragraphs, I would have scooped every single reporter and cemented my reputation as the best newshawk in the country.

But I didn't do it. As far as I was concerned, everything that went on in the presidential suite that night, no matter how newsworthy, was off the record.

I could go on working for the AP, but I knew I could no longer consider myself a journalist.

The next day, Saturday, March 4, was Inauguration Day, and I had one more official story to file: the first-ever on-the-record interview by a First Lady on her first night in residence in the White House. We began the interview in Eleanor's bedroom after we got back from the parade, but there were so many interruptions that we moved to her bathroom and shut the door. I learned afterward that this raised quite a few eyebrows among the backstairs gang, who had never before seen a First Lady retreat to a White House bathroom with a reporter. They were sure that there was more to our interview than would appear in print.

It was a day for raised eyebrows. Old-time Washington socialites were aghast when Mrs. Roosevelt opened the august East Room to accommodate the overflow crowd of three thousand—including the press—who came to tea. Nothing quite so shocking had happened in that room since Abigail Adams hung the family undies there to dry, or Andrew Jackson parked his giant cheese in the middle of the floor and invited the common folk to help themselves. And when the Roosevelts' seventy-five guests arrived for dinner that evening, the First Lady greeted them at the door of the Red Room rather than making a grand entrance after everyone was seated, as previous First Ladies had done. She was making it clear that if Washington wanted to visit the White House, it would be on her terms.

After dinner, the president went back upstairs—to work, he said, although the backstairs gang whispered later that he met for a little while and privately with a very pretty lady. Mrs. Rutherfurd, I assumed. Eleanor and I went to her suite, which included Abraham Lincoln's bedroom, a spacious room with a brick fireplace and windows overlooking the Rose Garden and Andrew Jackson's magnolia tree, and a smaller room that she would use for a bedroom. There, I helped her get ready for the inaugural ball. She looked stunning, I thought, as I watched her get into the limousine —the only First Lady to go to the gala without the president. And she didn't get home until nearly two a.m.

I know, because I was waiting up for her, with a plate of cookies and a pitcher of hot chocolate. I wanted Cinderella to tell me all about her ball.


Before I left the White House on Sunday evening, Eleanor and I talked about our letters.

Ah, the letters, those dangerous handwritten pages that record the progress of a love affair, two people coming together, holding on, falling apart. The letters, which, if I'd followed Bess Furman's advice, I would have burned. The letters that will be locked up for a good long time after I'm dead. The letters that are the reason I'm writing this memoir.

Well, then, to the letters. Eleanor and I began writing to one another after our night on the train from Potsdam. In those first few months, the letters were intensely, passionately personal, and neither of us were very discreet. They were too revealing, and we kept only a few. But we had agreed that I would write her biography, so when the new First Lady assumed her public duties, I asked her to be sure that every letter included an account of what she had done that day. Staying in touch in this way would help to ease our separation, and later, I could excerpt the material I needed for her biography.

Eleanor wrote her first letter after I left on Sunday night, on both sides of two large, thick sheets of cream-colored stationery embossed with the gold White House seal. *Hick, my dearest,* she began. *I cannot go to bed to-night without a word to you. I felt a little as though a part of me was leaving to-night, you have grown so much to be a part of my life that it is empty without you even though I'm busy every minute.*

"Empty without you"—yes, oh, yes, how I understood that! The next evening, we talked on the phone for a full hour, and the letter she wrote afterward rejoiced. *Hick darling, Oh! how good it was to hear your voice, it was so inadequate to try and tell you what it meant, Jimmy was near and I couldn't say "je t'aime et je t'adore" as I longed to do...*

The next day, March 7, was my birthday. She had thought of us all day, she wrote that evening. *Another birthday I will be with you... oh! I want to put my arms around you, I ache to hold you close. Your ring is a great comfort, I look at it and think she does love me, or I wouldn't be wearing it!*

And a few days later, finally settled into her new home, she wrote, *My pictures are nearly all up and I have you in my sitting room where I can look at you most of my waking hours! I can't kiss you so I kiss your picture good-night and good-morning. Don't laugh!*

Laugh? Now, really. Of course, I could not laugh. I cried easily and often, missing her, wanting to be together. Her letters and our telephone calls were an oasis, but the nights without her were a black well of loneliness. I was glad for the company of friends. Eva Le Gallienne's production of *The Cherry Orchard* had just opened at the New Amsterdam, with Josephine Hutchinson playing Anya, and I was invited to the glittering party on opening night. Jean Dixon, who had been in Hollywood to star in *The Kiss Before the Mirror*, was back in the city and helped to take my mind off the separation.

And there was work, of course. The Mitchell case was coming to trial, and Tammany Hall was in the news with another scandal of sex and corruption. I was back on my beat.

Toward the end of March, Bess Furman invited me to be her guest at a dinner given at the Hotel Willard by the Women's National Press Club. I took the train down and stayed at the White House. Eleanor had arranged for me to have the room across the hall from her whenever I was in town. But the house was full of guests that week. It gave her an excuse to have the Val-Kill daybed in her suite made up for me (which inspired another ripple of gossip among the backstairs gang). I had a handsome new dress for the Press Club dinner, a long black silk that swirled around my ankles and threatened to trip me as I went down the stairs. Eleanor enjoyed giving me a lesson in how to walk in it. Tommy and Mabel said I looked "stunning." Looking at herself in the mirror, the hired girl was amazed.

Perhaps it was the hired girl who made such an immediate connection with Mabel Haley, Mrs. R's personal maid. Mabel had worked for the Roosevelts when they lived on R Street years before, and she already knew the family secrets—including the Lucy Mercer affair. Mabel, who was the soul of discretion, did everything for Mrs. R: maintained her wardrobe, made her bed, packed and unpacked, and even shopped and ran errands. Over the next several months, while I was still a regular guest in the White House, she also did my mending and personal laundry.

Mabel introduced me to the other staff who worked on the second floor: Mrs. Maggie Rogers, the "First Maid," who had served every president since Taft; Mrs. Rogers's daughter Little Lillian, who did the sewing and (a polio victim) walked with a crutch under one arm and quickly became a favorite of FDR's; Lizzie McDuffie, a household maid whose husband Irvin was one of FDR's two full-time valets, on duty around the clock; Bluette Pannell, who kept everybody moving in the right direction; and Angelina Walton, the bath maid, whose tongue wagged at both ends, as Mabel said disapprovingly. Angelina, no angel, would cause me—and the First Lady—a great deal of grief in the months ahead.

The maids wore white uniforms with black shoes for daytime, and for evening, black taffeta uniforms with white collar and cuffs and an embroidered organdy apron. Most of the staff lived out, although a few (the McDuffies and Bluette) had sleeping rooms on the third floor, where Missy LeHand also had a small apartment. Everyone seemed to be loyal to their new master and mistress and I never picked up any special animosities, except for their understandable grumbling about the number of guests the Roosevelts entertained and the extra work created by the frequent comings and goings of the ever-expanding Roosevelt clan, which included in-laws, grandchildren, and even the children's nurses.

But it wasn't just family. Throughout the first term, Mrs. R's old friends—Nan and Marion, Elizabeth and Esther—came often, and at least once a year, Marion would bring a dozen Todhunter students. During FDR's second term, Mrs. Roosevelt would become involved with various student and political groups and impulsively bring people home with her for overnights or a weekend. Later, in the war years, heads of state, visiting royalty, and their entourages often stayed for two weeks or a month at a time. The White House often had the look of a busy hotel, with arriving guests waiting with their luggage in the hall while the departing guests were still packing and the maids were hurrying to ready the rooms, which had to be swept and dusted, and the linens and towels replaced.

And like a fine hotel, each guest room was provided with a vase of fresh flowers every day. The flowers were exchanged for a bowl of fresh fruit in the evening, when the maids turned down the beds. Ah, yes, those were the days—and for me that first year, when I was Eleanor's guest at the White House, happy days. Very happy days.


But back in New York, I had come smack up against the biggest dilemma of my professional life. I had realized that I couldn't be the First Lady's first friend *and* a responsible AP staff reporter. Now, it was becoming apparent to Bill Chapin.

If I had cared less deeply for Eleanor, I might have simply avoided the issue, as I tried to do for as long as I could. But it got harder and harder. On one occasion, my pay was docked because I withheld a story about an awkward gaffe of hers that was caught— and reported—by a UP journalist. At other times, Bill would ask me for specific information about what she planned to do, where she was going, and with whom. I would reply that my official coverage of the First Lady had ended and remind him that Bess Furman was covering her out of the Washington bureau. I couldn't refuse to cover her New York activities, however, and as it turned out, the First Lady spent about half of her time in New York that spring. She had given up teaching, but she continued to meet with various women's groups, work at her Democratic office, and spend most of the evenings with me. Under pressure from Bill, I filed brief, factual pieces about her daytime activities in the city—our evenings were off the record, of course.

I was also frequently quizzed about the continuing marital misadventures of the Roosevelts' daughter Anna and son Elliot, both of whom were on their way to the divorce courts. Divorces in prominent families were headline news in those days, and divorce in the First Family would produce hundreds of column inches in newspapers all over the country. But I refused to spy for the AP. As far as I was concerned, the whole family was off the record.

It was an increasingly uncomfortable situation, and I knew that sooner or later, I would have to make a choice. I could give up my friendship with Mrs. R, which seemed utterly impossible, or I could give up my job.

But how could I do *that*? I was at the top of the AP pyramid and I'd worked damned hard to get there. My byline, which was my connection with my colleagues and readers, was vital to me. My job was my professional identity. Apart from Eleanor, it was all I had, it was all I *was*, all I had ever wanted to be. That was what made it such an important sacrifice. If I left the AP, it would be a declaration to Eleanor: I choose to give up my profession for you, my work, my job, my identity. I am taking a pledge, making a statement, asserting a truth. My old life is over, my new life is ahead. I'll accept whatever that life brings, wherever it takes me, as long as we are together.

So it was settled, and I began to look for other work. I was hoping, of course, to find work that I could be proud of, where I could feel I was making some sort of difference in the world. I'm a realist, however, and I understood the situation. I needed a salary that would let me keep the Mitchell Place apartment, and I had to be based in Washington or New York so that Eleanor and I could be together. But the nation was in the fourth year of the worst depression in its history. Reporters were being let go everywhere, and positions for forty-year-old women were as scarce as hen's teeth. Another reporting job, assuming I could find one, would put me in the same uncomfortable box vis-à-vis the Roosevelts. Editors everywhere are alike. What they want, *all* they want, is the story. I would still be asked to provide the inside dope on what was going on with Mrs. R, with her children, even with the president. "Off the record" would not be an acceptable answer.

Eleanor appreciated my dilemma and tried to be comforting, but she didn't understand all the issues. "Well, if you don't feel comfortable with another reporting job," she said, "how about writing for the magazines? You're such a good writer, my dear— I'm sure they'd snap up anything you sent them."

I could try, yes. But for the most part, my writing had always been fact-based and crisply reportorial. I'm not very lyrical and I couldn't create the breezy, soft-edged style that most of the magazines wanted. As for fiction—well, I'd tried that, when Ellie and I were living in San Francisco. That episode taught me that I was a journalist, not a novelist or a short story writer, and that my writing had to be anchored to real people, to the real world.

"Well, then, write about me," the First Lady said, quite reasonably. But I couldn't do that, for the same reason I couldn't write about her for the AP. I wouldn't trade on her friendship. So I muddled along, trying to find other options, until what had been merely awkward and uncomfortable suddenly became exceedingly difficult.

I learned that I had become *persona non grata* at the White House. Eleanor and I had been found out, and there was hell to pay.

# CHAPTER EIGHT

# The Left Hook

It was Angelina Walton, the bath maid, who let the cat out of the bag. At least, that's what Louis Howe told me.

From the beginning, I'd had concerns. I was engaged in an intimate friendship with a very visible lady who—when her heart was touched—was not always discreet. She was charmingly warm and impulsive and she often said (and wrote) the first thing that came to her mind, without thinking that someone might be listening, or might pick up one of her letters. She could be shrewd and politically astute in one moment, and in the next, almost child-like in her expressions of affection and in her need for touch: a tender caress, fond fingers to the cheek, a brushing kiss.

I'm no psychologist, but I understood the reasons for Eleanor's almost desperate need to be touched. Her mother had rarely embraced her when she was a child, her father was mostly unavailable, and her Grandmother Hall, with whom she lived until she was sent to school, was an austere, undemonstrative Victorian. In her letters to her husband, Mrs. R called him "Dearest Honey," but the two of them rarely touched. Her children never hugged her; in fact, the boys (as many young men do) made a show of keeping their mother at arm's length. Earl Miller would gladly return her playful touch when it was offered, but he was out of reach now, and while she and Tommy were devoted, they came together over

147

work. Their relationship was brisk and businesslike. Eleanor was starved for touch, physically isolated from almost everyone on earth.

But not from me. Eleanor often said that what she loved about me was my ability to *feel* deeply and passionately. Touch—compassionate, caring, trusting touch—was simply the physical expression of that. She could feel deeply too, when she could temporarily stop being a Roosevelt by blood and by marriage and become just a woman with ordinary human needs: the need to be held, to be comforted, to be loved. She once told me that as a child, she felt most useful when her mother had a headache and she was allowed to stroke her forehead. And there are a great many instances in her letters to me when she lovingly recalls or looks forward to a touch, an embrace, to moments when we could lie close together. Touching was what she wanted, what she needed, and I wanted and needed it, too, very much.

But there were dangers, and if she wasn't mindful of them, I had to be, for both of us.

My first concern, of course, was for the president. Not long after the election, I asked Eleanor how much he knew, or imagined, about our friendship. She didn't answer my question. Instead, she let me know, in that casually dismissive way of hers, that when it came to us, she didn't care what he thought.

"Whatever is between us is *ours*, Hick, dear, not his. Franklin understands that I have my own life to lead, and my own friends, just as he has his." She didn't mention Missy, but I knew she was thinking of her. "I don't ask for his approval," she added, with a toss of her head, "and he doesn't ask for mine."

With that encouragement, naive or not, I tried to set aside my concerns. This had been easier in the four months between the election and the inauguration, when both Eleanor and I were in New York and FDR was someplace else—usually accompanied by Missy—for days or even weeks at a time. But after the inauguration, he and Eleanor were living in the same house, the White House. When I visited, I was his guest as well as hers. And he was the *president*, for Pete's sake. Of America. Of the most powerful nation in the world. Of course I was apprehensive.

So I insisted on discretion, especially where the servants were concerned. When I was in the house, I kept to myself, in the small bedroom Mrs. R had assigned to me. Her suite was across the hall, so it was easy to visit one another whenever we wished. A quick glance down the hall would tell us that the coast was clear.

But the young bath maid, Angelina, apparently witnessed a careless embrace or overheard a indiscreet conversation and talked about it to her cousin Minnie, who was Alice Roosevelt Longworth's upstairs maid. Minnie didn't waste a moment in telling the story to Mrs. Longworth (whom Bess Furman had called Princess Alice of Malice). Mrs. Longworth, an Oyster Bay Roosevelt, was delighted to whisper it to Eleanor's Oyster Bay cousin Corinne, who passed it along to her son Joseph Alsop, a bright young journalist working for the *New York Herald Tribune* (the Republican rival of the *New York Times*), who ran into Louis Howe at a New York press corps dinner and took him aside for a private word.

"I'm not being malicious, you understand," Joe told Louis, although, of course, he was. (Joe would later write a bitter book about his cousin Franklin's campaign to pack the Supreme Court.) "Neither my mother nor Cousin Alice think there's a shred of truth in it. The very idea of dear Eleanor—" He giggled nervously. "Well, it's just preposterous. But if it's being whispered among the servants, God only knows who else is talking. I thought you should know."

"Thank you," Louis said. "I appreciate it." Good political operative that he was, he recounted the incident to the president at their next staff meeting.

And then Louis recounted it to me, several weekends after the inauguration, when I was staying at the White House. That Saturday had been warm and rainy. Mrs. Roosevelt had gone riding in Rock Creek Park with Elinor Morgenthau, then attended a luncheon at the Mayflower and after that, a meeting of Democratic women. When she returned, she had brought me an armful of white cherry blossoms, now in a vase on the little mahogany writing desk in my room, where I was working. I was penciling edits on Mrs. R's first-draft chapters for a book that would be titled *It's Up to the Women*. It was quite a subversive book, I thought, for all its homely examples.

I had helped her with the other two books she was working on that spring—a collection of her father's letters and a little book for children called *When You Grow Up to Vote*. Mrs. R wasn't yet the skilled writer she would become in later years. But she had a clear idea about what she wanted to say, she was passionate, and she was willing to use the Roosevelt name to push her passions. She also saw her writing as a potential source of independent income in the future, and I knew that with a little help, she was going to do very well as a writer.

There was a tap on the door, and when I called out "Come in," I looked up to see that it was Louis. Over the past few weeks, we had shared train rides to and from New York and I had occasionally bumped into him in the White House. It was hard to be friends with Louis, but I thought we were almost there.

Now, he was holding two scotches, and he handed one to me.

Then he lit a cigarette, kicked off his shoes, and lay down on my bed. Sipping on his scotch, he launched into the story Joe Alsop had told him in New York—the tale Angelina had told to her cousin, who told it to Princess Alice of Malice, who told it to Corinne, who told it to Joe. And which he had that afternoon relayed to FDR.

According to Louis, the president heard it in silence, but his first remark was heavy with sarcasm: "Well, I'd say our Joe doesn't have much room to talk." Alsop made no secret of his sexual preferences. Even Alice Longworth had been heard to remark that "dear Joe" was "queer as a plaid rabbit."

"What did the president say next?" I sat back in my chair, knowing I didn't want to hear the answer to that question.

Louis gave me a straight look. "He said, 'You know, once Corinne and Alice sink their teeth into a juicy secret, it doesn't matter whether it's true or false. It will be all over town. For the record, I have no wish to forbid any friendship my missus might want to have with Lorena Hickok or anybody else. What she does behind closed doors is her own business. And I can't tell Hick what to do, either. I'm just the president, not a dictator. Not yet, anyway.'"

"That's comforting," I said.

Louis turned his glass in his fingers. "You may remember the Earl Miller affair."

I lit a cigarette, then got up and opened the window. My Pall Malls were nothing compared to the foulness of Louis's Sweet Caporals. I stood for a moment, looking out the window. In the rainy twilight, people hunched under umbrellas were hurrying along the sidewalk, and a bus was letting off passengers at the corner of Pennsylvania and Seventeenth, with a belch of purple exhaust smoke.

"I remember." I turned. "The marriage, the Hyde Park property, the job."

Louis nodded. "The president has the same worries about you and Eleanor that he had about Eleanor and Earl—attempted blackmail, by some third party. But in your case, he's more concerned about this thing getting into the press, since you are who *you* are." Leaving that ambiguous assertion hanging in the air between us, he lit a fresh cigarette from the butt of the one he'd been smoking. Ashes drifted down from his cigarette onto my coverlet.

I came back to my chair and my scotch. "I doubt that's an issue," I said, with greater conviction than I felt. "The press won't—"

Louis interrupted. "The responsible press won't be direct, but they'll suggest. 'The First Lady's First Friend,' that sort of thing. They'll leave it to people to take the hint. The tabloids, though, will milk the story for all it's worth." He squinted at me through the smoke. "The president knows that. And you do, too."

Yes, of course I knew. I had worked at one of the tabloids when I came back to New York.

"I suppose he has a plan," I said uneasily. "Or you do."

Louis held up his glass. "For starters, he's asked me to find another place for this maid, an agreeable job at an increase in pay." He drained his scotch. "Outside the White House."

"Well, at least she gets to keep her head. What does he have in mind for me?"

Louis tried to speak, coughed, tried to stop, and couldn't. He kept on coughing as I got up from my chair, went into the small adjacent bathroom, and got him a glass of water. Everybody who liked Louis (not all people did) worried about that hacking cough of his—and we were right to worry. He wouldn't live to help elect FDR to a second term.

He took the water gratefully, and when he could speak again, he said, "Of course, the president is aware that you were an enormous help during the campaign, and he's confident that you wouldn't want anything disagreeable to reflect on the First Lady." He eyed me. "Or on the administration."

I nodded. Yes. Those things were true.

"He's also aware that you are considering leaving the AP. So he suggested that I look around for a situation that might engage your capabilities and interests." He sat up and swung his feet off the bed. "'She's a smart one, that Hickok. You do right by her.'" He coughed. "That's a direct quote. But off the record, of course."

There it was. The left hook. Buried in a compliment and off the record, but a hard jab just the same. I pulled on my cigarette, exhaled, and watched the smoke eddy toward the open window.

"Engage my capabilities and interests in another city, I suppose," I said. "As far away as possible. What's it to be? Seattle? San Francisco? He could probably work a deal with Hearst to put me on the staff of the *Chronicle* or the *Post-Intelligencer*."

I sounded bitter, but I had to admit that it would be a smart move, from FDR's point of view. Washington might titter about the rumor for a few weeks, but most would attribute it to servants' nonsense. Once I was out of the picture, it would be forgotten—or more accurately, overwritten by a later, juicier rumor about somebody else.

"Now, now, Hick." Louis stood up, giving me a beetle-browed frown. "Don't get the wrong idea. The president isn't out to get rid of you. I'm not, either. What we're thinking of is temporary, just until the gossip quiets down. And helpful to you, professionally speaking." Head down, cigarette dangling from the corner of his mouth, he clasped his hands behind his back and prowled around the room in what FDR called his "Felix the Cat" posture, after the famous 1920s cartoon cat. Outside on the rainy street, a car honked. In the hallway, a tray rattled. It was teatime, and Mrs. R would soon come looking for me.

"Well?" I asked. "What's it to be?"

He stopped, turned, and regarded me. "The president would like you to have a talk with Harry Hopkins. It's not an order, mind you. Just a suggestion."

Not an order? Of course it was an order. But I was so surprised by his mention of Hopkins that I didn't dispute him on that point.

"Hopkins? Talk to him about what? I'm a reporter, not a social worker."

Harry Hopkins was the recently named head of the Federal Emergency Relief Administration, or FERA. He was in charge of all the government-funded relief in the country—to the tune, I had heard, of half a billion dollars. People were calling FERA the most important card in the entire New Deal deck.

"Harry doesn't need any more damn social workers," Louis growled, resuming his pacing. "He's got enough of those. What Harry needs is an experienced, sharp-eyed field investigator who can walk into the worst trouble spots around the country and find out what's happening. He needs somebody who's independent, knows how to ask a question and when not to, and refuses to suffer fools gladly. *Any* fools. At any time. For any reason." His grin was crooked. "The president would like to see you take the job."

"And if I... decline?"

"We didn't get that far."

The threat was plain as day, and I heard it. I was to be a field investigator who would do a lot of traveling. Who would be on the road for weeks, maybe months at a time. A convenient way to separate Eleanor and me and keep us out of the way of the press—with the obvious hope that by the time my travel assignment was finished, one or both of us would have found new interests.

"And what do *you* think, Louis?"

He stopped pacing. "I think," he said quietly, "that a reporter should never get too close to her source."

After a moment I said, "So now you've delivered the president's message. Are you supposed to talk to the First Lady, too?"

Outside in the hallway, a small silver bell tinkled. It was teatime. Louis sat down on the bed and began pulling on his shoes.

"I already have."

Of course. He would go to her first, push her for her cooperation, then tell me that she believes it's the right thing to do.

"And she says?" I asked, knowing the answer.

"She knows you're not happy at the AP." He bent down to tie his shoelaces. "She's fond of Harry and likes the idea of your working with him. She thinks it's an excellent place to put your journalistic skills and experience to work. She thinks you need a mission. She likes the idea that you would be helping get relief to people who need it." He sat up. "FERA is something *she* believes in and supports."

Yes, there was that. If I went to work for Harry, I would be doing something that Eleanor thought worthwhile. In a sense, she and I would be working together, on an agenda that was personally *hers* as well as the administration's. And it was true that I needed a mission.

He began coughing again and reached for the glass of water. "The job pays a pretty decent salary, too."

"Oh, really? Like what?" I'd been temporarily cut back to sixty dollars a week at the AP for failing to turn in the story on Mrs. R's gaffe, but that was still good money in comparison to what was being offered by other newspapers. Government work couldn't come close.

"Six thousand a year," he said. "Five dollars a day for food and lodging plus five cents a mile, if you're driving, train fare otherwise. Harry said he'd be glad to give you the details." He stood up and a shower of silvery ashes drifted toward the floor. "He knows your work, Hick—especially your Tammany Hall investigative pieces and your coverage of the Mitchell trial. He thinks you'd be a swell choice."

I was speechless. *Six thousand dollars a year?* Ye gods and little fishes, that was twice what the AP was paying me! FDR's left hook was a fistful of money.

Louis started toward the door. "Harry's set up his office in the Walker-Johnson Building. He'll be working over the weekend. I'll be glad to arrange a meeting for you tomorrow."

"It won't hurt to talk to him, I suppose." I was still thinking of the six thousand—and the alternative. "Not promising anything," I added hastily. "I need to think about this."

"Please do." He opened the door. "And you'll want to discuss it with Mrs. Roosevelt." He paused, his hand on the knob. "You will keep this between the two of you."

I heard that threat, too. "Of course," I faltered.

"Good. I'll let the president know you'll be talking with Harry. He'll be glad to hear it." He gave me that cat-like grin of his. "In fact, he'll be *dee*-lighted."

I'll just bet he would.


Hopkins had been on the job for just a week. On Sunday morning, I found him alone on the tenth floor of a dilapidated yellow brick office building a couple of blocks from the White House. He was sitting in a wooden tilt-back chair that had seen better days, behind a battered gray government-issue desk. The windows needed washing, the bookshelves needed painting, and Hopkins needed a clean shirt. But he was already spending money. When I came in, he was two-finger typing a yellow telegram flimsy on a Royal that probably dated back to the Wilson administration. He rolled it out of the typewriter and flung it at me. It authorized two million dollars to relief efforts in the state of Illinois.

"Chicago's dying," he said, dropping another flimsy into the typewriter. "If they don't get money fast, the city'll be dead inside a month." The next day, the *Washington Post* would remark, "The half-billion dollars for direct relief to the states won't last long if Harry Hopkins maintains the pace he set in his first week. He's a man with a mission."

The guys in the AP office were saying that FERA was the toughest top job in all the New Deal programs. Hopkins had to figure out how and where to spend the bales of money Congress was giving him, put people to work, and—most difficult of all—insert the federal government into the state and local agencies that had always administered relief. Some of these agencies were run by state and county political bosses who were in the habit of using local relief funds to build little empires for themselves. In other words, it would be no surprise if there was already a fair amount of graft and corruption out there. When the big federal money hit, some folks would start looking for a score.

And there would be big money. Roosevelt had managed to convince Congress—at least for the time being—that relief wasn't charity or a handout. It was a civic duty. In this view, giving people cash grants to tide them over the rough places meant that they had something to hang onto until they could stand on their own. But this philosophy flew in the face of the American tradition of sink-

or-swim self-reliance and personal responsibility, and the squawk-
ing from the right wings of both political parties was already
getting loud and louder.

In the midst of this cacophony, Hopkins was building a
distribution system for funneling cash to those who needed it. "We
didn't have much to go on," he would say later. "We had to invent
the whole goddamned thing. It was like asking the Aztecs to build
an airplane."

Now, he lit a cigarette and started to talk. Ten minutes later, he
was lighting another cigarette and finishing his spiel. "Well, there it
is, Miss Hickok. I need to know what's going on across the country. I need an investigator, somebody smart, somebody who can go
out and turn over a few rocks, look in the corners, open the closet
doors. I don't want statistics. I don't want the social worker angle. I
just want somebody to tell me, confidentially and objectively,
what's happening out there. All of it, the good, the bad, the hellish.
Without pulling any punches. You interested?"

I was interested, yes. But I hedged my bets.

"How about if we agree to a test run? I'll take one assignment,
and we'll see how it works out. But I can't start until the end of
July. I'm covering the Mitchell trial for the AP, and it's likely to go
another couple of weeks. After that, I'll need a vacation." I didn't
give him the details. Eleanor and I were trying to keep it quiet.

"You're on." He eyed me through the smoke. "But I want you
to remember a couple of things. First, don't get involved in what
you're seeing. Stay out of the story. Second thing, keep your head
down. No byline, no recognition. You're an objective eye, that's
all." He pursed his lips. "And keep quiet about your Washington
connections—to me, to the White House." With a dispassionate
emphasis, he added. "Especially the White House."

"Understood," I said.

He nodded. "Good. Glad to have you with us. I'll get the paperwork started."

So it was settled. I would go to work for Hopkins after the Mitchell trial was over. And after Eleanor and I returned from the three-week summer trip we were planning.

The Roosevelts were in the habit of taking separate summer holidays. FDR would go ocean fishing or sailing with friends and spend a few weeks in the pool at Warm Springs. Mrs. R would travel to Campobello and along the way, visit friends and relatives who lived on the Northeast coast. This year, she had decided that —having dutifully met her First Lady obligations in Washington— we would take a holiday trip, just the two of us, alone, a romantic escape to New Hampshire, Vermont, Quebec, and the Gaspé Peninsula. She would drive her sporty blue Buick roadster. We would be incognito.

"It'll be such fun, Hick," she said, with her usual enthusiasm. "We'll drive with the top down and see the sights and stay wherever we want. We'll be Jane and Janet Doe. We'll be *ordinary*."

"But won't people recognize you?" I asked doubtfully. It was hard to believe that the First Lady could get away with what she was planning. "And don't forget the press. Every chance they get, they'll want photos." The thought of seeing photos of us in the newspapers made me shrink.

"They won't know who I am." She smiled confidently. "They're all Republicans and Canadians up there."

I had to laugh at that. "But what about the Secret Service?"

Another smile, and a wave of the hand. "The Secret Service isn't going either. I've already told Franklin."

The Secret Service was furious. Bill Moran, the man in charge, was quite sure we'd be kidnapped, which Mrs. R pretended to think was very funny. It wasn't, of course: the Lindbergh kidnapping had occurred just the year before, and kidnapping-for-ransom was almost a national sport. At the end of May, a twenty-five-year-old Kansas City woman was taking a bubble bath when four armed men broke into the house and abducted her. She was released (dried and clothed) after her wealthy father paid a thirty-thousand-dollar ransom. At the time of our trip, the case was still a media sensation, and Bill Moran brought it up as an argument for sending a Secret Service car escort.

Mrs. Roosevelt rolled her eyes. "What would they do with us? Haul us out of our baths and cram us into the trunk of a car?" With a laugh, she added, "They'd find us quite a handful. One of us is six feet tall and the other weighs nearly two hundred pounds."

She was exaggerating my weight by twenty-five pounds, just to make a point. But it didn't matter. Mrs. R prevailed, although Bill Moran insisted on giving her a gun, which she locked (unloaded) in the glove compartment of her roadster. Thank heavens, we didn't need it.

As it turned out, Eleanor was surprisingly right about our anonymity, and we enjoyed a wonderfully private holiday, driving without a plan or a schedule through the mountains of Vermont and New Hampshire and north into Canada. She was determined that we would stay wherever we felt like it, small tourist cottages, a secluded hotel on a lake, a log cabin hideaway, and as we made our way north, that's what we did. In Quebec, we indulged ourselves for several glorious nights at the grand Château Frontenac, a castellated and turreted hotel in old Quebec City, overlooking the Saint Lawrence River. The First Lady had one official function, but after that, we were free.

The July days were lovely, the landscape was delightful, and best of all, we were entirely alone and utterly anonymous. Of all the time I would spend just with her, over all the years we knew one another, those three weeks would be the brightest, the happiest. Perhaps I can be forgiven for believing that, since we had these days of focusing entirely on one another, we could have them again someday, when she was no longer First Lady. She believed it, too —then, when both of us could imagine a future together.

On the coast of the rugged Gaspé Peninsula, we met a priest who invited us to his rectory for a lunch of fresh-caught fish, garden vegetables, chunks of warm, buttered bread. Learning that one of his two unexpected guests was a "Mrs. Roosevelt," he asked if she might be related to President Theodore Roosevelt. The man was charmed when he learned that the woman at his table was TR's niece. Back in the car, we decided that he didn't know that another Roosevelt was now living in the White House.

"Isn't that delicious?" Eleanor crowed. "I absolutely *love* being incognito. I'll have to write and tell Franklin about it." Which she did, for she wrote to her husband regularly while we were away. "I don't want him to worry about me," she explained. She addressed the envelopes with a flourish: *Mr. F. D. Roosevelt, 1600 Pennsylvania Ave. Washington D.C. U.S.A.*

Worry? Did he, really? By this time, I knew something about the way the Roosevelt marriage functioned, but its inner life was still an intriguing mystery. She had been in love with him once, as a very young woman—did she love him still? In what ways did she love him, exactly? As a wife, or as a sister? How were devotion and love related? Both husband and wife were committed to a common cause—their political universe of beliefs and goals and actions. Did it create enough of a bond to keep them connected, despite the forces that pulled them apart? The answers to these questions would forever elude me, and close as I was to her, then and in later years, I would never fully understand her relationship with FDR.

We stayed for several quiet days at Campobello, then drove back to Washington. The night of our arrival, we had dinner with the president, who wanted to hear about our travels. He was attentive and pleasant and laughed at his wife's stories and—most heartily of all—at my report of her pleasure when she learned that the Canadian priest had no idea that there was another Roosevelt in the White House.

But I kept thinking about that left hook and wasn't surprised when he asked me—pointedly, I thought—how soon I planned to see Harry Hopkins and get my first FERA assignment. His genial smile masked the suggestion I heard in his tone: I wasn't to linger in Washington, where gossip still linked my name with hers. (I would later learn that Princess Alice had exclaimed, loudly, and in a fashionable Washington restaurant, "I don't care what they say, I simply cannot believe that Eleanor Roosevelt is a *lesbian*.")

"Tomorrow, Mr. President," I replied. "I have an appointment with Mr. Hopkins first thing tomorrow morning."

"Bully!" He lit a fresh cigarette. "Your boss is a man with a mission—yours. He has your first trip all planned, I understand. Should be interesting."

"Oh, really, Franklin?" Mrs. R leaned forward. If she had caught the suggestion in his tone, she didn't let him know. "Did Harry tell you where Hick will be going?"

*Into exile*, I thought, trying not to look at her. We had been allowed to have our trip together. Now it was time to pay the piper.

"Pennsylvania," the president replied in a cheery tone. "And West Virginia. And Kentucky." He chuckled. "That's pretty country you'll be seeing, Hick. Coal mining country—or it was at one time, before the mines played out. I understand there are pockets of poverty there, but you'll like the people, I'm sure. Salt of the earth. Yes, indeedy, salt of the earth."

West Virginia it was. Scotts Run, West Virginia.

Whether it was intended as a punishment or not, I would never know. But the day I arrived in Scotts Run, I knew I'd been sent to hell.

## CHAPTER NINE

# "Deeply and Tenderly"

I've always been a practical, let's-get-the-details person, and as a reporter, I had internalized the cardinal AP rule: *Report what you see, not how you feel. Don't get involved. It's not your story, it's his, or hers, or theirs. Don't become part of what you're seeing.*

I went out for Hopkins and FERA with the same expectations. I was a reporter doing a job: collecting details, assembling the most meaningful into a coherent narrative, giving the whole a story shape that would convey its truths to its readers. And that was it.

But I wasn't prepared for what I saw and heard out there in the country in 1933 and 1934. Ragged, barefoot children hauling water from a stream polluted with sewage and mining refuse. A family of six—*six!*—sleeping, head to foot, in one filthy bed. Young girls on a Houston street selling their bodies to men for "just a dime, only a dime, Mister, please?" A South Dakota farm wife offering to share the tumbleweed soup she'd made for her family: "It don't taste so bad, dearie, but it ain't very fillin'."

I had been a reporter for nearly twenty years, and I'd honed the skill of assembling the stories of people's lives, detail by detail. But in my decades on the job, I had never seen such sights or heard such tales. For the two years I worked for Harry Hopkins, it sometimes seemed impossible to keep from being swallowed up by what I saw and heard. But my mission was even more impossible:

165

to witness these horrors and then recount them in a way that would get the attention of people inside the bubble that was Washington, people who were cocooned in their comfortable lives, bolstered by their possessions, buttressed by their firm belief that everything was working the way it was supposed to work. I wrote ninety-some reports for Hopkins in those years, and each time I sat down to write, I was submerged in hopelessness. I felt I was simply putting words on paper, words that could do nothing to heal the country's wounds. Still, the stories had to be told. Someone, some-day, might find something important in them.

Coping with the challenges of everyday existence was hard in those years, too. As a traveler, I was setting out in the worst year of the Depression. The trains rarely ran on time, banks and businesses were closed, utilities (public and private electricity, water, and sewage) had failed. The muddy country roads were appalling, the city streets downright dangerous. The food was usually unappetiz-ing and often inedible and the accommodations simply dreadful. Unheated hotel rooms in the dead of winter, beds crawling with bedbugs, toilets overflowing in bathrooms where we lined up to get a bath, howling drunks in the room next door.

And through all these difficult months, I was grappling with my longing to be with Eleanor and with the growing sense that I had been exiled from the life we had together. Worse, as one lonely month followed another and a crowd of new people and activities filled her letters, I began to understand that she was being pulled away from me, into a world where I didn't belong. She was chang-ing, becoming a person I didn't know. Toward the end (and yes, there was an end), she was becoming a *personage*, a figure who be-longed to everybody, to the country, to the world.

And I was changing, too. Maybe loving Eleanor had softened my hardboiled reporter's shell. Maybe I was learning to see with softer eyes, to look through the outside to what was within. Whatever it was, however it happened, what I witnessed over the next months would drive a lance into my heart and take me to the farthest edge of my capacity to see, experience, and record.

And that, in the end, would be *my* story.

The sun was barely up, but it was already hot as hell when my train pulled into the Market Street Station in Harrisburg. The thermometer would top one hundred on that first day of August. The capital of Pennsylvania stood on the banks of the brown, fetid Susquehanna River, and the stench of the city's ugly industrial pollution hung heavy in the air. As I left the train station, I stopped to pick up the latest edition of the *New York Times*, which headlined the lethal heat across the Northeast (at least thirty would die before the weather cooled), two more kidnappings, a plague of bank robberies.

As an antidote for the unpleasant news, I had a letter from Eleanor in my purse, asking me to send her the details of my investigations into the coalfield relief situation, so she could stay connected with my work. Our letters had already settled into a comforting routine. Long and diary-like, they were filled with the details of our work and framed by assurances of love. We wrote about the future, not just our next time together but that longed-for time when FDR was out of the White House and she could drop back into anonymity and we could spend all our time together. At least, that's what I thought then.

She thought so, too. *Darling,* she wrote, *I love you deeply and tenderly and oh! I want you to have a happy life. To be sure I'm selfish enough to want it to be near me but then we wouldn't either of us be happy otherwise, would we?* We often wrote about what we might do, where we might go, the kind of home we might have together. At one point, she had her eye on a Val-Kill piece she planned to buy for us. *One corner cupboard I long to have for our camp or cottage or house, which is it to be? I've always thought of it as in the country but I don't think we ever decided on the variety of abode nor the furniture. We probably won't argue!*

The daily reports of our doings kept each of us connected to the other's life and helped to make up, if only a little, for being apart. Now, looking back over the letters, I see how valuable they are and hope, when they are opened (although perhaps by people who may be dismayed by what they read), that the details will reveal something of the lives of two women who lived through— and wanted to do something about—a time of great national pain and turmoil.

I spent the first week on the road learning who the chief political players were. As in many states, the people with power proved to be the biggest barrier to getting help to people who needed it. In coal country, the relief situation was complicated by the total control of the mine owners. One payroll I saw credited a miner with $2.08 for ten hours of work but debited $2 for fuel for his lantern, leaving the poor man with a check for eight cents. South of Pittsburgh, I met thirty or forty jobless and forgotten men, stooped, malnourished, and ill with the lung disease they'd contracted in the mines. They were living in abandoned coke ovens, like hermit monks in caves.

The guide for the southwestern leg of that first trip was the soft-spoken, highly respected Clarence Pickett, who worked with the American Friends Service Committee, the Quakers. Pickett had been working with coal mining communities in Pennsylvania and West Virginia since 1928 and understood the situation better than anybody else. He took me to Scotts Run, a five-mile-long coal hollow south of Morgantown in Monongalia County, West Virginia

—a nightmare example of the way unregulated mining created unrelenting human misery.

Mining had exploded during and after World War I, when coal was needed to fuel the national war machine and the postwar economic expansion. During the boom, Scotts Run had been one of the most intensively developed coal districts in the United States. Now, the coal was exhausted. Most of the mines were closed, the miners had been out of work for five years or more, and the people along Scotts Run were stranded, unable to leave and powerless to change the situation.

"Looks like hell, doesn't it?" Pickett remarked as we stepped out of the car.

It didn't just look like hell, Scotts Run *was* hell. Ill-maintained company houses and tarpaper shanties, black with coal dust and infested with rats, lined the main dirt road. The creek that ran beside the road was contaminated by drainage from the mines, tipples, refuse dumps, and—worst of all—from the privies on the slopes above the stream. But the filthy water, streaked with iridescent reds, yellows, and greens and thickened with algae, was all the residents had for drinking, cooking, bathing, and laundry. People were so hungry that they couldn't wait for their pitiful hillside gardens to mature: they ate the tomatoes before they could ripen and tiny, bitter potatoes that they pulled out of the ground. Forty percent of the children were suffering from malnutrition. One calamitous outbreak of disease was followed by another: measles, typhoid, diphtheria, polio. The children couldn't go to school regularly because there was only one dress or one pair of trousers in the family, and no winter coats. I was dumbfounded. I thought I had known poverty in my childhood, but we'd been rich, compared to this. I had never seen people reduced to such despair.

"So," Pickett said, watching me. "What are you going to do?"

"Write a report to Harry Hopkins," I replied. "Tell him what I've seen. That's my job."

"A report? What else?" He frowned. "There's so much to be done here. Can't you *help?*"

"It's a horror," I said. "I understand how you feel. But I'm just a reporter, that's all." I looked around me, thinking that no matter how many people offered to help, this hell couldn't be fixed.

"But you know people in Washington," he protested. "Surely one of them could help. How about Mrs. Roosevelt? I've read your articles about her. She's interested in social problems."

"Well..." I hesitated. *Keep your head down,* Hopkins had said. *You're an objective eye, that's all. Keep quiet about your Washington connections... especially the White House.*

"Well?" Pickett repeated. "Isn't there something else you can do?" His tone was challenging, but his shoulders were slumped. He wore an air of defeat.

"No," I said, knowing it was the wrong answer. "I'm just here to write a report."

The next day, I went into Kentucky, driving with another guide over twisting dirt roads through the mountains of Knox County, then parked and walked a mile to a mining village. On the steep, rain-slicked trail, we met a woman wearing a calico sun-bonnet and feed-sack dress, stumbling along on bare, gnarled feet, leaning heavily on a walking stick. Her name was Cora. She was suffering, my guide said, from pellagra, a usually fatal disease caused by a diet of fatback, cornmeal, and molasses. When I asked her how old she was, she said she was forty, just my age. But she was stooped and toothless, her face a mass of leathery wrinkles.

As I turned to go, she seized my arm with her callused claws and rasped, fierce and hard, "Don't you forget me, honey. You go back where you come from and tell 'em what you seen. Send somebody to help us—you hear? You send 'em soon."

I stared at her, my heart thudding in my ears, beating time to Hopkins's dispassionate instructions: *Keep your head down. Don't get involved in the story.*

But in the end, I would forget Hopkins's caution. It was Cora I would remember. Thirty years have passed since that day, but I can still hear her cracked voice and see her face, wrinkled and wizened as a windfall apple. "Don't you forget me, honey. You go back where you come from and tell 'em what you seen."

In my hotel room that night, I wrote my report, ten typed pages about Scotts Run, about Cora, about all the rest. Ten typed pages, a story of horrors, of boys with old men's faces, of women bearing a child a year, of Cora's gnarled feet. Detail after grotesque detail, pointing to a truth too dark to be seen, too large to be comprehended. Finished at last, I dropped my hands in my lap and sat, staring at the paper, thinking of the people who would read this and would not understand. Could not understand, because they were too far away, too rich, too safe.

*Listen!* I wanted to cry. *Something has to be done. Pay attention!*

I sat there for a moment. And then—not wanting to put the call through the hotel desk—I got up and walked through the pitch dark to the pay phone on the corner, where I made a long-distance collect call to the White House.

"Oh, no," Eleanor murmured, when I told her about Cora. "Oh, Hick, that's horrible! I don't know what I can do, but surely there's something. Something!"

Several days later, she arrived—alone, no entourage, no Secret Service, no reporters—in her Buick roadster. Wearing a simple white blouse and dark blue skirt, a white bandeau around her hair, she got out of her car and walked toward me, her eyes warm, smiling.

"Hello, my very dear one," she said, and took my hand. "Show me what you want me to see. I'll help if I can."

*Show me.* For the rest of that day, Eleanor and Clarence Pickett and I walked up steep trails on Cheat Mountain, stopping to talk with miners and their families. The men, and especially the women, were silent at first, but quickly warmed to the First Lady's obvious interest. Several invited us into their homes, and if they had coffee or tea and extra cups, they shared with us. She sat down with them and asked the kind of ordinary questions one concerned woman asks another: the price of bread and bacon, and whether the hens she saw in the yard were able to keep the family supplied with eggs, and how the garden had fared in the summer heat and drought. When there were children, she asked their names, and one little baby proudly showed her his new tooth.

She looked, listened, asked questions and then more questions. Later, at dinner in Morgantown, she talked with Clarence and his fellow Quakers about what ought to be done, what was possible to do, who could best do it, and how. On the brink of this new idea, she was filled with energy and imaginings. In our room, we talked late into the night, an unexpected and wholly delightful reprieve from the loneliness and sense of exile that had already begun to wrap itself around me like a chilly blanket. Now, wrapped in her arms, I could feel myself coming to life again.

The next day, Eleanor went back to Washington, rolled up her sleeves, and got busy. That was the birth of Arthurdale, the experimental homestead community that over the next few years would be built on twelve hundred acres of rural land in Preston County, West Virginia, not far from Scotts Run. Once she became passionate about something, it was impossible to stop her, and I watched and cheered her on as Eleanor turned the project into a crusade, getting government funding, raising tens of thousands of dollars from her friends, and pouring most of the money she earned from her writing and speaking into the project. She fussed over it, Tommy once wrote to me, "like a mother hen with one chick."

Arthurdale—along with the ninety-eight other New Deal Communities planned or initiated by the Division of Subsistence Homesteads—was hugely controversial, and there was a continuous political barrage from critics who insisted that these settlements smacked of socialism or might even be part of a Communist plot aimed to undermine American capitalism. There were continuous practical challenges, too, from the way the houses were built and the difficulty in attracting industry to the selection of the people who would live there. Eleanor was deeply unhappy when she learned that Arthurdale's residents had voted to exclude Negroes.

But for the stranded families who were lucky enough to find a home at Arthurdale, it would be a story with a happy ending. Over and over, they said the same thing: "We woke up one morning in hell and went to bed the same night in heaven. We *love* Mrs. Roosevelt."

I'm glad I was there at the beginning of a project that became Eleanor's passion—one of them. Later, I would wish that she had left a little more room for me in her increasingly long list of passions, or at least kept me close to the top. But there's no dictating the directions a heart can take, or how far it will go to follow its urgings, or how many large loves it will embrace.

*Deeply, tenderly.* That was the way Eleanor loved. It would be one of the lessons she would teach me.

"Oh, there you are, Hick!" Tommy exclaimed. "Sit down and have some breakfast, dear." She pulled out a chair for me at the small table in front of the wide lunette window.

We were seated at the west end of the hall that ran through the center of the First Family's White House residence. Tommy was as brisk and cheerful as always, but under her trimly dressed, neatly combed surface, there was something rather sad. I wished I dared ask her whether she got everything she needed from the First Lady, and if not, where did she go to get it? It was a question I would begin asking myself in another year or two.

"You've just missed the Boss," Tommy went on. "She's gone riding. She said to tell you she'd be back in an hour." She nodded toward several chafing dishes on a small sideboard. "Scrambled eggs, bacon, Mrs. Nesbitt's hot biscuits, and—" She put her hand on a stack of newspapers. "The morning papers, with all the news that's fit to print. Help yourself."

I filled my plate, poured myself a cup of coffee, and sat down across from Tommy. I had returned from the coalfields to meet with Harry Hopkins and tell him I would take the job. The decision had actually been pretty easy to make. The scenes I witnessed were heart-wrenching, but I could feel myself learning, changing, growing. And working for FERA, I felt I was furthering Eleanor's agenda and doing my bit, for what it was worth, to support the New Deal. I would be meeting with Harry later that day to get my next assignment.

While I was in Washington, Eleanor insisted that I should be her guest. After Louis Howe had sent me packing earlier in the year, I wasn't sure this was a good idea. For one thing, the Roosevelts' daughter Anna was staying in the White House, trying to avoid the press until arrangements could be made for her divorce from her Wall Street broker husband. She was sleeping in my room, so Eleanor wanted me to share her suite. There was no keeping this from the servants, and I knew that tongues would wag at both ends, endlessly.

When I talked to Louis about it, he seemed to think that the tempest in the gossip teapot had blown over. (Which made me wonder if it hadn't been blown out of proportion in the first place, just to get me out of town.) He gave me a measuring look and said, "I don't see any problem with your being around for a week or ten days at a time, Hick—now that you're officially on the job at FERA." He added another drift of cigarette ashes to his already ash-covered vest. "But you might want to make yourself scarce around the president, at least for now."

He didn't have to tell me twice. Avoiding FDR would be easy. The Roosevelts' territories had been staked out from their first week in the White House, and—according to the backstairs gang—the two might as well be on separate planets. The First Lady had screened off the hall in front of her sitting room and bedroom, turning it into an informal dining and conversation area. It was cozy with comfortable cretonne-covered sofa and chairs, a walnut Val-Kill dining table, a radio, and bowls and vases of fresh flowers. This was where Eleanor ate her breakfast, glanced through the papers (before Tommy sent them off to be clipped), held morning meetings with her staff, and relaxed over late afternoon tea or an informal supper with her friends and guests.

The center and east end of the hall belonged to FDR. After a day in his West Wing office, he presided over evening cocktails in his study with *his* friends and guests. Unless he had to attend an official dinner, he usually had supper sent up on trays and ate with Missy and an advisor or two. Afterward, he and Missy worked on his stamp collection or, with family and staff, watched a movie on a screen set up in the center hall, with Missy operating the 16-mm projector that Bell and Howell had given the president. It was reported that he disliked films that were too long or too sad and that he was especially fond of Mickey Mouse cartoons and Myrna Loy. His favorite was a movie produced by media mogul William Randolph Hearst called *Gabriel Over the White House*, about an American president who assumes dictatorial powers to end an economic crisis. He and his friends and colleagues almost never ventured down to the First Lady's end of the hall, and she and her friends and guests rarely joined him. I didn't especially like his choice of movies and preferred to eat with the backstairs gang when Eleanor wasn't available.

Tommy filled my glass with orange juice from a pitcher on the table and handed me a plate of buttered toast. "The Boss asked me to remind you that today is Monday. Since you're here, she would love to have you attend this morning's press conference." She smiled. "Your press conferences have given her a job to do, you know."

"I have an idea for another one." I took a piece of toast. "I think she should write a newspaper column."

Tommy rolled her eyes. "Don't suggest it, please, Hick. She's already working eighteen-hour days. Anyway, what would she write about? Politics? FDR would never let her do that."

"She can write about what *she* does," I said. "Not what the president does. She could call it 'My Day.' People will be amazed when they read about the First Lady's doings—consequential things, not just society page stuff."

Before the inauguration, Eleanor had often confided to me her greatest concern: that, once in the White House, she would have nothing to do but stand in reception lines. She had obviously been mistaken. Now, some six months into her husband's term of office, there wasn't a single empty moment in her days. Not one.

Her morning began with an early, hour-long horseback ride

with her friend Elinor Morgenthau at Rock Creek Park. (She was still riding Dot, the mare Earl Miller had given her. The horse was stabled at Fort Meyer and saddled and driven to the park every morning.) Back at the White House by eight-thirty, she had breakfast and then met appointments all morning, with brief breaks to attack her correspondence. One morning a week, she met the women's press corps, and one afternoon a week she had lunch with Frances Perkins, secretary of labor (and the first female cabinet member), and a few other influential women. On other days, she gave talks, visited hospitals, and met with women's groups. When the Senate was in session, she often attended debates and hearings. She held formal teas for various groups on most afternoons, and there were official receptions and dinners in the evenings.

Eleanor's heart was in the right place, I knew. Or places, rather —too many of them, I thought. Loving Eleanor meant sharing her with multitudes. But when I tallied the hours she gave away to others, my jealousy was tinged with guilt. The First Lady's causes were so important and deserving that I really couldn't wish that she would neglect any of them. Just squeeze them a little, maybe, to make room for *us*.

Because her days were crammed full, late nights were our best times together. Her sitting room was cozy, with a fire, a pot of hot chocolate, and a tray of cookies—and if Lincoln's ghost wisped through the room, envying us our comfort, I never saw it. I read or wrote letters while she worked on her correspondence and we shared a few moments of quiet relaxation before bedtime, often not until one or two in the morning. But I could see that if we were ever to spend any significant amount of time together, it wouldn't be at the White House, where the First Lady was on the job—as she defined it—from six in the morning to well past midnight. She was tireless. I wasn't.

Tommy reached for a cigarette as the uniformed maid picked up her empty plate and poured her another cup of coffee. "The idea of another project for the Boss makes me shudder," she said. "But I have to admit, that the press conferences have been very good for her. I'm glad you came up with the idea, Hick. I don't think she would have accepted the suggestion from anybody else. Until you came along and showed her how she could use the press, she had the feeling that they were all out to get her."

"They probably were," I said, only half joking. "The press is a predatory bunch. How's she doing? Is she less nervous than she was?"

The First Lady's first press conference had been held in the Red Room just two days after FDR's inauguration—and two days before *his* first press conference. Steve Early had credentialed forty women from the Washington press corps, and they all showed up. Forty questioning pairs of eyes, forty notebooks, forty scribbling pencils. It must have been a daunting prospect for Eleanor. Tommy had told me that she was so nervous that her hands were trembling, her voice had gone squeaky, and she'd forgotten how she'd meant to begin.

"She's getting better at it," Tommy said. She flicked her lighter to her cigarette. "She's begun to realize how important these women are to her."

"I hope so," I said. "They *are* important—if they're used right." The press conferences might be risky, but they gave the First Lady the ability to shape the way the press saw her, which in turn shaped the way she—and the Roosevelt administration—would be presented to their readers all around the country. If any of the previous first ladies had understood this, their husbands had not.

But the Washington women's press corps, like women's right to vote, was a recent phenomenon, and if earlier First Ladies had dared to meet the press, the press would have been male, to a man. I shuddered to think how those fellows would have presented Mrs. Hoover, or Grace Coolidge, or Florence Harding—and especially Edith Wilson, who stood in for her husband Woodrow after he suffered a severe stroke. One editorial called Mrs. Wilson the "Presidentress" who had "promoted herself from First Lady to Acting First Man." If she had held a press conference, they would have made hamburger out of her.

Tommy waited until the maid had freshened my coffee and left, then lowered her voice. "The Boss is doing okay, but it's not always easy for her. She tries to avoid controversial subjects and won't answer anything she thinks is too political. I attend every conference and take down all the questions and answers in shorthand, so there's no mistake about what's said. But sometimes she says things that…" She gave a helpless little shrug. "You know."

"Like that unfortunate business about the inaugural ball," I said.

"Exactly."

That little ruckus had happened several weeks before the inauguration, when Eleanor had questioned the wisdom of holding an elaborate, expensive ball when so many people were going hungry. "I would think that this would be a good year to dispense with the ball," she'd said to a reporter, who immediately rushed to her typewriter and made a headline of it. *Mrs. Roosevelt Advises 'Cancel the Ball!'*

Privately, I was on Mrs. Roosevelt's side, but it wasn't the thing to say in public. There had been a chorus of wounded howls

—in print—from everybody who stood to profit from the ball: dress designers and dressmakers, men's clothiers, hairdressers, florists, musicians, waiters, and especially from the Shoreham Hotel, where the ball was to be held. The loudest were the anguished wails from the society page reporters. For them, the ball was the most important story of the year, bigger even than the inauguration. The First Lady's *"dispense with the ball"* smacked of *"surrender the Alamo."*

Tommy tapped her cigarette into the ashtray on the table. "She's getting better at it, though. She's less nervous, more sure of herself. And I think most of the newspaperwomen like her very much. They're perfectly aware that without the press conferences, some of them would lose their jobs, so if she makes a little mistake, they don't jump all over her. Even Steve Early has to admit that she puts the White House on the women's pages every week. Which is something dear Missy can't do for the president." She gave me a mischievous glance. "See what you've done?"

"Well, if I've helped Mrs. Roosevelt demonstrate that she can do something for her husband that his secretary can't, I'm delighted," I said cattily and went back to the buffet for a second helping of scrambled eggs and another of Mrs. Nesbitt's biscuits.

Ah, Mrs. Nesbitt. From the beginning, there had been nothing but complaints about the White House food, a litany that would only grow louder over the next twelve years. The villain of the piece was the White House housekeeper, Mrs. Henrietta Nesbitt, a small-town housewife and Hyde Park neighbor of the Roosevelts who had set herself up as a home-kitchen baker when her husband lost his job selling barrels after the Crash. Mrs. Roosevelt had been her most enthusiastic customer, and when FDR went to the White House, the First Lady invited Mrs. Nesbitt to come to Washington.

I had to feel sorry for poor Henrietta, who had none of the

management skills needed to handle a kitchen full of cooks and a housekeeping staff of more than thirty—and was an inexperienced, sadly uninspired cook, to boot. The president grumbled about her food, the Roosevelts' sons made snide remarks about it, and cabinet members advised each other to eat before they came to dinner. In Henrietta's defense, I have to say that the First Lady made a tough job even tougher by insisting that the menus should set an example in hard times by being simple and almost impossibly cheap, like the humble seven-and-a-half-cent-per-person luncheon she had served on not-so-humble White House china. I wasn't there, but I read about it in Katherine Brooks's society column in the *Washington Star*: deviled eggs covered thinly with tomato sauce, served hot with mashed potatoes, whole wheat bread, prune pudding, and coffee—hardly *haute cuisine*.

But the First Lady and the White House cook were caught between a rock and a hard place. If they gave their guests something extra nice, somebody in the press would criticize them as extravagant. If they pinched pennies, they weren't living up to White House culinary traditions. And whenever the press got wind of a rumor that the president had refused to eat his boiled spinach or take another mouthful of Mrs. Nesbitt's sweetbreads, they played it to the hilt.

I sat down and buttered the biscuit. Mrs. Nesbitt's boiled beef might be boring, her vegetables might be mush, and I didn't blame people for griping when chipped beef or broiled kidneys put in their second or third luncheon appearance of the week. But her biscuits were simply unbeatable.

And on the heels of that thought came the image of Cora, the woman on the mountain. Cora, who would have been astonished by the silver chafing dishes of scrambled eggs and bacon, the crystal plate of butter, the pretty jars of sparkling jellies, jams, and marmalades, the pitcher of orange juice and pot of hot coffee, the bowl of sugar, the pitcher of cream. Who would have been thrilled to the bone by chipped beef or broiled kidneys on toast, no matter how often they appeared on her table.

I put down my biscuit, my appetite suddenly flagging. *Don't you forget me, honey,* Cora had said. Here she was, damn it, joining me for breakfast and bringing with her all the sad, sick women and men and children I'd met out there in the mountains. *Pay attention,* they were crying, all together, all at once. *Pay attention!*

# CHAPTER TEN

## "It's a Good Thing You're Not a Man"

The press conference got off to a noisy start.

The reporters—thirty-seven of them—gathered in the Green Parlor downstairs, chattering and buzzing. When the usher gave the signal, they threw decorum to the wind and raced up the grand staircase, jostling to claim the front row of straight chairs in the Monroe Room. I waited until it was nearly filled, then slipped in and found a seat in a corner. Most of the reporters knew me, of course, and there was a flurry of *hello, Hick* and *good-to-see-you* greetings that made me feel almost like one of the press corps again. Almost. I wasn't, and I knew it—and the awareness was unnervingly painful.

After a few moments, the light chatter hushed under the weight of the stodgy formality of the Monroe Room. The room had been used for cabinet meetings under several presidents, and the presence of women here was a departure from a wholly masculine tradition. The declaration, "Here the Treaty with Spain was signed," was carved into the marble mantel, and an immense painting of the 1898 treaty ceremony occupied pride of place on the opposite wall. Over the mantel hung a gilt-framed portrait of Mrs. Roosevelt's grandfather, Theodore Roosevelt Sr., looking remarkably like General Grant. A hint of cigar smoke lingered on the air like a gentlemanly ghost reluctant to leave, mixed now with the blended scents of the women's perfumes and the music of their female voices, which seemed to me an omen of change.

Bess Furman dashed in late and dropped breathlessly into the chair next to me. Plump and perspiring, she was wearing a navy jacket and skirt, a red blouse with pearls, silk stockings, and shiny patent pumps—a city reporter's working clothes. She sat down and rummaged in her large navy handbag, pulling out her notebook.

"Oh, hello, Hick." She brushed her hair off her forehead and fanned herself with her notebook. "When did you get back from your trip? Are you going out again?"

"Late last week," I said. "And yes, I'm going out again, although I don't know where yet. I have to go back to New York first, though. I've sublet my apartment and I need to move my stuff."

Since I was going to be on the road for at least the next twelve months, I could save a great deal of money by letting one of my AP friends have the Mitchell Place apartment. Prinz had been staying with another friend while I was in the coalfields, but I had located an excellent kennel for him and was anxious to see him settled where he could have room to run.

"Mrs. R read us a few paragraphs from your report about the West Virginia situation." Bess blew a stray strand of hair out of her eyes. "It sounded like a pretty tough slog. Especially having to see those dilapidated shanties and all the sick, malnourished people." She shuddered. "I'm not sure I have the stomach for that kind of reporting, Hick."

"You'd do it if you had to, Bess," I replied. And then I thought (but didn't say), no, Bess, you wouldn't. Not in those patent pumps and silk stockings, anyway. In the coalfields, style was the least of anyone's worries. Cora and her people needed three square meals a day. The children needed shoes and winter coats. The women needed contraceptives. The men needed *jobs*.

"Well, maybe I could, but I wouldn't want to." Bess was back in her purse again, scrabbling for a pencil. "At least, not the way you're doing it. Mrs. R says the physical effort is exhausting."

She was missing the point. It wasn't how hard it was to do the work, it was how painful it was to look at what I had come to *see*. But I couldn't correct her. "It's brutal," I said.

"And yet you're going back for more?" Bess favored me with a bright smile. "Hick, dear, I swear to God, you are *hungry* for punishment."

Was I? I looked around at the nicely coiffed, well-dressed professional women, sitting in comfortable chairs in an ornate room in the house at the heart of the government of the most powerful nation on earth. Suddenly, I heard Cora's voice and saw her stooped figure as clearly as if she had hobbled into the room on her bare, gnarled feet. She stood in front of me and thumped her walking stick on the floor.

*Don't you forget me, honey. You go back where you come from and tell 'em what you seen.*

Tell them? I could tell them, and they might listen, but would they hear? *Could* they hear? Or would their pleasant surroundings so muffle the message that hearing was impossible?

And then, just for a moment, I saw this world—the self-important world of the White House, the political world of the Roosevelt administration, the hurly-burly carnival of the press—through different eyes, through Cora's eyes. I had thought that this world was real. It wasn't. The real world was out there in the coalfields, the mountain hollows, the poverty-stricken villages along the polluted creeks. The real world was filled with hungry, cold, sick people, and I was suddenly struck, as if by a blow, by the despairing sense that—New Deal or not—nothing that went on *here* could possibly change the situation out *there*. And yet the government had to try, for to do nothing was to admit that nothing could be done, and that was even more unthinkable.

Business-like now, Bess stuck her pencil behind her ear and opened her notebook. "Well, if somebody's got to go out there and find out what's happening in the hinterlands, I'm glad it's you, Hick. You're more experienced than the rest of us." She waved her hand at the women in the room. "You can handle that kind of stuff without letting it get to you."

I was about to reply that experience wasn't much help, out there in the hinterlands, and that Cora and the mountain people were getting to me in a big way. But she lowered her voice, leaned closer, and changed the subject.

"I heard something totally screwball a little while ago, Hick, and I think maybe you ought to know about it. A couple of months ago, a maid—Angelina, her name is—left the White House and went to work as a custodial shift supervisor over at the State Department. I know it sounds crazy, but—"

I stopped her. "You don't want to believe everything you hear. I never do."

"*I* don't believe it. But some people do." Bess chuckled nervously, but she wasn't backing off. "Angelina is refusing to talk, to me or anybody else. But Cissy Patterson told me—in the strictest confidence—that Alice Longworth has been saying that you and Eleanor..." She frowned, biting her lip.

I tried to conceal the rush of anxiety I felt. Since Louis Howe hadn't objected to my returning to the White House, I had thought that the gossip—if there was any—had been safely squelched. But here it was again, rearing its ugly head like a poisonous snake that refused to die. Angelina had probably been told that her job depended on her silence. Bess Furman had too much journalistic integrity to spread idle gossip about Mrs. Roosevelt. And Cissy Patterson, the editor of the *Washington Times-Herald*, was the First Lady's friend and longtime admirer. All three of them could be counted on, for different reasons.

But if Bess and Cissy had heard the story, chances were good that other reporters had heard it, too. I glanced furtively around the room, feeling sharply paranoid. Several of the women here wrote for conservative newspapers and were critical of Mrs. Roosevelt on issues like women in the workplace and birth control. If they heard the story, they wouldn't be able to resist using it. Not in print, surely—they would be too discreet for that. But they would use it. The question was how, and when. And how much damage it would do to the First Lady.

Bess saw my distress and put her hand on my arm. "Please don't think I'm suggesting that any of this is true," she said in a low, fierce whisper. "Everybody knows that Alice Longworth hates Franklin and Eleanor and will say the most outrageous things just to cause trouble for them. In fact, since the story comes from Princess Alice, I'm sure that people discount it as one of her malicious little fictions."

I thought swiftly. It was true that Mrs. Longworth was so outrageously anti-FDR that what she said about Mrs. FDR was likely not to be believed. Her upcoming memoir, *Crowded Hours,* was said to be a notorious tell-all that sniped at all her friends, sparing none. She probably wasn't in the best repute herself these days. Maybe the damage wasn't so—

At that moment, the door was flung open. Mrs. Roosevelt, with Tommy at her heels, rushed in, and a muffled gasp rippled around the room. Eleanor cut a striking figure in her tailored riding jacket, trim breeches, and polished boots. I'd bet my next month's paycheck that she was the very first woman to have entered this august room in breeches—and under the darkly accusatory gaze of her Roosevelt grandfather, at that. It was an emancipation declaration, and I could only applaud it.

But that wasn't what had made everyone gasp. The right sleeve of the First Lady's jacket was ripped from wrist to elbow, the right side of her face was scraped and bruised, her dark tie was askew, and her hair had come loose from her white bandeau.

"So sorry to be late, ladies," she said. "My mare had an untoward encounter with a fence, and I stayed to make sure her leg was patched up properly." She raised her hand with a smile. "But please don't worry. Dot is just fine, I assure you. She's already back in her stable, enjoying a bucket of oats and looking forward to a nap."

Margaret Hart rolled her eyes. Margaret was a society reporter for the *Washington Star,* and I could guess how this little incident would play in her column. The First Lady had such disrespect for the press that she kept them waiting while she catered to her horse. Had such disdain for her position that she wore torn riding clothes to a press conference in the White House. It was the equivalent of hanging the Adams undies in the East Room. All the more reason, I thought, for Eleanor to have her own newspaper column—as a counterweight to the influence of columnists who would interpret her activities according to their own political inclinations. Press conferences were good as far as they went, but she needed to make her *own* voice heard.

"But what about *you,* Mrs. Roosevelt?" someone else asked anxiously. "Are you all right? Was it much of a fall?"

"Oh, I'm quite indestructible," Eleanor said cheerfully. "I have tumbled off more horses than I can count. And you don't need to mention this trivial affair. Let's make it off the record, shall we?"

There was a disappointed murmur, and she looked around the room for a moment, reconsidering. "Really? You think it might make an interesting story? Well, then, ask Tommy this afternoon and she'll give you a couple of sentences you can use. I'm sure we can come up with something that doesn't make me look like a complete nincompoop."

Amid general laughter, she looked around and spotted me in the corner. "Oh, there you are, Hick. Ladies, please welcome Miss Lorena Hickok back from her reporting assignment for Mr. Hopkins. It was Miss Hickok who introduced me to the frightful conditions in the coal mining areas. I'm very grateful, and I hope we'll soon be able to do something about the appalling situation there."

Paranoia reached up and grabbed me by the throat. After what Bess had just told me, I felt like hiding under my chair. But a smattering of applause was echoing around the room and there was nothing for me to do but stand, offer a quick smile, and sit down as fast as I could.

Mrs. Roosevelt nodded at me again and said briskly, "Well, then, ladies, are we ready? There are several things I want to tell you about this morning."

She didn't start with a recital of what she had for breakfast, but she did go quickly over the upcoming week's social calendar, which included a visit from the Canadian prime minister, a delegation from Mexico, and a tea in honor of Dame Rachel Crowdy of the League of Nations. After that, she went on to talk—in quite a persuasive way, I thought—about the Bear Mountain forest work camp for women that was a part of the new Civilian Conservation Corps program. Camp Tera (derisively called a "she-she-she" camp by its male critics) was designed to help jobless, homeless single women become more employable. There was already plenty of backlash from those who argued that real jobs, if there *were* any, belonged to the men. The women belonged at home.

As I watched and listened, I felt a rush of admiration for Eleanor. There were some two million women looking for jobs across the country. If Camp Tera was successful, it could help. And the women in this room were the ones who could help get the story out, the *real* story of women who needed work, needed training, needed a new start. The reporters were scribbling fiercely in their notebooks and when Mrs. Roosevelt was finished, they raised their hands and began peppering her with questions. I could think of several questions, too, but I held my tongue. It was *their* press conference and hers, not mine. They would go back to their city rooms and write their stories and see their bylines—some of them, anyway—in newspapers across the country.

And for several painful moments, I envied them, every single one of them. I had been the top female wire service reporter in the country, with a standing byline and tens of thousands of daily readers. I'd been a member of an important team, one of an influential group of journalists. And who was I now? An anonymous government field reporter, charged with the disagreeable task of looking at—and writing about—some of the ugliest Depression-era hellholes in the country. No byline, no acknowledgment, and readers I could count on the fingers of one hand.

But then Eleanor looked out over the heads of the women reporters and caught my eye. She smiled with that special softening of her mouth that I knew and loved, and I reminded myself that I hadn't given up my position as an AP front-page reporter to do Harry Hopkins's dirty work. I had given it up for *her*. She was what mattered to me now.

And then I thought of Cora, and all the other sad, stranded

people I had met in the past two months. *Don't you forget me, honey.*
Cora mattered, too. Her story—their stories—had to be told.

*Pay attention.*

I didn't tell Eleanor what Bess Furman had told me—she would
just have smiled and advised me not to worry. Like her cousin
Alice, she was fundamentally indifferent to what other people
thought. But unlike Alice, it wasn't because she was arrogant or felt
superior to others or wanted to flaunt social conventions. She was
simply guided by her own moral compass. In her heart, Eleanor
knew that she was doing what was right, which made her
impervious to criticism.

Nevertheless, I thought it prudent to cut my Washington stay
short. I took the train to New York and began the job of putting
my things in storage so the apartment could be sublet. The next
day, Eleanor came up to the city and invited me—and Prinz, too—
to stay with her while I was finishing up at Mitchell Place. The
Sixty-Fifth Street house was rented and she was borrowing (and
would later rent) a pleasant third-floor walk-up from Esther Lape
and Elizabeth Read in the brownstone they owned on East
Eleventh, a block east of Fifth Avenue. Madam called it her "hiding house," away from reporters, the Secret Service, and her
mother-in-law. A hiding house, I told her, was exactly what we
needed. I enjoyed cooking in the well-equipped kitchen, and we
spent evenings with Esther and Elizabeth, or at the theater or the
opera.

"When I'm in New York," she said once, "I always feel that
I'm an unofficial person leading a quiet life." She wasn't exactly
anonymous, but New Yorkers are blasé about celebrities. And I

was completely anonymous. Nobody ever gave me a second look, which was exactly the way I liked it.

Being with Eleanor in New York had another important payoff, for it gave us a chance to talk, away from the White House, about the daily newspaper column I was urging her to do. We discussed it with Esther and Elizabeth over tea one afternoon, in Eleanor's apartment. She had already put up dozens of the framed photographs that helped her make any place a home, as well as a couple of paintings I brought from my now-sublet apartment.

"But I'm already doing the press conferences," Eleanor protested, pouring Esther a cup of tea. She'd brought the silver tea service from Sixty-Fifth Street—the same one I remembered from that long-ago day in 1928, when we first met. "Isn't that enough?"

"The press conferences are good as far as they go," Elizabeth replied. "But you're always at the mercy of the way the reporters write your story. And you know for a fact that they don't always tell it the way you'd like."

"Exactly," I passed the plate of rugelach that I'd bought at the deli down the street—a favorite that was hard to find in Washington. "With a column, *you* will tell your story, Eleanor. You'll be in control of the way people see you and your ideas." I slid a glance at her. She was nodding.

"You don't have to do it right away," Esther said. "People are just getting used to the press conferences."

"But certainly in the next year," I said, "before all the hulla-baloo of the 1936 presidential campaign. We don't want people to see it as just another political thing."

"Do you think FDR will run?" Elizabeth asked Eleanor.

"How should I know?" Eleanor gave a wry chuckle. "I'm only his wife. I'm always the last to know anything." She turned to me.

"The idea is a good one, Hick. But a *daily* column? What in the world would I write about?"

"You'd write about what you're doing, that's what. You're a woman who has her own interests, earns an independent income, and raises her own voice on issues she believes in." I grinned. "You won't have any problem in filling the space."

"I'm not sure that Franklin will like the idea," she said slowly. "And Steve Early—"

"Steve Early is a PR man," I said. "He'll see the advantages. And so will the president."

"I think you should do it, Eleanor," Elizabeth said.

"Do it," Esther echoed emphatically. "You'll be educating women—and men, too—to things they need to think about."

"Tell you what," I said. "I'll help you write a few sample columns. We'll show them to Steve and the president and get their approval. Then we can submit them to a syndicate. I think United Feature will jump at them." I added something I knew would entice her. "And they'll pay well."

She cocked her head. "How much, do you think?"

"A couple of hundred a week," I said. "Depending on the number of newspapers that subscribe."

With Elizabeth and Esther behind the idea, she agreed. "I like the thought of having more control over the way people see and hear me," she said. "And educating women on important issues."

Years later, when "My Day" would appear in as many as ninety newspapers and reach tens of thousands of readers every day, we would remember the conversation and smile about her initial reluctance. And I had plenty of reason to view her column with not a little irony. "My Day" helped to create Eleanor the *personage*, turning her into the woman the whole world loved.

In early September, I set out across New England on my second field inspection for Harry Hopkins. This time, though, I had a car. For my travels through coal country, I'd had to depend on guides and drivers to take me where I needed to go. An automobile would give me more flexibility and allow me to make unexpected appearances—and as every investigative reporter knows, there's a certain advantage to catching people by surprise. That was proving to be especially true in the work I did for FERA, where too many people had things to hide.

My little car wasn't brand new, but she was the first one I'd ever owned and I thought she was simply splendid. She was a little blue Chevy two-door roadster, undeniably female, and when Mrs. R and I went together to pick her up, we decided to call her Bluette, after my favorite upstairs maid at the White House. I developed a great fondness for that little Chevy. She had good tires, a sound motor, and even a radio. Her top leaked when it rained and her heater wasn't worth a plugged nickel. But Bluette and I would be fine travel companions for thousands of miles, and I loved the freedom she gave me.

The second trip was different from the first. In the worn-out coalfields of West Virginia and Kentucky, the human pain was inescapable. It lay like an open wound across the landscape. The placid farms and villages of New England had a prosperous look, but the serene surface concealed a sense of angry betrayal and despairing loss. In New York and Massachusetts, the price of milk had plunged and dairy farmers were forced to slaughter their herds. In Vermont and New Hampshire, the timber industry had failed. In Maine, the fisheries were in deep trouble, and the shipyards—once the largest employer in most coastal towns—were idle. Throughout the Northeast, people were desperately needy, but out of pride, they hid the depths of their need. The farms and shops and factories and houses might be clean and neat, but every door opened into a world of hidden hurt.

Back in New York City, the scale of the challenge was simply breathtaking, a tsunami of despairing poverty that threatened to sweep the entire metropolis away. One city block might house some two hundred families on relief, recent immigrants who couldn't speak a word of English as well as lawyers and bankers and stockbrokers who had been in the highest income brackets and were now lucky to have a fifth-floor walk-up. I visited one woman who was living with three small children in a single room not much bigger than Eleanor's White House bathroom. I found her trying to heat milk by burning newspapers under a pan. The gas in her building had been turned off and when she'd tried to use a borrowed electric grill, she'd blown the fuses. The landlord refused to have them replaced, so she had only candles for light.

It was hard, hard, *hard*. My work took me out among the neediest people, and all day long, I met families—upper-, middle-, and working-class families—who had no food, no shelter, and no hope. In many areas, the Depression had destroyed the old comfortable class distinctions. In some ways, I thought, the poor had it easier, for they had long ago learned to cope. The upper- and middle-class families, who remembered what it was like to have more than enough of everything, now had to scrape by on next to nothing.

Need was everywhere, everywhere, and the more I looked, the more I saw. It was now impossible for me to simply collect and consolidate details, to objectively witness, to write the day's reports and move on. I couldn't just go into a town or a neighborhood or a city block, get the story, and get out. By now, I had become *part* of the story. I spent hours every day trying to get federal relief to those who needed it most and hours every night pleading with

FERA for more money, more food and blankets, more compassion. I was always glad to hear that Eleanor had handed one of my reports to FDR. It gave me hope—a thin thread of hope—to hold on to.

For her part, Eleanor spent those autumn months trying to get houses built for the people who had been selected to settle Arthurdale, but flimsy construction created problems that would plague the project for years. She was worried about the Jewish refugees who were fleeing the German Nazis, but she couldn't move her husband or his administration to offer help. And she was trying to get a recalcitrant Congress to clean up Washington's festering back alleys where the mostly black residents were charged exorbitant rents to live in Dickensian squalor—a problem that even her powerful Uncle Teddy had been powerless to solve. But she was putting her heart into it—into creating Arthurdale, persuading FDR on the Jewish issue, cleaning up Washington's squalid alleys.

Two women, each with her own mission. Or in the First Lady's case, *missions,* plural, none of them easily solved.

Which would, in the long term, be the reef on which the two of us would founder.

The second field trip finished, I went back to Washington to brief Hopkins and his staff on the situation in the Northeast. I stayed at the White House for ten days, and the First Lady managed to clear enough of her schedule so we could spend a few hours of every day together. Anna still had my room, so I once again took the daybed in Eleanor's suite. The hours of intimacy encouraged me to dream of a future when the two of us would have all the time in the world, just for one another. But the days passed all too swiftly, and when I left again, Anna (who needed a car) kept Bluette. This trip would take me to the upper Midwest in winter—I wouldn't be back until almost Christmas—and it seemed smarter to travel by train.

Wherever I traveled, I did my best to minimize my connection to Washington, and especially to the First Lady. This was harder than it might seem, for her letters, like a flock of birds, followed me everywhere I went. Eleanor wrote every day, and her gold-embossed White House stationery was bound to attract the attention of curious hotel clerks, especially when two or three letters arrived on the same day, each addressed to me in her extravagant script. With discretion in mind, I had given her a box of plain blue writing paper and envelopes printed with the address: 1600 Pennsylvania Avenue, Washington D.C. I learned to wait until the day I left a town to send her a Western Union wire listing my next one or two stops, so she would know where to write. Telegraph clerks were just as nosy as hotel clerks and most of them had a direct line to the desk of the nearest newspaper editor. I would occasionally be met at the next train station by an eager-beaver reporter who could only have gotten the word from a buddy at the telegraph key.

Given my efforts at professional and personal anonymity, I think I can be forgiven for being annoyed when the *Literary Digest* —a widely read general-interest weekly magazine published by Funk & Wagnall—published a story about me in their November 8, 1933, issue. The writer called me Harry Hopkins's "chief investigator," charged with keeping public relief money out of private pockets. There was a photo, too, captioned "Gets Facts for White House." Anybody who saw it could recognize me. So much for working undercover.

I was irritated. This kind of media attention only made it more difficult to do my investigative work. Worse, some might use it to connect me to the First Lady. I complained to her about it, and especially about the mention of the White House. Her response was a little off the mark but comforting nonetheless. *Darling, I know they bother you to death because you are my friend, but we'll forget it and think only that someday I'll be back in obscurity again and no one will care except ourselves.*

I was comforted by her remark about returning to obscurity. That was the important thing for me in those difficult, lonely days: believing that her stay in the White House was—in the nature of things—temporary. There would be a time—perhaps not far distant—when she would be out of the public eye and we would be together and able to shape our own lives. I shake my head at this hope now, for it seems so naïve, given the way her interests and her work expanded. But that belief buoyed me up and kept me going on even the bleakest days.

Madam might tell me to forget about the reporters, but she had her own problems with the press. The week before Thanksgiving, she was upset because some of the tabloids were speculating about the *two* Roosevelt divorces—Anna's and Elliott's—currently in the news. The gossip bothered her. *We can't hide things, can we?* she wrote sadly, adding, *It's a good thing you're not a man, Hick.*

I had to smile at that. People might talk about us, yes. But under the circumstances, being a woman had a definite advantage. If I were a man, tongues would wag a hundred times harder.

By the next day, she was braver. *So you think they gossip about us. Well, they must at least think we stand separation rather well! I am always so much more optimistic than you are. I suppose because I care so little what "they" say!* I remembered that she had to deal with the gossip about Franklin and Lucy Mercer. Perhaps, I thought, her skin had grown tougher than mine.

Eleanor spent Thanksgiving in Warm Springs with the rest of the Roosevelt tribe—including her mother-in-law and Missy. She wrote, forlornly, I thought, that she'd wished that FDR might realize that she would like me to be there, too. *You know how one dreams?* she added. *I do so wish you were here, Hick.*

I was a dreamer then, and I knew how one dreams, knew it all too well. But I also knew that I would have been miserable in Warm Springs. I would have wanted us to have time for one another. But Eleanor—wife, daughter-in-law, mother, grandmother—would be pulled in a dozen different directions by a dozen different people. And she was almost never happy there herself. Conscious that it was FDR's and Missy's retreat, she felt like an intruder. It was better to be apart for now and to look forward to our Christmas holiday together.

And I needed something to anticipate, to pull me into the future—oh, how I needed it. That third trip was a journey into the farthest, darkest reaches of my past. To Wisconsin, where I was born over a creamery in the tiny, leafy town of East Troy. To the Dakotas, where I was first a girl and then a hired girl. To Minnesota, where I earned a place in my profession and learned to love Ellie. Harry Hopkins had sent me to farming country, where it was feared that too many years of crop failures and rock-bottom prices might fan the farmers' discontent into outright rebellion. Looking back now, it seems a little far-fetched, but at the time, the New Dealers in FDR's administration were afraid that Communist organizers would invade the Midwest and rally the desperate communities. Fast relief and plenty of it would calm the storm, they thought. I was supposed to tell Hopkins how much money was needed and where it should go.

In New York City, the need for aid had been so great that there wasn't enough money in the New Deal pocket to meet it.

Here, the problem was different. While there was a growing bitterness among the farmers, they seemed to me more despairing and desperate than violent—and while federal money might have temporarily eased their pain, relief was no real remedy. What the farmers needed most of all was *rain*.

From horizon to horizon, the prairie had been destroyed by drought. The winds whipped up maniacal dust storms and howled and screamed and sobbed around the windows of the small-town hotels where I slept at night. Every day, everywhere I looked, I saw the crushing drabness of life and felt a nameless, formless dread like a lid of gray cloud over the bleak landscape. I was nearly overwhelmed by the suffering of people and animals on the farms, in the towns. I had lived and worked here, too, scrubbing floors and emptying chamber pots in other people's houses, and by some miracle of grace, I had broken out, as from a prison. Looking around me, I wondered now how I had managed to escape, when all these others were still here. Was it simple luck? Or had there been something in *me*, urging me outward, onward, farther?

But what if I had stayed? Who would I be?

Would I be the gaunt and toothless mother, whose only cow had just gone dry, leaving her baby with no milk? Would I be the woman who had so few dishes that she and her husband and their four elderly parents, all living in the same house, could not sit down together for a meal?

Or would I be the woman who had ten children—so many that she couldn't remember all their names—and was pregnant again and begged me, *begged* me, to ask Mrs. Roosevelt to send her something that would keep her from having more babies? Could that life have been mine?

These unanswerable questions haunted me day and night, and when I reached the next dreary hotel in the next sad little town and found a letter from Eleanor, I snatched it up and held it to my heart. It was my lifeline back to her—and to civilization. I cried when I read what she had written in one letter, that she was prouder to know me than she could ever tell me, *because anyone who is "you" after all you've been through need never be afraid of anything or anyone.*

Later, I would think about that and take a kind of bleak refuge in the thought that, while the miseries I witnessed daily were changing me, I was still my*self*, at the core. For now, Eleanor's words gave me courage to face the next day and the next. They helped to carry me into the next week. They gave me a horizon to look toward and a sweet wind at my back. Now, all my attention was focused on mid-December, when this endless, awful journey would be over and I would be back in civilization, back with her.

I was in far northern Minnesota that last week, in Bemidji, in the timber country, where it was bitterly cold and government relief—in the form of money for warm clothes or help with the rent or with jobs—had been very slow in coming. I was doing my job: noting what was needed (blankets, clothing, food, and money, lots of money), where it should be sent, and how the distribution should be handled in the sparsely populated northern counties. And at the same time, I was trying to cope with my diabetes.

I had lived with mood swings for years, but now they seemed to intensify. Whether it was the disease or the stress of travel or the bleakness of the lives I was witnessing, I couldn't be sure—most likely, it was a combination of everything. But there were many days when I was exasperated, frustrated, physically exhausted, and weighed down with the sadnesses I saw and felt around me. Depression was a constant dark shadow.

And all of this, of course, intensified my longing. Eleanor was a lighthouse, a lifeline, my hope of salvation. My heart was already in Washington, with her, and I was counting the days and hours, as lovers do. At the end of a long December letter, I wrote, *I've been trying today to bring back your face—to remember just how you look. Most clearly I remember your eyes, with a kind of teasing smile in them, and the feeling of that soft spot just north-east of the corner of your mouth against my lips... Good night, dear one. I want to put my arms around you and kiss you at the corner of your mouth. And in a little more than a week now—I shall!* It was true. My surroundings were so bleak and people's needs were so overwhelming that I could only survive by living in the future, with her.

She was counting the days, too. *Less than a week now*, she wrote. *I know I won't be able to talk when we first meet but though I can remember just how you look I shall want to look long and very lovingly at you.* Long and loving looks, touches, kisses. These were the future hopes that warmed me through the cold, dark present of that journey into the bleak heart of the country I had come from. In her letters, I read the same eager hope. But I was—and I think she was, too—creating a fantasy so fabulous, so miraculous, that its reality could only be a bitter disappointment.

It was the Christmas season—the first for the Roosevelts in the White House—and Edith Helm, the First Lady's social secretary, was determined to fill her calendar with holiday events. I arrived expecting that Eleanor and I would be able to spend evenings together, but Edith had other plans. In fact, there were so many holiday events heaped on top of Mrs. Roosevelt's usual heavy load of daytime activities that there was not a single evening left for *us*. I was relegated to a few breathless catch-as-catch-can conversations during the day and a late-night half-hour before bed, when I was tired and Eleanor was completely exhausted.

While I waited for Eleanor to return from whatever holiday event Edith had scheduled, I used the time to write my wrap-up reports for Harry Hopkins and catch up on my mending and reading. I had almost run out of things to do when at last Madam promised, *promised*, that we would spend one whole evening together, decorating the little tree in her sitting room and exchanging our gifts. She cancelled her attendance at the event that Edith had scheduled for that night and asked Mrs. Nesbitt to make something special for our dinner. She even asked the head usher to chill a bottle of bubbly.

But Anna arrived late in the afternoon, once again in tears over her coming divorce, and Eleanor gave her *my* evening. I had grown fond of Anna and her daughter Sisty, and the three of us would remain friends over the years. But I was hungry for time with her mother, a hunger that our separation had intensified to a starvation. It hurt like hell to be put aside, like a book that Eleanor could open and close—or simply ignore—whenever something else came up.

I didn't blow up or stage a dramatic scene punctuated with accusations and tearful recriminations. I waited until Anna had gone to bed across the hall and Eleanor had changed into her nightgown and her old chenille robe. I had packed a bag with what I needed, and I set it beside the door.

"Goodbye," I said, pulling on my coat.

"Goodbye?" She looked at me blankly. "You're not leaving, Hick. *Why?* Where are you going? It's the middle of the night. And it's snowing!"

I took a deep breath and recited the little speech I had prepared. "People who love one another keep the commitments they make. Tonight was our time—finally, our time together—and you gave it away to someone else."

"But… but Anna is my daughter," Eleanor said blankly. "I love her. She *needs* me!"

I managed a small smile. "I love you and need you, too, my dear. Anna will be here next week and next month and the month after that. I won't." Then, at nearly midnight, I left the White House and checked in for the night at the Powhatan, a few blocks away. The next morning, I took the train to New York and retrieved Prinz from the kennel. We went to stay with Jean Dixon.

That night, Eleanor called. "I'm sorry, Hick," she said contritely. "Oh, so sorry. Sometimes I— Sometimes I let things get the better of me. I've told Edith and Tommy to clear the calendar. I'm coming to New York. Will you and Prinz come and stay with me?"

I agreed, of course. We had a lazy three days, reading, walking, going to see *As Thousands Cheer,* Irving Berlin's hit musical revue, at the Music Box. The revue was made up of witty songs and satirical sketches based on recent newspaper headlines. In one, President and Mrs. Hoover gloomily leave the White House, Hoover giving his cabinet a Bronx cheer. Eleanor tried not to laugh at that one, but she couldn't help herself.

Best of all, there was time for the talk that seemed to make things right between us. When she went back to the White House, she wrote, *Dearest one bless you and forgive me and believe me you've brought me more and meant more to me than you know and I will be thankful… every day for your mere being in the world.*

Now, with decades of hindsight, I can see that what happened during that holiday season was a preview of times to come, when it would be increasingly difficult for me to find a place in her overscheduled, overcrowded life. But I didn't understand it then. Only one thing seemed different to me, and important: that I had stood up for myself when I felt she was using me. I loved her, but I had left her when I couldn't be with her for just one evening on *my* terms, even when those terms were terribly compromised.

The significance of this eluded me then. But after I had done it once, I would find that I could do it again.

## CHAPTER ELEVEN

# An Infinite Succession of Things

My first FERA trip of 1934 took me south, to Georgia, where the new Civil Works Administration had created enough construction jobs—primarily bridges and roads—to blunt the worst effects of the Depression. The situation was bad, yes, especially for the Negroes who were competing with white people for the available jobs. But life didn't seem quite as dire as it was in the upper Midwest or in coal country, perhaps because the weather was warmer, or perhaps because I didn't get out into the rural areas. In the cities and large towns and among the local business people, I found a spirit of optimism and a sense that the future held brighter prospects.

And I was optimistic, too. Madam and I were planning a weekend together, a *quiet* weekend, just the two of us. On a Friday in mid-January, Bluette and I picked her up at the Atlanta airport and drove to Warm Springs. The president was in Washington, so we would be alone there.

Warm Springs had been FDR's haven for nearly ten years. He had invested nearly two hundred thousand dollars of his own money in the purchase of the old run-down Meriwether Inn and much more in new buildings and facilities: a riding stable, a golf course for his friends, and pools and treatment facilities for the "polios" who came there to recuperate. The 88-degree springs were the powerful attraction, for the minerals in the bubbling water buoyed a polio victim up, allowing him or her to exercise paralyzed limbs in ways that weren't possible anywhere else.

Just two years before, FDR had built a white clapboard, green-shuttered cottage on a rise overlooking a dense stand of Georgia pine. In the center was a large living-dining area, with Missy's bedroom on the right and his on the left, with a smaller room for Eleanor and a porch in the back that overlooked the ravine. When she was there, Missy presided over the Little White House with a happily proprietary air. She was in charge, and more nearly FDR's wife than she was anywhere else.

For visitors, including the president's mother, there were comfortable cottages in the woods, some of them furnished with Val-Kill beds, sofas, and chairs. Eleanor, who thought of herself as a visitor, preferred the guest cottages—and that's where we stayed. Our meals were brought to the cottage, where we ate, and in the evenings, we read aloud to each other in front of a blazing fireplace.

The weekend was lovely, an intimate foretaste, I thought then, of the best times to come, when the First Lady had stepped out of the national spotlight. On Saturday, we slept late, then swam in the heated water of the pool, and went riding. That is, *she* went riding. I stayed behind with a book, feeling pampered and lazy, loving the way the tall Georgia pines clustered around our cabin, closing it in from the world. In the days before white conquest and settlement, the warm, spring-fed pools had been a healing sanctuary, and the warring Cherokee, Creek, and Choctaw came there under truce. There would be no fighting at the springs. It was a refuge. That's how I felt there: that Madam and I were a pair of refugees from a contentious world—shut away, shielded, sheltered from the openly disapproving or the merely curious. We were just *ourselves*. We were just two women who loved each other.

On Monday, I took her to Atlanta and put her on a plane. And on Monday night, I wrote to her. *Each time we have together that way —brings us closer, doesn't it? And I believe those days and long pleasant hours together each time make it perhaps a little less possible for us to hurt each other. They give us better understanding of each other, give us more faith, draw us closer.* If it wasn't quite all that I might have wanted, that long, sweet arc of hours at Warm Springs created a dream of the future for me, and I held it in my mind for a long time. That was what our life together could be, *would* be, if we could only get through the arid desert of Eleanor's years as First Lady.

She felt as I did. That night, she wrote that she had loved every minute of our time together. *I am going to live on it during these next few weeks,* she added tenderly, sounding resigned to a heavy schedule. The next day, she wrote that she always had a "lost feeling" after we parted, but *then the infinite succession of things takes hold and though I'm not always interested at least I am numb!*

Numb to what? I wondered. To the job of being First Lady? To whatever private demons might be driving her? When she gave in to the infinite succession of things, was she trying to outrun the dark? Whatever it was, she was constantly busy. There were her press conferences and radio broadcasts, as well as her Washington alley project, which was now a bill moving through Congress. She designed the costumes, decorations, and favors for FDR's birthday gala, attended three charity balls, and stayed with her son John when he had his appendix removed. (Unhappily for me, this meant that she had to cancel our plan to meet for the weekend in Charleston.) And Arthurdale clamored for her attention, as always, with a thousand management questions. Arthurdale *loved* the First Lady, and their needs were always on her mind.

In the Deep South, I was dealing with another kind of clamor, the noisy opposition to the Civil Works Administration. The CWA, a short-term, temporary job creation program, promised to be the most controversial New Deal agency. But in less than a year, it put more than four million people back to work, built or improved 40,000 schools, 469 airports, and 255,000 miles of roads. It was designed to use government funds to pay unemployed people to do useful work for close to the prevailing wage, which was opposed by those on the political right as "socialist."

In the South, though, the opposition wasn't philosophical. It came from white planters and businessmen who balked at paying blacks the 30 cents an hour imposed by the CWA, which was more than twice the 12 1/2 cents an hour they had been paying. Stacey Turner, a local banker and chairman of the relief program in Jackson County, Georgia, was dead set against 30 cents an hour. I wrote to Eleanor about his reaction when I told him what he had to do. *"It's charity and nothing else," he roared—he's the kind that roars and then looks out of the corner of his eye to see if you're scared. "Pay 'em 12 1/2 cents an hour and let 'em play checkers for it. They ain't doing any work that amounts to anything, anyway."*

I'd grown up in the Dakotas and had never given racial issues much thought. When I first came to Dixie, I saw things through the eyes of the business people I was interviewing—white business people. But even in my ignorance, I couldn't help seeing the cruel and violent racism, the poison that infected the entire South. There would be fifteen lynchings of blacks in 1934, but to a man, every Southern senator would oppose a bill designed to make lynching a federal crime. Eleanor told me that FDR refused to back the bill, adding candidly that he was afraid that if he pushed for anti-lynching legislation, the Southern Democrats would retaliate by refusing to fund his New Deal bills. And when the CWA and

FERA money was gone, field hands would go back to earning 12 1/2 cents an hour.

It was Gay Shepperson, Georgia's FERA director, who pushed me up against the ugliest truth and made me see it and *feel* it. She showed me that in the rural areas, there was no work except sharecropping, which gave a family a shack, a few sticks of stove wood, some grits and a little pork, and the sweet potatoes and collards they raised in their garden. There were no schools worth the name, and no medical facilities to cope with the epidemic tuberculosis and pellagra. But these problems weren't caused by the Depression and they couldn't be remedied by short-term government-funded employment. They were caused by prejudice and race hatred, and things would never be different until hearts and minds were changed. And change would be a long time coming.

In the meantime, Eleanor and I had another trip to look forward to. In December, Harry Hopkins had told me that he was sending me to Puerto Rico in March to survey the situation there, and I had asked her to go with me. It would be a lovely vacation, just the two of us. I would have to work, of course, and the First Lady would most likely have a few official duties. But we could surely manage a weekend to ourselves, and I had imagined the two of us enjoying a private, sun-blessed tropical holiday. In Puerto Rico, we would be as anonymous as we had been in French Canada the summer before. We wouldn't attract attention, much less any media attention.

I was wrong on all counts. It was no vacation. It wouldn't be "just the two of us." And the media attention would begin with a vengeance even before we left Washington. Conservative, anti-New Deal *Time* magazine put Harry Hopkins on the cover of its February nineteenth issue and a photo of me (a very attractive one, actually) on page thirteen, where I was named FERA's chief under-cover investigator.

The accompanying text wasn't as complimentary as the photo. *Time*'s Miss Hickok was a "rotund lady with a husky voice, a per-emptory manner, baggy clothes… in her day one of the country's best female newshawks." And then it got even more malicious. After Miss Hickok had covered the candidate's wife during the presidential campaign, she and Mrs. Roosevelt had become "fast friends" and now traveled together "a lot." Oh, and incidentally, Miss Hickok had gotten the job with FERA because Mr. Hopkins was "a great admirer of Mrs. Roosevelt." When Mrs. Roosevelt went to Puerto Rico in March, Miss Hickok would naturally go along, "to look into relief work there."

The piece gave me heartburn. I couldn't complain about "rotund" or "husky" or even "baggy." On the job, I wore comfort-able clothes that I didn't have to fuss with and that didn't set me apart from the poverty-stricken people I was there to interview. But "businesslike" would have been more accurate than "peremp-tory," and I resented the suggestion that I had been given the job because I was Mrs. Roosevelt's "fast friend." Hopkins wouldn't have hired me if I hadn't been a damn good reporter. What's more, I wasn't tagging along on the First Lady's trip to Puerto Rico. It was the other way around: she was "going along" with me.

But while the trip may have begun with my invitation to her, that's not how it worked out. Not only was *I* going with *her*, but so were four other women reporters: Bess Furman of the AP, Ruby Black of the UP, Dorothy Ducas of the International News Service, and Emma Bugbee of the *New York Herald Tribune*. Sam Schulman, a press pool photographer, would fly in from Miami. None of this press extravaganza could be laid to the First Lady's charge, of course. The scheme was concocted by Steve Early and

Louis Howe, and Eleanor was in tears when she told me about it during one of our long-distance telephone talks.

"Four reporters and a photographer?" I exclaimed. "I like those women and Sam is a good guy. But with them on our heels, we'll never have a private moment."

Eleanor sighed. "I am so, so sorry, Hick. I didn't intend this to happen. It was meant to be just the two of us. The trip was taken out of my hands."

I believed her, then, because I understood that Steve and Louis would want to take advantage of her travel in Puerto Rico—and who better to send with her than the four top women in the Washington press corps?

"I know," I said. "It's just so hard."

"Yes, it is," she replied. "I'll try to make it up to you, even if just a little."

And she did—at least as far as our accommodations were concerned. On Haiti, we stayed in the sumptuous National Palace. On St. Thomas, where the First Lady was welcomed by a crowd that serenaded her with a chorus of protest and union songs, we were the guests of the governor and slept on the third floor of the impressive Government House. (We didn't understand about the union songs until we heard, later, about the ongoing labor union strike—one of the things the First Lady wasn't supposed to know about.) The next morning, we went swimming with the press at the governor's gorgeous private beach, where Bess and Dorothy filmed a sequence of Eleanor in a bathing suit, skipping rope.

For our stay in San Juan, Madam arranged for us to share a splendid room in the magnificent seventeenth-century La Fortaleza, the Puerto Rican governor's mansion. The old fort had been transformed into a palace many decades before, and its pale blue-and-white facade, tiled roof, and many fountains recalled the

Moorish elegance of colonial Spanish architecture. Our room—with marble floors and opulent gilded ceilings and wall panels—looked out onto the Caribbean, and that evening, we stood arm in arm on the balcony, enjoying the tropical breeze and marveling at the blue, blue water. Bess, Dorothy, Ruby, and Emma, all having a wonderful time on their own, were booked into a hotel some distance away. So Madam and I were able to dine quietly in our room and go for early morning ocean swims while the reporters were still asleep.

For me, the luxury of our surroundings was a sad contrast to the island's misery, and my connection to the First Lady's eager entourage made it difficult to do much meaningful investigating. But I saw enough, and the lengthy report I wrote for Harry Hopkins (it went to the president, too) outlined the difficult situation. Economically, Puerto Rico was in a bad way indeed, and the people—American citizens of an American territory—were even worse off than the rural blacks I had met in Georgia.

But as in Georgia, the Depression had very little to do with Puerto Rico's poverty, and government-funded relief, while it might put food on a few tables, wasn't going to create any fundamental change. The island was suffering from serious over-population, dangerous malnutrition, an epidemic of tuberculosis and malaria, and a chronic lack of decent jobs. The coffee plantations had been wiped out by several recent hurricanes, and sugar cane was now the only viable crop. But sugar was a seasonal industry that barely paid a living wage and left the workers with nothing during the six months they were idle.

The depth of the island's poverty was illustrated in the photographs that Sam Schulman took as the First Lady and her press entourage walked through the filthy streets of the "swamp slums," where refugees from the 1932 hurricane still lived in huts cobbled together from storm debris. Eager to catch a glimpse of Mrs. Roosevelt, they trailed wherever we went and darted ahead to toss flowers in her path.

Their plight touched her heart, and after she returned to Washington, she spent nearly as much time on projects for Puerto Rico as she did on Arthurdale. My recommendation for a change in administering the island (from the War Department to the Department of the Interior) was implemented, and other changes we recommended were in the works: new school buildings, higher prices for Puerto Rican products, and a minimum wage scale for women seamstresses. It had been a hard trip, and I had begun it with the sense that I had been ill-used. In spite of everything, though, we had managed some private time together. The trip was good for Puerto Rico—and for us. But it was the last good trip we would take together.

We were back in Washington by St. Patrick's Day. A little more than a week later, Bluette and I were on our way again, bound for a ten-week swing through Alabama and points west. I wouldn't be back until the second week of May. That night, Madam wrote: *Hick darling, I believe it gets harder to let you go each time, but that is because you grow closer... I ache for you... and always much love dear one.*

The busyness of our work swallowed both of us, but our personal concerns were eclipsed by waves of violence that seemed to engulf the whole world. After a year-long robbing and killing spree, Clyde Barrow and Bonnie Parker were ambushed and killed by a Texas posse on a rural road in Bienville Parish, Louisiana. Notorious outlaw John Dillinger went to the Biograph Theater in Chicago to see Clark Gable in *Manhattan Melodrama* and was gunned down by police when he came out of the movie. A strike by San Francisco longshoremen shut down U.S. ports all along the Pacific coast and spelled disaster for businesses that relied on shipping. Fierce dust storms blew an estimated 350 million tons of topsoil from the Plains states all the way to the Atlantic, ironically engulfing Washington in the same week that Congress was hearing testimony about soil conservation. On the other side of the world, German chancellor Adolf Hitler made a state visit to Italy, building closer relations with Mussolini; back home, he got rid of nearly eighty of his enemies in a slaughter that came to be called "The Night of the Long Knives."

For me, the long swing through the Southern states felt endless, and what I saw seemed to get worse and worse the farther I went. And it wasn't just the poverty, either. There was political interference, graft, and outright thievery. In northern Alabama, I reported to Harry that I had visited a county with a population of twelve thousand, of whom ten thousand were on relief. It was a coal-mining area and the union bosses, who were out to line their own pockets, were telling people that in order to get a relief check from the government, they had to join the United Mine Workers.

In Louisiana, I wrote that New Orleans, where 85 percent of the case load was black, looked simply hopeless, and that the office where people went to apply for relief was revoltingly filthy and smelled so that the odor clung to me for hours after I left.

And in Houston, in mid-April, I wrote that Texas was a god-awful mess, with the relief rolls so overburdened that single women were getting a food allowance of thirty-nine cents a week. In Beaumont and Port Arthur, relief workers told me that they were taking the white applications first and turning the blacks away. "We've got to," they said, "because of the attitude of the whites. We've been threatened with riots here."

There were a couple of bright spots, though. One was Arnaud's famous restaurant in New Orleans's French Quarter, where I had the best meal in years. Two legal gin fizzes, shrimps Arnaud, pompano baked in a paper bag, potato soufflé, crepes Suzette, sauterne, and chicory coffee. To which Eleanor, when I reported my gluttony, replied with a sigh, "Oh, how I wish I could enjoy food the way you do, Hick!" The indulgence wasn't healthy, I knew, and I would pay for it. But after all I'd been through, I damn well needed it, and I refused to feel guilty.

The second bright spot was Fort Worth, where I spent an afternoon with the Roosevelts' oldest son, Elliott, and his pregnant wife. Ruth was a "vast improvement," I told Madam candidly, over Elliott's first wife, Betty, whom I had met often at the White House. During the visit, I told Elliott that I was worried about what people were saying about the president—this, after a pair of Texas businessmen had told me that in their opinion, FDR was in danger of becoming another Mussolini. Elliott had a very different view.

"The trouble with Father," he said, "is that he has too much of a tendency to compromise. He hates to say no to anybody." Which didn't sound very much like Mussolini to me.

It was in Arizona that Bluette and I had the wreck that nearly ended my career as an investigator—and my life. I had spent several dispiriting days in New Mexico and Arizona, where the public works jobs were handed out to Anglos only in an entrenched system of political patronage, and where the economic gap between the whites and the Mexican-Americans seemed as wide as the Grand Canyon. On the last Sunday of April, on a gravel road that was notorious for producing a fatality every few months,

Bluette skidded on loose gravel, went briefly airborne, and rolled twice. I rolled with her, taking her weight on my neck as we went over. The state patrolman who showed up a little later could only shake his head and mutter that he couldn't believe I had crawled out of the wreckage alive.

I ended up in the hospital for a day, but other than some scratches, bruises, and a very sore neck, I was undamaged. But for poor Bluette, it was the end of the road. I said a tearful goodbye as she was hauled off to the wrecking yard and then took the train east.

I arrived back at the White House on the eleventh of May, looking forward to the quiet two weeks Eleanor had promised me. But our time together was an infinite succession of interruptions. The First Lady's days were scheduled full, from early morning to late at night—not just with meetings and the usual press conference and fundraisers and lunches with the "press girls" and Democratic women, but with magazine articles and radio speeches to write and stacks of mail to answer.

I thought often of Tommy's remark about demons and wondered once again whether this radical busyness was Eleanor's way of holding them at bay. Whatever it was, her life was simply *full*. In the short time I was at the White House, she had official guests for dinner every single night. One evening, she held an East Room reception for the Swedish minister, his delegation, and 334 guests. The next, she presided over a formal dinner for eighty-five guests honoring the governor of New York and his wife, followed by an orchestral evening. Knowing my love of music, the First Lady invited me to that event. I wore my black lace gown and she wore her silvery blue. We looked splendid, I thought. We sat together during the performance, but I would rather have had the evening to ourselves.

The president seemed to have forgotten whatever animosity

he'd held toward me and asked Eleanor and me to join him and Missy for a weekend cruise on the presidential yacht, the USS *Sequoia*. It was a lovely, relaxing trip down the Potomac and into Chesapeake Bay, in a yacht that seemed (to me, anyway) like a floating palace. While the president and Missy fished for bluefin tuna, Madam and I read the Sunday papers and talked in a sheltered corner of the deck. At one point, I got up from my chair.

"Where are you going, Hick?" Madam asked idly.

"Downstairs," I replied and turned to go. "Can I bring you anything?"

"Below, Hick! Be-*low!*" the president shouted over his shoulder. "I'll make a sailor out of you if it takes me two full terms in office." Two terms? Eleanor and I rolled our eyes and the president laughed. But it wasn't funny, at least for me. We were only in the second year of a first term.

The next morning, I set off on another trip for Harry Hopkins. We didn't get to say a proper goodbye because—yet another in the infinite succession of things—the First Lady was swamped by a flood of Girl Scouts. She regretted that in the letter she wrote that evening, but reminded me that we would have years of happy times together, and in the meantime, there was our summer trip to look forward to. *July is a long way off,* she added, *but when it comes, we'll be together.*

Ah, July. We were planning to spend nearly three weeks together, just the two of us, in California. We were clinging to the hope of it as pilgrims crossing a desert might cling to the vision of a faraway mirage, shimmering and dreamlike at the far edge of the world.


The next few weeks were strenuous, the June heat was terrible, and

I exhausted myself with day-long visits, one after another, to Tennessee Valley Authority sites. But my physical weariness was lightened by what I saw of the TVA, where nearly ten thousand people—both men and women—were at work on various parts of the project, earning a "really living wage," as I wrote to Harry Hopkins. That number barely made a dent in the need for paying jobs, but the mood throughout the region was upbeat and hopeful, a contrast to that in next-door West Virginia, where I had visited nearly a year before.

In Dayton, Ohio, I met with Elizabeth Nutting, who was managing the homesteading cooperative there. Elizabeth (we were on a first-name basis immediately) held the wonderful if enigmatic title of Director of the Division of Character Building for Dayton's Council of Social Agencies. To Eleanor, I wrote of my admiration: *Elizabeth is a very attractive woman and yet has the mind of a man.* Eleanor took exception to my remark: *Why can't a woman think, be practical and a good business woman and still have a mind of her own?*

I stood corrected. Yes, of course, she could. Elizabeth Nutting did—have a mind of her own, that is. She and her partner, Margaret, knew exactly what they both wanted and how they were going to get it. The war intervened, but afterward, the two of them established the American Homestead Foundation and built the community of Melbourne Village in Florida, where they spent the rest of their lives together.

From Ohio, I traveled across the Midwest on to the sugar beet fields of Colorado and beef-producing Wyoming, but always and every day with one golden destination in mind. California in July, with Eleanor, for three lovely weeks—as delightful, we both hoped, as our French Canadian adventure of the previous summer, a sweet dream of a holiday that neither of us would ever forget.

We would never forget the California holiday, either. But not because it was a sweet dream.

# Chapter Twelve

## The End of the Beginning

Every trip you make with someone teaches you something important about the person you travel with—and about yourself. The three weeks that Eleanor and I spent together on the West Coast revealed some truths about each of us, truths that changed the way we understood each other. In those weeks, I was challenged in ways that showed me who I was, essentially, what I wanted in my life, and what I *didn't* want. It reminded me of something I already knew from personal experience: every love affair has a beginning, a middle, and an end. California would be the end of our beginning. Eleanor and I would go on loving each other for the rest of our lives, dearly, deeply, tenderly. But not in the way we began.

After Puerto Rico, I drew the line. When we were traveling together, there would be no more First Lady doings, no entourage, and no media. "I absolutely agree," Eleanor said when we discussed it on the phone. "That's what I want, too, Hick. The California trip will be our private getaway."

Well, almost. We would be driving—I had replaced Bluette with a used gray Plymouth roadster—and planned a few days with friends and family. Otherwise, we would be alone. We would be tourists, as we were when we drove through New England and

Quebec. And we would be anonymous: no fanfare, no fuss, no Secret Service. If reporters asked about her vacation plans, she would tell them her trip was off the record, and that would be that. After Puerto Rico, she understood. *We must be careful this summer and keep it out of the papers when we are off together,* she wrote.

That pleased me. I was glad to see that Eleanor was being discreet. But I knew how determined reporters could be when they're on the trail of a story, and a visiting First Lady was a very juicy story indeed, especially when she's trying to avoid the press. It wasn't going to be as easy to keep ourselves out of the newspapers as it had been the year before. But when I tried to suggest some ways we might escape press scrutiny, she brushed my concerns aside with a blithe, *I can't quite understand why you are so worried, dear. We'll just be natural. We'll have a wonderful time together.* I hoped so— oh, how I hoped so!

The longer I thought about our trip and the more deeply I looked into myself, the more clearly I understood why it was so important to me. The time we had together was precious—and terribly, terribly brief. The best times had been the summer Northeastern trip the year before and the weekend at Warm Springs. She shared Val-Kill with Nan and Marion, who didn't welcome me. The White House was a three-ring circus, complete with clowns— and lions. We'd had some lovely moments in Puerto Rico, but it had been a publicity stunt, with that gaggle of girl reporters tagging along.

I didn't ask myself whether the antagonism I felt toward the press might have something to do with the fact that I was no longer a respected member of that profession. More likely, I thought, my desire for anonymity had to do with the fact that, like other women who have loved women, I had learned how important it was to keep my friendships private.

But I *did* know one thing. I didn't want to spend a day, or three weeks, or the rest of my life traveling with the First Lady of the United States. I wanted to spend it with Eleanor. For me, the California trip was beginning to feel like a test case. If we couldn't make it work now, I was afraid it might never work.

Things couldn't have gotten off to a worse start. Eleanor was flying to Sacramento from Chicago, and somebody—most likely an airline ticket agent—tipped off the *Bee* that she was coming to town. When I got to our hotel the evening before her arrival, they were already camped out in the lobby, a noisy, clamoring swarm of reporters. I was chagrined when they recognized me, but I wasn't surprised. My photograph had been in *Time* magazine and in the newspaper reports of the Puerto Rico trip. Like it or not, I was recognizable. And I was news.

Early the next morning, I picked Eleanor up at the airport and drove her back to the hotel, where I told the waiting reporters that she was going upstairs to wash her face and would meet them in the lobby in a few moments. Thinking ahead, I had planned to use the old elevator-and-alley-door trick and had recruited a pair of California state troopers to help with the deception. We took the elevator upstairs, then took another elevator down to the rear entrance, where a uniformed trooper waited at the wheel of my car, another in a squad car behind. We tossed our luggage into the Plymouth's rumble seat, squeezed in beside the trooper, and off we went.

A few minutes later, we were on the highway, heading out of town. The top was down, the sun was bright, and I was happy. So was Eleanor. "As they say in the movies, we've made a clean getaway," she said, patting my knee. "Good work, Hick."

"Uh-oh." The trooper checked the review mirror. "Afraid we've got company."

I turned to look and there they were, a half-dozen reporters crammed into an old green Buick. They had cut in ahead of our police escort. "Damn," I muttered.

"Hold onto your hats, ladies," the trooper said cheerfully and jammed down the accelerator. "We're going to outrun them."

The Plymouth began to fly. Sixty, seventy. My hat whirled off, and Eleanor's silk scarf whipped like a flag in the wind. Eighty, ninety. The Plymouth had wings. But the Buick was heavier, with more horsepower. It stayed on our tail.

"Stop!" Eleanor cried breathlessly, as we took a sharp curve. "Oh, please stop! This is too dangerous—not just for us, but for them."

Personally, I wouldn't have cared if that damned Buick had careened off the road and killed the whole damned carload. But if that happened when they were chasing the First Lady's getaway car, the headlines would stretch not just across the country but around the world.

"Yeah," I said, between gritted teeth. "Stop. We have to talk to them."

"You're the boss," the cop said and pulled off the road. I got out and walked back to the Buick, which had pulled in behind.

"Okay, fellas." I bared my teeth in a grin. "You got us. Let's cut the Keystone Cops act." I had seen a billboard advertising a coffee shop in Roseville ("Jim's Coffee Shop, Booths for Ladies"), a few miles ahead. "How about meeting Mrs. Roosevelt over a cup of coffee at Jim's?"

A burly guy stopped popping photos of the car and growled, "You're not going to try to outrun us again, are you?"

"Nope. See you at the coffee shop, boys." I walked around to

the driver's side of the Plymouth, thanked the trooper, and sent him on his way with his colleague, then drove off with Eleanor. I was seething, but if she was angry, she didn't show it. To my surprise, she seemed to be rather enjoying herself.

We ordered breakfast while the reporters clustered noisily around our table, shouting questions. For me, it was worse than Puerto Rico—much worse, actually, since the women journalists on that trip had been friends. Here, I felt like a carnival sideshow. But Eleanor was her usual First Lady self, casually eating her breakfast and pleasantly answering questions, all but one. She refused to tell them where we were going.

"I am simply trying to get away from the White House for a few days," she said with a smile. "This little auto tour is my vacation. It's off the record."

The reporters grumbled, but they had to content themselves with reporting that the First Lady breakfasted on California peaches, toast, and coffee, while her friend, Lorena Hickok, smoked a cigarette and scowled—which I certainly did, since I knew what to expect. The next day's Sacramento *Union* headline read, *President's Wife Tells* Union *She Plans "Secret" Auto Tour of California.* The implication was inescapable: Mrs. Roosevelt had something to hide.

For the moment, we seemed to be safe. When we got in the car and headed for the little town of Colfax and Ellie Dickinson's house, the reporters drove off in the other direction. I knew they had photographs of my automobile and its license plate, however. They wouldn't leave us alone.

But they did—at least for a while. Ellie was a perfect hostess and our two days with her and her husband Roy were exactly what I had hoped for. A pleasant picnic in the mountains, suppers on the back porch of their small cottage, evenings talking and listening to music on the radio. Long before, I had told Eleanor about the eight years Ellie and I had spent in Minneapolis and her sudden decision to elope with Roy. She knew we'd kept in touch since the marriage, both of us holding on to the memory of an important chapter in our lives. Eleanor had admitted then that she was nervous about the meeting. *I know I've got to fit in gradually to your past and with your friends,* she had written to me, *so there won't be any closed doors between us later on.* "Fitting in" wasn't any problem. It was an easy, comfortable time, and both of us felt very much at home.

When we left Ellie and Roy, we crossed the Sierras at Donner Pass and drove north to Pyramid Lake, to a sprawling Nevada ranch named the Arrowhead D where the Roosevelts' daughter Anna had been staying, waiting to get a Nevada divorce. The ranch was owned by Bill and Ella Dana, longtime friends of the Roosevelts. During the four days we were there, Madam and I played with Anna's children, swam in Pyramid Lake, and sang cowboy songs to the accompaniment of Bill's banjo. And we went horseback riding, Eleanor on a golden palomino with a platinum blond mane and tail and I on a sleepy gray horse named Old Blue. Blue was retired from active duty and needed to be nudged with a toe every few minutes to keep him awake and moving.

Riding wasn't my idea of fun, but I thought I'd better get in some practice, for when we arrived at the ranch, Eleanor had a surprise for me—not a very pleasant one. As we were unpacking, she told me that she had asked Tommy to look for a couple of quiet tourist cabins for our trip back to San Francisco. Tommy had written to Bill Nelson, the chief ranger at Yosemite National Park, thinking he might be able to recommend a place or two.

"I'm afraid Nelson misunderstood," she said apologetically, handing me a packet of information. "He's asked us to be guests of the Park Service. It's to be my first official visit to Yosemite."

I opened the packet warily. "Official visit?"

"Just for a night or two." She added hurriedly, "I'm so sorry, Hick. I know it's not what we planned, but—"

"And what's this about horses?" I said, looking down at the sheets of National Park Service stationery she had handed me. As I scanned the page, I saw that the First Lady's "official visit" included a backcountry camping trip and that a horse had been requested for me: "'A quiet, gentle horse,'" I read aloud, "since Miss Hickok has not ridden for some time.'"

"Well, you haven't, have you?" Eleanor asked.

I shook my head. "Riding is your thing, dear, not mine. And you could have told me ahead of time, so I could bring the right clothes." I took a breath. "But that's not the point, Eleanor. The point is this 'official visit' thing. You promised there wouldn't be any of that. You *promised*."

"I know, and I'm sorry." Contritely, she added, "But it's just a little camping trip—nothing like a banquet or a reception line. This will be fun, Hick. We'll be getting into the backcountry wilderness that tourists rarely get to see." She smiled happily. "And it's really quite fitting, you know, dear. Uncle Teddy camped in Yosemite with John Muir in 1903. Just thirty-one years ago this summer."

"Another chapter of Roosevelt history," I growled. "There's no getting away from it." I was only half-teasing.

Ella had dug up some corduroy trousers and a blue plaid shirt for me, and Old Blue and I spent several hours of every day together. By the end of our time at the ranch, I was reasonably comfortable in the saddle. I loved the slow, sunlit days, the cool star-studded nights, the noisy hours with the kids, the private times for talks—and even the riding. If Eleanor and I could have spent the rest of our vacation with the Danas, I would have been entirely happy.

But that wasn't the plan. A few days later, a pair of rangers arrived to pick us up in a Park Service car. With one of the rangers following in my Plymouth, the other drove us over Tioga Pass to Yosemite's Tuolumne Meadows. There, we met the escort for our backcountry camping trip: four rangers plus Chief Ranger Nelson, seven saddle horses, and five—*five!*—pack animals loaded with gear. A little camping trip? More like an African safari.

If Eleanor was surprised, she hid it very well, greeting Ranger Nelson with what seemed like genuine pleasure and shaking hands with each of the other rangers. That's when it dawned on me that she had been expecting this, or something like it, and hadn't wanted to tell me, perhaps because she didn't want to spoil the time we had together at the ranch. But the size of the rangers' entourage and their respectful attention to her was a reminder to me (as if I needed one) of just who my companion was: like it or not, the most famous woman in the United States—perhaps in the world. The awareness was disconcerting and added to my uneasiness about the "little camping trip" we were about to take.

The pack train was ready to leave when we arrived, and I was introduced to my mount, a little brown mare named Sweetie Pie. She was easygoing, mild-tempered, and actually fun to ride, although I was grateful for the saddle time at the Arrowhead D. We started off single file and rode for several hours along narrow, straight-up and straight-down mountain trails, to the lowest of the three Young Lakes, lovely alpine lakes above the timberline.

The altitude was bothering me and I was glad that I could sit and watch the rangers—experts, every one of them—set up our camp. The lake was around eleven thousand feet, high enough to be a serious problem for somebody who wasn't used to the mountains, especially since we had gotten up that morning at thirty-seven hundred feet and hadn't paused to acclimate ourselves to the higher altitude.

It didn't bother Eleanor, though. The woman was indefatigable. She helped set up camp that evening, got up at dawn the next morning to swim in the lake's icy waters, then climbed to thirteen thousand feet to help Bill Nelson stock another lake—named Lake Roosevelt, in her honor—with rainbow trout fingerlings. She clearly enjoyed being the center of the rangers' attention. When one of them remarked admiringly on her stamina, she tossed her head. "It's just my constitution. People tell me I'm like my Uncle Teddy, always on the move." She laughed when she said this, giving the ranger the same kind of flirtatious glance I had seen her give Earl Miller. She enjoyed having men admire her. Nothing wrong with that, I thought, although I had to confess to feeling sidelined—and maybe a little bit jealous.

Our camping partners went out of their way to make sure we enjoyed ourselves. We were well fed by a ranger whose flapjacks, fried trout, and baked beans were beyond belief. The days were warm, and while Eleanor rode off with Nelson, I lazed beside the lake. At night, we sat around a blazing campfire and listened to the rangers' stories about wilderness life. An umbrella tent had been set up for us, but we carried our sleeping bags out to the edge of the camp and slept on the ground, with the enchanted stars filling the sky over our heads. The only thing I could wish for was some private time for Eleanor—and a hot bath and change of clothes. I might have to burn Ella's shirt and trousers when we got back to civilization.

On the way back down to the valley, though, my relationship with Sweetie Pie turned sour. We were fording a narrow river when, with a great splash, she stepped off into the deeper water and began to roll. I managed to slide off before she rolled on me, landing in icy water up to my chin. As it turned out, this wasn't the first time the little mare had pulled this dangerous trick. When she saw a pool she liked, she simply stopped to take a bath, no matter who was in the saddle. It would have been kind, I thought darkly, if someone had bothered to warn me.

In Yosemite Valley, Eleanor checked us into the room reserved for us at the luxurious Ahwahnee Hotel while I headed straight to the El Dorado Diggins Bar—wet clothes and all—and ordered a double scotch, followed immediately by a long, hot bath. By the time I was dressed, Eleanor had ordered dinner to be delivered to our suite, which had a magnificent view of Yosemite Falls. We dined on prime rib, with broiled potatoes, fresh asparagus, Yorkshire pudding, and a lemon chèvre cheesecake. And Eleanor ordered an elegant Cabernet for me.

"I didn't realize that the camping trip was going to be such a big effort," she said contritely. She reached across the table for my hand. "I'm sorry, dear. I should have told Tommy it was a mistake."

I took another sip of wine. I was beginning to feel human again, and charitable. "But you had a good time, didn't you? You were obviously in your element. And once I got used to the altitude, I was fine—until Sweetie Pie dumped me in the river. Humiliating, that's what it was."

But now, fortified by a fine dinner and an excellent wine, I could see the humor in it. I chuckled when Eleanor said, quite seriously, "I thought you were clever to dismount so quickly, Hick."

There were no reporters in Yosemite, but the enormous swarms of tourists made up for the lack. They recognized Mrs. Roosevelt immediately and followed us around the park all the next day, snapping photos and demanding autographs. But it wasn't just the recognition that troubled me, or the rudeness of their cameras poked in our faces wherever we went. It was the realization, unavoidable and undeniable, that Eleanor Roosevelt had become a public figure. She was a *personage*, and everyone who had read a newspaper or seen a Movietone newsreel in the past year was half in love with her. They thought she belonged to them.

What's more, she seemed to enjoy the celebrity. She smiled and chatted amiably with those nearby and signed any scrap of paper that was thrust into her hand. For my part, I was struck by the irony of the thing. I was the one who'd encouraged her to seek the spotlight and had coached her in ways to get her message across to the media. She was a star, while I was reaping the predictable harvest of my good intentions.

We left the following morning. "Thank God that's over," I said as I put the Plymouth in gear and began inching forward through the mob of tourists who had gathered in front of the hotel to see us off. The top was down, and Eleanor was smiling and waving cheerily. It took a while to escape the crowds, but at last we were on our way.

"It'll be better in the city," she comforted me, as we swung onto the highway. "We can be anonymous there, dear. We'll be tourists, like everybody else, and have a simply wonderful time."

I had made reservations for us at a hotel on Post Street where I had often stayed. It was a small place and not well known, but very nice, and the manager and I were acquainted. I hadn't mentioned that Mrs. Roosevelt would be accompanying me, but when we checked in, the desk clerk recognized her. We sent the Plymouth off with a valet to a nearby parking garage and were still unpacking when a large basket of flowers arrived from the manager, along with a note promising that he would personally make sure our privacy was respected. When I read it aloud to

Eleanor, she crowed, "There! What did I tell you, Hick? Nobody will know us. We'll just be Jane and Janet Doe."

It was Saturday night in the city, and the streets and restaurants were crowded. While Eleanor attracted a few startled glances, we walked comfortably to my favorite French restaurant, a nondescript little place on Pine known just to the locals. After a wonderful dinner, we took the cable car to the top of Russian Hill, where I pointed out the apartment house where Ellie and I had lived. We walked a few blocks to a tiny green park on Chestnut Street and sat in the silvery moonlight, gazing at Alcatraz Island moored like a lighted ship in the middle of San Francisco Bay.

On the way back to the hotel, we stopped for ice cream sodas. "An evening like this is such a treat," Eleanor said as we slid into a booth. "I can't tell you how glad I'll be when I can be myself again. Sometimes I think I've created this other woman who does the First Lady's job." She turned her straw in her fingers. "She's the president's wife, not me. And I sometimes feel that she's taking over—taking *me* over, I mean."

I wanted to reach for her hand, but I couldn't, not in this public place. I held her glance instead. "That may be the only way to survive," I said. "But you're still *you*. You're not the persona, the performer. Somewhere deep down inside, that's where *you* are, the real you."

"I used to think so, my dear, but now I'm not so sure." She gave me a long, sad look. "She's strong, stronger than I am. She gets stronger every day. I'm afraid that pretty soon, there won't be anything left of *me*."

I was startled. I had never heard her talk about herself in such a way, and it alarmed me. I shook my head. "Don't say that, Eleanor. It's not *true*."

"But what if it is?" she asked quietly. "What if I will never be *me*—the person you loved—ever again?"

That question stopped me, and I didn't know how to answer it. Later, I would think that this was as close as we would ever come to understanding what was happening to her—and not just to her, to *us*. But it was already too late. What was to come had already been set in motion. There was nothing either of us could do about it.

We finished our sodas and started back to the hotel, talking about our plans for the next day. At the corner, we were met by the manager of our hotel. "I didn't tip them off!" he cried frantically, waving his arms. "I swear I didn't! It must have been the bellboy!"

"Oh, no," I groaned, understanding his panic. "How about the alley? Is there a back entrance?"

He shook his head. "I'm afraid they're camped out there, too."

"Well, then, we'll just have to face them," Eleanor said matter-of-factly.

We walked into the hotel lobby and straight into a barrage of exploding flashlamps—not the flashbulbs that photographers use now, but trays of flash powder that ignited with a sharp *bang*, a flash of blinding light, and a puff of acrid smoke. We made it to the elevator with the manager running interference for us and the First Lady smiling nicely and saying, "Thank you, but I'm really rather tired tonight. Thank you, thank you. Perhaps tomorrow. Thank you. Goodnight."

Upstairs, we found another gang of reporters jamming the hallway outside our door. They wouldn't leave until the manager threatened to call the police.

On Sunday morning, it was the same story. We walked a block to the Hotel Clift for breakfast, trailed by another, even larger gaggle of reporters and photographers—and by that time, tourists, as well. After breakfast, the same rabble followed us to Fisherman's Wharf and boarded the ferry to Sausalito with us. It was a gorgeous day, the blue sky decorated with puffs of white cloud, the waters of the bay glinting in the sunlight, and in Sausalito, the resinous scent of eucalyptus, fresh and invigorating. But the clamoring crowd pursued us everywhere we went, and we couldn't get more than a dozen private words.

What's more, I was beginning to be deeply worried. Neither of us had imagined such crowds when Eleanor refused to allow the Secret Service to protect her on our trips. Her husband had been shot at by a crazy anarchist—what's to say there wasn't one of them in the mob around us? I found myself, apprehensive, searching the faces of the people pressing in close to get a glimpse of her. They seemed to be admiring, even loving, but as they reached out to touch her arm or her shoulder, I could feel a knot of fear tightening inside me. If anything happened to her, I would blame myself. And the president of the United States would certainly blame me, too.

I wanted to get the Plymouth and drive up to Twin Peaks to show Eleanor the view, but both of us were tired. And what if we found ourselves at the head of a parade of cars, trailing us to see where we were going? We could create a traffic jam that would keep us out until all hours of the night.

"Better just give it up," I told Eleanor, and she agreed.

At dinner time, we crept down the back stairs and hurried into a taxi waiting in the alley. It took us the few blocks to the St. Francis Hotel, where the menu was too pricey for the average tourist and reporters were not allowed in the dining room. We enjoyed our dinner. But we had to fight our way to the taxi through the noisy crowd waiting on the sidewalk out front, and there was another mob in our hotel lobby. Finally alone, we collapsed into bed, both of us utterly exhausted.

After a few moments, Madam spoke into the darkness, so low I could barely hear her. "I hate to say it, but I think we might as well leave in the morning. Don't you agree, Hick?" She took my hand. On her finger, I could feel the shape of the ring I had given her with such eagerness, such hopes. She sighed. "Now that they've found us, they'll be after us everywhere we go. This isn't what either of us wanted."

I wished I could disagree, but I couldn't. "Well, then, we'd better get up very early," I said at last. "With luck, we can get out of town without being followed." I turned toward her and touched her cheek. It was wet. She was crying.


We weren't followed, as it turned out. But we were utterly dismayed when the Plymouth was brought from the garage where it had been parked. Souvenir hunters had stripped the automobile bare, taking anything they could carry off—sunglasses, chocolate bars, maps, suntan lotion, a pair of my favorite gloves, cigarettes and my lighter, even the dear little St. Christopher medal Eleanor had given me after Bluette took her fatal tumble on that Arizona road.

As we drove off, I kept looking in the rearview mirror, fearing that a gang of reporters might be on our tail, but finally, we were out of the city. We were headed to Portland, where Eleanor was to meet Steve Early and Louis Howe, and then go on with them to meet FDR in Seattle.

The three-day drive up the coast was scenic, calm, and without incident—until nearly the end. We managed to visit Muir Woods without attracting the attention of tourists and spent a lovely, almost-anonymous night at the guest lodge on the southwest rim of Crater Lake, where we sat under a pine tree, holding hands and watching the full moon swim in the silver waters.

The next evening, we stopped at the Pilot Butte Inn, a lovely rustic hotel in Bend, Oregon. We'd been driving with the top down and both of us were sunburned and wind-blown. We were hungry, too, so we didn't bother to wash off the dust—we just headed for the dining room. But at the door, the hotel manager stopped us. "Mrs. Roosevelt!" he cried excitedly. "I was told you were here! Several people have seen you and the news is spreading fast. Everybody loves you, you know, for all you're doing to help people. They'll want to meet you."

Eleanor shook her head. "Thank you but no, please. My friend and I have been driving all day and we have to leave early in the morning. We'd just like a quiet dinner, if you don't mind."

In the dining room, we sat down, alone, to a breathtaking view of snowy mountains painted pink and lavender by the setting sun and a splendid dinner of planked trout fresh from the Deschutes River, not twenty yards away. But we stepped out of the privacy of the dining room and into the apologetic arms of the mayor, who had been powerless to turn away the town fathers and mothers who came to greet their unexpected guest. The reception line stretched across the hotel lobby and out the front door. While I stood and watched, the First Lady shook everyone's hand and hugged those who wanted to tell her how much they admired and loved her.

Back in our hotel room at last, she sat down on the bed and began to cry, low, soft sobs that wrenched my heart. I sat beside her and put my arm around her shoulders.

"It's no use, is it?" she said, after a few moments. "We can't do this again, Hick. It's not just the press, it's *everybody*. They'll hound us as long as Franklin is in the White House. And even after, I imagine."

I pulled her closer, her face against my shoulder. I could see myself, see her, as if from a great distance, huddled together, holding each other against the forces that threatened to pull us apart.

"No," I said, very softly. "We can't. We can't do it again." The words were a physical pain.

She sat back a little, her eyes on my face. "But it's not the end, Hick. For *us*, I mean. I don't want us to change. Tell me we can wait it out, until this is over. Until I'm *me* again."

I picked up her hand and kissed her ring, but I couldn't tell her what I already knew. It wasn't the end, and with luck, we might be able to wait it out. We could hope that her celebrity—her notoriety, really—would fade after she was out of the White House, and people would forget who she was. Perhaps they would even forget that they loved her.

No, it wasn't the end. But it was the end of the beginning. And that was what I could not say.

# Part Four

1935–1945

# CHAPTER THIRTEEN

# Loving Eleanor

Love changes, you know. It's silly to believe that people love some-one in the very same way day in and day out, year after year. Circumstances change, needs change. Lovers change and grow, discovering new desires and new energies, dreaming new dreams. The California trip changed me. It showed me very clearly what I wanted, what I needed, what I dreamed of: a relationship that was the center and anchor of my life, not a bottom-of-the-page foot-note to a busy day's activities. I accepted the fact that an infinite succession of things pulled Eleanor in hundreds of different directions, and it was hard to imagine a future when she would no longer be a national celebrity. I loved her still, but loving Eleanor was loving a dervish, whirling, whirling, whirling away.

After we said goodbye in Portland, she wrote in much the same way she always had. *Darling, how I hated to have you go. It is still a pretty bad ache and I've thought of you all day.* Later: *I wish I could lie down beside you tonight and take you in my arms.* She looked forward to the autumn months, she wrote, when we would be together in New York, *quietly and unobserved.* I found her phrase ironic. She knew now what I had always known: how important it was to our friendship to be *unobserved.*

I also knew, if she didn't, that our relationship had sailed into new waters. I had felt sidelined and even jealous during our camping trip in Yosemite, while Eleanor had enjoyed the young rangers' admiring attentions. And I knew that even though she was annoyed at the crowds of reporters and tourists in San Francisco, some part of her was fed by their attention. I was afraid she'd been right when she said she felt as if she was being taken over by the woman who does the First Lady's job.

I was reminded of this one night at the White House. It was late October, and I was there for a few days between trips for Hopkins. She changed her schedule so we could be together, but I didn't get the message and we missed our connection. Her response made me aware that she might be thinking of me as just another of the First Lady's appointments. *I was back at 6:45*, she wrote later that evening, *and I lay on the sofa and read from 7:15 to 7:45 which was the time I had planned for you.*

The time she—or the First Lady—had planned for me? Well, as I said, love changes, lovers change. One day you look at the person you loved and see someone you haven't seen before—and then you look at yourself and you see that you are altered as well. Eleanor was becoming someone else, and while I continued to love her—yes, deeply and tenderly—I began to think it was time to find a new direction for myself.

I had been pushed into the FERA job by Louis Howe and FDR because it served their purposes to get me out of Washington. But the work had quickly become absorbing, and it wasn't long before I realized that I had a unique, firsthand view of the effects of the Depression in all parts of the country—east to west, north to south —and on all levels of American society, from the poorest to the richest. What I saw wasn't pretty, and it tore at my heart like a thousand lions. But someone had to take the journey, someone had to look at what was out there and tell the truth about it, the whole, ugly truth. I began to understand that the reports I was writing provided a documentary history of a remarkable era, an era that should never be forgotten.

But I was already thinking seriously about what I would do when the FERA money ran out, as it was bound to do. I couldn't go back to newspaper reporting, for the same reasons I had left the AP in the first place. I could have found a job in the burgeoning federal bureaucracy—Harry Hopkins would have been glad to recommend me—but if I wanted a new direction, Washington wasn't the place to find it.

Then Harry came through by sending me to work in New York City. The sublease on my Mitchell Place apartment had expired, so Prinz and I were back home. 1936 was an election year, and while the president was playing his cards close to his chest, Eleanor was certain that he intended to be the Democrats' nominee. For her part, she might protest that she would love nothing better than to be simple Jane Doe and live in the country with me. (*I've always thought of it as in the country,* she had written, *but I don't think we ever decided on the kind of house we wanted.*) But it was clear that she hadn't tackled all of the items on her progressive agenda. Still playing the role of a reluctant First Lady, she might say that she wished Franklin wouldn't run. But Tommy and I both knew that secretly, she was hoping for four more years of getting things done.

For myself, I had thought of something else. Internationally, there were dark rumblings of troubles to come. Mussolini's occupation of Ethiopia and Franco's fascist challenge in Spain were making international headlines, and it was clear that these conflicts might well become a dress rehearsal for another world war. Before it was over, a half-dozen well-known American writers and journalists would make their way to the Spanish front: John Dos Passos,

Josephine Herbst, Lillian Hellman, Langston Hughes, Ernest Hemingway and his friend (and mine) Martha Gellhorn. It was Martha—a compatriot of mine at FERA and, later, Ernest Hemingway's third wife—who first suggested that I put my reporting skills to work as a foreign correspondent.

As it happened, I knew just who to ask for advice: my old friend Mark Sainsbury, who had worked out of the New York AP office when I was there and who was now covering the Italian-Ethiopian conflict for the wire service. Mark knew my work and offered to help me get credentialed.

"It's true that all the world's a stage," he told me that spring, "and we're all just goddamned bit players. But this particular stage has a lot more action than most, and there's plenty of room for walk-ons. You'd love it, Hick. And you'd be good at it. Very good."

In the beginning, Eleanor hadn't liked the idea, but when the Spanish conflict became more heated, she wrote, *I think the war idea is a good one*, and offered to speak to Roy Howard, one of the owners of the Scripps-Howard newspaper syndicate.

"Of course," I told her. "Please do." And I began to think seriously about getting back into the business as a war correspondent.

But before that could happen, something else did—something beyond my control. I had just left on another investigative assignment in the Midwest when I found myself suddenly slammed flat, barely able to summon the energy to get dressed. When I got to a doctor, I was disheartened to hear that the diabetes I had been living with for the past decade was going to require not just diet control, but insulin. Not the kind of thing I could pack in a suitcase and take to war-torn Spain. I was disconsolate, but in the end I had to accept it. Diabetes was going to limit my options.

So I would finish out the year for FERA and then look into a possibility that Tommy had suggested, a job on the World's Fair publicity staff. That appealed to me because I could work and live in New York. And the World's Fair was one of the more exciting things going on at the time, with its "I Have Seen the Future" theme and its portrayal of science as the bridge between the past doleful decade and an exciting tomorrow.

But in the meantime, something else happened. Or rather, someone.

Her name was Alicent Holt, and she had been my favorite teacher at Battle Creek High School, twenty-five years earlier. I was working in Michigan for FERA in the spring of 1936, and when I heard that Miss Holt was recuperating from surgery in a hospital in Grand Rapids, I dropped in to see her. Her delighted, open-arm welcome quite took me aback. She remembered my school-girl nickname, Rena—short for Lorena—and she saw "her" Rena as having created an impressively successful professional life. Seeing Rena through her eyes, I could be a little impressed as well, which lifted my spirits and (I confess) made me regard her with a greater interest.

From my teenaged perspective, Miss Holt had been a sophisticated older woman, and I had been silently, secretly smitten by her intelligence and experience. But, in fact, she was only five years older than I, with a fragile, delicate prettiness and quiet confidence that age only underscored. Alix (as she soon began signing her letters to me) had never married and was still teaching English. When I sent her white roses on her birthday a couple of months after seeing her in Grand Rapids, she was thrilled. It was, she said, the first time she had ever been remembered in such a tender way.

Looking back, I think now that tenderness was the mooring of our friendship, which gave me what I most needed in those uncertain months—and what Alix needed, too. For in the lovely weekends and longer holidays that we spent together, we were not quite ourselves, or rather, I should say, we were somewhat more. Alix was more adventuresome and funnier and more flirtatious than Alicent. And Rena—Carissima, as I soon became in her letters —was more tender and observant, less eager to take offense, less argumentative than I. Alix and Carissima took care of one another, each with an attentive awareness of the other's needs. Alix would write: *We will do all we can for each other, and be happy in this good friendship of ours... Dear, I love you a very great deal, and need you and your love more than that!*

There it was again, loving and needing. It felt very good to know that Alix needed me, for Eleanor needed me less. When we first came together, I had been the one—the *only* one—who bolstered her, supported her, made her feel strong and competent, admired and even adored. Now, there were others around her who could satisfy almost all those needs. And I didn't have to share Alix, which was a boon. When we set aside time to spend together, we made each other the center of attention, not letting anything or anyone else intervene—a relief to me, after the infinite distractions that pursued Eleanor.

But we both knew, without saying so, that this friendship had its limitations and that it might not last long. While Alix was well read, she had little experience of the world outside her Midwestern classroom. Beyond books and music—and our relationship—we shared only a few common interests. I could almost see the end of our affair in its beginning, and she understood. *I suspect I shall love you*, she wrote with a wry understanding, *as long as you do me, at least, and perhaps a little bit longer.*

That was the summer of the 1936 presidential campaign, and I was traveling in the Midwest for FERA. Remembering the California debacle, I didn't even try to arrange a vacation with Eleanor, who would be constantly on the telephone, writing letters, or working on her daily "My Day" column, for which she was now earning $1,000 a month. Instead, Alix and I spent a week at a resort on the shore of Lake Superior. It was exactly what I needed, as I wrote to Eleanor, rubbing it in just a little: "So quiet. So very, very restful…"

Eleanor's response to my friendship with Alix was interesting. While I was in Minnesota, she wrote me wistfully, *I miss you, dear, and often wish I were Alix.* I did, too, but I refused to tell her so. When I couldn't accept her last-minute invitation for a weekend in Chicago because Alix and I had already planned to drive up-country, she replied with asperity, *Are you taking the absent treatment because it helps?* And when I skipped writing for several days, she sent me a snappish note: *I shall be glad to get some letters from you tonight! I'm not accustomed to being so long without news and I don't like it.* That one, I thought, sounded more like the First Lady than Eleanor.

But while there might be someone else in my life, loving Eleanor was still at the center of it. Our daily letters continued to be a comfort to me, and to her as well. The campaign that ramped up in the summer and fall of 1936 was much nastier than the 1932 campaign, and our friendship became a refuge for her. We were together for a week at Val-Kill at the end of August—Nan and Marion were gone—but the cottage was no longer the relaxing retreat it had once been for her. These days, she never seemed to stop working. Tommy had come to Val-Kill with her so the two of them could manage her correspondence and her column. Hours we might have spent reading and walking through the woods vanished into her work.

And there was the vexed issue of her fraying relationship with Nan Cook and Marion Dickerman. The furniture factory had never been a paying concern, and the three women finally closed the business. Eleanor took over the large workshop behind the cottage and renovated it into a home for herself, with an apartment for Tommy and plenty of space for guests. The next year, there would be an irrevocable break that would shatter their fifteen-year friendship. Nan and Marion would keep the cottage for a while, living uncomfortably on the fringe of the Roosevelt activities, then sell it to Eleanor and move to Connecticut.

Even more calamitously, Louis Howe was dead. He had been sidelined by illness during the last two years of FDR's first term and died in April. If he had been in charge of the 1936 campaign, the First Lady would have played an active role. But her out-spokenness had made her the target of a vicious press, and the president's new advisers kept her under wraps. The loudest criti-cisms had come from Southern newspapers after the White House garden party she had hosted for students of the National Industrial School, all girls, all black. Even friendly newspapers, like the *New York Times*, wrote that she was "both an asset and a liability" to the campaign. And a Republican campaign button declared, "We don't want Eleanor, either!"

As a result, her role in the campaign was reduced to standing behind the president, a smile pasted across her face. To me, she wrote, *How I hate being a show*, adding with a wry self-approval, *but I'm doing it so nicely.* In her memoir, *This Is My Story*, she remarked, "It is as though you lived two lives, one of your own and the other which belonged to the circumstances that surround you." To a reporter who asked about her future plans, she said bleakly, "My dear, I don't know. I go where the president goes."

The president went back to the White House, riding on a landslide of 62 percent of the popular vote. Eleanor would be in Washington for another four years. Shortly after, FDR celebrated by sailing to Samoa and Hawaii on the USS *Indianapolis*, while Madam and I enjoyed the vacation we had missed in the summer. We spent several very quiet days together at the White House, then drove, alone, to Arthurdale. We stopped on the way back to visit friends in Virginia and had only a few minor skirmishes with the press. For me, it was a wonderful time. The erotic passions of my obsession with Madam had ebbed. I was finding it easier now to love Eleanor, and to include the First Lady in that love.

A week after the election, I was interviewed by Grover Whalen, the chairman of the 1939 World's Fair planning committee. When he offered me a publicist's job at $5,200 a year, I took it. But I wouldn't start until early in 1937, so I spent the two intervening months on a book project.

Harry Hopkins and Mrs. R had both encouraged me to organize my FERA reports into a book about the Depression. Eleanor's literary agent, George Bye, thought it was a "grand idea" and encouraged me to get started on it. Staying at the White House, I settled down to several weeks of writing and reading, not just my reports to Harry, but my letters to Eleanor, which also contained a great many details about the places I'd been and the things I had seen.

Ah, there they are again, the letters. She had kept them all, and I stumbled onto a small packet of the earliest ones, written during the four months between the 1932 election and her move to the White House. Reading them made me weep for what we had shared, and even though the passion may have diminished (even the hottest, brightest blaze burns itself out, sooner or later), I knew that love still endured. *Dear,* I wrote to her, *whatever may have happened since—whatever may happen in the future—I was certainly happy*

*those days, much happier, I believe than many people ever are in all their lives.*
*You gave me that, and I'm deeply grateful... I love you—now and always.*

Aside from what the letters revealed about the course of our love affair, they also contained a great deal of important information about the lives of two energetic women, each engaged in important work during one of the most difficult periods in America's history. But I never wrote the book about the Depression. George Bye shook his head when he read the sample manuscript. "It's too depressing," he said. "It'll never sell." Perhaps he was right—or perhaps not. If I had been smart, I would have given the manuscript to a couple of other agents for a look. But I had a demanding new job and very little time to write anything of my own.

There would come a time when Americans would be too ironic about themselves to take a World's Fair seriously. But at the end of the Thirties, people turned to the Fair to lift them out of their personal depressions. For many, it was a cheering landmark in an otherwise bleak decade. It was for me, too. While I wasn't exactly challenged by public relations work and the office politics were often tiresome, I was glad to be relieved of the constant traveling and, of course, grateful for the paycheck.

And I loved being back in New York. I was working in the Empire State Building, where the World's Fair Corporation had its temporary offices, and then later, in the new administration building at Flushing Meadows. There, my office had a view of the twelve-hundred-acre site, where the spire of the Trylon and the enormous globe of the Perisphere seemed to fill the sky. And on my desk were all the astonishments the Fair would offer when it opened in the spring of 1939.

There would be fluorescent lights, nylon stockings, and artificially generated bolts of lightning. There would be a twelve-foot-high electric shaver, electronic milking machines, and robots with movable fingers and their own intentions. In one pavilion, an aproned "Mrs. Drudge" would plod through her kitchen chores the old-fashioned way, while "Mrs. Modern" (wearing a revealing red cocktail dress and a stylish perm) would fry an egg in thirty seconds in her revolutionary microwave oven and breeze through the kitchen chores with her amazing Westinghouse electric dishwasher. In the same pavilion, a strange new semicircular sofa would transform the Living Room of Tomorrow into a home theater, so the American family could watch the greatest miracle of all, the RCA television set.

Everybody who left the Fair would wear an "I Have Seen the Future" button and believe that they had been afforded a dazzling glimpse of the world that was to come. Back home in *their* world, things weren't all that good yet—some would even find it difficult to come up with the seventy-five-cent entrance fee. But the material promises of the Fair would give them the hope that things would be better and brighter someday, and that hope might help them endure the unhappiness that clouded their lives today. I might sometimes feel that the Fair's promises were trivial and even false, and that electric dishwashers and sofas would not guarantee a better world. But I was paid to do a job, and I did it as well as I could.

In the meantime, something every bit as wonderful and amazing as the World's Fair had happened for me, a surprising gift of that otherwise disastrous California trip. After leaving Eleanor in Portland, I had driven back east, stopping at the Arrowhead D and spending a few days getting better acquainted with Bill and Ella Dana. A month or two after I began working at the Fair, they telephoned me. They had left the ranch and were back home at the family estate on the Atlantic side of Long Island, near the village of Mastic. Would I come for the weekend? Of course I would.

The huge Dana estate—called Moss Lots, on the Forge River estuary, along Poospatuck Creek—was only two hours by car from the city. Built by Bill's grandfather in the 1890s, the sprawling house was reached by a lane that wound through dense pine and coastal oak forest, then opened onto a sloping seaside meadow and a heart-stopping view of the great, gray Atlantic. Bill had inherited the estate and the Nevada ranch from his wealthy publisher father, along with the *Financial Chronicle*, a well-known Wall Street journal. But he preferred boats, horses, and dogs to a publisher's desk and rarely went into the city. Ella was lovely, generous, and impulsive. From her parents, she had inherited the neighboring Floyd estate and joked that Bill had married the girl next door.

The three of us got along famously. They invited me for a weekend, and then another and another, and before I quite understood what was happening, Ella had offered to rent me a house—the Little House—on the Floyd estate. Small only by comparison to the Danas' baronial mansion, it was surrounded by own three secluded acres. The living area was filled with sunshine, the pine-walled kitchen was large and convenient, and the dining room ceiling was beamed with dark oak. There was an upstairs deck, two screened porches, three brick fireplaces, four gabled bedrooms, and a library.

A library! with built-in bookshelves, polished pine floors, and its very own fireplace. I loved it. The house would be furnished, Ella said (she had *lots* of furniture in her attic), and newly painted (she loved to decorate, and this house would be a special treat for her). Clarence Ross, their handyman and caretaker, lived nearby with Annie, his wife. Ella would have him do a little landscaping, mow the grass, and tidy up the garden—if only I would agree to come and live there on weekends.

I tried to refuse. The Little House—furnished, painted, and landscaped—was a dream, so much more wonderful than anything the hired girl and I could have imagined for ourselves. But Ella wouldn't take no for an answer. The place desperately needed to be lived in, she said, but she wanted to rent it to someone who would appreciate the seclusion. There was no telephone, which made it even more appealing to me. It would be a perfect weekend retreat. It would give me the peace and quiet I needed as a refuge from the city and the stress of the work at the World's Fair.

Because we were friends, Ella was asking only thirty-five dollars a month, half what I was paying for Mitchell Place and much less than she would get if she advertised the place. But I had taken a pay cut to work at the Fair and I wasn't sure I could swing it alone. The rent would be much more manageable if I could share it with someone. And since the Little House was certainly large enough for two, sharing it would also be quite practical. As it happened, I knew exactly who to ask. Howard Haycraft, whom I had known since my days with the Associated Press.

A fellow Minnesotan and a dozen years my junior, Howard was like a younger brother. He worked as an editor at the Wilson publishing company and in his spare time was writing a book called *Murder for Pleasure*. (It would be published in 1941 and hailed, as time went on, as one of the very best histories of the mystery genre.) He and his girlfriend, Molly, and I had dinner together at least once a week and the two of us—Howard and I—often spent Sunday afternoons listening to Mahler and Wagner recordings. The previous summer, he and Molly and I had shared a week at a cottage at Oak Beach.

Howard and I went out to the Little House for a weekend in

March. He and Bill went fishing; I helped Ella hang new drapes and cook the fish the guys brought home. Howard liked the place just as much as I did, and before we went back to the city, we had agreed to share the Little House. It would be my personal paradise for the next eighteen years.

But still and always in those months, there was Eleanor. Our letters continued, four or five, even six a week. We saw one another whenever she was in New York and could break free of the infinite succession of things—her endless list of places to go, people to see, causes to support. "Eleanor Everywhere," some wag called her, and the name stuck. One of my favorite *New Yorker* cartoons of the time shows two miners, shoveling coal in a mine shaft. One looks up and says, "For gosh sakes, here comes Mrs. Roosevelt!" Another cartoon showed her on a magic carpet, her typewriter on her lap, flying around a spinning globe. Her stamina seemed boundless, her energies had become the stuff of legend. Even Tommy—who looked older and more frazzled every time I saw her—confessed that she simply couldn't keep up with "the Boss." Loving Eleanor came with a price tag, and Tommy (whose husband would divorce her the next year on grounds of "voluntary separation") was paying a heavy cost.

Eleanor and I were often together. Early that year, I spent several days at the White House for some Democratic party doings, dressing up in my new black velvet gown—although Bill Dana (who was also there) later told Ella that I looked "like a royal Bengal tiger with the sulks." In March, Eleanor and I spent ten pretty days in the Smoky Mountains (she hiked, I didn't) and then drove on to Asheville and Charleston. We avoided tourists and the press and were almost able to recapture—or at least to remember

—the romantic magic of our early months together. Then she went back to the White House and I went on the road for Hopkins.

And there were lovely evenings in New York, where we enjoyed dinners, the theater, and opera. In October, she came to the Little House for her birthday weekend—one of our very best times together. She asked me to reconsider going with her to Val-Kill, but I refused. "There's just no privacy there," I told her, "too many people and altogether too much friction. Sorry, dear, but I covet my peace and quiet."

Later that month, Harper & Brothers published her memoir— *This Is My Story*—and dispatched her on a lengthy speaking and book-signing tour, with Tommy going along to help manage the practical details. When she got back, we celebrated an early Christmas together with a tender sweetness that cast a lovely halo around the holiday. As always, loving Eleanor was a work in progress.

I had the usual professional ups and downs that year and the next, the downs mostly precipitated by the stress of office politics, but also by my health. Diabetes isn't easy to cope with. It was harder in those days, before insulin was perfected and the emotional effects of blood sugar spikes were still a mystery. I was often prickly, swearing at the traffic, biting the heads off my colleagues, and feeling sometimes that my life wasn't worth a helluva lot. I used my letters to Eleanor to blow off steam. As I read them now, noting my strings of whiney complaints, I can see what a difficult time I was having on the job, doing PR work I didn't always entirely believe in, with people I didn't always like.

But those unhappy weeks were balanced by the restful seclusion of weekends at the Little House, the home of my heart, where I could relax and be myself. I was delighted when Eleanor promised to spend a full week with me there the next summer, and I couldn't help hoping that the week might rekindle our dream of living together someday, somewhere. She changed the date a half-dozen times, but it finally happened in late July. We had picnics on the beach at Fire Island, dinners with Bill and Ella and Clarence and Annie, walks in the woods and along the shore with Prinz, and sunsets and sunrises and splendid weather.

And it was just the two of us, since Eleanor hadn't brought Tommy. I had put my foot down on this issue months before, in spite of the fact that I was very fond of Tommy. *The reason is,* I wrote, *that when you and Tommy are together you can never forget your darned jobs for more than fifteen minutes at a time.* But Eleanor fretted without her work, and especially without the telephone. "It's like being cut off from the world," she complained.

We tried to laugh about it, but our time together showed both of us how hard it was for her to disconnect from her infinite succession of projects and showed me how fruitless it was to try to hold onto our old dream. If we lived together, I would have to live *her* kind of life. At one time, I would have said yes to that proposition and happily buried my needs in the service of hers. But I was no longer the woman who had fallen in love with Eleanor six years before, just as she was no longer the woman I'd fallen in love with. When our vacation was over, I went back to Mitchell Place and my friends and my work with a stronger sense of being my own person, still loving Eleanor but in a different, more sisterly way.

She also had her own homes now. She kept her rented apartment on Eleventh Street in Greenwich Village, and her renovation of the Val-Kill furniture workshop was finally finished and she was able to invite friends to stay there. The Sixty-Fifth Street townhouse was rented and would soon be sold. And the White House seemed, she said, to be less like a home and more like a hotel, where she stayed when she was expected to perform her official duties. It had always been divided into two courts—FDR's and

ER's—but now that Louis Howe was dead, the division seemed deeper and colder. Louis had connected Eleanor and Franklin, and now there was no one to bridge the gap between them. Even Harry Hopkins, who had originally been her friend, now found it politically expedient to become FDR's man, and Missy was constantly on hand to meet the president's every demand.

Still, things seemed a little easier for her. She was looking forward to the end of the second term and a return, she hoped, to something like a normal life. FDR hadn't told his advisors whether or not he would try to break the no-third-term tradition, which wasn't embodied into law until the term limit amendment was ratified in 1951. He had told Eleanor privately, however, that he wouldn't seek the nomination again—unless a major war broke out and he felt obliged to stay at the helm.

But she shook her head sadly when she told me this one evening over dinner at Mitchell Place. She understood that FDR had said only that he wouldn't *seek* the nomination. He hadn't said he would refuse a draft. And whenever she looked in the direction of Europe, she could see the clouds of war, dark and ominous on the horizon.

The headlines in those years were grim. In July 1937, Amelia Earhart and her navigator, Fred Noonan, disappeared in the Pacific. A massive naval search was launched, but there was no sign of her plane. I heard some whispered speculation that FDR had sent her on a secret mission to spy on the Japanese, but even though I was always suspicious of his left hook, I didn't believe it.

But the international situation was clearly deteriorating. In the same month that Amelia was lost, Japan invaded China. Early the next year, German troops marched into Austria, and Hitler annexed it as part of the German Reich. Six months later, Italy ordered Jews to leave, and two months later, Nazi troops and civilians destroyed Jewish shops, burned synagogues, and killed Jews in a violent rampage across Germany and Austria that came to be known as "Kristallnacht," the "Night of Broken Glass."

And on September 21, a hurricane swept the East Coast of the U.S. and changed the lives of everyone who lived there.

Eleanor and I had been out to lunch that Wednesday when we heard a newsboy hawking the *Daily News*: a hurricane was blowing in our direction. The Weather Bureau had been predicting that it was going to hit Miami, but it had suddenly shifted to the north and was barreling up the coast. The "Yankee Clipper," they were calling it. But like everyone else in the city, I was skeptical.

"A hurricane in New England?" I said to Eleanor. "I don't think so."

"Not very likely," she replied, and we both agreed that we had other things to worry about. Still, I was concerned for Prinz. During the week, he stayed in the yard at the Little House, and Clarence and Bill looked after him. His kennel would keep him dry and warm in an ordinary storm, and if it got worse than that, I hoped they would remember to bring him in.

New York City escaped the worst of the wind and storm surge. That night, there were sixty-mile-per-hour winds in Central Park and twice that on top of the Empire State Building. The storm surge was nearly nine feet at the Battery and in New York Harbor, the waters rose seven feet in thirty minutes. Still, other than street flooding and closed schools, the damage was minor.

It was a different story across New England, where hundreds were dead, buildings were destroyed, roads were impassable, and all the wires were down. The newspapers reported that the eye of the hurricane had come ashore at Bayport, some twenty miles west of the Little House, and that the towns along the Atlantic coast of Long Island had been swept away by a tidal wave.

I was frantic with worry but the phones were out and I couldn't reach the Danas to find out what had happened. The fair site had been damaged, too, so it was late afternoon before I could get away from Flushing Meadows. Normally, the drive wasn't much more than an hour, but it was slow going on the Montauk Highway, which was littered with storm debris. Trees were down everywhere, the Mastic railroad station was destroyed, and sections of the Long Island Railroad tracks looked as if they had been ripped up by a bulldozer. At the entrance to the Dana estate, a huge pine tree lay across the road, and when I got out of the car, the stillness stunned me. The nights there were always filled with the sounds of tree frogs and katydids and night birds. Now, there was only silence, except for the thudding of my heart in my ears. I had covered a great many disasters as a reporter, but I had seen nothing like this.

It took me an hour to climb over and crawl under and scramble through the downed trees to the Dana mansion, just two miles away. Twilight was falling and the farther I went, the more hopeless it seemed. If the storm had been so terrible here in the thick woods, how could anything have survived close to the shore, where the houses stood? But then I saw a light and heard the sound of a motor, and ten minutes later, I stumbled into the meadow, where a generator was running, providing electricity for Bill and Ella's house.

And there they all were, alive and unharmed—even Prinz. During the storm, Clarence and Annie had taken him to join Bill and Ella in the mansion, which suffered almost no damage from the wind. It was the flooding that did the most harm. The hurricane had coincided with the autumnal equinox and a full moon, producing tides as high as eighteen feet across Long Island. My Little House had several inches of water and all of its lovely old locust trees were gone, utterly gone. But my friends and Prinz, dear Prinz, were safe, and that was all I cared about.

The very next week, that disaster was capped by another, even more devastating. In Munich, Neville Chamberlain of Great Britain and Edward Daladier of France agreed to Hitler's demand that part of Czechoslovakia be ceded to Germany. In return, Hitler pledged not to lay claim to the rest of that country. But in England, Virginia Woolf's husband Leonard called it a "peace without honor," and Winston Churchill thought it no peace at all. "We have sustained a defeat without a war," he said somberly. "This is only the beginning." Trying to convince an isolationist Congress of the threat of war, FDR replied, "Normal practices of diplomacy are of no possible use in dealing with international outlaws." From Washington, Eleanor wrote to me: *F said he's done the last thing he can do and we can all pray.*

As the year neared its dark close, a different door opened for me—that is, it opened a crack just wide enough for me to see through. Molly Dewson, the powerhouse head of the Women's Democratic Committee, would be leaving her post in another year. Eleanor asked if I would consider it.

I would. In fact, there was nothing I would rather do. The Fair would be opening in April, and after that, the excitement would go out of my work, like air out of a balloon, and I'd be left with just the daily hurly-burly. But it was a good thing I wasn't in any great hurry to make a move. It took a year for the door to fully open.

And in the meantime, 1939 had brought nothing but gloom, for Bill Dana was dead. A heart attack, according to the *New York Times* obituary. But his family and friends knew that Bill—cheerful, amiable Bill, always smiling, always helpful—had put a gun to his head. He was in trouble with the IRS over a mistake his accountant had made years ago, and he owed so much in back taxes that he and Ella would have to sell both Moss Lots and the Arrowhead D to pay it off. His life insurance was enough to cover the debt, though, and until the check arrived, Ella crept around the place, pale and ghost-like. A few months later, she went out to Nevada and when she came back, she brought with her a blue-eyed cowboy, fifteen years her junior.

I know from experience that hearts have their own will, but I had admired and cared for Bill and I was saddened that Ella could so easily forget him. When I told Eleanor how I felt, she replied archly, "I'm amused by Ella's cowboy. She deserves to be happy, doesn't she? Why should anyone care who she loves?"

Eleanor may have been thinking of something else when she made that remark. For by that time, she had already begun a relationship with young Joe Lash—romantic on her part, quite practical on his. She would love Joe with as much intensity as she had once loved me, although (I think) without the physical intimacies that marked our own first years together.

Was I jealous? Yes, certainly, although I already understood, and very clearly, that our friendship would never again be as richly passionate and consuming as it was in that first year. But my jealousy was outweighed by my concern, for I felt that loving this young man was personally and politically perilous to her, a threat to his welfare, and a hazard to both of them.

Still, she loved him. And her love, like the irresistible storm tide that had swept across Long Island, would sweep across Joe's world and turn it upside down. He would discover, as I had, that loving Eleanor—and being loved by her—was utterly life-changing

# CHAPTER FOURTEEN

# On the Record

Eleanor met Joseph Lash on the train to Washington in late 1939. Joe, who was Jewish, was good-looking, tall, slender, and nearly the same age as her favorite son Elliott. Politically idealistic, he was executive secretary of the American Student Union, a coalition of radical youth groups that HUAC—the House Un-American Activities Committee—suspected to be communist sympathizers. Eleanor took him home to dinner and introduced him to the president. Joe visited the White House several times that winter, and as 1939 turned into 1940, she invited him to Val-Kill, where they spent hours talking beside the fire and in the woods. They met often in New York and Washington, and the next year, she took him and his youth group to Campobello for a month.

Tommy, who rarely criticized her boss, felt that Eleanor was flinging herself into a relationship that would endanger both her and Lash. "She *says* her feeling is maternal," she told me worriedly, "but she's not fooling me one bit. And while Joe is a nice enough boy, he's an opportunist. All this attention from the First Lady—who knows how he'll use it?"

I frowned. "What does Anna think?" Eleanor and her daughter were close, and Anna's opinion might carry some weight.

"Anna has already told her mother that this is ill-advised, and it hasn't helped." Tommy grew plaintive. "The Boss listens to you, Hick. Please talk some sense into her."

But if Anna couldn't change her mother's mind—or her heart, rather—I would surely fail. And what the hell could I say that wouldn't sound like a mouthful of sour grapes? There was nothing that Tommy or I could do but hold our breaths and watch while Eleanor's infatuation with Joe became an obsession. No matter that he was involved with someone else—a German woman named Trude who was married to a well-known New York philanthropist and who worried that she would lose her small children in a divorce. When Joe moved into an apartment in Manhattan, Eleanor sent him an expensive armchair from Wanamaker's. For his birthday, she gave him a new Pontiac convertible. When he was at the White House, she didn't make any secret of her affection, and he seemed to enjoy telling everyone about their friendship. Anyway, it wasn't long before Washington society was buzzing about Eleanor and her young man.

Official Washington had plenty of things to talk about, for 1940 was a whirlpool of international chaos and the United States was caught between a desire for neutrality and the fiery realities of European war. Backed by Hitler and Mussolini, Franco's fascist rebels defeated the Spanish Republican government. Russia invaded Finland. Germany took Czechoslovakia and Poland. France, Great Britain, Canada, Australia, and New Zealand entered the war, while the United States stood on the sidelines. The British fleet was mobilized, the Royal Air Force attacked the German navy, and British mothers began sending their children out of London into the countryside, out of danger.

The door to my new adventure opened with the new year and I stepped into the wild world of politics. I would be working for Charlie Michelson, the publicity director of the Democratic

National Committee, in the DNC's office at the Mayflower. Eleanor suggested that I live at the White House and I accepted. Living there might present a few problems, but it would allow me to give up the pricey Mitchell Place apartment. I would spend my weekends and holidays at the Little House, where Prinz could stay in the care of Clarence and Annie Ross.

And, yes, Eleanor helped me land the DNC job, which was a damn good thing because employment for forty-seven-year-old women was exceedingly scarce. But I do have to say that I was exactly the right person. Charlie wasn't quite sure how to use me at first, but he quickly figured it out and sent me on a cross-country trip to assess the voters' feelings about the possibility of a third term for FDR.

A *third* term? Both Washington and Jefferson had refused third terms, so no other two-term president had dared to consider it. Nobody was sure how the electorate would respond.

I was quite aware of the multiple ironies. When the president was asked whether he would run, he would cast his eyes toward the ceiling and exclaim dramatically, "I am a tired and weary man"— which was very likely true but said nothing about whether he would or wouldn't. The First Lady insisted publically that *she* did not want a third term (which may or may not have been true), but added that if her husband decided to run, she would support him. To me, she wrote: *If FDR wins I'll be glad for him and for the country and if he loses I'll be glad for myself and the kids!* Which put it quite succinctly, I thought. Loving Eleanor as I did, my own personal interest was clear, and everywhere I went, I listened for a chorus of opposition to the idea of a third term. But I had to tell Charlie that it looked like the president had a green light. To Eleanor, I wrote that everything I heard made FDR's nomination seem inevitable: *Darling, I'm sorry, but it's all Third Term!*

Ironies aside, my new job was a tonic, improving my disposition and even my health. I worked with the DNC in Washington during the week and took the train to Long Island on weekends. It was a glorious spring in the Little House garden, especially splendid because I didn't have a radio to tell me that the world was going to hell—as it was. Hitler's forces overran Scandinavia, and his armies simultaneously invaded Holland, Luxembourg, Belgium, and France. In June, the British army was evacuated from Dunkirk by a fragile armada of small boats. On the campaign trail, Eleanor wrote despairingly: *With the state of the world as it is, campaigns seem unimportant.*

But my heart was in that campaign, for I believed (and still do, to this day) that FDR was the only man who could lead the United States through the wilderness of war. When I boarded the Liberty Limited for Chicago ten days before the 1940 Democratic convention began, I was on a mission. A third term wasn't in *my* best interest, but for the sake of the country, I would do everything I could to see that it happened.

Eleanor wasn't expected to attend the convention—at least, not until her husband was nominated. And that nomination, it began to appear, was no sure thing. The fifty thousand delegates at the Chicago Stadium were nearly unanimous in their support of FDR, and he was speedily nominated. But conservative Southern and Midwestern Democrats were fiercely opposed to Henry Wallace, the president's choice as a running mate. They insisted that Wallace was too liberal, and as agriculture secretary, his New Deal farm programs had been disastrous. They threatened revolt unless he withdrew.

It was the First Lady who settled the matter. She was at Val-Kill with Joe Lash when Jim Farley, FDR's convention manager and chair of the DNC, telephoned and asked her to come to Chicago and talk with the delegates. She told Farley no, she wouldn't come. "I have a guest, and I'm very busy," she said.

I was in the room, so Farley handed the phone to me. "She's your friend, Hick—see what you can do."

Eleanor and I talked, she checked with FDR, and a little later, she boarded a plane to Chicago. She was on the platform when Wallace's name was entered into nomination and the rebellious delegates began to boo. But when she stepped up to the podium, the huge audience fell silent. She spoke for only a few moments, without a prepared text, without notes. At the end, she reminded the delegates that, with war everywhere beyond our shores, no one knew what might come.

"This is no ordinary time," she said. "No time for weighing anything except what we can do best for the country."

*No ordinary time.* The organist began to play "God Bless America," the crowd erupted into a wild cheering, and the convention united behind the Roosevelt-Wallace ticket. I was prouder of that amazing woman—that *personage*—than I had ever been. And proud of myself, for whatever role I had played in her growth.

But when the cheering was all done, Eleanor returned to Val-Kill, where Joe Lash was waiting for her. He spent most of that summer at the cottage, and she was there as often as she could get away.

In good conscience, though, I couldn't lecture Eleanor about Joe. That summer—the summer of 1940—was no ordinary time for me, either. I began a relationship that would anchor me during the emotionally difficult years of the war. Did I do this because Eleanor was otherwise preoccupied? Was I feeling left out, abandoned? Did I need someone to ease the pain? Perhaps, but that was long ago and time does dull some darker feelings. All I know is that when I met Judge Marion Harron, I found her irresistibly charming, a smart, funny woman who wasn't afraid of her emotions. She made it easy for me to care for her, and for the next five years, there would be no barrier to our caring, deeply and in all ways, for one another.

Marion had taken her law degree at the University of California at Berkeley, filled several banking positions, worked for the National Recovery Administration, and—when she was only thirty-three—won a much-coveted presidential appointment to a twelve-year term on the U.S. Board of Tax Appeals. As a judge, she traveled extensively across the U.S., hearing tax cases in various cities. In 1942, she was nominated for a vacancy on a federal district court and endorsed by then Attorney General Francis Biddle. But FDR didn't appoint her. I've always wondered if that was another left hook.

In Washington, Marion had an office not far from the White House and lived with her mother in an attractive little home in Chevy Chase. We met at a Democratic fundraiser and it wasn't long before we were seeing each other for lunch when we were both in town. By August, she was taking weekends with me at the Little House, and when we traveled, we exchanged letters. Eleanor met Marion and found her "interesting." But Joe was much more interesting, and that's all there was to it.


I had been relieved when Eleanor suggested that I stay at the White House, for as the probability of war rose, national defense spending ratcheted up and people began crowding into Washington. Apartments were nearly impossible to find and rents were sky-high. I was making six thousand a year, but I couldn't have afforded to rent an apartment in D.C. and keep the Little House. As well, living at the White House gave me the chance to see Eleanor at breakfast when she was in town, or slip across the hall to say goodnight. We were even able, occasionally, to set aside an hour just to sit and talk, as we used to.

And we continued to exchange letters. During 1940, when we were both working on the campaign, we wrote some 350; during the next four years, more than 260. But these letters were different from the earlier ones because our relationship had changed. She was infatuated with Joe, and I had Marion. But Eleanor and I still loved one another, with a sweet, distant echo of the old passion. Her letters to me were filled with her political doings, worries about the international situation, family news—but always there was a personal paragraph of concern about my health, a plan (often more wishful than not) to get together, a regret that the plan had to be canceled. They were signed *Much love* or *Devotedly* or *A world of love, dear.*

My letters to her in those years reported my work activities; my weekends at the Little House; thanks for her frequent gifts (a turkey at Thanksgiving, a box of handkerchiefs, material for a new suit); and White House activities. I signed them *Much, much love, always* and *All my love* and *My love to Tommy and you.* One bright July day in 1943, I sent sad news: *The thing I've dreaded for a long time has finally happened. Dear old Prinz died Wednesday afternoon.* Clarence and I buried him at the Little House, near the path where we always took our walks. We had been together for fifteen years. I would miss him the rest of my life.

But that was later. 1940 brought its own trials and tribulations, and 1941 would be almost too much to bear.

If the president was concerned about my living at the White House, I didn't hear about it, and I was pleased when Eleanor told me, "Franklin says he never even knows when you are in the house." That was the way I wanted it. I tried not to call attention to myself, and I went to some lengths to keep my friends and colleagues from learning my real address. I didn't need to be bombarded by appeals from people who wanted something from the president and might try to use me to get it. I didn't want a return of the old gossip, either. I no longer feared Alice Longworth; even Republicans were offended when she told the press that FDR really stood for "Fuehrer, Duce, Roosevelt" and that she'd "rather vote for Hitler than for Franklin" for a third term. But Eleanor's friendship with Joe Lash (a "former Communist-Front leader, close friend of the First Lady," according to the newspapers) was causing her a great deal of grief. I didn't want to cause her any more.

So I created the fiction that I was living at the Mayflower, where I worked. When someone offered to give me a lift home from a party or a dinner, I said good night in the hotel lobby and when the coast was clear, I walked or taxied to the White House. When my job required me to escort a group of Democratic ladies to the White House for a formal tea, the ushers had instructions not to recognize me as a resident. And if Eleanor happened to be presiding behind the silver teapot, she would smile at me and say, with evident surprise, "Why, hello, Miss Hickok, so good to see you again!"—just as if we hadn't had breakfast together that very morning.

I enjoyed my job, and I enjoyed working for the presidential campaign—not an easy task, because while the First Lady had silenced the party rivalries at the convention, they were out in full force a week or two later, prompting me to stew and fret. *My God, dear,* I wrote to her, *these men are children, small quarrelsome children... They don't deserve to win this election if they keep on the way they've been going.*

And FDR's election was not a sure thing. The isolationists were in full cry, pushing for a negotiated peace in Europe. On August 4, at Soldier Field in Chicago, Charles Lindbergh spoke to forty thousand cheering opponents of the war, most of whom were suspicious of a Britain they saw as irredeemably imperialist and dominated by a discredited ruling class. Conscription was another hotly debated issue. When the House of Representatives stopped bickering and managed to pass the first peace-time draft in the nation's history, the isolationists saw it as another straw in the winds of war.

And while Americans had supported the president during the summer, when Hitler's advances struck fear into their hearts, that support faded in October, when German troops appeared to be stalled. Joe Kennedy, ambassador to Great Britain (and rumored to have his eye on the presidency), was hinting that FDR had made a "secret deal" with Winston Churchill to bring the U.S. into war as soon as he was reelected. FDR was forced to promise an audience that "your boys are not going to be sent into any foreign wars." When his adviser, Sam Rosenman, objected that it was a promise that couldn't be kept, the president replied grimly: "If we're attacked, it's no longer a foreign war."

Given the challenges and uncertainties, and especially given the strength of the GOP candidate, the liberal Republican Wendell Willkie, I wasn't at all sure that FDR would win in 1940. On election night, I couldn't eat any dinner, and when I went to the press headquarters on the Biltmore's mezzanine, I was glad to be kept on the run, gathering the numbers. Willkie had been polling well, gaining momentum in the last weeks with the charge that the president had been scheming for years to take the country to war. The first returns looked bleak. Willkie was winning in small towns and rural areas.

But the balloting in the big states—New York, Illinois, Ohio, Pennsylvania—was heavily Democratic, and I began to breathe easier. By midnight, it was nearly over, and by two a.m., it was only a question of how many states the president would carry. Lynn Bryce, one of my DNC colleagues, invited me to her apartment, where we had two stiff brandies and a plate of bacon and eggs. When I got up around noon, I saw the headlines. FDR had gathered 55 percent of the popular vote and 85 percent of the electoral votes. He had won his third term, and I was out of a job.

But not for long. I had done good work for the DNC on the election, and as 1941 dawned, I was named executive secretary of the Women's Division. This time, Eleanor had nothing to do with it. I had earned the position myself.

Later, I wrote to tell her how proud I was of the woman she had become in the eight years since that 1932 election night at the Biltmore. *My trouble,* I wrote, *has always been that I've been so much more interested in the* person *than the* personage... *I still prefer the person, but I admire and respect the personage with all my heart!*

It was true. Loving Eleanor, I still very much preferred the person. And by the autumn of 1940, as her husband began his third term in office, I always felt blessed when I caught a glimpse of her behind or inside the personage she had become.


*No ordinary time.* For the Roosevelts, 1941 was a year of extraordinary personal losses.

On June 4, Missy LeHand collapsed at the annual office party that she and FDR always hosted for his top staffers. Lillian Parks, the White House seamstress and my favorite of the backstairs gang, told me she remembered the evening clearly because she'd had to hunt for the chef's apron she'd made for the president. He liked to wear it, along with a tall chef's hat from the kitchen, to serve the party food, which was catered by the Willard Hotel. (He didn't trust Mrs. Nesbitt to cook for this event.) After drinks and a buffet dinner, an aide began to play the president's favorite songs on a piano and everybody happily sang along. Suddenly, Missy gave a little scream and slumped to the floor, which put an end "real fast," Lillian said, to the party. She was carried to her apartment on the third floor, where Dr. McIntire, the president's physician, examined her.

"She's apparently had a slight heart attack," he said, although he was obviously puzzled.

The week that Missy was stricken, Eleanor was at Campobello with Joe Lash. When I phoned to tell her what had happened, she sighed. "This isn't the first time," she said. In 1927, Missy had suffered a perplexing illness, followed by a depression that was so acute that she was hospitalized and placed on a suicide watch. It had happened at Warm Springs, where Eff-dee (as Missy called FDR) was working with Helena Mahoney, an attractive physiotherapist. Eleanor thought that Missy collapsed because she feared that her boss had fallen in love with Mahoney.

Lillian, who knew about that episode, thought that this later collapse might have been triggered by a similar threat. FDR had promised his wife that he would never see Lucy Mercer again. But the backstairs gang knew that he *was* seeing her. He had invited her to his inaugurations in 1933, 1937, and 1941. He had received private telephone calls and letters from her—calls and letters that he apparently kept from Missy. Now, Lucy was appearing on the president's calendar, under the name of Mrs. Paul Johnson. On

June 5, she was scheduled to spend two hours with him in the residence.

"June fifth," Lillian told me, waggling her eyebrows to emphasize the date. "Missy's attack was on June fourth, the night *before*."

I frowned. Since I'd become a White House resident, I had heard the servants whispering about FDR's sexual abilities, in which they took a great interest. It was the majority opinion that FDR was fully capable.

"A man's got no secrets from his valet," Lillian said. "And the valets know that it's only his legs that're paralyzed." Irvin McDuffie, the president's long-term valet, had once made this perfectly clear. The kitchen crew, Lillian said, had been laughing at a sleazy tabloid cartoon with the caption, "Hoover was dead from the waist up. Roosevelt's dead from the waist down." McDuffie cast one scornful look at it and said, "I'll be damned if he is," and walked away.

Pale and grim, FDR was clearly devastated by Missy's loss. Whatever else they had been to one another, she had always been available to him. He had relied on her calm, quiet presence for twenty years. Bereft, he visited her and tried to cheer her up, but the visits were difficult for both of them, and after a few days, he simply stopped going to her apartment. He was convinced—and I was too, when I visited her—that Missy would never again be the person she had been.

I brought flowers and newspapers and tried to cheer her up, but Missy could only say how desperately she missed Eff-dee. I remembered something that Eleanor had said once, long ago, about herself and the children and Missy. They were like little moons, she'd said, all orbiting, inescapably, around a giant planet, around Franklin. Even Missy couldn't break away.

Two weeks after the first episode, on the day that Grace Tully officially became the president's private secretary, Missy had what was clearly a massive stroke. Unable to speak, partially paralyzed, she was moved to Doctors Hospital, where she stayed for several months, then—at FDR's urging—went to Warm Springs, with full-time nursing care. She returned to the White House after six months or so, but her speech was slurred and everyone knew that she would never go back to work. At last, FDR asked Missy's sister to take her home to Boston. There, she suffered another stroke and died, just forty-six years old. Franklin was on a ship in the Pacific when it happened. It was Eleanor who put on black and went to her funeral—the last sad irony of Missy's life.

When Missy collapsed, Franklin lost the one person in the White House on whom he could depend for uncritical, uncon-ditional, unquestioning love. Just three months later, he lost the only other person who gave him that kind of love. Sara Roosevelt had been slowly failing for some time, like an old soldier in sad decline but still unwilling to give up her post. In early September, Eleanor phoned her husband and asked him to come to Hyde Park. He was with his mother when she died and for her burial next to his father in the graveyard at St. James Episcopal Church. He returned to Washington looking haggard and desolate, with a black armband on the left sleeve of his coat.

I noticed, though, that Daisy Suckley, FDR's cousin, began coming more frequently to the White House and staying for longer visits. Eleanor said that they often saw one another at Hyde Park, where Daisy was helping FDR plan his own retreat, which he called Top Cottage. Daisy couldn't make up for the loss of Missy or his mother, but Franklin must have found that he could count on her for at least some of what the other two women had given him—and which his wife would not.

Just two weeks later, Eleanor suffered her own terrible loss, the death of her fifty-year-old brother Hall, an alcoholic. He had been her special charge since they were children, abandoned by their parents' deaths to the care of their strict Victorian grandmother. That night, when I went to her room, she was crying, and I held her until she grew quiet, thinking that I had never seen her cry before. In her "My Day" column for the next day, she wrote: *I remember him very vividly as a very small boy with curls and a round roly-poly face; whom my young aunts made much of and called the "cherub," thereby creating much jealousy in me because I could not aspire to any such name. By the time my brother was eighteen, he was an entirely independent person, and from that time on, the only way that anyone could hold him, was to let him go.*

I read that more than once and thought that it contained a lesson in loving Eleanor: loving and letting go.

In late November, weary to the bone from the constant push and shove of the campaign and the election, I took some vacation time and went up to Long Island. Howard had married his Molly and they had a place of their own, so the Little House was all mine now. The New England autumn had been lovely, but as winter came on, the weather turned blustery. It was never too cold or windy for me, though. I loved to walk with Prinz along the shore, feeling the chill sting of salt mist on my face and listening to the roar of the wild Atlantic surf and the shrill cries of the seabirds. Back indoors, I would build a fire in the library and curl up in my favorite chair with a book or work at my typewriter at the walnut Val-Kill desk that Eleanor had given me. Evenings were the best, as the silvery twilight fell across the ocean and the old house stood sturdy against the winter wind.

Marion came up to join me the first weekend in December, bringing Ernest Hemingway's new novel, *For Whom the Bell Tolls*, an excellent pinot noir, and a cherished pound of Brazilian coffee, so hard to get. On Saturday, I baked a chicken with dressing and Marion made her famous double chocolate cake, and we invited Clarence and Annie for supper—Ella, too, alone now, for money was scarce and the cowboy had moved on to greener pastures. On Sunday morning, I drove over to Mastic for the *Times,* and Marion and I were lazy and contented all morning. We had chicken soup and grilled cheese sandwiches for lunch and were washing the dishes when Clarence came running with the terrifying news. He had heard on the radio that the Japanese had bombed Pearl Harbor.

Marion and I stared at one another. At last, in a voice very unlike her own, she said, "This is it, Hick. It's finally happening." She put her arms around me. "War."

We clung together, each feeling the other's heart beating against the fear, against the darkness and death on the other side of the world, where war had become a fiery tide that would engulf all of us. I knew it would change our lives in ways we couldn't imagine. But it would change Eleanor's life even more, and I knew that the pain in my heart was nothing to the pain she must be feeling.

That night, listening to the radio, I heard her voice, her familiar voice, whose every lilt and dip and cadence I knew as well as I knew my own. She was speaking, live, before her regular pre-recorded Sunday night broadcast. The next day, the president would speak to the Congress and the nation. But tonight, she was speaking *for* all Americans, rather than *to* us, saying the words that each of us, all of us needed to say for ourselves.

"We know what we have to face," she said quietly, "and we know that we are ready to face it. We must go about our daily business more determined than ever to do the ordinary things as well as we can. When we find a way to do anything more in our communities to help others, to build morale, to give a feeling of security, we must do it. Whatever is asked of us, we can accomplish it."

*Whatever is asked of us, we can accomplish it*—words that rang with a confident certainty, inspiring that same confidence in every listener. Somewhere, Louis Howe must be smiling down on the reluctant First Lady who had proved herself a master strategist, always able to find the words that would bring people together and move them to do what had to be done. It was an inspired message, and by the end of it, I was overwhelmed with pride. Marion put her arm around me and gripped my hand, as if to hold me to her. But my heart was reaching out for Eleanor, loving her still, loving her always.

By the time I got back to the White House, the halls were filled with steadily purposeful activity. The cabinet was in continuous meetings, congressional leaders were coming and going, and State Department and military officers were in and out. The president's advisers were receiving continual reports about the damage to U.S. installations, ships, and planes in Hawaii, and newspapers all over the country were putting out special editions. Just after noon on Monday, the president went to Capitol Hill to address a joint session of Congress and the nation, asking for a declaration of war against Japan. It was five a.m. in London, but hundreds of thousands of Britons heard his address. A few hours later, as a gray twilight fell outside the Oval Office, FDR signed the declaration of war. A little later, he wired Prime Minister Winston Churchill: "Today all of us are in the same boat with you and the people of the Empire and it is a ship that cannot and will not be sunk."

Brave words on the first day of a long, bleak week. On

December 9, the Japanese seized Guam. On December 10, four thousand Japanese troops landed on the Philippine Islands, and Japanese aircraft sank the British warships *Prince of Wales* and *Repulse*.

And on December 11, Germany and Italy declared war against the United States.

Overnight, everything changed. At the White House, blackout curtains went up and, at the order of the Secret Service, some windows were painted black. A machine gun was installed on the roof of FDR's swimming pool, and soldiers armed with high-powered rifles were stationed on the roof of the White House. People left their offices after work and hurried home without stopping to shop. The lights were turned off on the Capitol dome, all the streetlights went dark, and the streets were silent and eerily empty. But all night long, I could hear the clanking and hissing of a giant steam shovel, digging a bomb shelter in the area between the White House and the Treasury Building.

Winston Churchill arrived on December 22, landing on the White House like a grenade. Eleanor had to find room for the prime minister and his large staff on the second floor. I set up a cot in Lillian's third floor sewing room for the duration, took most of my meals out, and tried to be invisible. That wasn't hard, for Churchill dominated all affairs for the three-and-a-half weeks he stayed at the White House. He rarely went to bed before three in the morning, slept until eleven, and took two hot baths and a long afternoon nap every day. He gave Alonzo Fields, FDR's butler, a standing drink order: a tumbler of sherry before breakfast, a couple of scotch and sodas before lunch, and brandy and French champagne before bed—in addition to the usual cocktails in FDR's study and wine at dinner.

On the afternoon of Christmas Eve, some twenty thousand Washingtonians came to watch the commander in chief light the nation's Christmas tree, a living, thirty-foot Oriental spruce planted on the South Lawn of the White House. After the usual carols, we heard from the president and the prime minister. Wrapped in his overcoat like a great wooly bear, Churchill wished that at this Christmas season, "each home throughout the English-speaking world should be a brightly lighted island of happiness and peace." I wondered why those who didn't speak English shouldn't be happy and peaceful too, but it didn't seem the time to quibble. On Christmas Day, Churchill's holiday was marred by a telegram. The British forces in Hong Kong had surrendered to the Japanese.

Washington was getting ready for war. In the basement of the White House, the president commandeered the ladies cloakroom and turned it into his map room, staffed twenty-four hours a day. At the Library of Congress, the Constitution and the Declaration of Independence were bundled up and secretly transported, via the Baltimore & Ohio Railroad, to Fort Knox, where at 12:07 p.m. on December 27 (everything at Fort Knox is exactly recorded), they were locked up in the vault where they would remain until the war's end. And out on the old Hoover Field across the Potomac, a huge building had begun going up, a monstrosity, people said, the goddamnest thing anybody ever saw. It was constructed in five wedge-shaped sections, with seventeen and a half miles of corridors and 150 stairways. Construction began on August 11, 1941, and moved with the speed of imagination. On April 29, 1942, three hundred employees from the Ordnance Department sat down at their desks in the new Pentagon.

April also brought the first good newspaper headlines of the war: *Tokyo Bombed!* The city was so far from any Allied airbase that everyone was astonished. Where had the planes taken off? How far had they flown? FDR, who ordered the raid, said teasingly that they had taken off from Shangri-La, the fictional Himalayan paradise—and the name of the presidential retreat. A couple of weeks later, we learned that the daring daylight raid had been led by Brigadier General James Doolittle and that the raiders had flown from the aircraft carrier *Hornet,* nearly seven hundred sea miles from Tokyo. American morale shot up. If FDR's chief aim had been to prove to the nation that the capital of Japan was in striking distance, he had succeeded beyond question.

April was also the month that Eleanor's friend, Joe Lash, put on his Army uniform. She had tried to get him a commission in the Naval Intelligence Service, but when the newspapers began to claim that the First Lady was attempting to install a "former Communist organizer" in an American military spy service, she had to drop her efforts. It would have been best if he had been able to go quietly off to basic training. Instead, Eleanor gave him an extravagant going-away party at the Brevoort Hotel in New York, with an eight-piece orchestra and a lavish menu and an eight-piece orchestra. Joe, Tommy said, was "terribly embarrassed" by the sendoff.

All over the country, the newspapers were cruel to her that year, and I cringed when I read the savagely critical stories. I didn't like to think what the administration's publicity people were saying about the president's wife, and Tommy kept shaking her head as she read, muttering "I try and try to tell her that young man is dangerous, but she just won't listen."

I'll admit to some resentment and perhaps even jealousy, but for the most part, I felt sorry for Joe. When he met Eleanor, he was very young and under attack by powerful forces, trying to find a place for himself in a world that challenged his political ideologies and cast him as an outsider. He must have been overwhelmed by her friendship, seeing it both as a refuge and as an opportunity. But I often wondered whether he felt that loving Eleanor—and being loved by Eleanor—was too great a burden to bear.

On the home front that year, the war meant getting used to shortages.

The military needed guns and ammunition, but before anything else, it needed uniforms—64 million shirts, 229 million pairs of trousers, and 165 million coats—which meant that there wouldn't be a lot of material left for civilian clothing. There would be restrictions on fabric, dyes, zippers, and even buttons. To reduce the amount of fabric needed, the War Production Board came up with a new "Victory" suit for men, with narrower lapels and cuffless trousers. For women, hems and belts were restricted to two inches and cuffs on sleeves were eliminated. Skirts rose alarmingly above the knee. Box pleats were out (too much fabric) and kick pleats were in. Patch pockets were replaced by smaller slash pockets.

And nylons? Forget it! DuPont, the only producer of nylon in the United States, stopped making hosiery and started making parachutes. You could sometimes find pre-war stockings on the black market for $20 a pair, or you could learn to use leg makeup and paint dark seams down the backs of your legs. If you were a shoe fancier, though, you were really out of luck. You could buy only one pair a year.

We women might be prepared to shorten our skirts and paint our legs, but when the rubber shortage threatened our girdles, we rebelled. The girdle companies came up with a "Victory Girdle" that had no stays, no rubber, and no silk, but nobody bought it. The War Production Board suggested that women should grow their own "muscular girdles" through exercise, but the idea never caught on. At last, after the women's magazines raised a nation-wide hue and cry, the WPB hung out the white flag. Foundation garments would be considered an essential part of a woman's wardrobe and would continue to be manufactured and sold, no matter how much rubber they took.

Getting used to shortages meant getting used to rationing. Every American civilian—even the children—got a book of stamps containing forty-eight "points" per month that could be spent on rationed goods, including meat, butter, sugar, shoes, and other scarce commodities. At the White House, Mrs. Nesbitt confiscated stamps from all the residents, including the president and the First Lady, and used them to buy groceries.

The phrase "Don't you know there's a war on?" was on everybody's lips, especially when you tried to buy cigarettes, which were being sent to "our boys overseas" by the shipload. One after-noon I heard that a drugstore at 15th and H Street had cigarettes, but after a half hour in line, what I got at the counter was a chocolate bar—also scarce and welcome enough, but not as satisfying as a pack of Pall Malls. When I joined Marion for drinks before dinner, she offered me a few puffs of the pipe she was smoking. But I had learned to roll my own cigarettes when I worked in the newsroom, so I pulled out my fixings and went to work. It didn't do much for my reputation, but I could smoke when others couldn't.

With tires and gasoline rationed, everybody learned to walk again. Government employees walked to work rather than wait for standing-room-only buses. Taxies were as rare as good cups of coffee, so Embassy Row diplomats took to their heels. In bars, beer was rationed, so beer drinkers got used to moving from bar to bar in the evening—walking fast or slow, depending on their thirst.

But the First Lady always walked with her long, swinging stride, with Tommy, steno pad in hand, trotting wearily behind, taking the dictation that the Boss tossed back over her shoulder. She spent three weeks touring England and another six visiting the troops in the Pacific—including a visit to Joe on Guadalcanal—as well as dropping in, unexpectedly, on military installations in the U.S. From Puerto Rico, where she was inspecting the troops, she wrote, *Hick dearest, I have thought of you so much ever since I arrived,* reminding me that it was almost ten years since our trip there together. Ten years? It seemed a century. A few days later, she wrote again as she flew over the Amazon River. *Gosh,* I replied wistfully, remembering that I had once wanted to go to war-torn Spain, *I'd like to go to South America sometime.* But the war kept me at home, as it sent her abroad.

The tone of our letters changed in those years, not because I loved her less but because our lives were taking each of us in different directions. She was Eleanor Everywhere, and her heart was set on Joe. I was in Washington for the duration, and so (most of the time) was Marion, who was a passionate partner in our relationship. Her office was just a few blocks from the White House, and she got into the habit of dropping off little notes with the White House sentries on her way home at night. Both of us enjoyed gardening and wrote about it often. Marion planted a dozen lilacs and swamp maple saplings at the Little House, and together we put in some peonies. When I took a week's vacation to work in the garden, she wrote: *I can't tell you how much it means to me to look forward to the weekend with you. I wish so much that I could be there all of this week with you. Some of our friends may have honeysuckle in their yard but we have our own trellis and vines, roses in summer and burning pine in the winter. I think we'll make out very well... All my love darling—and a kiss.*

For Christmas in those years, we gave each other practical presents: from me to Marion, two pairs of black-market nylons, a pre-war latex Living Girdle, and a new tire for her car; from her to me, a sweater and a ton of "black diamonds," coal for the Little House, which was the devil to heat in the winter. When I was in Chicago for the DNC, she sent me a postcard with a photograph of the Hay-Adams House at 16th and H Streets, with a hand-inked arrow pointing to a third-floor room that we had once shared. *X marks the spot,* she wrote on the back. *Let me go on the record to say "wish we were here," m'dear.* When she was in Louisville, hearing a tax case, she wrote, sweetly, amusingly poetic: *Hick, darling, I love to hear you laugh and see you smile. Do you know that your mirth is as light and bright as sunshine, and as warm?*

But there wasn't a lot to be mirthful about in those days. It wasn't until late 1942 that we had more good news about the war, when the Allied landing in North Africa went off as planned. But it was well into 1943 before the Germans were routed. After that, Sicily and then Italy, a long, weary battle. And then months and months of silence as the Allies prepared for D-Day, June 1944. In the Pacific, the victories were even slower in coming, and the casualties mounted alarmingly.

I read the newspapers with great attention, especially when I spotted the names of women correspondents who were covering the war. My friends from FERA days were there: Martha Gellhorn and Margaret Bourke-White. Janet Flanner of the *New Yorker,* Helen Kirkpatrick of the *Chicago Daily News,* Marguerite Higgens of the *New York Herald Tribune.* I thought back to the day in 1917 when I'd been told that females didn't cover wars and glowed with pride at their work. I often thought longingly of joining them, but I had to be realistic. Given my diabetes, it was physically difficult to do my job for the DNC in wartime Washington. I couldn't have done a reporter's job in wartime Europe or North Africa or the Far East. That was a landmark realization for me, and not a happy one.

I often saw Eleanor's name in the newspapers, too, especially in connection with the "Eleanor Clubs" that were supposedly being organized by Southern black servants who were demanding better pay and fewer hours. The First Lady heard so often about these clubs that she finally asked the FBI to find out whether they actually existed. J. Edgar Hoover wasn't Eleanor's friend, and I was sure he would've been glad to hand her a long list of clubs. But the FBI couldn't find even one. The report concluded that Mrs. Roosevelt—who had been arguing for better treatment of household help—was being blamed for the fact that Negro cooks and maids were leaving their white employers for higher pay in the wartime factories.

Eleanor was also taking plenty of flak for her energetic support of Congresswoman Edith Nourse Rogers's bill to create the Women's Auxiliary Army Corps. "Shame, shame, Mrs. Roosevelt!" the conservative newspapers cried. "Women don't belong in uniform!" And on the floor of the House, a congressman warned, "If Mrs. Roosevelt has her way and the women go into the armed service, there will be no one left to wear the apron—to do the cooking, the washing, the mending, the many humble homey tasks to which every woman has devoted herself."

I didn't read about Eleanor's greatest trouble in the newspapers, though. I heard it from Tommy, one morning at breakfast at the White House. When Joe finished basic training early that year, he was sent to Weather Observer School at Chanute Air Force Base in Illinois. One Friday in March, Eleanor and Tommy checked into a hotel in nearby Urbana. Joe spent two nights in Eleanor's room, while Tommy slept in the adjacent room.

"Bad idea," I muttered under my breath. It was one thing for Eleanor to share a room with me when we were traveling; that didn't raise many eyebrows. But the First Lady and an unmarried man—a much younger man, a soldier! "They weren't seen, were they?" I asked quickly. "I haven't read anything in the newspapers about—"

Tommy held up her hand. "There's more. A couple of weeks after the Urbana episode, the Boss and I were in Chicago. She paid for Joe's bus ticket from Chanute and he met us at the Hotel Blackstone. We stayed for the weekend. I had a separate room. Joe and the Boss shared a room."

I frowned. "I'm surprised that McCormick didn't send somebody to sniff around." Robert McCormick, the owner and publisher of the *Chicago Tribune*, hated liberals, the New Deal, and everything the Roosevelts stood for. He took every opportunity to lay the ills of the country at their feet. I gave her a quick glance. "He didn't, did he?" Maybe he had. Maybe he was holding the story as blackmail.

She shook her head. "It's worse than that, Hick. The Boss and I stayed at the Blackstone again, on our way back from a trip to the West Coast. While we were there, a hotel employee told her that the room she and Joe had shared was bugged."

I gasped. *"Bugged?"*

"Yes, bugged," Tommy said grimly, and told me the rest of the story.

Because of Joe's pre-war left-wing advocacy, the Army Counter-Intelligence Corps was keeping an eye on him—a suspicious eye. They searched his footlocker, read his mail, and put him under surveillance. The CIC had been watching when he went to the

Urbana hotel where he stayed with the First Lady. When they intercepted and read Mrs. Roosevelt's telegram inviting him to Chicago, they bugged her hotel room.

"Joe and the Boss didn't leave the room all weekend," Tommy said bleakly. "So there were hours of talk. Pillow talk. Behind closed doors. And they got it all on tape."

*On tape!* I remembered how she loved to be touched, and what we had said when we were touching. I didn't think she and Joe would share such intimacies, but I couldn't be sure. "Just… talk?" I asked.

Tommy darted me a glance. "I didn't hear the tapes, so I can't say." She paused to take out a cigarette. "Anyway, when the Boss heard what had happened, she was terribly worried for Joe, but also for herself—and the president. She was thinking about blackmail, of course. When we got back to the White House, she went to Harry Hopkins and asked him to find out what was going on. Harry went to General Marshall, the Army chief of staff, who dug around and discovered that it was true. The CIC actually bugged her room. They had hours and hours of tapes." She picked up a matchbook on the table. "And not just tapes, but typed transcripts. Somebody typed up the whole damned thing. Pages and pages of it."

I took a deep breath, bracing myself. "And then what?"

"Hopkins and General Marshall knew they had to tell the president, of course. FDR blew his stack. He ordered the tapes and transcripts destroyed and told Marshall to clean house at the CIC."

"Good for FDR!" I exclaimed, relieved. "He did the right thing." I didn't ask what he had said to his wife. I didn't want to know.

"Yes, the right thing—although somebody might have been tempted to keep a copy. Or give one to the FBI for Hoover's files.

You know how J. Edgar hates Mrs. Roosevelt. He could leak it, out of pure malice." Tommy shuddered. "Can't you just imagine what would happen if Westbrook Pegler got hold of this?"

"Oh, God, yes," I muttered. Pegler, a right-wing columnist for the *Washington Post,* was a vocal critic of the administration. Recently, he had written that Mrs. Roosevelt was "impudent, presumptuous, and conspiratorial," and that "her withdrawal from public life at this time would be a fine public service." I got up to pour myself another cup of coffee and sat back down again. "But at least the CIC files have been cleaned out."

"We can hope." Tommy opened the matchbook and lit her cigarette. "But there's more, I'm afraid. The Boss got a letter from Joe yesterday. He'd been expecting to go to Grand Rapids, where his Weather Observers class was assigned to a six-months advanced school." She dropped the match in an ashtray. "But he and several others got different orders. They're going overseas."

I raised my eyebrows. "Overseas?"

Tommy blew out a stream of smoke. "To the Pacific. He's already on his way."

It was that left hook again.


As 1943 ended and 1944 began, the war ground on endlessly, battle after battle. In January, the German siege of Leningrad finally ended. But the same month, the Germans pinned down 150,000 Allied soldiers at Anzio, and it wasn't until May that they could break free and liberate Rome. In February, Allied air forces began an intensive bombing of German cities. The next month, German forces occupied Hungary. All the while, subterranean whispers about Operation Overlord—the invasion of German-occupied Western Europe—blew like a chilly wind through government corridors. While none of us knew when or where, we knew that Eisenhower and his generals were planning to send an Allied army across the channel. If the invasion succeeded, it could end the war.

But what if it failed? Washington was seized by a shivering anxiety. War Department workers wore grim faces. Newspapers fretted. Pastors preached anxious sermons. In May, Eleanor told me that for weeks, she hadn't been able to sleep through the night. "I feel as though a terrible sword is hanging over our heads," she told me. "It has to fall, and I dread it."

The sword fell on June 6, D-day. War correspondent Ernie Pyle reported that the invasion had turned from "a vague anticipatory dread into a horrible reality," as tens of thousands of soldiers poured out of their landing crafts onto the beaches of Normandy. *INVASION! Allied Armies Land in France.* The headline was cried by newsboys and shouted from radios that morning. *Vast Sea and Air Operation. Armada of 4,000 Ships.* Church bells tolled, school bells rang. Horns blared. *Hitler's Sea Wall Is Breached.* Stores closed, people filled the churches and synagogues, and FDR offered a national prayer on the radio. *Mighty Allied Force Fighting Way Inland.* Three weeks after D-day, a million men had been put ashore, and Americans were coming to realize that the war wouldn't be over overnight. It would be eleven more months before the Allies reached Berlin and the war in Europe ended.

And in July, just six weeks after D-day, FDR was nominated for a fourth term.

The 1944 presidential campaign was a hard one for me. After the July convention, I worked for the president's campaign against his Republican opponent, Thomas E. Dewey, whose pencil-thin black moustache made him look like the "little man on the wedding cake," in the scathing words of Alice Longworth. But the president looked like a cadaver, and his health was a constant worry. Despite that, and the usual opposition from conservatives, Americans could not imagine the leadership of the country and the war in any hands but Roosevelt's. He led Dewey in the polls throughout the campaign and on election day, scored a comfortable victory, taking 36 states for 432 electoral votes to Dewey's 12 states and 99 electoral votes. FDR—and Eleanor—were committed to four more years in the White House.

But I was leaving Washington. Now that the election was over, it was time for me to give up the travel, the late nights, the political confrontations, the exhausting work. I had saved enough money to support a six-month sabbatical, and my health demanded it. I was fifty-two, severely diabetic, and ready for some peace and quiet. I resigned from the DNC, wrote farewell notes to all my friends, and a deeply felt letter of thanks to Eleanor. *Dearest, I wish I had the words to tell you how grateful I am for your many kindnesses these last four years—and especially for letting me stay at the White House. It did two wonderful things—kept me near you and made it possible for me to hang on to my Little House, which is so infinitely precious to me.*

The Little House. I had made up my mind to live there fulltime, with the woods and meadows all around me, the open sky like a blessing over my head, and the wild Atlantic at my door. There, I would have time to myself, all the time I needed to read, to write, to think, to just *be.*

To Marion, my decision was inexplicable. "You can certainly leave the DNC, Hick, if that's what you want to do." She said this in her firm, executive tone. "But I simply cannot see why you have to move to Long Island. We have a lovely apartment here in D.C. You can read and write here just as easily as *there.* And we'll be together."

Strictly speaking, the apartment wasn't ours, it was Marion's. She had at last moved out of her mother's Chevy Chase house, found a very nice place to live, and furnished it beautifully. We lived together there for a month or so after the election, and it went well enough. We liked the same music, food, books. We enjoyed each other and we liked each other's friends. We were compatible.

But I knew it was time for a change, and I chose the Little House. Marion was ten years younger than I, energetic, ambitious. Her career was—or ought to be—her highest priority. She couldn't live with me on Long Island, and I couldn't live with her in the city.

So, in August, when she came to spend her two-week vacation at the Little House, I told her it was time to end our exclusive relationship. I tried to make it as easy as I could, saying once again that it wasn't *her*, it was me. I simply didn't want to live in Washington, and I needed to step back and be quiet for a time. And there was my health. I'd had a diabetic crisis just a few weeks before. I'd had to learn how to give myself daily insulin injections —not an easy matter for somebody who's always been afraid of needles.

"I want to be friends," I said. "I want to see you often, dear. But I can't make a commitment to a life together. It wouldn't be fair to you—or to me, either, come to that."

She wasn't going to make it easy. "But I don't want us to end it, Hick." She reached for my hand. "I *love* you. I'm not ready to give you up."

I shook my head. "We don't have to give each other up. You're a sweet, warm generous person and I'm terribly fond of you. I just can't manage an exclusive commitment, that's all. I want you to feel free to—"

Her eyes darkened and her jaw was working. "It's Eleanor, isn't it." It wasn't a question.

"No, of course it's not Eleanor," I said, quickly, but she was rushing on, the anger building.

"Don't try to fool me, Hick. Val-Kill and her New York apartment are both a lot closer to you here at the Little House than in Washington. You have that arrangement to work on her papers, which brings you together often. And after what happened in April, everything's changed. You're thinking that the two of you will—"

"No," I said. "No, really, Marion, please. It's not like that at all."

But Marion was right, of course. Eleanor and I *were* working together on the papers she wanted to give to the FDR Library, now established at Hyde Park. And in April, everything *had* changed.

The disappointment brought out the worst in Marion, and I replied with the worst in me. We ended our relationship. It was just a few days after America dropped the atomic bomb on Hiroshima and Nagasaki, killing a quarter of a million people outright. The long, terrible Pacific war was over. Life could begin again.


Many Americans felt the single death that happened on April 12 far more deeply than the hundreds of thousands of Japanese deaths four months later.

I had left Washington on the twenty-first of March. For the next three weeks, I relaxed at the Little House, catching up on my reading, puttering in the garden, enjoying the sunshine. It was a lovely April, with the dogwoods blooming in the woods and the lilacs a feast of lavender blossoms along the edge of the garden. Mr. Choate was with me then, a frisky English spaniel that Eleanor had given me after Prinz died, and he danced beside me that late

Thursday afternoon as I walked to the mailbox on the main road to post a letter to Eleanor. She was in Washington that week, coping with the usual infinite succession of things. That afternoon, I knew, she was with Mrs. Woodrow Wilson, giving a talk at the Sulgrave Club.

Back home, I was brewing a cup of tea when Clarence appeared at the kitchen door, out of breath and frantic. The Little House still didn't have a telephone, but I had left Clarence's number with several friends, in case they needed to reach me. One look at his face told me that the message was a terrible one.

"It's the president," he said, barely able to get the words out. "He's dead."

Howard Haycraft had called to tell me. He was in Washington, in the Army Special Services, where it had just been announced that the president had been fatally stricken in Warm Springs. It was as if the sky had suddenly splintered and crashed to the ground and lay in slivers and crazed shards around my feet. I sat for a long while, trying to get used to the idea of a world without FDR in it, then walked to Clarence's and telephoned Tommy at the White House. She told me that Eleanor was getting ready to go downstairs to the Cabinet Room, where Harry Truman would be sworn in at seven. When the ceremony was over, she was leaving for Warm Springs. She had asked Tommy to wire me with the news.

After a sleepless night, I called Warm Springs in the morning. Within a moment, I was talking to her. "I love you," I said. "And I'm so very, very sorry, dear."

"I know," she said quietly. "We're all sorry." There was a long pause, and a breath, and I heard the heartbreak in her voice when she said, "Lucy was here, Hick. With him. When he died."

"Oh," I said, and then there was nothing left to say. Nothing at all.

FDR was buried at the Big House in Hyde Park, in his mother's rose garden. At the Little House, I sat outside in the sunshine and read aloud Walt Whitman's elegy for Abraham Lincoln, dead on that same day, April 15, eighty years before:

> When lilacs last in the dooryard bloom'd,
> And the great star early droop'd in the western sky in the
>     night,
> I mourn'd, and yet shall mourn with ever-returning spring...

As I read, I thought of FDR, of the man I had known and the president I had worked for, of his strength and vitality and magnetism—and his cunning and secretiveness and willingness to use people for his own ends, some good, some bad. And like millions of others in our country around the world I felt bewilderment and terror at the thought of the then-unfinished war and could not imagine how it could be won without him. But it would be, of course. Peace in Europe would come in only three more weeks; in the Pacific, four more months. Life and death go on, love goes on.

A week later, I gathered an armload of lilac and peonies from the garden and went to the Washington Square apartment Eleanor had rented in 1942, when she was looking ahead to the end of Franklin's third term. I was arranging the flowers when she and Tommy arrived, both of them utterly exhausted. They had packed up all the Roosevelt furniture and possessions at the White House, had it loaded into Army trucks (eleven, Tommy said), and sent to Hyde Park. Eleanor's next job was the unpacking and all the decisions that had to be made—while all around her people were celebrating the announcement of Hitler's April 30 suicide and the German surrender on May 7. Things were happening too quickly, too much, too overwhelming. It was hard to make sense of it all.

For Eleanor and her future, I had no worries, just the hope that she would find the time for rest and a little peace. Joe Lash married his Trude and the controversy over Eleanor's friendship with him died down after the war. But another one quickly erupted. After the annulment of his second marriage, Earl Miller (then a Navy reserve lieutenant commander) had married for the third time in 1941. When his wife Simone filed for divorce in 1947, she threatened to name Eleanor as a co-respondent, and her lawyer gave the court copies of Eleanor's letters to Earl. The judge awarded a substantial settlement to Simone, along with the custody of the two children, named Eleanor and Earl. He also ordered the letters sealed. Westbrook Pegler would later write several nasty columns about the divorce. But at the time, the only publicity was a single exclamatory sentence in Ed Sullivan's New York *Daily News* column: "Navy commander's wife will rock the country if she names the co-respondent in her divorce action!!!"

But most of the newspaper coverage of Eleanor's activities was positive and she would be revered for her efforts as First Lady. She was her own agent now and freer to act than she had been for more than forty years. When she spoke to me about her plans, not long after the president's death, she was very firm.

"I am nearly sixty-one," she said emphatically. "I'm going to be a homebody and enjoy my friends. I want to spend time with my children, and with you. Tommy is getting my papers together so you can start organizing them for the library. It'll be good to get that job finished."

Did I hope, as Marion believed, that with Franklin gone, Eleanor and I would at last be able live together? Perhaps I did, in some secret cranny of my heart. But I knew very well that the person I had loved had become a personage. Too many now loved her—and she them—to allow herself to love and be loved by one.

And a homebody? I smiled at that. I wanted to believe her, but I couldn't. I had no idea what new projects, large and small, might land on her desk, but I was sure they would come, and they wouldn't be projects she could manage at home. I could only nod and smile and remember what she had written in her "My Day" column after her brother died, that the only way we can ever hold anyone is to let them go. Loving Eleanor had been a work in progress for more than a decade. For me, it would go on for nearly two more decades.

The projects weren't long in coming. Some months later, President Harry Truman asked her to serve in the American delegation to the United Nations. No longer First Lady of the United States, she was embarking on a new journey—this time, a journey of her own. "First Lady of the World," President Truman called her.

And so she was, First Lady of the World—still First Lady of *my* world, anyway. But I had to laugh at something that happened when I went to see her off to the Netherlands, where she was to meet the rest of the U.N. delegates. As we boarded her ship, we found a gang of eager reporters waiting on the deck. An eager young lady asked, "Mrs. Roosevelt, what's the most important thing about being on your own?"

Eleanor replied quickly—and honestly. "For the first time in my life, I can say anything I want, It's simply *wonderful* to feel free." When she heard what she'd said and realized what it meant, she added, "Maybe we'd better keep that off the record."

And then, at the disappointment on the reporter's face, she reconsidered. "Really? You think it might make an interesting story? Well, then, leave it on the record. It's true—I *do* feel free to say what I think. But we all have to be careful, of course." She slid me a conspiratorial smile. "We never know who might be listening, do we?"

Of course, we have to be careful. Some of the story—the part that goes on behind closed doors, in private places, in our hearts—will always be wordless and must be imagined.

But the rest of the story must be told, and so I have.

My story, her story, our story.

Our story.

# A BIOGRAPHICAL AFTERWORD

There's more to Hick's story, of course. She lived frugally at the Little House for another decade, supporting her island seclusion by working on ER's papers and as a researcher, speechwriter, and ghostwriter for two of her political friends, Congresswomen Mary Norton and Helen Gahagan Douglas. She also worked frequently for the Democratic State Committee in New York City and commuted to Washington when her work or events demanded it. She started to write an autobiography, but gave it up when she began to fear that a publisher would want the same thing that her AP editors had wanted years before: the inside scoop on her friendship with Eleanor Roosevelt. She certainly couldn't tell that story, and she felt that, without it, her own story wasn't terribly interesting. She abandoned the effort.

And then, at the suggestion of ER's literary agent, Nannine Joseph, another project came along. In 1952, Hick undertook the writing of profiles of women in political life called *Ladies of Courage*, an inspiring account of women's struggle for recognition in American public and political life since women gained the vote in 1920. ER lent the luster of her name to the book and Tommy typed the manuscript, but Hick spent the better part of two years on the research—including extensive interviews with her subjects—and the writing. Before she submitted the finished manuscript, she shared it with ER, who wrote: *At last tonight I've finished reading your material* [for Ladies of Courage] *and it is simply swell I think. Much more interesting than I thought it could possibly be made.*

The book, which included profiles of Frances Perkins, Clare Boothe Luce, Helen Gahagan Douglas, and Oveta Culp Hobby, was published in 1954. Thanks to ER's popularity, it received extensive newspaper attention, and Hick traveled around the country, speaking to women's groups about the book and about the challenges women faced in political life. In recognition of her authorship, ER assigned her the royalties, which cumulatively amounted to about $4,000 (about $35,000 in 2015).

Tommy Thompson did not live to see the publication of *Ladies of Courage*. She died of a cerebral hemorrhage on April 12, 1953, the eight-year anniversary of FDR's death. She was sixty-six years old. Hick and Tommy had always been friends, but they had drawn much closer after the White House years and Hick was bereft at her loss. ER was shattered. "When [Tommy] died," she wrote, "I learned for the first time what being alone was like."

As a journalist, Hick had always been deeply interested in people who had stories, who met extraordinary challenges. In the profiles of the *Ladies of Courage*, Hick had found a narrative voice that enabled her to tell these stories. After that book was published, she began work on what would be three biographies for young readers in Grosset & Dunlap's much-heralded Signature Books series: *The Story of Franklin D. Roosevelt* (1956), *The Story of Helen Keller* (1958), and *The Story of Eleanor Roosevelt* (1959). For Scholastic, Hick also wrote a biography of FDR, this one focusing on his early political life: *The Road to the White House: FDR, The Pre-Presidential Years* (1962).

Of the four books for young readers, Hick's biography of Helen Keller was the most successful. It was adopted by several school-affiliated book clubs, and sales were boosted even further by the Broadway launch of William Gibson's *The Miracle Worker* and the release of the 1962 film of the same title, starring Patty

Duke. When she was doing the research for the Keller biography, Hick became deeply interested in Keller's teacher and went on to write a biography for older teens called *The Touch of Magic: The Story of Helen Keller's Great Teacher, Anne Sullivan Macy.* The book was published by Dodd, Mead in 1961.

Hick felt a special admiration for Macy. "No author ever finished a book with greater regret," she wrote in her foreword. "During the months I worked on this book she became as real to me as a living person... I miss her." I can't help wondering if Hick saw something of herself and Eleanor in the relationship between Macy and her beloved pupil. Without her teacher and mentor, Helen Keller might have lived a life of dark and inarticulate silence. Without Hick—who encouraged the press conferences, supported her friend's early efforts as a writer, and urged her to begin her newspaper column—would Eleanor have found her own powerful voice? Perhaps. But it's a question that Hick might have asked herself.

While Hick was working on the Macy biography, she struck up a professional friendship with Allen Klots, her editor at Dodd, Mead. When the book was finished, Hick proposed to Klots the project that became *Eleanor Roosevelt, Reluctant First Lady,* the book for which Hick is probably best known. It sketches the period of their most intense friendship, giving only a few clues to its intimacy. Finished in 1961, *Reluctant First Lady* was published just prior to ER's death. Increasingly confident in her work, Hick pitched a third project to Klots: *Eleanor Roosevelt's Christmas Book,* a collection of ER's favorite Christmas writings, as well as a description of Christmas at Hyde Park and in the White House. Hick was working on that book when ER died. Published in 1963, it sold well and the royalties from that and her other projects provided Hick with something approaching a comfortable living.

She was well along with a biography of labor leader Walter Reuther (also for Dodd, Mead) when her failing eyesight finally compelled her to stop, not long before her death in 1968. That project was completed by Jean Gould and published under the title *Walter Reuther: Labor's Rugged Individualist*—with Hick's name on the cover, as well as Gould's. That title brought to nine the number of books Hick had produced in the last fifteen years of her life.

A tenth book would eventually be published under Hick's name: *One Third of a Nation: Lorena Hickok Reports on the Great Depression*, edited by Richard Lowitt and Maurine Beasley and published in 1981. It includes the passionate piece, "The Unsung Heroes of the Depression," that Hick drafted in 1937 as an introduction to a projected publication of her reports to Harry Hopkins, at FERA. *One Third of a Nation* is a collection of those reports, as well as a biographical introduction and selections from Hick's letters to ER. The reports, illustrated with photos of the period, provide us with the eyewitness view of a skilled journalist who listened with her heart to what people had to say—people like Cora, the woman she met on a Kentucky mountain and never forgot. Or the woman in Bakersfield, California: "It's this thing of having babies. You've got no protection at all. You don't have any money, you see, to buy anything at the drugstore. And there you are, surrounded by young ones you can't support." Or the Iowa woman who spent part of her husband's first Civil Works Administration check for oranges because she hadn't tasted an orange for three years. Hick became a part of their stories. She felt their despair and recorded it, so that those who came after would know what it was like to live through the terrible years of the Depression.

As Hick grew older, her activities were increasingly limited by severe diabetes. From the late 1940s, she suffered from diabetic retinopathy and often awakened in the morning to discover that she could not see out of either eye—a temporary but unsettling condition. Arthritis was beginning to slow her down, too. The Little House was expensive to heat in winter and often isolated by snow, and in the early 1950s, at ER's invitation, she began spending the cold months at Val-Kill. In 1955, she moved there. The relocation proved to be a help because she was working on the book that would become *The Story of Franklin D. Roosevelt*. Val-Kill gave her easier access to the FDR Library and acquainted her with the library's staff members, who quickly became her friends.

Hick stayed at Val-Kill for nearly a year, but it was an uncomfortable time. After the solitude of the Little House, ER's home was a noisy tumult of people, children, and dogs, some of whom were not compatible with Muffin, the placid successor to the irrepressible Mr. Choate. It was hard to find a quiet place and time to work on her book. As well, there were the uneasy currents of jealousy that often swirled around Eleanor. The Roosevelts generally accepted Hick or ignored her, but ER's East Coast Establishment friends saw the former newspaper reporter as uncultured and uncouth. As for Hick, she treasured the particular friendship she and Eleanor had shared for a quarter of a century and resented those whom she considered latecomers and hangers-on. Marion Dickerman and Nancy Cook were no longer around, but Hick had never liked or trusted Joseph Lash. And then there was David Gurewitsch, Eleanor's doctor, traveling companion, and New York housemate, to whom ER developed a passionate attachment—and whom Hick must have viewed with great jealousy.

In the fall of 1956, Hick left Val-Kill and moved to a small but comfortable motel cabin overlooking a little lake on the northern outskirts of Hyde Park, about three miles from Val-Kill. In 1958, when income from her growing list of books gave her more flexibility, she rented an apartment in the former Episcopal rectory on Park Place. She lived there until her death in 1968, two months after her seventy-fifth birthday. She seems not to have given clear instructions for the disposal of her ashes, and her sister Ruby did not take them. They were stored in an urn at a local funeral home for twenty years and then buried in an unmarked grave in Rhinebeck Cemetery in Rhinebeck, New York.

But Hick was not forgotten. On the anniversary of her death in 2000, friends and admirers dedicated a dogwood tree to be planted near the grave, with a bluestone bench and a plaque: *Lorena Hickok "Hick" AP Reporter, Author, Activist, and Friend of E.R.*


It appears that Hick may have begun donating materials to the FDR Library as early as 1958, although references in her own later letters suggest that she withheld the bulk of the correspondence— some thirty-five hundred letters—until after ER's death in 1962. It is also possible that a substantial cache of letters was found at her death. It is reported that her sister Ruby burned a dozen or more, saying that they were "none of anybody's business." Hick's donation to the library required that all the materials be sealed until ten years after her death. A description of the collection can be found in Rodger Streitmatter's book, *Empty Without You: The Intimate Letters of Eleanor Roosevelt and Lorena Hickok* (1998) and in Doris Faber's1980 biography of Lorena Hickok.

Faber had gone to the FDR Library to research a children's biography of Mrs. Roosevelt. She arrived shortly after the Hickok collection was opened and was confronted by the mass of altogether unexpected—and, for Faber, highly disturbing—material. She describes her reactions in "A Personal Note" at the end of *The Life of Lorena Hickok: E.R.'s Friend.* Traumatized by what she read, "in something like a classic state of shock," she attempted to persuade archivist William Emerson to suppress the materials, or at least lock them away for another three or four decades. Failing in that, she was left to decide whether to go on with her original project or try instead to deal with the new material.

With the enthusiastic encouragement of her editor at William Morrow and her husband (Harold Faber, a *New York Times* reporter and editor who knew a sensational story when he saw one), Faber decided to scrap the kids' project and tackle the letters. She would write a biography of Lorena Hickok for adult readers, "one of the hardest challenges that any writer could face," in Faber's words; "the Everest of writing," as her daughter described it. *The Life of Lorena Hickok* was published in 1980 to wide reviews and a great deal of newspaper coverage.

The work Faber produced reflected her personal dismay at the intense love story she discovered in the boxes of letters on her desk in the serene reading room at the FDR Library. Faced with what seems to have been a profoundly unsettling glimpse into the erotic life of the nation's most famous First Lady, she decided that the passionate language of the early letters simply did not mean "what it appears to mean" and did her best to reinterpret the material—and demean her subject. As Leila J. Rupp puts it, *The Life of Lorena Hickok* would make "fascinating material for a case study of homophobia." Faber goes out of her way to present Hickok in an unflattering and unsympathetic light: undercutting or completely overlooking her many professional achievements, failing to provide an adequate historical or political context for her activities, and diminishing her work as a journalist and the professional writing she did after she left the DNC in 1945. As a biography, *The Life of Lorena Hickok* falls sadly short.

Some of the damage has been undone. Blanche Wiesen Cook

has helped to rescue Hick and ER from the closet where Faber put them. "They were two adult women, in the prime of their lives, committed to working out a relationship under very difficult circumstances," Cook writes in her acclaimed and authoritative biography of Eleanor Roosevelt. "They knew the score. They appreciated the risks and the dangers.... They touched each other deeply, loved profoundly, and moved on." And Rodger Streitmatter's edited collection of some three hundred of the letters provides us with a broad look into the evolution of the relationship, from obvious physical intimacy to warm and enduring friendship. But we are still waiting for a serious, better prepared, less judgmental biographer who will take a longer, deeper, more open-minded look into Lorena Hickok's many-faceted life and place her relationship to Eleanor Roosevelt in the context of Eleanor's complex romantic relationships with FDR, Earl Miller, Joseph Lash, and David Gurewitsch.

In the meantime, I offer my own interpretation of the intimate friendship of Hick and Eleanor—a fictional interpretation. As a novelist, I am privileged to live not only my own life but also the lives of my characters, in their times and places and with an intensity that sometimes takes me entirely out of my own world and into theirs. I have based my fiction on a reading of the women's letters held in the FDR Library, on Hick's writings about ER, and on the multitudinous sources available in books and online, some of which are listed in "Resources."

Because of the controversy surrounding the friendship of Lorena Hickok and Eleanor Roosevelt, I have chosen to fashion a narrative that stays close to the facts as we know them and to the intense emotional truths that are documented in the letters, most of which were written by Eleanor and reveal her inner life, so far as she was able to express it to Hick. The italicized quotations from Eleanor's and Hick's letters appear in the narrative at the same times and in the same contexts in which they appear in the ongoing relationship. In describing the women's intimate relationship, I have used the letters as a guide to its depth, intensity, and sexual nature. Like a diary, they allow us to look into the inner lives of the writers, experiencing their anticipation and disappointments, their eagerness, their anxieties and fears—and especially, their feelings about each other.

Both women's letters tell us that during the first two-and-a-half to three years of their lengthy friendship, they longed to be physically intimate, to touch and kiss and hold one another, to spend as much time together as they could. Doris Faber protests that a woman of ER's "stature" could not have physically expressed her love for Hick, and that when ER writes to her that she wishes she could "lie down beside you tonight and take you in my arms," her feeling is maternal. The women's relationship was essentially Victorian, she claims, innocent of our post-Freudian, twentieth-century sexual awareness.

But Hick had lived with her dear Ellie for eight years (1918–1926) as what Rodger Streitmatter calls a "classic butch/femme couple." She would go on to a five-year romantic and sexual relationship with Judge Marion Harron (1940–1945). She was sexually experienced, as even Faber has to acknowledge. And as Lillian Faderman points out in *Surpassing the Love of Men*, both Hick and Eleanor were "worldly, literate women" who lived in a post-Freudian world. They did not have "the luxury of innocence." ER herself, before she met Hick, was close to two lesbian couples: she shared Val-Kill with Marion Dickerman and Nancy Cook, and she would go on to live for several years in a house owned by her life-long friends Esther Lape and Elizabeth Read.

Blanche Wiesen Cook may have had the last word on the matter. She quotes Hick's letter counting the days until they can be together: *Most clearly I remember your eyes, with a kind of teasing smile in them, and the feeling of that soft spot just north-east of the corner of your mouth against my lips....* "They wrote to each other exactly what they meant to write," Cook says. After Freud, "A cigar may not always be a cigar, but the 'north-east corner of your mouth against my lips' is always the north-east corner."

For readers who want to know what's "real" and what's imagined in *Loving Eleanor*, I should point out several significant departures from the historical record. Hick's first visit to Springwood and Val-Kill occurred in the spring of 1932, but I have imagined what she saw and did there. The events of the day after the November 1932 election (the trip to the Statue of Liberty and the flight with Amelia Earhart) are entirely fictional, as are several of the events of the interlude between the election and the inauguration. The bath maid's tittle-tattle is also made up, but it reflects the gossip that went on among the backstairs gang, as Lillian Rogers Parks describes it in her tell-all White House memoir, *The Roosevelts: A Family in Turmoil*, in a chapter titled "Eleanor and Hicky."

In terms of the plot, the most significant fictional creation is what Hick describes as "FDR's left hook." Its several manifestations are based on the assessment of the president as "manipulative" and "deceptive" by many historians and on contemporary speculation. At the time, some viewed Earl Miller's September 1932 wedding to the seventeen-year-old cousin of his first wife as a staged distraction from his continuing relationship with FDR's wife. A decade later, Joseph Lash believed that his military orders to the Pacific in 1943 came directly from the White House, following Army

Intelligence's bugging of the Chicago hotel room that he and the First Lady shared. Louis Howe's role in assigning Hick to Hopkins at FERA is nowhere documented, but logically fits with the strategies that may have been used to deal with Miller and Lash.

In the end, *Loving Eleanor* is a novel, not a history or a biography, and Lorena Hickok and Eleanor Roosevelt, like everyone else in the book, are fictional characters. However, I agree with Norman Mailer, who wrote that novelists who work with historical events and real people have a "unique opportunity—they can create superior histories out of an enhancement of the real, the unverified, and the wholly fictional." I confess to enhancements of various kinds in this book, in the hope that they may lead to a deeper understanding of who Lorena Hickok really was and what might have happened in those off-the-record moments when she and Eleanor were alone together.

I owe thanks to all those scholars whose work has helped me in the research for this book, but most especially to Blanche Wiesen Cook, upon whose outstanding biographical study of the life of Eleanor Roosevelt I have relied, and to Maurine Beasley, for her work on Hickok's influence on ER's use of the media. I very much appreciate the kindness of the staff at the Franklin D. Roosevelt Presidential Library, and Nancy Roosevelt Ireland's generous permission to quote from her grandmother's letters. I am grateful to the group of readers who read and reacted to an early draft of the manuscript: Betty Walston, Robert Goodfellow, Harriette Andreadis, Cindy Huyser, Neena Husid, and Candyce Rusk. Thanks are also due to my writing sisters @WorkInProgress of the Story Circle Network for their nurturing friendship, to Kerry Sparks and Michele Karlsberg for their unflagging enthusiasm, and to my husband Bill Albert, for his steadfast love and constant support, always.

# THE PEOPLE OF *LOVING ELEANOR*

Names within quotation marks are fictional characters; all others are real persons.

Ruby Black, reporter for the United Press news agency

Emma Bugbee, reporter for the *New York Herald Tribune*

George Bye, ER's literary agent in the 1930s and 1940s

Bill Chapin, city editor, New York City Bureau, Associated Press news agency

Winston Churchill, prime minister of the United Kingdom and visitor to the White House

Nancy Cook, ER's friend and coworker in the Women's Division of the New York State Democratic Committee; with ER and her life partner, Marion Dickerman, co-owner of the Todhunter School and partner in the Val-Kill Industries

Bill and Ella Dana, friends of ER and Hick, who hosted them at the Arrowhead D Ranch (Pyramid Lake, NV) in the summer of 1933 and rented the Long Island "Little House" to Hick, 1938–1955

"Reggie Davis," AP stringer in Albany

Marion Dickerman, ER's friend and (with her life partner, Nancy Cook) co-owner of the Todhunter School and partner in the Val-Kill Industries

Ella (Ellie) Morse Dickinson, intimate friend of Hick from Minneapolis

Thomas Dillon, editor-in-chief of the Minneapolis *Tribune* and
   Hick's mentor

Dorothy Ducas, reporter for the International News Service

Amelia Earhart, famous female aviator, friend of ER and Hick

Stephen T. Early, UP and AP reporter, White House press
   secretary, 1933–1945

James Farley, long-serving chairman of the Democratic National
   Committee, helped to ensure FDR's third-term bid

Elton Fay, Albany, New York bureau chief for the AP

Bess Furman, reporter for the AP Washington Bureau, assigned to
   cover the First Lady

Martha Gellhorn, journalist, war correspondent, and novelist;
   Hick's coworker at FERA (1934–1935); friend of ER and
   frequent White House guest

David Gurewitsch, ER's physician after 1945; after 1947, her friend
   and travel companion; her housemate, after his marriage to
   Edna (1958–1962)

Mabel Haley, ER's personal maid in the White House, also during
   the years when FDR was assistant secretary of the Navy

Marion Harron, U.S. Board of Tax Appeals judge; Hick's intimate
   friend (1940–1945)

Howard Haycraft, writer (*Murder for Pleasure*) and publishing
   executive; shared the Little House with Hick (1938–1941)

Ruby Hickok, Hick's younger sister; burned a packet of letters after
   Hick's death

Harry Hopkins, administrator of the Federal Emergency Relief
   Administration, Hick's employer (1933–1936)

Alicent (Alix) Holt, Hick's teacher at Battle Creek High School; a
   romantic friend (1935–1937)

Louis McHenry Howe, FDR's devoted friend and advisor; ER's
   political mentor

Nannine Joseph, ER's literary agent, 1947–1962

Esther Lape, progressive activist; close friend of ER (1920–1962); ER rented an apartment in a house owned by Lape and her life partner Elizabeth Read at 20 East Eleventh Street in New York City

Joseph Lash, close friend of ER, later her biographer; their friendship created difficulties for both

Alice Roosevelt Longworth, eldest daughter of Theodore Roosevelt and ER's first cousin, with whom she had a conflicted relationship

Marguerite (Missy) LeHand, FDR's devoted personal secretary (1920–1941)

Irvin (Mac) and Lizzie McDuffie, FDR's valet (1927–1939) and White House maid

Charles Michelson, publicity director of the Democratic National Committee and Hick's supervisor,1940–1942

Earl Miller, ER's bodyguard during FDR's governorship (1928–1932), close friend, confidant, champion, and correspondent. His two children (with his third wife, Simone) were named Eleanor and Earl. ER's letters to Earl have not been found

Bill Moran, chief of the U.S. Secret Service during the first two years of the Roosevelt administration. His tenure began in 1917; he served under five presidents

Henrietta Nesbitt, cook and housekeeper at the White House during the Roosevelt years

Lillian Rogers Parks, White House seamstress, maid

Clarence Pickett, executive secretary of the American Friends Service Committee; Hick's guide at Scotts Run, supporter of ER's efforts at Arthurdale

Byron Price, chief of the AP Washington Bureau during the first

Roosevelt administration. Director of the U.S. Office of
Censorship during World War II

George Putnam, Amelia Earhart's husband, publisher, and
promoter

Elizabeth Read, ER's personal attorney and close friend; ER rented
an apartment in a house owned by Read and her life partner
Esther Lape at 20 East Eleventh Street in New York City

Clarence and Annie Ross, caretakers at the Dana estate, Hick's
close friends

"Mark Sainsbury," AP correspondent in Ethiopia

Anna Eleanor Roosevelt Halsted, the Roosevelts' daughter

Eleanor Roosevelt, Hick's intimate friend

Franklin Delano Roosevelt, ER's husband, 32nd president of the
United States

Sara Delano Roosevelt, ER's mother-in-law and a dominant force
in the young ER's marriage

Lucy Mercer Rutherfurd, FDR's lover (1916?–1918) and later
friend; she was with him at his death at Warm Springs

Malvina (Tommy) Thompson, ER's personal secretary, confidant,
and close friend from 1923 to her death in 1953

"Angelina Walton," bath maid in the White House residence

# WORKS CONSULTED

Readers who are interested in learning more about the background of this novel will find details about people and places on the book's website: www.LovingEleanor.com.

Asbell, Bernard. *Mother and Daughter: The Letters of Eleanor and Anna Roosevelt*

Beasley, Maurine H. *Eleanor Roosevelt: Transformative First Lady*

Beasley, Maurine Hoffman. *The Eleanor Roosevelt Encyclopedia*

Brinkley, David. *Washington Goes to War*

Conn, Marjorie. *Lost Lesbian Lives: Three Plays*

Cook, Blanche Wiesen. *Eleanor Roosevelt, Vol. 1: 1884–1933*

Cook, Blanche Wiesen. *Eleanor Roosevelt, Vol. 2: The Defining Years, 1933–1938*

Davis, Kenneth Sydney. *Invincible Summer: An Intimate Portrait of the Roosevelts, based on the recollections of Marion Dickerman*

Faber, Doris. *The Life of Lorena Hickok: E. R.'s Friend*

Faderman, Lillian. *Surpassing the Love of Men: Romantic Friendship and Love between Women from the Renaissance to the Present*

Furman, Bess. *Washington By-Line: The Personal History of a Newspaperwoman*

Goodwin, Doris Kearns. *No Ordinary Time: Franklin and Eleanor Roosevelt: The Home Front in World War II*

Gurewitsch, Edna. *Kindred Souls: The Devoted Friendship of Eleanor Roosevelt and Dr. David Gurewitsch*

Hickok, Lorena A. *Eleanor Roosevelt, Reluctant First Lady*

Hickok, Lorena. *One Third of a Nation: Lorena Hickok Reports on the Great Depression*

Hickok, Lorena A. *The Road to the White House: FDR, The Pre-Presidential Years*

Hickok, Lorena A. *The Story of Eleanor Roosevelt*

Hickok, Lorena A. *The Story of Helen Keller*

Hickok, Lorena A. *The Touch of Magic: The Story of Helen Keller's Great Teacher, Anne Sullivan Macy*

Lash, Joseph L. *Love, Eleanor: Eleanor Roosevelt and Her Friends*

Lash, Joseph. *Eleanor and Franklin*

Mills, Kay. *A Place in the News: From the Women's Pages to the Front Page*

Parks, Lillian Rogers. *The Roosevelts: A Family in Turmoil*

Persico, Joseph E. *Franklin and Lucy: Mrs. Rutherfurd and the Other Remarkable Women in Roosevelt's Life*

Roosevelt, Eleanor. *On My Own*

Roosevelt, Eleanor. *This I Remember*

Roosevelt, Eleanor. *This Is My Story*

Roosevelt, Eleanor, and Lorena Hickok. *Ladies of Courage*

Roosevelt, James. *My Parents: A Differing View*

Rowley, Hazel. *Franklin and Eleanor: An Extraordinary Marriage*

Rupp, Leila J. "'Imagine My Surprise': Women's Relationships in Historical Perspective," *Frontiers: A Journal of Women Studies* 5 (Fall 1980): 61–70.

St. John, Robert. *This Was My World*

Streitmatter, Rodger. *Empty Without You: The Intimate Letters Of Eleanor Roosevelt and Lorena Hickok*

Tully, Grace. *F.D.R., My Boss*

West, J. B., and Mary Lynn Kotz. *Upstairs at the White House: My Life With the First Ladies*

# ABOUT SUSAN WITTIG ALBERT

Growing up on a farm on the Illinois prairie, Susan learned that books could take her anywhere, and reading became a passion that has accompanied her throughout her life. She earned an undergraduate degree in English from the University of Illinois at Urbana and a Ph.D. in Medieval Studies from the University of California at Berkeley, then turned to teaching. After faculty and administrative appointments at the University of Texas, Tulane University, and Texas State University, she left her academic career and began writing fulltime. Her bestselling and prize-winning work includes mysteries, historical fiction, memoir, nonfiction, and anthologies. She is the founder of the Story Circle Network, a nonprofit organization for women writers, and a member of the Texas Institute of Letters. She and her husband Bill live on thirty-one acres in the Texas Hill Country. Her website:

www.susanalbert.com.

# Books by Susan Wittig Albert

*Loving Eleanor*
*A Wilder Rose*
*An Extraordinary Year of Ordinary Days*
*Together, Alone: A Memoir of Marriage and Place*

The China Bayles Mysteries
The Darling Dahlias Mysteries
The Cottage Tales of Beatrix Potter
*Writing From Life: Telling the Soul's Story*
*Work of Her Own*

With Bill Albert
The Robin Paige Victorian-Edwardian Mysteries

Edited Anthologies
*What Wildness is This: Women Write about the Southwest*
*With Courage and Common Sense: Memoirs from
the Older Women's Legacy Circle*

www.susanalbert.com

CPSIA information can be obtained
at www.ICGtesting.com
Printed in the USA
BVHW071419300721
612903BV00006B/1111